MW01439813

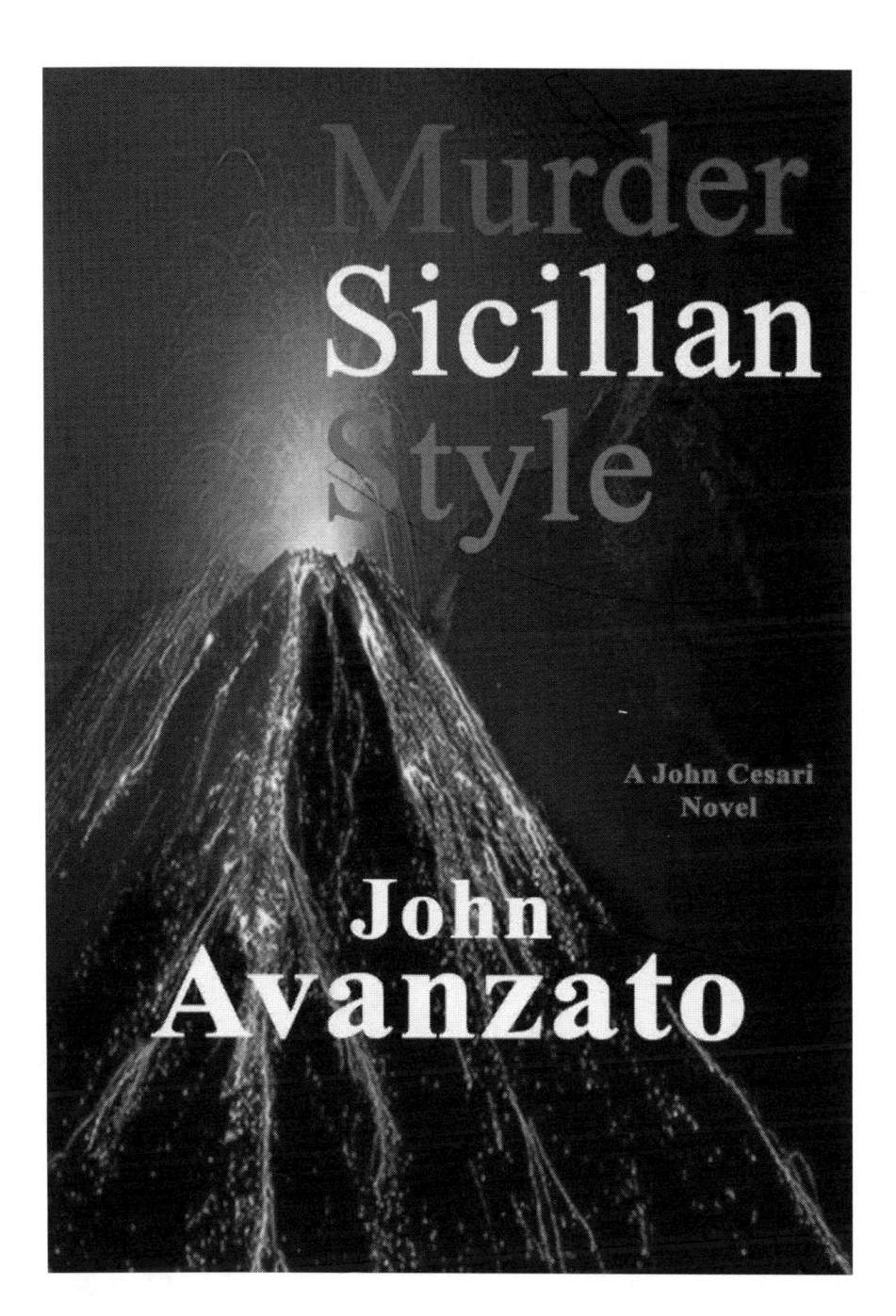

Murder Sicilian Style

A John Cesari Novel

John Avanzato

Murder Sicilian Style

Copyright © 2023 by John Avanzato
All Rights Reserved.

This content may not be reproduced in whole or in part, in any form or by any means, electronic or mechanical, including photocopying, recording, or by any information storage and retrieval system now known or hereafter invented, without written permission from the publisher.

This is a work of fiction. Names, characters, businesses, places, events, and incidents are either the products of the author's imagination or used in a fictitious manner. Any resemblance to actual persons, living or dead, or actual events is purely coincidental.

Murder Sicilian Style by John Avanzato

First Edition

Other books by John Avanzato

Hostile Hospital

Prescription for Disaster

Temperature Rising

Claim Denied

The Gas Man Cometh

Jailhouse Doc

Sea Sick

Pace Yourself

The Legend of the Night Nurse

Hilton Dead

Bleeding Heart

Under the Weather

The Pain Killers

Visit my author page at amazon

ACKNOWLEDGEMENT

I would like to thank Stephen Colo, Melisa Colabella, and Leslie Kisatsky Mariano, for their advice, their expertise, and most of all, their time. Murder, Sicilian Style is a story with multiple moving parts, and I needed all the help I could get.

A frequently asked question to all authors is how do you come up with your ideas? For me, there is no easy answer. Occasionally, something will happen at work or at home that will set off the little light bulb in my head. Sometimes, someone will say something that I find amusing and can't shake off, and from there I will build on it. Rarely, do I sit down to write without having some notion of where I want to go and who I want to take with me. For the most part, my tales are people driven, triggered by some seminal event or interaction I have had at one point or another.

My wife Cheryl and I have been travelling the globe in recent years both by land and by sea. To say the least, we have made many new friends in the course of our exciting adventures. As I typically do on vacation, I grab a cocktail wherever we happen to be and start pressing the flesh, always on the prowl for interesting characters. Some of my most productive book research has taken place during happy hour on cruise ships where inspiration can usually be found in abundance.

When I first sat down to write this particular novel, we had just returned from Switzerland where we met some of the nicest and most colorful people, including retired assistant director of the Secret Service, Stephen Colo, who I can only describe as a salt of the earth, made me proud to be American, kind of guy. Fascinated by his back story, I immediately began batting around ideas for a novel. In its first iteration, this book was titled, *Bern Notice,* and it was my original intention to have Cesari wind up at the hotel, Bellevue Palace, in Bern, Switzerland being chased by rogue Secret Service agents who in turn were being chased by the good guy Stephen Colo agent.

Halfway through that version of the story, Cheryl and I took off again to visit Sicily for an extended holiday and fell in love with the land, the food, the people, and most importantly our amazing guide, Melisa Colabella. Her enthusiasm, energy and passion for all things Sicilian was extremely contagious and had me seriously thinking about renting an apartment in Taormina. (I'm still thinking about it.) Returning home, I decided to blend the two vacations and came up with *Murder, Sicilian Style*. The rogue Secret Service agents are still lurking about, but now they all wind up in Palermo and Mount Etna instead of Switzerland, with a healthy dose of Sicilian wine, food, and culture thrown in.

There are several scenes in this book where I play it fast and loose with the facts, but it was all in the spirit of good fun. My deviation from reality is particularly on display in the fight scene between Cesari and the bad guy that takes place on an airbus traveling to Italy. The error of my way was explained to me by Leslie Kisatsky Mariano, my favorite flight attendant, whose advice and consultation were greatly appreciated. But after we discussed the weaknesses of that scene, she ultimately concluded, "Honestly, who's going to know?"

Good point. If it was real, it wouldn't be called fiction.

Cheryl, the most interesting person in the world.

Worthy of Trust and Confidence

U.S. Secret Service

The Heads

Table of Contents

Acknowledgement 7
Chapter 1 19
Chapter 2 23
Chapter 3 30
Chapter 4 36
Chapter 5 40
Chapter 6 46
Chapter 7 52
Chapter 8 58
Chapter 9 65
Chapter 10 70
Chapter 11 75
Chapter 12 81
Chapter 13 88
Chapter 14 93
Chapter 15 99
Chapter 16 104
Chapter 17 109
Chapter 18 116
Chapter 19 123
Chapter 20 129
Chapter 21 137
Chapter 22 144
Chapter 23 150
Chapter 24 155
Chapter 25 161
Chapter 26 166
Chapter 27 172
Chapter 28 179
Chapter 29 185

Chapter 30	191
Chapter 31	197
Chapter 32	203
Chapter 33	210
Chapter 34	217
Chapter 35	222
Chapter 36	228
Chapter 37	234
Chapter 38	240
Chapter 39	246
Chapter 40	251
Chapter 41	257
Chapter 42	262
Chapter 43	269
Chapter 44	275
Chapter 45	283
Chapter 46	290
Chapter 47	295
Chapter 48	300
Chapter 49	307
Chapter 50	314
Chapter 51	319
Chapter 52	324
Chapter 53	332
Chapter 54	339
The Author	345
A Sicilian Cat	349

Murder Sicilian Style

by
John Avanzato

Chapter 1

The door buzzer squawked insistently, and John Cesari looked up from his laptop. He was sitting at the kitchen table of his third-floor loft apartment at the north end of Washington Square Park. It was 7:00 p.m. and he was waiting for a pizza delivery. He had been working on a proposal for upgrading and expanding the endoscopy suite at St. Matt's medical center in lower Manhattan where he was the chief of gastroenterology and medical director. The department needed to accommodate several new physicians hired to meet the growing needs of the community for endoscopic services. Apparently, getting a camera stuck up your butt was all the rage these days. Perhaps it was a welcome distraction from cable news whose seeming sole purpose was to drive the viewing population insane with anxiety.

Salivating with anticipation, he did something he almost never did. He failed to look through the peephole before opening the door. It had been a long day and he had been on the move since entering the hospital early that morning. Black coffee for breakfast, a cafeteria hot dog for lunch while sprinting toward a budget meeting and more coffee later as a snack. At the moment, he was ravenous and not necessarily thinking clearly. In his defense, he didn't have a whole lot to be concerned about. He was six feet tall, two-hundred and twenty pounds, in great shape and kept a seven-pound crowbar in the umbrella stand next to the door. Combined with many years of street-fighting experience and generally good instincts for sizing people up, he would easily be considered the apex predator in most situations that would have left the average person wetting himself. But he wasn't a superhero and kept a loaded twelve gauge in his bedroom and a small handheld axe under one of the sofa cushions in case of emergencies. His personal credo was that he would rather explain to the police why he killed an intruder than be found by his landlord lying on the floor in a state of advanced decomposition.

The door swung open but instead of seeing a pimply faced delivery kid holding a fresh, hot, steaming pepperoni and sausage pie from his favorite pizza joint just a few blocks away in Greenwich Village, there stood a short, well-dressed guy named Gerry Acquilano chewing on a slice of pizza that looked very much like the one he had ordered. Cesari was momentarily confused by the sight. Gerry was five feet four inches tall, middle-aged, with a full head of curly brown hair graying at the sides. Feisty and pugnacious, Gerry tipped the scales at no more than one hundred and fifty pounds dripping wet. His nose had been broken and reset a number of times from a failed golden gloves experience as a teen. Now specializing in high end car theft amongst his many accomplishments, he had been recruited by Vito Gianelli to be his personal driver and all-around gofer type of indentured servitude to pay off a debt.

Vito Gianelli, in turn, was a local mob boss and Cesari's best friend. They had known each other since the first grade in the Bronx and despite the vastly different worlds they now lived in had managed to overcome the many paradoxes that defined their relationship. He hadn't seen or heard from Vito in more than two weeks which wasn't unusual. Vito frequently went radio silent for protracted periods of time depending on what projects he was working on or who he was trying to avoid.

Cesari glanced past Gerry, searching for the still expected delivery guy and with disappointment in his voice said, "Where'd you get that pizza, Gerry?"

Gerry swallowed the piece in his mouth and in a decidedly Brooklyn accent, replied, "There was a guy downstairs delivering a pie to this address. I was hungry so I grabbed a slice and sent him on his way."

More confused than angry, Cesari asked, "Why would you do that, Gerry? And why are you here?"

Shoveling the crust into his mouth, Gerry garbled, "I didn't think you would mind, and I'm here to pick you up."

Cesari's fuse had been lit, and he simmered at the smaller man, "What are you talking about?"

"Vito told me to pick you up at 7:00 p.m. and bring you to the La Bella Sicilia restaurant in mid-town. It's a new place. They had a soft opening two weeks ago to rave reviews, but tonight's the big night. The grand opening. Pretty nice too from what I heard so put on a tie or something. Rumor is all their ingredients are imported from Sicily. Wine, cheese, pasta, cured meats, olive earl... everything. Killer caponata they're saying."

Cesari was officially pissed off now and was having trouble suppressing his ire. "I got nothing against little people, Gerry, but you're walking a thin line here. That was my dinner you just ate and I'm not going anywhere. If Vito wanted me to meet him somewhere, he should have called. Now get out of my sight before I decide throwing you down the stairs isn't as unreasonable as it sounds. And it's olive *oil* not earl. Learn how to speak English."

Cesari stepped back with the intention of slamming the door shut but in one fluid motion Gerry whipped out a handgun and pointed it right at Cesari's chest. It was a big, black thing, a Glock 19, shiny and lethal.

Cesari stared at him in disbelief. "Are you out of your mind, Gerry?"

With a look of determination that didn't bode well, Gerry said coolly, "Vito said to get you and that's exactly what I'm going to do."

"Did Vito tell you to shoot me if I didn't agree to come along?"

"That's the thing. He didn't specify what condition you had to be in when I brought you. He said and I quote, "Go get the doc and bring him to Bella's." End of quote. As you can imagine, there's a lot that can be read into that and Vito's not exactly the kind of guy that likes to be disappointed so if you don't mind... I'd rather not have to carry you into the restaurant bleeding."

"You're an asshole, Gerry. Did you know that?"

In response, Gerry cocked the gun and pointed it at Cesari's left knee. "Sticks and stones, Doc. You coming or do I have to cap you?"

Cesari let out a deep breath. "Easy with that thing, Gerry. It's got a hair trigger."

Gerry smirked, "Don't I know it."

Cesari's gaze unconsciously drifted toward the umbrella stand with the crowbar, but Gerry read his mind and sneered, "Just give me a reason, Doc. That's all I ask."

Cesari knew there was no way Vito would have approved of Gerry shooting him over a dinner reservation. Problem was that was now a real possibility. Gerry was a borderline psychopath in addition to being one of the most concrete human beings he had ever met, and he was intensely loyal to Vito. If Vito said something wistfully in passing like, "Gee, wouldn't it be great to have a grandchild one day?", Gerry would immediately run down to Central Park and snatch the first kid he spotted at gunpoint.

"Can I at least call Vito?" Cesari asked in a conciliatory voice.

"You can do whatever you want from inside the car downstairs. We're running late."

Cesari rolled his eyes, "What about the tie and maybe a sport coat? They're in my bedroom. You said it's a nice place."

Gerry hesitated and then nodded, "Fine, but hurry up and don't come out with that shotgun I know you have in there."

"I won't. So how about we try to avoid an accident by you putting the pistol away? It's too big for you anyway. A guy your size ought to consider carrying a toy nerf gun."

Gerry ignored the barb, uncocked the weapon, relaxed a smidge, but didn't put it away. "I'm waiting."

Cesari knew that one day he was going to have to bitch-slap Gerry into submission but for now he decided to acquiesce. So cursing under his breath, he marched into his bedroom, put on a clean white shirt with a red striped tie, threw on a navy-blue sport coat and returned with his cellphone next to his ear listening as the call to Vito went to voicemail.

Outside the apartment, a brand-new black Cadillac Escalade was waiting for them. Another one of Vito's men wearing a suit stood at attention near the massive vehicle. He was as large as Gerry was diminutive. He opened the rear door and Cesari made himself comfortable. Gerry hopped into the driver's seat and the behemoth got into the front passenger side.

Cesari sat alone in the back fuming and wondering what the hell was going on. Despite the gun-waving and threats of bodily harm, he didn't feel as if he were in any real danger. Over the years, he had become used to Vito's machinations and drama. It was simply the price of admission to this particular party. So he nestled back into the soft and very luxurious leather seat and let the 700-horsepower engine escort him to the ball.

He was very hungry.

CHAPTER 2

La Bella Sicilia was located on West 43rd Street midway between Sixth and Seventh Avenues, a prime location just a short distance from Times Square. A place to be and to be seen as they say. Cesari stepped out of the Escalade and watched it zip away to some unknown parking location. He glanced around, taking in the crowd of people hanging out near the front entrance. It was a nice evening in early September and New Yorkers were ready to rumble. Apparently, the restaurant had just opened its doors moments before he arrived, and guests were piling in for the first seating. Sharply dressed, upscale clientele in their late twenties to early fifties mostly. An authentic Italian restaurant would just be starting to shift into high gear at this hour, so this place appeared to be the real deal. A large plate window allowed him a limited view of the bustling dining room and bar. Opening night appeared to be going very well. He scanned around but didn't see Vito. Bypassing a long line of waiting patrons, he strode confidently up to the entrance, whispered Vito's name into the greeter's ear and was promptly ushered inside.

A tuxedoed maître d' found his name on a guest list and escorted him past the main dining area to a private suite. As they walked, Cesari was immediately struck by the fact that this was no ordinary Italian restaurant with red and white checkered tablecloths, the smell of garlic drowning one's senses and a smarmy guy walking around playing an accordion for tips. Elegant and sophisticated décor with classy and chic design from top to bottom, somebody was trying to make a statement about Sicilian cuisine and doing very well at it.

Inside the private dining area, he found Vito holding court at a large rectangular table for twelve set for royalty. There was an embroidered linen table covering, sterling silver cutlery, brass candle holders, a crystal chandelier, tapestries depicting medieval life on the walls and white jacketed waitstaff pouring champagne into Murano glass flutes. The guests were already chowing down on fresh-baked bread dipped in olive oil and massive plates of delicious looking caponata, the quintessential Sicilian eggplant antipasto. The gentle and soulful sound of *Santa Lucia* drifted melodically overhead from an unseen speaker system sung by the maestro himself, Enrico Caruso.

Cesari was impressed.

Other than Vito, Cesari didn't recognize any of the other people who didn't seem to notice his arrival. Vito stood in the middle of the table and was about to make a toast when he suddenly spotted Cesari. The scene reminded Cesari of Da Vinci's *Last Supper*. To Vito's right was the only unoccupied place setting and Vito signaled him to take a seat.

"Glad you could make it, Cesari," Vito said.

"I wouldn't have missed this for the world."

Missing the subtlety of the sarcasm, Vito grinned. "I was just about to get the party started with a few words."

Cesari held back his desire to slap his friend's champagne out of his hand and demand an explanation. Instead, he sat down picked up his own flute and observed the other guests politely smiling at him. The room went quiet as if on cue as Vito cleared his throat. He looked uncomfortable standing there, front and center like that. Maybe his subconscious didn't like the idea of him being so exposed. Years of dodging bullets could do that to you, Cesari speculated.

There was a thin, frail woman of about seventy to Vito's left and a woman in her early to mid-thirties next to her. To Cesari's right was a woman with dark, Mediterranean skin tone and jet-black shoulder length hair. She looked to be in her late twenties perhaps just touching thirty. They were seated five on a side and one at each end. The rest of the table were an assortment of middle-aged, rough-looking men and women with stoic faces and dark brooding eyes. The men wore dark ill-fitting suits, and the women wore even darker dresses with little make up or accessories. This was a working class, serious crowd, Cesari thought.

It soon became obvious that most of them spoke little or no English. As Vito addressed them, the woman next to Cesari translated into Italian. Cesari saw that they eagerly hung on every word, nodding approvingly at various junctures in the speech. Apparently, this gathering was Vito's extended family from the old country. They had all arrived from Sicily just a few days ago to celebrate the upcoming marriage of Vito's cousin, Angelina, to the love of her life, Enzo, the owner and head chef of the restaurant who was busy in the kitchen. In Cesari's opinion, Vito gave a fine speech. He thanked and welcomed everyone who needed to be thanked and welcomed and congratulated the bride to be. It was also very clear that Vito was footing the bill for tonight's affair because he reminded everyone of that fact several times during his soliloquy. After close to fifteen minutes, Vito wrapped it up and they all raised their glasses, shouting *bravo!* and *salute!*

Vito sat down, full of himself. He clinked glasses with Cesari and sipped champagne. "You made it just in time, Cesari. How'd I do?"

Despite his irritation, Cesari smiled. He couldn't help himself. Vito was a mountain of a man. Six three, two hundred and sixty-five pounds of muscle and mean. He'd been running every illegal enterprise in lower Manhattan for the better part of twenty years. He'd killed men with his bare hands right in front of Cesari, and yet here he was looking for his grammar school bud's approval over a simple salutation. Cesari studied his friend's features, his large, oversized head with curly salt and pepper hair, strong jaw line, beaked nose, and piercing, even cruel gray eyes.

Softening up, he said, "You did great, pal. Thanks for inviting me."

"You're welcome. I knew you'd want to meet my family. Now let me give you the lay of the land. First off, you're sitting next to my cousin Teresa. She's the only one here that speaks any English besides you and me. She's the sister of the bride, Angelina, on my left side who's sitting next to their mother, my aunt Sofia. By the way, Teresa's a virgin and says the rosary three times a day so don't get any ideas."

That's what Cesari had always liked about Vito. Start with the insults and accusations before moving on to the niceties. He glanced to his right quickly and saw that Teresa was absorbed in an animated conversation with the guy at the end of the table and not paying attention to anyone else.

He then leaned into Vito and whispered, "Between you and me, I have no interest in women with mustaches but thanks for the tip."

Vito retorted angrily, "That's my cousin we're talking about, Cesari. Knock it off."

Cesari returned in kind. "Do you realize that I was kidnapped at gunpoint and brought here? I'm the victim, so tell your cousin to stay away from me, not the other way around."

Vito laughed. "That Gerry's a pisser, isn't he?"

"A regular riot."

As they spoke, waiters came through with massive platters of fried calamari, marinated sardines, clams oreganata, mussels in marinara, eggplant rollatini, grilled octopus, and even more caponata which appeared to be the most coveted dish on the menu tonight. Bottles of wine were uncorked, and more fresh baked bread, hot from the oven, were passed around to begin the family style feast. Remembering his hunger, Cesari scooped up a half-dozen clams and a plateful of calamari. From the way everyone attacked their food, he wondered how anyone was going to have any room to eat the main course.

Vito shoved a calamari ring into his mouth and said, "Let's get on with the background story. As you know, my mom and dad are no longer here. May they rest in peace." He paused a moment to make the sign of the cross. "And now that forty is just around corner for me, I'm tired of being an orphan. I've been reflecting on how nice it would be to reconnect with family. I knew my mother had a sister across the pond who I never met so I did some leg work and found out my Aunt Sofia's still alive and kicking in Palermo with two beautiful daughters, Angelina and Teresa. I reached out a couple of months ago and she was thrilled that I did. Anyway, that's when I learned about Enzo marrying Angelina and opening this restaurant. That turned out to be a huge opportunity for me as well."

Cesari was puzzled at that last part. "How so?"

"It seems Enzo's previous business partner had pulled out at the last minute and left him high and dry with the banks. Enzo was completely tapped out on a personal level and was scrambling for dough with opening night just around the corner when out of nowhere I showed up."

"And you came to his rescue like any good relation would."

"Something like that, but remember, Enzo isn't my relative yet."

"What's that supposed to mean?"

"What that means is that you are now looking at the fifty-one percent owner of La Bella Sicilia, the hottest new restaurant in Manhattan. Enzo was so desperate for cash that I practically stole the place from him for a fraction of what it should have cost."

Cesari was appalled. "You didn't? Please tell me you're joking."

"I don't joke about money, Cesari. You know that. He needed it and I had it. Best million bucks I ever doled out too. I mean look at this place."

"Enzo works for you?"

"Not exactly, but you get the picture."

"I can't believe what I'm hearing. How could you do that to the poor guy? And on the eve of his wedding to your cousin? Don't you have a soul?"

Vito chuckled. "Listen to yourself. Enzo's fine. Besides, if he wants his restaurant back, he can cough up the one point five million he owes me, and I'll walk away. Of course, I'll need that in cash."

"One point five million?"

"Only if he gets the money to me by midnight, the month's end. Then it will be two million."

Cesari shook his head. "I'm not sure this is the best way to reconnect with family, Vito."

"Well, it's his family that put him in this position."

Cesari asked, "And how pray tell did they do that?"

"Enzo's mother, Rosaria, and my aunt Sofia are best friends. Well, they used to be anyway. Rosaria is also an old lady and stubborn beyond all reason. Really old school if you know what I mean. She's got the control thing going on."

Cesari's interest began to wane as the first morsel hit his taste buds. Sipping wine, he said, "Can you speed up the story. I'd like to focus on my plate."

"Well, Rosaria's other son, Ernesto, owns and runs a vineyard and olive grove back in Sicily. You're drinking his wine right now."

"Really? It's pretty good."

"One hundred percent nero d'avola grapes grown on the north side of Mount Etna."

"Continue please. So what happened?"

"Angelina's what happened."

"You mean the mustache?"

"Stop it. This is serious. The two families grew up within sight of each other. Sunday dinners together, baptisms, confirmations, graduation parties, the whole nine yards. Ernesto is the older brother by two years and he's unmarried. It seems that in the old country, it's highly disrespectful even humiliating for the younger brother to get hitched before the older brother."

"You can't be serious?"

"I kid you not. This is some heavy shit, but it gets worse."

Cesari glanced past Vito at Sofia. She was wolfing down caponata as if she hadn't seen food in months. Cesari commented, "Does she always eat like that?"

"What? You're going to pick on my aunt now too?"

"Get to the point of the story, Vito. I'm hungry," Cesari said as he tore off a huge chunk of crusty bread.

"Okay… It's not that Rosaria doesn't like Angelina. Just the opposite. She adores her. But Rosaria feels that because Angelina is the older sister, she ought to marry the older brother…"

"But that's not the way love works," interjected Cesari.

"Don't say that to Rosaria. She says love has nothing to do with it. It's about respect and tradition. Trust me, I spent a whole week trying to get her to see the light and patch things up for the sake of Enzo and Angelina. Anyway, she demanded they call off the wedding, but Enzo and Angelina refused. They were planning on relocating here after the wedding anyway because of the restaurant but decided Palermo was getting too toxic for them so here they are."

"You're kidding? Is Rosaria here?"

"Not a chance. I went to Sicily. I wanted to meet my aunt Sofia and the rest of the family before the wedding. That's why you haven't heard from me for the last couple of weeks. While I was there, I heard the whole story. It sounded crazy so I went to meet Rosaria to see what I could do, but the woman has a mean streak in her the width of the Mississippi river."

"Not the compromising type, I gather."

"Compromising? Get this. When I went to see her, she was wearing black and sitting shivah, mourning the loss of her son, Enzo. As far as she's concerned, he's dead. And worse, she had Ernesto doing the same. He was the main investor in this restaurant and Rosaria ordered him to back out at the last minute to punish Enzo."

Cesari's jaw dropped. "Jesus…"

"Now, you understand. Imagine how I felt. I'm all sentimental about meeting up with my Sicilian roots and heritage and they're all at each other's throats, but it has sort of a happy ending. Right before I left, Ernesto called me and said that he was feeling somewhat remorseful about the whole thing, but that he couldn't go against his mother's will. He couldn't do anything about the money because he was afraid his mother would find out. However, he agreed to supply all the wine and olive oil to the restaurant at discounted prices for as long as Enzo wanted. In his mind a sale is a sale, so Rosaria wouldn't get too upset about that if she found out. He also said he was going to ship a case of his best cold-pressed extra virgin olive oil as a wedding present. I checked, the special olive oil arrived yesterday, gift wrapped and everything. It's supposed to be the best in all of Italy, the kind he usually reserves only for Michelin star restaurants. Enzo said he was going to use it in the caponata tonight, so there is a bit of a silver lining in all this."

Cesari thought it over for a moment before saying, "I'm proud of you, Vito. I really am. You went out of your way to make peace between two feuding families when you didn't have to. This is a side of you I don't think I ever really appreciated before."

Vito beamed at the compliment.

Cesari stood and raised his wine glass. He turned to Teresa who was watching him. "Would you mind translating for me?"

"Of course," she replied smiling.

All eyes were on him now. He intended to heap praise on Vito and to commend him on his newfound family values as well as applaud Angelina and her mother for having the resolve to align themselves on the side of true love. But as he started to speak, he noticed Vito's aunt Sofia looking a little pasty. She was sweating too. Before he could say anything, she began to vomit violently, over and over. At first food, then blood...

Lots of blood.

Angelina screamed in horror. Then one by one the other guests began to retch and heave their stomach contents onto the table or their neighbor. Cesari raced to Aunt Sofia's aid, ordering Vito to call 911.

Just when it seemed like it couldn't get any worse, the door burst open and a guy in a white smock and chef's hat came charging in with a shocked look of dismay on his face. That had to be Enzo. With the door wide open behind him, Cesari could see that the entire restaurant was in total free fall. Diners were either running for the door or on their hands and knees sick as dogs.

Aunt Sofia collapsed into Cesari's arms.

Chapter 3

By midnight it was all over, or just beginning, depending on your point of view. Aunt Sofia was intubated in an ambulance with Cesari squeezing a bag of blood into her veins travelling at breakneck speed to St. Matt's emergency room along with three dozen other people including half of Vito's relatives. Angelina, Teresa and Enzo were inconsolable, and Vito's dreams of a happy family reunion had been dashed irrevocably. Bella's had shuttered its doors and the place was crawling with police, health department officials, the press, and FBI agents. Multiple guests had called in the catastrophe and before long the rumor mill was churning that the nightmare unfolding in real time was the result of a terrorist attack.

Two hundred miles away, a torrential storm of epic proportions raged across the D.C. area causing power outages, flooding and motor vehicle accidents. Emily Hoffman steered her car into the driving rain with the wipers slapping furiously to maintain visibility. She was still twenty minutes from the Dulles International Airport on I-66 coming out of D.C. when she encountered a long line of cars trying to merge down to one lane, and then come abruptly to a halt. Up ahead in the distance, she saw roadside flares and the flickering beacons of emergency vehicles.

Not good.

A quick glance at the time told her that if the delay was more than a few minutes, her passenger would be at risk of missing her flight. There was an exit ramp about a hundred yards away, and making a snap decision, she drove onto the shoulder of the highway and pressed on the accelerator. She knew the area well and planned to pick up the Dulles access road in Tysons Corner five miles further on. Better to be moving at thirty-five miles an hour than not moving at all, she mused. Besides, at this hour she had no intention of adhering too strictly to traffic laws. With that in mind she pulled off the highway.

That was her first mistake.

Emily Hoffman was twenty-two years old, a recent graduate of New York University, and six months into a yearlong internship for Harlan McGuigan, the junior senator from North Carolina. After graduating magna cum laude with a B.A. in political science, she had decided to take a year off to learn the congressional ropes and make connections before pursuing her law degree at Yale where she had already been accepted.

As an intern, she wasn't a federal employee per se. None of the thousands of interns were, but she did receive a pittance of a stipend in order to maintain herself while she fetched coffee, made copies of not so important documents and took notes for the boss. It wasn't all mundane. She got to meet very important and frequently interesting people. The senate building was the playground for the power players of the greatest country on earth. These were the king-makers and the king-breakers. She'd sat in on some very high-level meetings and was starting to become a fixture in those hallowed halls where the laws of the land were hammered out over coffee, scotch, and red-faced men and women shouting epithets at each other.

Most internships were only several weeks to several months long, but she had decided to make a statement to the world that she had arrived, and that they had better take her seriously. Her twelve-month commitment to a certain degree was working in her favor. People were taking notice of her diligence and perseverance. At six months, she had become a senior intern and a go-to girl for several congressmen and women besides Harlan McGuigan. There was no task too big or too small for her. Other senators were starting to question why she didn't rotate her time with them. One even suggested that a rule be passed that no intern be assigned for more than three months at a time to any one senator so that the intern could get a more well-rounded experience. This was met with derision from most of the other senators. Everyone knew that McGuigan had lucked out and if the shoe were on the other foot, they would never give Emily up.

Besides being smart and friendly, Emily was a quick learner. An athletic build, five feet six inches tall with shoulder length brown hair and eyes, she was as attractive in blue jeans as an evening dress. Her father was a police lieutenant in a suburb of Philadelphia and had warned her repetitively about the perils lurking for her in Washington. He had even given her a small revolver, a Smith & Wesson snub-nosed .38 special, to protect herself. It was quite illegal in D.C., and they'd had quite a row over it, but in the end she tucked it away in her suitcase to appease him. You're swimming in shark-infested waters young lady was his favorite admonition. There are people in this world that will rob you, rape you, kill you, and not think twice about going out for pizza an hour later. Her father was slightly north of cynical about the human condition, but she discovered after just a short time in D.C that his words of caution weren't completely unfounded. The nation's capital was an extremely dangerous city, and before long, she began carrying the .38 with her whenever she went out at night.

And don't trust men of any persuasion was his second favorite saying. I don't care what god they worship, what color they are, or what their party affiliation is. They only want one thing. They're all savages without exception. If you keep that in mind you should be okay. She used to just shake her head at that and had long since stopped being embarrassed by those types of conversations with him. He couldn't help himself and her mother had long since stopped trying to change him.

But once again, he was right. The sexual pressure from every direction was relentless. Fortunately, she had no problem handling men, young or old. Her quick wit, decisive mannerism, and maturity imbued her with an air of confidence that withered even the most stalwart pursuer. If anyone thought they had set their sights on a fresh-faced, wide-eyed, impressionable college girl they were unabashedly disabused of the notion. A stern look of rebuke from her could freeze the majority of would-be casanovas dead in their tracks. She was driven, goal-oriented and had no intention of being side-tracked by romantic interludes no matter how tempting. Emily was on the fast track and intended on staying there. Elected office somewhere down the road was not out of the question.

If only she could keep her damn Crohn's disease under control. She had been tormented by it since early adolescence with frequent doctors' visits and even the occasional hospitalization. Her stressful years and poor diet while living in Manhattan attending NYU had been particularly trying for her. Fortunately, she had met a very caring gastroenterologist there who had managed to get her through all four years with minimal complications. By graduation, she was doing so well she had almost forgotten she had a chronic disease. The every other week self-injection with a biologic agent, however, was a constant reminder that hers was no ordinary life. Was Dr. John Cesari her hero? Very possibly, she thought. He was certainly easy on the eyes… for an older guy, anyway. That thought gave her a chuckle. Easy to talk to and relaxed, he explained things in a way that anyone could understand. She had called him once or twice since leaving New York to discuss mild symptoms and he had continued to advise her and prescribe medications, but she knew the time was coming when she would have to find a new physician. She actually dreaded the thought of that just as much as she dreaded a Crohn's flare-up which tended to occur at the most inopportune times such as being stuck in traffic in the middle of a cataclysmic thunderstorm.

She glanced over at her passenger, a woman who was almost her polar opposite both physically and mentally. She could only be described as glamorous with made for Hollywood looks. Insanely beautiful, everyone stopped to gawk in awe when she sauntered by, men and women alike. At least when she was made up and not crying which she had been doing continuously since Emily had picked her up at her apartment in Foggy Bottom. In the car, she had barely acknowledged Emily's presence because her face was buried in a handkerchief, sobbing uncontrollably. She was ten years older than Emily and was secretary to Remington R. Taylor, the senior senator from Virginia and currently the majority leader. Some would say he was the second most important man in the country with only the president himself wielding more raw power and influence. It was rumored that the senator was tired of sitting on the bench and was on the verge of announcing his candidacy for the main office itself and thus have world leaders kiss his ass for a change.

Emily was both shocked and flattered when he had called her personally on her cellphone that afternoon to request a favor. It was a big favor he knew and thanked her profusely. He needed someone to drive his secretary, Claire, to the airport. She had a family emergency in Miami and had booked the first flight she could which is why she was flying out of Dulles and not Ronald Reagan Airport, a much shorter ride from the city center. It was also why she was flying out at this unholy hour. She was very upset, and the senator didn't want her to be alone or to have to take a cab.

Senator Taylor had concluded the phone call saying that he owed her one. Emily had repeated it over and over in her head. The words sent a rush through her like nothing else ever had. The second most powerful man in the country, the world, owed her one. It was like hitting a grand slam in the bottom of the ninth. Six months in Washington and she had already made the big league. Without hesitation she had agreed of course, and had reassured the senator that it was her pleasure to help out, no strings attached. So enthralled was she at the call that it never dawned on her to ask the obvious question. Why her? She barely knew Claire and had only briefly met the senator himself on two, perhaps three occasions. The fact that he even knew her name should have struck her as nothing less than miraculous.

She turned to her companion. "I know my way around this area very well. We'll pick up the highway again in a few miles. We should be all right, timewise."

Claire nodded. She had seen the massive line of red taillights back on the highway. Glancing at her watch, she said, "It'll be fine."

"Claire, I don't know what happened, but whatever it is, I'm very sorry for you and your family."

"What do you mean?" Claire asked genuinely curious.

Emily was confused. "Senator Taylor told me you had some sort of family emergency and that's why you're leaving for Miami."

Claire hesitated and then replied, "Oh, yes…Thank you, I guess."

Emily thought that was a strange response but didn't press her. They drove on in silence for a few minutes before Claire offered, "Don't fall in love, Emily. It's a bitch."

Emily grinned. Her first thought was that maybe Claire had a beau in Miami that was giving her a headache. She said, "I'll keep that in mind… Is that what's going on? Somebody back home's gone off the reservation?"

Claire shook her head. "No, Em. Somebody right here's gone off the reservation. And now I'm the one paying the price. I can't say any more about it, all right?"

Emily was slowly catching on. She nodded. "Got it. You didn't even have to say that."

"I know, and I probably shouldn't have, but I felt you deserved something. Thank you for driving me on such a miserable night."

"It's no problem," Emily said, thankful Claire was finally opening up a little. "When the senator called, I was happy to help out."

Claire snorted derisively. "Do yourself a favor and stay as far away from him as possible."

Emily didn't say anything to that, and Claire turned away to snuggle into her seat, signaling an end to the conversation. Emily thought about that exchange for a while as they traveled along an isolated stretch of Great Falls St., a couple of miles from Tysons Corner. Her curiosity had been aroused and she was dying to know the details but didn't want to pry. This had all the earmarks of a juicy story. Her father's repeated warnings about men bleated loudly in the back of her mind. In her mirrors, the strobing multicolored lights of a police vehicle suddenly caught her attention.

Looking down at her speedometer, she whispered, "Damn it…"

CHAPTER 4

Claire felt the car slow down and asked, "What's the matter?"

"There's a cop car behind us with his lights on."

Claire looked back over her shoulder and sighed, "How fast were you going?"

"Too fast, apparently," Emily replied drolly. "I was doing forty-five in a thirty-five zone... I can't believe they're going to do a pullover at this hour. There's an overpass just ahead. I'll stop there. No point in getting soaked. He might even appreciate the gesture and have mercy on us."

Seconds later, she drove her car off as far onto the shoulder as she could and waited. Shielded from the downpour, she could see much better, and in her side mirror, observed an unmarked SUV pull up behind her with a swirling red light on its dashboard. A large man in a black trench coat got out and walked toward them. His coat was buttoned up with a belt fastened in the front. He had his right hand in his pocket.

He wasn't in uniform.

Alarm bells went off in Emily's head and the hair on the nape of her neck stood up. Officers out of uniform in unmarked cars almost never made routine traffic stops especially not in the middle of the night. Granted she was speeding, but there was too much risk involved for everyone. She wondered if it would have been smarter to keep on driving to the nearest gas station or all night mini-mart. But to suddenly step on the gas now and drive away would certainly cause an even greater problem. And then, without doubt, Claire would miss her flight and they would both very possibly spend the night in a local jail. The senator would be very disappointed in her.

The second most powerful man in the United States would be disappointed in her. That thought made her cringe. Not a chance was she going to let that happen. Still, she didn't like the feeling she was getting. She needed some reassurance.

She pulled her bag onto her lap and reached inside with her right hand for her wallet. Next to it was the .38 special her father had given her. It was hammerless and had a five-round capacity. He had taken her to the range so she would have some familiarity with it, but she had never intended on ever using it. Her father had told her it was terribly inaccurate at more than a few feet. The idea with the .38 was only to shoot someone who was violating your personal space against your wishes. She wrapped her hand around the grip for security and waited as her heart pounded.

The man was tall and broad shouldered, clean cut and shaved, wearing a black cap tilted slightly over the front of his face. He was dripping wet. Overall, his appearance and posture certainly suggested law-enforcement. He tapped on the window and Emily rolled it down. Her finger rested on the trigger guard with the barrel pointed in his direction. It would be no big deal to let go of the weapon and take out her wallet.

When the window fully opened, the man placed his left hand on the frame of the car and looked inside, studying the two women. Then he scanned the rear seat. It was if he was trying to determine if he had the right car. Just then Emily noticed something else that sent her into a frantic tailspin. He wore a latex surgical glove. Something was really not right here. Her finger went from the trigger guard to the trigger.

"Please turn the engine off ma'am."

"But it's cold officer."

"It won't be for very long ma'am. I promise."

She didn't want to take her right hand off the gun, and reached over with her left to turn the engine off, hoping he didn't notice the slightly awkward move, but he didn't. He was preoccupied with studying Claire.

The man asked, "Are you Claire Tompkins?"

Claire paused a beat, looked puzzled and replied, "Yes, that's me, but I don't understand."

The man looked at Emily said, "You must be Emily Hoffman."

Even more surprised, Emily nodded, "Yes, I am."

Claire leaned closer to Emily to get a better view of the guy. "Hey, I know you. We've met at the senator's office…"

Emily relaxed a hair and turned slightly toward Claire. The familiarity she voiced was comforting. She never saw the smooth motion as the man slid the handgun from his pocket and into the car. Even with a silencer, the sudden explosion was deafening, and burnt gunpowder filled the small confines of the cabin. The flame from the end of the barrel singed the side of Emily's face and hair. The back of Claire's head burst open splattering the inside of the vehicle and the bullet rocketed through the passenger side window. Time slowed down as Emily froze with shock and fear. She was mostly deaf from the report as her gaze followed the large pistol moving back toward the open window on her side. Cold damp air rushed at her, reviving her senses.

The man grabbed her chin and said, "Open your mouth, sweetheart. This needs to look like a murder suicide. You won't feel anything. I promise."

The words sounded muffled as if she were under water. She was confused and the heat from the hot barrel so close to her face was uncomfortable. She nodded and pulled the trigger of her .38 special. The shot rang out, blasted through her bag and hit the guy square in the throat. His fingers contracted reflexively, and as he fell backward, he fired off a wild shot that screamed past Emily's head, missing her by an inch, plowing into the upholstery of the car. He dropped his pistol and landed on his back, clutching his neck.

Emily opened the car door and stumbled out onto her hands and knees, gasping. The guy was three feet from her, gurgling and wheezing as a fountain of his blood shot through and around his fingers and hands. His eyes were wide open, but he wasn't seeing anything. He was dead. He just didn't know it yet. She quickly searched his pockets to see who he was. She found his wallet and opened it. Flipping through his credit cards, his driver's license, and other paraphernalia, she came across a photo ID and a badge that made her jaw drop.

Franklin Mills, Special Agent, Secret Service.

Shit.

She also found a small photo of Claire taken during happier times. Emily threw the wallet to the side and got back in her car. She was trembling uncontrollably and had to struggle to regain her composure. Claire was dead. She thought about calling the police. She ought to, right? And tell them what? She shot and killed a Secret Service agent with an illegal handgun? Would anyone believe he murdered Claire and was about to murder her too? Being raised by a cop had made her incredibly jaded. Why did he murder Claire? Her mind raced. He had asked for her by name, but he obviously hadn't known her well. She recognized him though, so their acquaintance had been casual at best. But he had a photo of Claire. What did that mean?

He also knew her name was Emily Hoffman. How? She had never met him before. Her eyes suddenly went wide with comprehension. This was an assassination. This agent had been sent for them both and wanted to confirm his targets before pulling the trigger. The last thing he had said was this needed to look like a murder suicide, but why?

Who could order a Secret Service agent to commit a double murder? That thought made her shudder. Not the kind of people who would appreciate their plot being thwarted. That was for sure. Her heart sank as she realized that her whole world had just been turned upside down and inside out. She looked around. She needed to get out of there in a hurry. Shots had been fired. Someone might have heard and dialed the police. A car might pass by at any moment.

She didn't know what to do but she knew she didn't want to try to explain this mess to anyone. She glanced at the agent. He had stopped struggling. He was too big for her to move off the road. Claire deserved better than to be left here while she ran away. The car was registered in her name, so she couldn't just abandon it either. A thousand thoughts at once begged for her immediate attention. She thanked God she wasn't prone to crying because if there ever was a time, this was it. She took a deep breath, started the engine and drove off with Claire slumped against the passenger door and the dead agent lying in the road with his SUV lights flashing.

Safely away, she dialed home. Her father answered on the third ring. She pictured him looking at the time and becoming alarmed. He was.

"Emily, are you all right?" he asked with all the stress in his voice that any father would have at an unexpected call from his daughter in the middle of the night.

"Dad, I'm in trouble."

Chapter 5

Cesari inserted the tip of the endoscope into Aunt Sofia's esophagus at exactly 1:15 a.m. They were in room 2 of the ICU at St. Matt's hospital on Third Avenue between East 9th and East 10th St. Aunt Sofia had blood pouring in through a central line and she was already on her sixth unit of packed red cells. The hum of mechanical ventilation droned rhythmically in the background as Cesari advanced the scope. She was now heavily sedated and motionless. Her initial labs indicated that in addition to her having hemorrhaged away half her blood volume, the shock had provoked a heart attack as well. Surgeons stood at the ready, but Cesari knew that realistically her likelihood of making it through the night rested on his ability to stop the bleeding. The chances of a woman her age surviving emergency surgery while experiencing an acute cardiac event were slim to none. Even if he succeeded, he didn't think her odds were that great. Vito, Enzo, Angelina and Teresa were in the waiting area while the rest of the family were in the emergency room receiving intravenous fluids and antiemetics.

Cesari looked at the screen. They were in the distal esophagus and fresh blood obscured much of the visibility. He cleaned up the area as best he could with bursts of fresh water from a pump attachment. Eventually, he identified an artery spurting bright red blood from the center of a two-centimeter tear in the mucosal lining at the gastro-esophageal junction.

He turned to his nurse. "Debbie, give me a syringe with epinephrine and then set up the heater probe. She has a Mallory-Weiss tear."

Debbie was young and relatively inexperienced and hadn't seen a lot of GI bleeds yet. She handed him the equipment he requested and asked, "What's a Mallory-Weiss tear?"

It was a reasonable question. As he manipulated a thin plastic catheter through the scope, he replied, "When people vomit forcefully or repetitively the internal pressure generated can actually rip apart the lining of the esophagus exposing and even rupturing arteries. Kenneth Mallory and Soma Weiss were physicians who first described this phenomena in 1929. They were at Harvard of course."

Standing at the head of the bed, the anesthesiologist added sarcastically, "Naturally…"

Jaskaran Singh, Jay to his friends, was a Sikh from Queens, New York. His traditionally long hair was tucked discreetly under his OR cap which was a shame because Cesari really liked the colorful turbans he usually wore. And even wearing a surgical mask, he couldn't hide his famously bushy beard. Jay claimed he was descended from warriors, but Cesari was somewhat skeptical about that. Regardless, he was one of the best anesthesiologists Cesari had ever worked with.

Cesari responded with equally deep sarcasm, "Now, now, Jay. We shouldn't cop an attitude towards our friends in the Ivy League. If it wasn't for them, we wouldn't have Oxford shirts, loafers, and crew neck sweaters... How's my patient doing?"

Jay glanced at his machines and replied, "Rock steady, Cesari. Blood pressure's a little soft and pulse is a little high as to be expected, but I'm working on it. She's oxygenating well."

"Good. Keep her alive. I hate to think of the international implications this will have."

"So what happened?"

The catheter Cesari was sliding down the length of the scope suddenly appeared on the screen in front of them. He said, "Not entirely sure, Jay. Mass food poisoning or food borne infections can happen. If one of the kitchen workers was ill and didn't wash his hands well, he might have tainted some common food that was served. However, Salmonella, Shigella, E. coli or viruses such as norovirus don't usually manifest symptoms this quickly. Usually, an illness that acts this fast is the result of some type of preformed toxin like staph that's just sitting around waiting for somebody to ingest it, but even that can take several hours to kick in. There's something very unusual about the way everyone got sick all at once."

"Is that why the police and the FBI are involved? They're crawling all over the ER."

Cesari nodded, cleaned the area again with water and then injected the vessel with epinephrine a couple of times until the bleeding subsided somewhat and he could see things clearly. He said, "Unfortunately, we live in the age of terrorism and insanity, and they have to be concerned about the possibility that this might have been deliberate using some type of poison or chemical toxic to humans. The Department of Health and Poison Control Center are all over this already. They shut the restaurant down and are testing everyone and everything in it for arsenic to anti-freeze. Debbie, hand me the heater probe. I want to coagulate this vessel into oblivion."

Cesari withdrew the epinephrine catheter and replaced it with the heater probe. After he jockeyed it into position, he stepped on a pedal and applied microbursts of heat and energy to the site. The flesh burned and smoked and after several applications, he was satisfied with his work. The bleeding was no more. He then examined the rest of the stomach and duodenum for any other problems. Not finding any, he withdrew his instrument, thanked everyone, and spoke with the intensive care doctor taking care of Sofia. Then he went to find Vito and his family.

They were sitting in the ICU waiting room talking to a large man wearing a brown tweed suit, red bowtie and bowler derby hat. He was clean-shaven, fifty years old, and jawed on the unlit stub of a sixty-ring cigar dangling out one side of his mouth. He was jotting notes down onto a small pad with a tiny number two lead pencil. Very old school, Cesari thought. On the small wood table in the center of the room rested a large Starbucks latte. Cesari could practically smell the pumpkin spice from where he stood.

Cesari entered the room and said, "I thought we agreed you were going to cut back on the pumpkin spice lattes, Detective."

The man turned and said, "Cesari, glad you could join us, and I'd rather give up my cat than my pumpkin spice lattes."

Detective Robert B. Tierney was a retired Marine who had spent one too many tours of duty in Iraq and Afghanistan, leading to chronic insomnia and post-traumatic stress. On more than one occasion, Cesari thought he was about to get shot because Tierney had him confused with some murderous Taliban chieftain he had been hunting, but tonight seemed to be a good night for the detective. Cesari's curious connection to a underworld figures such as Vito had caused him to interface with the detective on more than one occasion. Oddly, these interactions had led to a somewhat cordial relationship.

Cesari said, "The NYPD isn't convinced of the randomness of tonight's events, I presume?"

Tierney smirked. "You presume right. I was just taking statements. Gianelli already told me his version. Maybe you can tell me yours?"

"Certainly, but first let me update the family about their mother." Cesari walked past Tierney to where the others sat. He said reassuringly to Teresa, "Tell Angelina and Enzo that everything went well and that I was able to stop the bleeding. Sofia's resting comfortably and for the moment appears stable. She's been through a lot, and we've decided to keep her on the ventilator for the rest of the night. If all goes well, we'll remove the breathing tube in the morning."

Teresa translated and everyone let out a sigh of relief. Cesari added, "Although I am encouraged, the situation is still uncertain because of the heart attack she suffered. A cardiologist is on his way in to see her, and we are doing everything we can."

After Teresa relayed this, Enzo stood and shook Cesari's hand, saying, "I thank you so much."

Cesari turned to Tierney who said, "Very compassionate, Cesari."

"Thanks, now how can I help you?"

"Gianelli says nothing at all was out of place, and that the meal had just begun, more or less, when all hell broke loose. Is that how you see it too?"

"I was there less than an hour, but yes. I didn't get to eat very much, just a few clams, some calamari, and a few sips of wine. Everyone else was nibbling on olives and bread before I arrived. We were maybe thirty minutes into the hot antipasto course when everyone got sick. Nothing seemed out of the ordinary to me."

"Nothing at all? No suspicious characters lurking behind giant wheels of parmigiano reggiano?"

"Nothing at all, but I was quite distracted chatting with Vito."

"Yeah, that's what he said too. Big family get together from the old country. Lots of personal drama to fill you in on. He told me all about Romeo and Juliet over there."

"That's about right. We'll know more about what happened when the toxicology comes back. The Department of Health is performing an investigation to determine if it was something in the food or drinks. Anything's possible right now."

"Including attempted murder?"

"Murder?" Cesari asked. "I know terrorism is on the table, but honestly, that seems unlikely."

"I didn't mean terrorism. I meant good old-fashioned guinea on guinea crime."

Vito, who had been sitting quietly with his family, heard that and jumped to his feet, bridling with hostility. "C'mon Tierney. You're out of line. Every time an Italian lands in the emergency room, you call them criminals. That's racist."

Tierney shot him a look. "Is it? Being a little touchy, aren't you, Gianelli? Besides, you had your turn. Now let Cesari speak."

Cesari said, "Give him a break, Detective. This is his family. He didn't even know he had any until a short while ago, and I'm not sure I understand what you're getting at."

"That's right. You weren't here when Vito's cousin, Enzo, gave his statement."

"He's not my cousin," interjected Vito, fuming.

"Not yet, you mean," retorted Tierney.

Cesari stepped in between them. "What are you talking about? It's late, I'm starving, and I still have things to do with Sofia."

Teresa had been listening intently and joined the conversation. "Before you arrive, Enzo tell the detective that his mother, Rosaria, is responsible."

Cesari's eyes went wide. "What?"

Tierney grinned triumphantly. "See what I mean?"

"Please explain, Teresa," asked Cesari.

"Enzo say that his mother, Rosaria, do to him the malocchio. How do you say in English? She give to him the evil eye. He is cornuto… cursed. Because he no do what she say and marry Angelina. Enzo is very superstitious."

Cesari rolled his eyes at Tierney, "You can't be serious?"

"Why not? It's not that far a stretch. People cast evil spells on others all the time and then orchestrate bad things to happen for real knowing that the more gullible the victim is the more likely they'll blame it on the magic. What do you think the basis for voodoo is?"

Cesari shook his head dismissively, "Some old woman in Sicily poisoned an entire restaurant in New York because her son is marrying the girl she wants for his older brother? That's your theory? This is a joke, right? Please let me know when you give your press conference. I want a front a row seat and a bucket of popcorn."

"Think about it, Cesari. Opening night in Manhattan is an unmitigated disaster. The Department of Health shuts him down. His reputation is shot to hell. Enzo loses his shirt. Angelina is humiliated. The wedding is called off. The entire gang high tails it back to Sicily where Angelina finds solace in the arms of Ernesto."

Teresa said, "Rosaria è la suocera dall'inferno."

Cesari and Tierney looked at her confused.

She added, "Rosaria is the mother-in-law from hell."

Chapter 6

At the break of dawn the next day, Emily was sitting at the kitchen table in her parents' home in a suburb of Philadelphia. Staring blankly at each other over steaming mugs of hot coffee, the mood was decidedly morose. Emily's parents were in their late forties, fit and healthy, just starting to gray. Her mother was an ER nurse and her father was on the fast track for chief of police in their small town. Right now they were both pale and in shock. Their only child had left them to make her way in the world and had returned with a dead body in her car.

"Are you sure he was a Secret Service agent, Emily?" her father asked grimly, breaking the ice.

She thought about it for a minute. "The ID on him looked real enough. Why else would he have it?"

"People make false ID's all the time these days. It's the way predators disarm people. Show them the phony badge or ID and people relax. It happens all the time."

"He didn't show us any ID, Dad. He just started shooting. I found the ID after I shot him. Besides, he knew who we were by name, and Claire knew him from the Capitol building. Just before he killed her, she said she'd recognized him from the senator's office."

Her mother said, "Fred, she's exhausted. Don't interrogate her now."

"I'm sorry, Kathy, but I'm not sure we have much time. First of all, there's a dead body in our garage, and if the man really was Secret Service and was sent to kill Emily and her friend, then they will have a great deal of resources at their disposal to figure out what happened and where they might be."

"Why would anyone want to kill our daughter? That doesn't make sense."

"I don't know why either, but that's not the point. Clearly the agent was looking for them or maybe he was looking for Emily's friend and Emily was just collateral damage." He turned to Emily. "Do you know of any reason why someone would want Claire dead?"

She shook her head. "No, not really."

"What was the big crisis in Miami that she had to leave in such a hurry?"

"I don't know. I was told it was a family emergency, but she didn't talk that much in the car. She cried most of the time."

"Think hard, Emily. Did she say anything that seemed odd?"

"She told me to not fall in love... I don't know. It seemed like girl stuff... She also told me to stay away from the senator."

"Which senator?"

"Her boss, Senator Taylor. She said to stay as far away from him as possible."

"Why?"

"She didn't say... But she said something else. When she told me to not fall in love, I asked if that was why she was going to Miami. I thought maybe she had a boyfriend there and that maybe they were having problems. She said no. That it had to do with someone in D.C. and that she was paying the price... What are we going to do with her? Her family needs to know what happened."

"Right now, Em, we have to decide what to do with you. I don't like the idea of government agents trying to murder my daughter. Whatever happened to Claire has now involved you, and I'm concerned that it will shortly embroil your mother and myself as well. It won't take them long before they come sniffing around here looking for you. Claire didn't make her flight so they will very correctly assume she's with you."

Emily's mother covered her mouth in horror. "Can't we call the FBI or state police?"

"We can," he countered, "and they'll arrest Emily on numerous charges from murder to obstruction of justice to possession of an illegal handgun to transporting a corpse across state lines. Not to mention, they'll destroy us in the process."

"But it was self-defense," she argued back.

"Yeah, our Emily vs. the Secret Service. I can see the trial now. If she makes it to trial, that is. Obviously, we're not dealing with people who worry too much about laws or morality."

"What do I do?" Emily asked apprehensively.

"You can start by ripping up your credit cards and throwing away your cellphone. Your friend's cellphone too. That's the easiest way to find someone." He sighed deeply, looking worried. "Depending on how determined these people are, they could track you all the way here just by following the pinging of your phones as they passed each cell tower."

Emily and her mother groaned.

"It's water under the bridge. Besides, I have an idea how to throw them off the cellphone trail. Look, the timer starts now. I have two thousand dollars in cash in the safe in the basement, I'll give it to you, and we'll get you a cheap phone with pre-paid minutes. I'll take care of your car, but you're going to have to leave, and I mean immediately."

"Fred, don't you think you're overreacting? She has to sleep. The poor thing has been up all night."

"She needs to pack a duffle bag. Travel light and keep moving. Don't call anyone. We'll call you. As for overreacting, keep in mind there are two dead people now and one of them is in my garage. So no, I don't believe I'm overreacting."

Emily felt sick to her stomach. "Where am I going?"

He said, "I have a friend in New York. We served together in the Marines. He's a detective in Manhattan. His name is Robert Tierney. We haven't talked in a while, but he's a good man. I'll ask him if you can stay with him for a few days while we try to piece together the big picture. In fact, I'll have him buy you the cellphone. Then there'll be no way of tracing it back to me."

"How do you know he'll help?"

"Because Emily, once a Marine, always a Marine. We covered each other's asses for multiple tours in Iraq and Afghanistan. If he's alive, he'll help. I know it. Now please go pack some clothes while I call him."

"And Claire?"

"No one can know about Claire, Emily. Not even her parents. Not now anyway. Maybe when this is all over, but not now. Our best chance is secrecy. Whoever sent that man for you will be confused this morning when his guy doesn't check in. They'll try to sort it out before taking any action. If her body shows up, it will tip our hand."

Emily said flatly, "I left my Crohn's medications in my apartment."

Both parents stared glumly at her. In the heat of the moment, they had momentarily forgotten the albatross around Emily's neck. "How are you feeling right now?" her mother asked.

"Lousy, but mostly just from the stress of it all. I'm not flaring yet but at the rate this is going, it won't be long until I do."

Her father said, "One thing at a time. You're still in touch with that doctor in New York? The one who took care of you in college?"

"Yes, Dr. Cesari. He's still prescribing my meds. I haven't found a new doctor yet."

"When you're in New York you can give the doctor a call for more medications. I don't think we should go back to your apartment until this blows over."

"You mean if this blows over."

Everyone was quiet for a moment digesting that last part. After a minute, her mother rose from the table, tears streaming down her face. "I'll make breakfast for you, Emily. You'll need to eat before you go."

Emily left the table and went to her room to pack. Though she had an apartment in D.C. much of her stuff was still there. She was still at that age where one foot was out the door but the other still at home. Her mother occupied her troubled mind by making pancakes and sausage while her father stepped into the living room to call Detective Tierney of the NYPD.

"Sergeant Tierney, this is Corporal Hoffman."

"Fred, long time no talk."

"Too long, Gunny. Semper fi."

"Oorah, brother. What can I do for you?"

Fred explained the situation leaving nothing out. The last thing he would ever want to do was to mislead a fellow Marine he was trying to recruit for his own personal battle.

When he was done, Tierney whistled, "I assume you've thought it through. A lot of people are going to be looking for her."

"I know. That's why I'm worried. This is all happening real time, Bob. I'm running on instinct right now trying to protect my daughter. A guy with the Secret Service wearing latex gloves was about to shove a pistol in her mouth a few hours ago for reasons as yet unknown."

"I see your point and I agree. Better to keep her under wraps while we sort it out. How do you plan on getting her up here?"

"It's a two-hour train ride to Grand Central Station from here. I'll pay cash for the ticket. I can get her there by noon. She's going to be a basket case."

"I don't like the idea of public transportation, Fred. Too many cameras and paper trails even with cash. And I don't like the idea of her travelling alone either."

"I can drive her there."

"No, I like that idea even less. You're going to have your work cut out for you down there. I'll come down to you and pick her up. I'll leave immediately."

"Bob, I can't put you out like that."

"Are you trying to make me angry, corporal?"

"No Gunny, I'm not, and thank you."

"What about the car and the dead girl?"

"I feel terrible about it, but I think I should dispose of them both."

Tierney didn't like that idea either. "That's going to be rough on her family."

"I know, but I'm not sure what to do. I can't just ship the body to them, and if she shows up somewhere, someone will put it together. I was thinking Emily's best chance was if whoever did this was kept in the dark about what happened."

"I think we can keep them off-balance and still give the family some resolution, Fred. What do you drive?"

"An old pickup. Why?"

"Wrap the girl up in a tarp and place her in the back of the pickup. Clean the blood from Emily's car as best you can and take it to a car compactor. You can pay those guys under the table to crush it off the books. That'll take care of the car."

"And the body?"

"You've got to get it away from where you live. These guys aren't stupid. If it shows up anywhere near you, they'll know you're involved. Bring it back down to D.C. tonight and leave it somewhere, maybe in the Potomac or behind the Lincoln Memorial. Is she a big girl? Hard to lift?"

"Not at all. Slender. I could fit her into a large suitcase."

"Whatever you do, do so carefully and wear gloves. After you drop her off, call the D.C. police anonymously, and get rid of the gun Emily used. Are you down with this?"

Fred Hoffman took a deep breath and let it out slowly. "I'd rather wipe my ass with steel wool, but it's my daughter, so yeah."

"Good, then start coaching your wife so you guys stick to the script if and when they come."

"And Emily?"

"One step at a time. Does she have a passport?"

"Yes…"

"Tell her to bring it. She may be leaving the country for a while. If it's the government that's looking for, she won't be able to stay under the radar for very long. Meanwhile, I'll pick us up burner phones. Don't call me again on this line. Do you have that?"

"I do. Anything else?"

"Go through the dead girl's personal effects. You might find some clues as to what's going on. Later today, you should report Emily missing. It won't seem natural if you don't. What about Emily and the girl's cellphones? They'll trace them right to your house once they regroup."

"I already thought about the phones. They'll know Emily came here or near here. I'll stick with that and go to downtown Philly where I'll plant her phone somewhere on a train bound for Pittsburgh or Chicago. I wasn't sure about Clair's phone, but I think I'll bring it back to D.C. with her body."

"That's a reasonable plan, corporal. A lot of plausible deniability in it. They can't be one hundred percent sure that Emily didn't just pass through without stopping. And they won't really know what happened to Claire. I like it. Lots of confusion. I can see the pointy heads who are pulling the strings sitting there scratching their chins. Good job."

"Roger that, Chainsaw, but there is one more thing you need to be aware of."

Tierney smiled. It had been a long time since anyone had used his Marine call sign. "I'm listening, Hawkeye," he replied.

"Emily has Crohn's disease."

Chapter 7

Cesari heard pounding on his apartment door. It was 7:30 a.m. and he was exhausted. He didn't get to bed until well after 3:00 a.m. and felt like he had a massive hangover. Sofia had stabilized and was doing as well as possible under the circumstances. Vito had taken his family back to his apartment where they could console each other in comfort. Everyone else that had become ill were either treated and released or were still in the emergency room under observation. Sofia was the only one that night who warranted admission. Rolling out of bed, he threw on a robe and stumbled into his living room, squinting as sunlight hit him through a window. He looked through the peep hole and opened the door.

"Detective Tierney. What can I do for you?"

Detective Robert Tierney was wearing the same three-piece brown tweed suit from the night before. Instead of holding one gigantic Starbucks in his hands, he held two. One was for Cesari.

He had a serious look on his face as he said, "Wake up Cesari, I brought you coffee. Black, right? French roast? We have things to do. How's your aunt Sofia?"

"She's not my aunt. She's Vito's aunt, and all things considered, she's doing okay. Thanks for the coffee, and what things do we have to do?"

"An hour ago, I received a call from an old friend, Fred Hoffman. He was my corporal in the Marines. He's now a cop in Lansdale, Pennsylvania. He has a daughter in her early twenty's named Emily. She's your patient. Sound familiar?"

"Emily Hoffman, of course I remember her. Is everything all right? And come on in," Cesari said, suddenly very interested.

He stepped aside to allow Tierney room to enter the apartment. They went to sit on the sofa and Tierney placed Cesari's venti in front of him. Cesari picked it up and inhaled its aroma before taking a sip.

"No, there's something wrong, very wrong," replied Tierney tersely and then summarized the story, adding at the end, "Can you get her medications and provide her medical care without formally documenting it? It's a big favor, I know, and I'd owe you one. It's important that she lay low, and the government's tapped into everything these days."

Cesari sat back with his coffee. "This is unbelievable. Yeah, I can do that as long as she doesn't require hospitalization or emergency care. Is she okay now?"

"Emotionally, she's a wreck as you can imagine, but Fred told me her Crohn's seems to be holding its own for the moment. Emily's very concerned that all the stress is going to bring on a flare-up. Is that possible?"

"Very much so."

"Well, that brings me to the second part of why I'm here. Fred asked me if I would let her stay in my place. I have no problem with that but because of her medical condition and the need to keep her away from hospitals and doctor's offices, I'm asking you if she can stay here. You'll be in a much better position to evaluate her if a problem with her health should arise."

Cesari thought it over. It did make sense, at least for a few days anyway. "Did Emily agree to that? She's half my age, and it's a fairly creepy proposition to share a flat with her close to middle-aged gastroenterologist."

"I don't know yet because I didn't ask her. I didn't think of it until after I hung up with Fred, and now I don't want to call him back because I can't be sure who's listening in on his line. My plan is to pick up some burner phones right after I leave here. We're talking about the Secret Service, Cesari. One of their guys is dead and we have no way of knowing who sent him, why they sent him, and just how unhappy they are that he can't tell them what happened."

"They probably know that Emily has Crohn's disease, and that she'll require medical care at some point."

"That's a safe assumption. She's a congressional intern, and I doubt she would have lied about it on her application."

"Okay, I'll pull up her chart and find out what meds she needs. Then I'll check my office to see if I have samples to give her. If not, I'll hit up a pharmaceutical rep for what we need. When will she arrive?"

"As soon we go get her, so get dressed. It's a two-hour drive from here. My car is gassed up downstairs and ready to go." He glanced at his watch. We'll be back in time for lunch."

"Why am I going?"

"Emily was ten years old the last time she saw me. You've been taking care of her more recently. She trusts you. It will be very reassuring for her to have someone she feels comfortable with along for the ride, and the idea of staying here will be better received coming from you personally."

"Do I have time to shower?"

****

Vito poured coffee for Teresa while Enzo and Angelina slept. It was her second cup. They were in his heavily guarded apartment on Mulberry Street in Manhattan's Little Italy and Vito was feeling a variety of intense and very conflicting emotions. He had no family, and then suddenly he did, and now he was very close to losing his mother's only sister. Not to mention, the euphoria of the reunion had now been replaced by dark thoughts of revenge. He had been brooding all night. So much so, that he hadn't even bothered trying to sleep. Mocha pot after mocha pot of espresso fueled his rage. At his core, Vito was not a very complicated man. If you hit him, he hit you back harder. He would never stop to ask the question of why you hit him. That was completely irrelevant to him.

The possibility of attempted murder had been raised and now that it had, he couldn't shake it. Somebody had rained on his parade, and his anger was mounting as was his need to counterattack. The question was who the object of his wrath should be.

"How's the coffee, Teresa?" he asked, trying not to wear his emotions on his sleeve.

She looked depressed and worried, but smiled weakly. "It is very good. Thank you."

"I think your mom is going to pull through. I really do. I trust Dr. Cesari with my life."

"If you trust him, then I will to trust him also, but mama is old woman."

"I know what you mean. At her age anything can happen, and much of it already has, but let's be positive. You know, day by day."

She nodded but didn't say anything to that. Vito gently prodded her, "Tell me a little bit about Ernesto and Rosaria. I met them briefly a couple of weeks ago and I know how strongly they felt about the wedding, but I guess I thought it was mostly just acting out. What's your take on it?"

"What means acting out?"

Vito rephrased the question. "I may have underestimated how serious their objections to the wedding were. I thought they were just being dramatic. What do you think?"

She sipped her espresso and said, "They are very serious. They consider Enzo and Angelina's marriage a great infamnia... insult."

"A big enough insult to get revenge?"

She thought it over before saying, "I know you are Sicilian, Vito, but you were raised here in America where things are different. In Sicily, the codes of honor, respect, and family traditions are as real and present now as they were in Middle Ages. Defying Rosaria's wishes was terrible offense. But whether or no Rosaria or Ernesto would do something like this is wrong question. Could they do is better way to look at it. In America, everyone thinks every Sicilian is Mafia but that is no true. Mafia is tiny percentage of Sicily and growing weaker every day. To reach out and poison a restaurant in America would take great resources and planning that Rosaria and Ernesto no have. Rosaria and Ernesto no are Mafia. They simply would not have the ability to do what happened last night."

Vito nodded. What she said made sense, but if Rosaria and Ernesto weren't behind the attack, then who was? Maybe it was just an unfortunate coincidence like Cesari said. Some infected kitchen worker got everybody sick. They should string the bastard up.

He said, "You make a valid point, Teresa. I'm sorry for bringing it up like that. I'm just thinking it through."

"I understand, and believe me when I say there is no love lost between me and Rosaria. She is a hateful woman."

"I got it. Rosaria will never be person of the year, but that doesn't mean you think she would kill anyone."

"Esattamente... exactly."

"And Ernesto?"

"Ernesto does whatever Rosaria tells him to. He is mama's boy."

"Okay, then. We'll just have to wait and see what turns up."

"Is very difficult situation I know."

"But you know something? Ernesto sent a case of olive oil as a wedding present to Enzo and Angelina. It's possible that it may have been tampered with."

She picked up on where he was going and shook her head. "If that had happened, then I would be lying sick in hospital too. I was there when it arrived, and I helped Enzo in the kitchen that morning. I tasted plenty of the olive oil… enough to kill a horse if it was poisoned."

Vito let out a loud sigh. He knew he was grasping at straws. It was always like this. You went after the obvious targets first and wound up missing something big in the process. Sure, Ernesto and Rosaria had motive, but maybe someone else had motive too, but who? Who would want to hurt Enzo and Angelina like this?

He asked, "Out of curiosity is there anyone else who might have had a grudge against Enzo?"

Teresa seemed surprised by the question. "I don't think so. Enzo is very nice person. Help everyone, kind to everyone. All the girls in Palermo love Enzo. Want to marry him and make the baby."

Enzo was a good-looking guy but not that good-looking. For a second Vito wondered if Teresa needed glasses. On the other hand, a winning personality and sense of humor frequently overcame physical obstacles to romantic success. He was a prime example of that, he mused. What he lacked in looks, charm, and wit, he more than made up for with rippling muscles and overactive scent glands which sprayed pheromones into the atmosphere when unsuspecting females walked by.

As he mulled over the conversation, Teresa stood and thanked him for the coffee. She said, "I go wake Angelina and Enzo now. We should go visit mama."

She walked away leaving him with more questions than answers. His nerves were on edge, and he felt the need to beat someone senseless. What he really needed was a cigarette, and a reason to not get on the first flight to Palermo to discuss the matter personally with Ernesto and his mother. He wasn't entirely satisfied that they had nothing to do with it.

In fact, he was deeply dissatisfied with that assessment. This was one of those situations where if it looked like a duck and quacked like a duck then it was definitely a duck. Maybe there wasn't enough for law enforcement to pin it on them but that was the beauty of being him. He didn't require proof beyond a shadow of a doubt. All he needed was his suspicions and he would let his fists do the rest of the research necessary to determine innocence or guilt. He suddenly wondered what the weather was like there right now.

Palermo….

He took out his cellphone and called Gerry Acquilano. "Yeah, boss," was the quick response.

"Gerry, go find me a pack of Camels and bring them up here, and make it snappy."

Gerry hesitated and then said meekly, "But boss, you're on the patch."

"Gerry, I don't think I heard you right. It sounded almost as if you were questioning me."

"I'll be there in five minutes, boss."

Chapter 8

Deputy Director, Grayson Morehouse, entered 950 H St. NW, Washington D.C., closed his umbrella, shook himself off and passed through security, flashing his ID with a nod at the guard as he strode to the bank of elevators lining the far wall. Under his raincoat, he was dressed in a navy-blue suit, white shirt, and dark tie. Fifty years old, six-feet-two inches tall with a full head of hair that hadn't even started to thin or turn gray, he had successfully warded off the assault of time and the effects of a stressful job by eating healthy and hitting the gym hard four and sometimes five times a week. His only vice was a good glass of scotch. He arrived at the office of his boss, Travis Burke, the Director of the Secret Service and knocked politely before entering.

Burke was on the phone and waved him to a chair in front of his desk. Morehouse hung his London Fog on a coat hook behind the door and took a seat. The Director was ten years his senior and had been the man in charge for the last decade. The bureaucratic machine had ground him down, caused most of his hair to fall out, and etched a perpetual scowl on his face. Mandatory retirement was on the horizon, and he had been grooming Morehouse to be his hand-picked successor. There were generally two paths into the Secret Service. One was through the military and the other through law enforcement. Occasionally both. Burke had been an Army Ranger and from there had drifted into Army Intelligence before entering the Secret Service. Morehouse had been a hardboiled D.C. cop. Both men were dedicated and professional. Either would step in front of a bullet without hesitation to protect their president, even if they personally thought the man was a complete jackass.

Thankfully, Burke's tenure as Director had been uneventful. Despite the numerous threats and cranks that had to be dealt with on a regular basis, nothing even came close to being serious. There were no scandals under his watch either which always came as a great relief and was no small feat in the modern era of watchdog groups and fire-breathing media ready to pounce on every misstep no matter how minor. That is, until that morning.

Burke hung up the phone and exhaled loudly. He was exasperated and said, "Do you know who that was?"

Morehouse briefly considered cracking a joke about Hollywood calling but knew it wouldn't be well-received under the circumstances. He shook his head, "Tell me."

"That was Maureen Hennessy, the White House Chief of Staff. All of a sudden, she's my best friend. Wants me to call her day or night."

Morehouse glanced at his watch and remarked, "That was fast."

"Before she called, I had calls from the ATF, FBI, NSA and Homeland Security offering their assistance."

Morehouse smiled. "It's nice they want to help in our time of need."

"Bullshit and you know it. They're like piranha who smell blood in the water. Something happened and they all want to know what, and how they can work it to their advantage."

"Awfully cynical this morning, aren't you, boss?"

"I have a right to be. So tell me what you know, Grayson."

"Only what I heard on the news. That one of our agents, Franklin Mills, was found dead early this morning in Tysons Corner by a civilian on his way to work."

Burke nodded. "Yes, he was found dead but there's much more to it. How well did you know him?"

"As well as anyone can get to know one of three thousand special agents, I suppose. He seemed like an all-right guy. I've had a few beers with him. He liked football and the usual stuff. I reviewed his dossier on the way over here. Thirty-seven, single, ex-navy SEAL, saw service in Iraq, Afghanistan, and Africa. Exemplary record. Came directly to us after he mustered out. No real blemishes. Just a couple of minor dustups with the D.C. police over jurisdiction. Nothing big. Recently assigned to lead Senator Taylor's security detail now that he's decided to run for president."

"The senator hasn't made that announcement yet."

"No, he hasn't, but everyone knows he will. And since polling suggests he's the hands-on favorite to win, it was decided to go ahead and assign him protection, despite the lack of any real threats at the moment, but you know all that."

Burke was prone to mental exercises of this nature and continued, "Mills was requested personally by the senator's chief of staff, Rufus Youngblood, to head the detail."

"I am aware of that too. They were SEALs together. What are you thinking?"

"Just talking out loud... So, is that all you know? That Mills was found dead in Tysons Corner?"

"Yes..."

Burke nodded and said, "The first call I received this morning was from, Bud Morrison, the officer in charge of the Mclean district of the Fairfax County police department. He wanted to give me a head's up that we had a situation in Tysons Corner. At 5:00 a.m. this morning, the body of Franklin Mills was found lying face up in an underpass on Great Falls Street. A Secret Service Suburban with its engine on and lights flashing was not too far away. It was Mill's Suburban. He'd been shot in the throat with a small caliber weapon. The time of death was probably just a few hours before he was found, somewhere between midnight and 2:00 a.m. They think he died more or less instantly. The citizen who discovered him called 911. EMS arrived first, followed shortly by the local cops and the coroner. The circumstances were highly irregular, and the uniforms woke up Bud. He concurred with his men that we had a problem and called me. I, in turn, have been fielding calls all morning culminating in the last one you walked in on."

"Nothing travels as fast as bad news."

"It gets much worse, Grayson."

Morehouse didn't say anything.

"Problem number one... Details are still a bit sketchy, and so far, they've been able to keep the media at bay, but Mills was found with a silenced Ruger several feet from his body. It wasn't issued by us, and the serial number had been filed off. The police there speculate that the shooter threw it away after he shot Mills. It had been fired twice, they think. They've recovered one bullet from the cement wall of the underpass, but they haven't found the second bullet."

Morehouse was confused. "What's the dilemma? The other bullet is probably still in Mills. I assume that was the murder weapon."

"Maybe... They can't be sure. The Ruger was a .45 caliber. The entry wound in Mill's neck appears much smaller than that, but he'll need to be examined more thoroughly, so there's the possibility the assailant or assailants may have had a second weapon with them."

"Okay, let's say they had a second weapon. Why do they think the Ruger was fired twice?"

"They're assuming. The magazine had a ten-round capacity and there were only eight bullets left. Seven in the magazine and one chambered."

"Still, that's a presumption. Like I said, if it's the murder weapon, the other round might still be in Mills. We won't know until the autopsy."

Burke nodded. "Problem number two... Mills' service issue Glock19 was still holstered. It's all preliminary of course, but there are some very troubling aspects to the case so far."

"I agree. A silenced, untraceable handgun makes this very disturbing, and why would the shooter leave his gun at the scene?"

Travis Burke strummed his fingers on the surface of his desk. "This is where it starts to get ugly. The reason Bud Morrison pressed the alarm bell is that it seems from the way everything was positioned, the silenced weapon may well have belonged to Special Agent Mills who may have dropped it when he was shot. At least that's one way of interpreting things."

Morehouse let that sink in. An agent with a silenced untraceable weapon. He was about to respond when Burke added, "Before you try to rationalize why, you should also know that Mills was wearing latex gloves."

Morehouse had a hard time wrapping his head around that one. Now it was an agent wearing latex gloves with a silenced, untraceable weapon in a deserted underpass. Beginning to think the unthinkable, and trying to fathom the unfathomable, he said, "There has to be some logical explanation other than what this is starting to look like."

The Director shook his head. "I wish there was. From the way Mill's Suburban was found on the road in relation to his body, it appears that he had done a pullover. That's all we know right now. We're damn lucky this guy, Bud Morrison, out in Tysons Corner isn't a complete asshole. He's kept almost all of this out of the press and even more importantly has agreed to not spill his guts to the other agencies until we've had a chance to look into the matter ourselves. He'll keep it in stall mode for as long as he can, even with his own chief."

"Why's he being so nice?"

"Now who's being cynical? Anyway you're right. He's got a kid in the D.C. police department. A five-year veteran. He wants in on the

Secret Service and plans on taking the SAEE next year. Our friend, Bud, would like us to look favorably at his application when the time arrives."

"I like Bud already."

"At least he knows how to play ball, but obviously we can't keep the FBI completely out of the loop. The murder of a federal agent on U.S. soil is their territory, but we can piggyback along on their inquiry and use their advantage in manpower and resources to aid our own parallel investigation. Clearly, we'd like to be the ones to reach the finish line first in order to control the narrative and limit the fallout."

"Roger that."

"Okay, let's get started. We have both a sensitive and time sensitive situation on our hands. You first, Grayson. What do we know and what does it look like?"

Morehouse rubbed his chin in thought before saying, "A veteran agent pulls over a motorist in Tysons Corner in the middle of the night out in nowhere with intent to do what? Things go awry and the agent gets killed."

"I disagree already," interrupted the Director. "You're being too nice. We know why he pulled the motorist over. There's only one reason why he would wear latex gloves and whip out a silenced, untraceable weapon. Agent Mills went there to assassinate someone. After that I agree with you. Something went terribly wrong, and the tables got turned on him. I want to know who the intended target was and who authorized agent Mills to do this, and I don't care how far up the food chain this goes. They're fucking with me now and they've just made a big mistake."

Morehouse nodded. He hated the idea of it, but they needed to run on the facts not sentiment. "I assume you want me to handle this personally?"

"You assume correctly. Other than you, me, and Bud Morrison, no one knows the full details, and after today, he's out of the loop. I want you to keep it that way. On many levels, this is going to require extreme discretion. To a degree, you're going to have to play ball with the FBI, but you know how to handle them. I don't want you to mislead them or feed them falsehoods, but we have to be careful. The FBI is like a sieve when it comes to sensitive information, and in some cases, they're a direct conduit to the press."

"Understood."

"Good. Start by finding the owners of every cellphone that pinged in the area of where Mills' body was found from the hours of say an hour or two before midnight to 6:00 a.m. Cross reference those with the contact list in his phone, any known acquaintances and fellow employees or anybody who even had the most remote connection with him. I want you to go over to Tysons Corner and review what they have. Reassure this Bud Morrison character that we here at the Secret Service are fully committed to honesty and fairness in the application process but that his son sounds like a fine and promising candidate who we would be thrilled to consider. Scour the area looking for cameras at traffic lights, rest stops and minimarts. Also check every hospital within a one-hour travel distance from Tysons Corner. Whoever was in that car might have been wounded and in need of medical attention."

"Mills' apartment?"

"I've already dispatched a team to scrub it down for fingerprints and DNA. I'm hoping they'll get there before the FBI. After they search it and take photos, they'll disassemble everything and bring it all to our forensics lab for further inspection. I told them to rip up the carpets and take the appliances. I want everything analyzed, down to the used condoms in his trash cans. If he had a girlfriend, bring her in for questioning. If he had a boyfriend, bring him in too."

"Won't the FBI consider that interfering with their investigation?"

The Director grinned slyly. "Why, was Mill's under investigation? If he was, I was unaware of it. Besides, I thought he was the victim. In any event, if an agent gets murdered, we have the right to recover anything that could potentially jeopardize one of our protectees. I'm pretty sure I could find a sympathetic judge to agree with that."

"What about Senator Taylor? This could affect him."

"Without question. You'll need to speak to him and his chief of staff about it, but go gently with those guys. Taylor could very well be the next president and your boss in a year's time."

"Full disclosure?"

"No, hold the particulars back for now. Tell them what we're going to tell the press. Mills died in the line of duty. As far as we know, he was conducting an independent investigation that led him to Tysons Corner and was driving back to D.C. when a disabled vehicle caught his attention. He stopped to lend a hand like the good Samaritan he was and was ambushed. He died a hero."

"Will they buy that? It smells too clean."

"Of course they won't buy it, but this is Washington. They'll understand the need for double-speak. While you're at it, try to pin Rufus Youngblood down for any information he might have about Mills' personal life. They were friends. He should know something."

"I'll need a team."

"Keep it small. Only people you can trust to keep their mouths shut."

Morehouse stood to leave, hesitated, and said, "Is it possible that this was personal? Maybe Mills had an axe to grind with an individual that doesn't involve some bigger conspiracy?"

Burke sat back in his chair as he thought about that. In time he said, "Not a chance. Mills was up to his eyeballs in something, and I want to know what."

CHAPTER 9

After picking up Emily and dropping off the burner phones with the Hoffmans, they drove back to Manhattan in Tierney's Buick. It was a very quiet journey. Emily had been surprised to see Cesari show up at her home and just as Tierney had predicted, she was both pleased and reassured to travel with someone she knew personally and trusted. Without hesitation, she agreed to stay at his apartment. Her parents were suddenly overwhelmed with confidence that everything was going to be all right. The good guys were mobilizing. Her medical condition was starting to weigh heavily on their minds and Cesari's presence miraculously lifted that burden. But exhaustion and worry were taking their toll and ten minutes into the ride, Emily dozed off in the rear seat with a hoodie covering her face.

Cesari glanced back at her sympathetically. He'd first met her four years earlier. She was eighteen and just starting NYU when she'd had a flare up of her Crohn's disease. They came to know each other very well over the next several months as he brought her symptoms to heel on a combination of medications. As she got better and better, he saw her less and less. It finally reached a point of biannual visits and blood work and then she graduated and moved away. She'd call occasionally to discuss problems as they arose, and he continued to call in prescriptions for her. Like most people her age, she wasn't particularly motivated to find a new physician until she had to, which had been okay with Cesari for the time being.

Tierney asked, "She sleeping?"

"Yeah."

"Pretty sick stuff what's going on."

"To say the least... Nice family."

"Salt of the earth, Cesari. I wish I had stayed in touch with them more."

"That's the way life is, Detective. We all move on."

Tierney sighed, "Yup..."

I-95 was straight, flat and monotonous from Philadelphia to New York. If it wasn't for the occasional tractor trailer trying to muscle them out of their lane, they might have passed out from boredom.

"Any ideas, Cesari?"

"Me? What would I know about this?"

"C'mon... You heard the story. Nobody likes conspiracies as much as you. You must have something popping around in your head."

"Thanks for the vote of confidence, but you forget I was up half the night trying to keep Vito's aunt alive. I can barely see straight. We'll know more when Emily gets some rest, and we can talk to her under slightly less stressful conditions. Plus, we have to go through her friend Claire's suitcase. Fred didn't have a chance to do that."

"I know. We probably shouldn't have taken the bag. It could tie us to the murder in a way that can't be easily explained."

"I think we're already tied to it in a way that can't be easily explained. I believe this is called harboring a fugitive."

Tierney snorted. "She's not a fugitive yet."

"Semantics aren't going to help anyone."

Tierney didn't say anything to that.

Cesari took his cellphone out and called Jaskaran. "Good morning, Dr. Singh. How's my favorite Sikh?"

Jay chuckled into the phone. "I'm good. If you're calling about Sofia, she's doing very well. I extubated her an hour ago and so far, no problems. Cardiology is in there now doing an echo, but I don't think they have any great plans for her other than observation. The intensivist said she can have clear liquids. Your big friend is here."

"Vito?"

"I don't know his name. He's pretty ugly. I'm having trouble picturing his parents."

Cesari laughed. "That's him. Is he bothering anyone?"

"No, not really but he's quite intimidating. He should wear a hazardous material sticker on his forehead, so people know to steer clear of him."

"I'll bring that up with him. Anyway, never mind him. Just don't show any fear. He's just worried about his aunt. So everything's good?"

"Everything's good."

"Thanks. Are you still in the ICU?"

"No, I'm on my way to the OR to do a hip replacement with that A-hole orthopedic surgeon."

"You just described every orthopedic surgeon I ever met. Which one in particular are we talking about?"

"That new guy Bell. He's an hour late for his case and had the nerve to blame me."

"How's it your fault?"

"Because it's always anesthesia's fault when something goes wrong. Didn't you get the memo? He says that he's late because we're always behind schedule so therefore he shouldn't be expected to show up on time. Can you believe this? He told the nurses he's going to file a complaint about it with administration."

"He's got some serious psychopathology going on."

"You're telling me? Who names their kid Alexander Graham Bell and then expects him to grow up normal?"

"Parents with a great sense of humor, I guess," reasoned Cesari. "Alexander's an okay name, but adding the Graham part was over the top… You know what? Why don't you and I take him out to the parking lot after work and ring his bell a few times? Get it? Ring his bell… Are you in?"

Jay chortled into the receiver. "I love the idea, but he's a pretty big guy. That's the other problem with orthopedic surgeons. They always come in triple extra-large."

"Seriously, Jay, you're worried about his size? I thought you had warrior blood in you. You told me so yourself. Didn't one of your ancestors single-handedly drive off an invading horde of Pathans to save his entire village in the Punjab?"

"True, true and true, but that was a long time ago, when men were men, and the goats were scared."

"Then it's settled. We'll lure the great Alexander Graham Bell into the parking lot after work where we can reach out and touch him."

"You're killing me with the Ma Bell jokes, Cesari, and I'm also a little worried that you're serious."

"Fine, I'll let you off the hook this time, but I'm not going to forget this."

Cesari clicked off the call and turned to Tierney. "Vito's aunt is doing much better."

Tierney shook his head. "That's good, and I'm sure I don't want to know what the rest of that incriminating conversation was about."

"Just the usual hospital politics."

"Why do you hate orthopedic surgeons?" asked Emily groggily from the rear seat.

Cesari looked over his shoulder and saw her yawning and stretching. "How much longer till we get there?" she added.

"We're fifteen minutes out from Manhattan," Tierney responded. You've been asleep for a little over an hour and a half."

"Wow, it feels like we just left Philadelphia."

Cesari said, "You were pretty out of it… Feel like talking?"

"Sure, but tell my why you hate orthopedic surgeons first."

He grinned. "I don't hate orthopedic surgeons… I loathe them."

"What's the difference?"

"You lived in Manhattan, Emily. Did you ever see a rat in an alley eating garbage out of a dumpster?"

She scrunched her nose at the all too familiar image of life in the Big Apple. "Eww…"

"Exactly. I have too. I don't hate the rat, but I definitely loathe the rat. It fills me with dread, and I think the world would be better off without rats, but I'm sure they must serve some important role in nature. I just haven't figure out what that role is."

Emily giggled. "You think orthopedic surgeons are the same as rats?"

"I never said that," protested Cesari. "I was just trying to explain the difference between loathing them and hating them. The truth is, I just don't like the way many orthopedic surgeons act. Because their procedures generate so much revenue for the hospital, they get treated special. And because they get treated special, they tend to feel entitled and more important than everyone else. They can be real divas at times."

Emily smiled. "So you're jealous?"

Tierney guffawed. "She nailed you right between the eyes with that one, Cesari. Glad to see you still have a sense of humor, Emily."

Cesari said, "I'm not jealous. I'm outraged that one particular medical specialty has been artificially raised in importance over all the others based on arbitrary reimbursement scales, not necessarily rooted in medical necessity, but that's neither here nor there. Anyway, would you mind very much talking about what happened last night?"

"No, I don't mind, but there's not a whole lot to say beyond what I've already told everyone."

Cesari nodded. "You said you worked with Claire, but how well did you know her? Were you friends outside of work?"

She shook her head. "No, not really. We would chat once in a while in the hallway. I had lunch in the congressional cafeteria with her once a couple of months ago, but we didn't go out together or call each other to talk. She was older and travelled in different circles. I didn't really know too much about her on a personal level."

"She cautioned you about Senator Taylor. What was your take on that?"

"I didn't really have time to think about it before the shooting started, but I suppose it could be interpreted in several ways. Maybe he's a handy kind of guy and she was warning me, but I personally never witnessed him to be anything but professional and courteous. I never felt uncomfortable around him if that helps."

"It does. Go on. How else would you interpret her warning?"

"Well, you don't get to be in the senator's position without stepping on a few toes. Let's face facts, politics is a full contact sort of sport and I'm sure that the senator had to climb over more than a few bodies to get to where he is. It's the nature of the beast."

"Agreed... so she may have been implying that you should watch your back around him."

"Possibly... or that he's the type of guy that uses people and then discards them when they've served their purpose."

"And the bit about not falling in love?"

"I really don't know. I was told she had a family emergency in Miami. My first reaction was that maybe there was some drama going on with a boyfriend there. I'm pretty sure now that had nothing to do with why she was leaving. But if she was involved with anybody at work, I never heard about it."

"Do you think you would have? What if it was a married man? A very important married man...like maybe a senator?"

She thought it over and then said, "I think if she was involved with the senator, or some other high-ranking person, I would have heard about it. That's the kind of juicy story the water coolers thrive on, especially amongst the women. They love that stuff."

"How long have you been an intern, Em?"

"Six months."

"You've learned a lot about people in six months."

"Politics ages you really fast. It's sink, swim or be eaten alive."

Cesari said flatly, "Or get shot."

Chapter 10

The phone rang sharply, breaking her concentration. She was dreading the call. She had turned on the news that morning and had been horrified. The worst case scenario had happened. A quick glance at the number and she knew things were about to get a lot worse.

She put the phone to her ear. "You've heard?" the voice on the other end asked gruffly without any preliminary pleasantries.

"Yes…"

"What went wrong?"

"I don't know."

"You don't know wasn't the response I was hoping to hear. The big guy isn't pleased. He didn't expect incompetence on this level."

She said nothing.

"When was the last time you heard from him?"

"At about 9:00 p.m. last night. He had them under surveillance. We finalized the plan and he said he would call me when he was done."

"Can I ask you something?"

She said nothing. It was a rhetorical question.

"How the fuck did he survive eight years in Iraq and Afghanistan and then get ambushed by a secretary?"

"I don't have an answer for that."

"Well you better start thinking of one because it's your turn at bat. We've lost track of the women and the car, and I mean completely. The secretary never made her flight, and the intern didn't show up for work this morning. We need to know what happened to them. Start checking hospitals. You already have the make and license plate of the car they were driving. The intern was from somewhere around Philadelphia. That's not too far from here. I'll text you the address. If she was frightened or wounded, she may have gone home to mommy and daddy. Needless to say, if anyone finds them before we do then we're all going down."

"I can't just up and leave."

"I don't think you fully understand the implications of what just happened. Everything else in your life just got put on hold. Your boy screwed up and you need to make this right. Am I being clear enough?"

"Perfectly. Do we have a lead on their phones?"

"Not yet, but I'm working on it. Don't call me. I'll call you."

The man hung up abruptly and she threw her phone angrily into a sofa cushion. She was pissed off. Involuntarily, she paced back and forth trying to sort out the night's events. Mills was a large, well-trained agent, a born killer with great instincts. Yet somehow, two young women with absolutely zero combat experience left him dead on the side of the road.

It was inconceivable.

****

Cesari got off the elevator and headed toward the ICU to check on Sofia. When he left his apartment, Emily was sleeping on his sofa and Tierney was at the kitchen table rummaging through Claire's suitcase looking for clues. He had a lot to do, starting with telling his secretary that he was taking the rest of the week off, and then ransacking the medication cabinet in his office on Emily's behalf. If that didn't pay off, he would call a pharmaceutical representative for samples. As a last resort, he would call in a prescription for himself to his local pharmacy and pray they didn't report him to the state. It was generally frowned upon to self-medicate, but as long as he didn't prescribe himself narcotics, he figured he should be okay.

Sofia was resting comfortably with her eyes closed. Teresa was at her side saying the rosary. Vito, Enzo, and Angelina were nowhere in sight. Cesari smiled at Teresa but didn't say anything so as to not disturb Sofia. He studied the monitors and determined that Sofia's vital signs were stable with a healthy rhythm. Then he signaled Teresa to join him outside the room.

When she did, he asked, "Is everything all right?"

She nodded. "Yes, mama is feel good but very tired."

"I'm glad. I'm going to speak with the cardiologist and ICU doctor in a few minutes to see what they have to say. How are you and your sister doing?"

"We are good. Cousin Vito has been very kind to us. Treat us very well."

"I'm glad to hear that."

"Mama say her throat hurt from where the breathing tube was."

"That's normal and will go away in a day or two. I'll tell the nurses to give her some lozenges. That will soothe her discomfort. She hasn't said anything about being short of breath or having chest pain?"

She shook her head. "No, she say she is hungry. When can she eat?"

"Let me talk to her doctors so we're all on the same page. If everybody is in agreement, we'll start feeding her. We usually begin with clear liquids to make sure she's not going to retch again. If she tolerates that, then we'll advance to a regular diet, which in a hospital means some type of bland chicken and steamed carrots. I'm afraid that our supplies of pancetta and tiramisu are a little low."

Teresa smiled. "I don't think she will mind."

"I'll talk to you later."

"Thank you, Dr. Cesari."

She turned and went back into the room with her mother as Cesari watched. She was kind of cute, he thought; slender, about five-four, brown eyes, long dark hair, olive skin with a certain kind of innocence about her. Meandering over to the nursing station thinking about her, he wondered if she had a baby, would the child be born with a mustache. Shuddering, he put it out of his mind, and found the intensivist sitting in a conference room staring at his laptop.

Herb Bronstein was a chubby guy in his late thirties, with curly brown hair and generally unkempt appearance. He was munching on a bagel with cream cheese and lox.

Cesari said, "A little late in the day for breakfast, isn't it Herb?"

Herb looked up from his computer. "First of all, it's never too late in the day for bagels and lox, but more importantly, when you work night shifts for three months and then suddenly switch to days, you get a little disoriented as to what time of day it is and what food groups you should be eating. What's up, Cesari?"

"How's the little Italian lady in room 2 doing from your perspective?"

"She's doing well. I just got off the horn with cardiology. Her echo shows minimal damage and she's been rock stable. He feels the event was demand mediated because of the stress of the GI bleed and doesn't require any further work up. We'll watch her for another day. If nothing happens, we'll transfer her to a floor bed. All her labs look great, and she's had no bleeding since last night. How would you feel about feeding her?"

"Start her on clears. Wait a few hours and if she doesn't toss it back up advance her diet. Leave her on the pantoprazole drip and IV antiemetics for another twenty-four hours and then switch her over to oral meds."

"Will do… It's pretty unbelievable what happened, isn't it? I mean who would want to do such a thing?"

Cesari looked at him puzzled. "What are you talking about?"

"You didn't hear?"

"Hear what?"

"Poison Control was here earlier. They were all poisoned. It was the caponata. Specifically, it was the olive oil used to make the caponata."

Cesari's jaw dropped. "You can't be serious? This wasn't viral or bacterial?"

"I kid you not. They found traces of ipecac in the eggplant and in one of the bottles of olive oil they used at the restaurant."

"Ipecac? I didn't even know people used that anymore."

"They don't but it's still widely available for sale. Anyone can buy it off the internet. And since there's no natural way for anything to be contaminated by ipecac, it had to be deliberate."

Cesari was speechless and just stared at him for a long moment before saying, "There was a big guy here. That's his aunt in room 2. Did you mention this to him?"

"Of course. I had to, and I have to tell you, he wasn't too thrilled. I wouldn't want to be the guy who did this when he catches him."

"I agree with that assessment. Thanks, Herb. Keep me posted if anything happens."

Cesari left to go find Vito. A calm Vito was hard enough to control. An angry Vito was like a cruise missile with a malfunctioning guidance system. As he walked past Sofia's room, he noticed she was still sleeping. He stopped by the door and Teresa came over to him.

"Were you here earlier when the doctor talked to everyone?" he asked.

"Yes… Why?"

"So you know what happened?"

"You mean about the poison?"

He nodded. "Yes."

"Yes, he tell us. Is terrible person to do this."

"I agree. So everybody knows about the ipecac?"

"Yes, but what is ipecac? He did not explain well. He just say make everyone sick."

"It's a drug that was once commonly used to induce emesis in patients who ingested poison. The idea was to help them get the substance out of their bodies as quickly as possible. Ipecac is very good at that, but the medical community stopped using it. Over time, we found better ways to neutralize poisons without the risks of ipecac."

She looked confused. "You used a poison to treat poison?"

He took in a deep breath and let it out as he tried to explain, "Yes, sort of. You see, ipecac doesn't usually kill anyone. It just makes them sick for a short time. Your mother had a secondary complication unfortunately. Ipecac doesn't directly cause people to bleed or have heart attacks."

"I see."

"Do you know where Vito is?"

She shook her head. "No, he was very angry when doctor tell to us. I think he is planning to give someone a secondary complication."

Cesari nodded and was becoming increasingly concerned. "I'll talk to him. The important thing is to make sure your mother is taken care of properly."

"I agree."

Cesari's phone buzzed with a text message from Xi Hong, the chief of anesthesiology and a good friend. He was late for a budget committee meeting he had forgotten all about, and the one absolute truth in hospital politics was that you didn't skip budget meetings. He said, "I'm sorry, Teresa, but I have to go. I'm late for a meeting, but I'll drop by again in a few hours."

"Thank you, Doctor," she said and held up her rosary beads. "I will be here praying for mama."

CHAPTER 11

Deputy Director Morehouse hung up the phone and faced the three agents in front of him. He had just finished telling his wife, Ellie, that he probably wasn't going to be home in time for dinner. In fact, he wasn't even sure when he would be home at all. She had been watching the news and understood there was a crisis going on that would require his full attention. They were sitting in his office down the hall from the director. These three special agents were in Morehouse's estimation the best he had ever worked with. Angela Munoz, Dirk Bradbury, and Ben Forman stared at him with solemn faces. Word of their comrade's untimely demise had raced through the halls of D.C. with unparalleled alacrity and the deputy director doubted that the bubonic plague could have spread more rapidly.

"Dirk, I want you to handle the phone angle," Morehouse began. "Get a warrant and find the owner of every cellphone that pinged within a five-mile radius of Tysons Corner plus three and minus three hours of the estimated time of death. Get Mill's phone and do a dump on it. I want to know who he called, messaged or emailed and who called, messaged or emailed him back within forty-eight hours of his time of death. The same for his laptop. Check all his online activity, social media accounts and internet searches. You report your findings directly to me and will not discuss anything with anyone not even the other agents here in this room. Is that understood? The same goes for the rest of you."

They all nodded. The importance of the moment was not lost on them. A dead agent could mean almost anything, and they all assumed that national security was on the table.

"Ben, go to Mills' apartment and see what you can dig up. Take pictures. Make a mental image. Was he a slob? A sports enthusiast? A playboy? Whips and chains in his closet? Kiddie porn? Stuff like that. The director already sent a forensics team there. Work with them. I need to go out to the crime scene itself while it's still warm. In the meantime, find out if he had a second car. If he did, go through it. Start interviewing the other agents on his detail. Find out if he was close with anyone. He may have had a girlfriend, but was he banging anyone else? That kind of stuff. Also call every hospital within reasonable driving distance of Tysons Corner to see if anybody showed up in their emergency department early this morning with a gunshot wound. The director will handle the family, the media, the other agencies and the brass. There's going to be a lot of chatter and speculation coming from every direction. Ignore it. The FBI has the lead on this investigation, and they have agreed to let us tag along, but they will undoubtedly want their pound of flesh in the form of information. You will defer to them, but keep your opinions to yourself. All you know is that an agent was murdered in the line of duty. That's all you will ever know until I say differently. Got it?"

The three heads bobbed up and down in unison. He then turned to Angela Munoz. Dark-haired and lithe, she was second generation Cuban-American and the senior of the three special agents sitting in front of him. At thirty-five, she had ten years in, and her record was exemplary. Morehouse looked at her. It was time to take the training wheels off.

He said, "Angela, I want you to come with me to Tysons Corner to examine the crime scene and talk to the local cops. All right people, let's get started. We'll re-group later today. Tell your friends and family that they won't be seeing you for a while."

Morehouse and Munoz went down to the Secret Service garage and found Morehouse's Suburban. On the way to Tysons Corner, they discussed what they knew. He had given the group a redacted version of events, withholding the part about the silencer and latex gloves. He thought about full disclosure now but decided to hold back just a little longer. He wanted a fresh pair of unprejudiced eyes considering the problem. When they arrived, he pulled the Suburban to a stop by the police barricade blocking off Great Falls Street. They had kept the road closed off as a favor for him to inspect the scene although the body had been carted off to the morgue hours earlier. Mills' SUV was parked as he had left it. It was still raining, and he and Munoz hustled their way into the underpass where they were greeted by a uniformed Tysons Corner police officer. The man handed Morehouse an iPad with digital photos of Mills and the scene in general when law enforcement had arrived.

Morehouse studied the images while Munoz examined the underpass and the environs in general. Then they walked over to Mills' Suburban together and got in, with Morehouse in the driver's seat. The vehicle had recently been dusted for fingerprints. Morehouse glanced around trying to place himself in Mills' mind while Munoz rifled through the glove compartment.

He said, "It looks like Mills must have been following some car and placed his lights on as they approached the underpass. The vehicle pulled over and he came to a stop behind it. The first question that comes to mind was whether the meeting was pre-arranged or not? If it was then why flash your lights?"

"To keep any passerby from stopping and asking questions or offering assistance perhaps," Munoz replied.

"Maybe… Or maybe the meeting wasn't pre-arranged and the person in the car thought he was guilty of some type of traffic violation."

"An equally valid possibility, but it seems unlikely that an agent would make a traffic stop in the middle of the night."

"Unless he thought something was seriously off. Anything of interest in the glove compartment?"

She shook her head, opened the console between the two seats and peered inside. There was nothing there. They searched the rest of the vehicle as a matter of routine but didn't find anything. Exiting the SUV, they traced Mills' path to where his body was found. Morehouse acted as if he was approaching a parked car the way Mills might have.

He said, "Tell me how you see it going down, Munoz."

She thought it over and replied, "Okay, so for whatever reason, Mills pulls the guy over, or perhaps the vehicle appeared to be disabled. He then approaches the driver's side window. Maybe the guy in the car had a warrant out on him. He freaks, pulls out a gun and shoots. Mills staggers back a few paces, collapses, and dies. The guy drives away. That much is obvious. The real question is why was Mills here at that hour in the first place?"

"Good question. How good are you at thinking outside the box, Munoz?"

Slightly puzzled by the question, she hesitated. "Better than most, I think."

"I want you to start thinking outside the box now. Go back to Mills' Suburban and retrace his steps again. Re-enact the scene and see if you can come up with at least one or two other scenarios."

She walked back to the SUV, turned around and returned to where they estimated the other car must have been. She pretended to speak to an imaginary driver and then to fake a gun battle with said driver. When she was done, she ran it through her mind for a minute.

She said, "There could have been someone else in the car. Maybe several people. Okay, scenario one is that Mills pulled the car over for some reason. Things go sideways, he gets shot. Scenario two is that the car might have been parked or disabled and Mills just happened to be driving by and was ambushed. Maybe he interrupted a drug deal or something completely unrelated to his work as an agent. Quiet underpass in the middle of the night. It's possible."

"Very good, Munoz, but I need you to think it through some more. There's at least one more scenario we need to consider. Remember, think outside the box."

She looked around and scratched her head. While she did that, Morehouse took the Tysons Corner officer to the side and asked, "Were there any tire tracks that could be made out?"

The officer nodded and walked over to a spot ten or twelve feet away from Munoz and pointed at the pavement. "We think these rubber burn marks belonged to the car. They're still working on it, but it looks like a small model, such as a Civic or a Corolla. It appears that after the shooting, someone peeled out in hurry. What do you want us to do about the Suburban? Technically, it's part of an ongoing criminal investigation."

"Then do what you always do. I'll send someone to pick it up after you're done with it."

The officer nodded and walked away to make a call. Morehouse walked back to Munoz and signaled her to scan the cement wall with him. The police had marked the spot where the bullet had been found embedded after it had passed through Claire's brain.

He said, "Remember, I said Mills was found face up with a bullet wound to the throat, but I also said that a round was found in the cement wall which we just examined. There was no exit wound in the back of Mill's neck so that bullet must still be in him. So how do you explain a second round in the wall on the other side of the car from where Mills stood?"

After a moment, she concluded, "He must have returned fire at least once before going down."

"I agree that he must have fired, but before we continue with that come with me."

They then walked back to where the scene took place. Morehouse stood at the imaginary driver's side window and said, "Mills was six feet three inches tall."

Munoz nodded. "What are you thinking?"

"The officer said the car was probably a compact judging from the tire marks, so he'd have had to bend down or stooped a little to see into the car, right?"

Munoz agreed.

"The bullet hole in the cement wall is at least as high as the window of a Civic or its equivalent. Are we agreed?"

"Sure, and?"

"Have you ever fired your weapon in the heat of battle?"

"No."

"I have, and when somebody aims a gun at you by surprise, your first reaction is to take a step back as you pull out your own weapon. It's a reflex. Can't be helped." He re-enacted the scene pretending to withdraw his pistol as he stepped back and with the pretend gun fired into the imaginary car. "I'm six feet two inches tall Munoz. What's my trajectory?"

"Downward." She glanced back at the wall. "Your shot would have been lodged at least a foot, maybe two feet lower in the wall."

"What's that tell you?"

"That he was leaning down or perhaps even crouched when he fired."

"Like he was talking to someone in the car just before the action started."

"But that would make sense if he stopped to help someone or check out something suspicious."

"Not really because when they drew their gun, he would have jumped away from the car to withdraw his own weapon and would have returned to full height to regain his balance. Have you considered any additional scenarios like I asked you to?"

"I've tried, but I've come up short."

"In all of your scenarios, you depicted Agent Mills as the victim. You failed to consider the possibility that he may have drawn his weapon first as he bent down to look in the car. And that when he discharged his weapon from that angle the bullet went straight out the other side. Consider for a moment that it was the occupant of the car who may have returned fire in self-defense."

Her eyes went wide. She hadn't thought about that possibility for a moment. She stammered, "I don't understand. What are you trying to say?"

He continued, "I also mentioned that a large caliber handgun was found a few feet from the body of Agent Mills. His service Glock was still holstered and apparently hadn't been fired. The officers first on the scene assumed it belonged to the man or men in the car who shot Mills and then threw it away. The serial number on the gun had been filed off, and we're still waiting on prints, but how can you reconcile agent Mills being shot in one direction and a second bullet being found in the cement wall on the other side of the car if both shots came from the same gun?"

She pondered that for a moment and then stepped to where the driver of the car might have been. She aimed left to shoot Mills and then realized she would have had to spin one-hundred and eighty degrees to the right and fire out the passenger side window to achieve the result.

She shook her head. "It doesn't make sense."

"I want you now to consider a new scenario. That Agent Mills may have brought two guns to the party last night when he made the pullover, and that possibly he drew his first, leaned into the car and fired the round which ended up in the wall on the other side. Unbeknownst to Agent Mills the occupant was armed, and thus provoked, returned fire. When Mills died, he dropped his gun to the ground. That would explain why his service issued weapon was still holstered."

It wasn't easy to make Angela Munoz speechless, but Morehouse had successfully done so, and she stood there quietly. He continued, "I'm not saying that's what happened, but you need to consider all aspects of a situation before drawing conclusions based on sentiment or loyalty to one's own. You think on that for a while. In the meantime, let's go to the morgue to see how they're making out with Mills' autopsy. After that, we'll drop in on the Tysons Corner station house and see how our friend, Bud Morrison, is doing."

CHAPTER 12

Cesari entered conference room C in the basement of the hospital and quietly took a seat at the oval table. There was a generic coffee urn, a stack of styrofoam cups and a plate of house-baked cookies in the center of the table. He was twenty minutes late and trying hard to keep a low profile. The meeting was in full swing, and he nodded at several of the people there. The only thing he hated more than morning meetings were afternoon meetings. But budget meetings were the key to survival as every department head was there to slug it out for every last dollar they could scrounge out of the limited resources the hospital could provide.

This was supposed to be a big year for GI. Six months earlier, it had been decided to upgrade and expand the endoscopy unit to accommodate the arrival of two new gastroenterologists. The equipment was outdated, and the physical space was old. They were long overdue for the makeover.

In attendance were representatives from surgery, anesthesia, internal medicine, pediatrics, ob-gyn, psychiatry, emergency medicine, podiatry, rehab medicine, and neurology. The various subspecialties of medicine and surgery, such as cardiology and vascular surgery did not participate at this level of financial administration. They relied on the heads of medicine and general surgery to represent them. As chief medical officer, Cesari's attendance was required but since he was also the chief of gastroenterology, he was in the unique position of being able to promote his department and ward off the swarming predators trying to pick off a piece of his pie. In this regard, the GI department had an advantage over the other subspecialties. Who Cesari didn't see was Arnie Goldstein, the CEO, his seat being noticeably unoccupied.

Greg Polanski was the chief financial officer of St. Matt's and ran the budget committee. Forty-five, clean-cut, lean and corporate looking, he started out life as an accountant, progressed to an MBA and eventually obtained a law degree specializing in taxes, or more accurately, how to avoid paying them. Unfortunately, the firm where he was a partner avoided paying taxes too much and found themselves in the crosshairs of a criminal investigation for tax fraud and evasion. Unlike some of his partners, he narrowly escaped prison time in lieu of punitive fines which nearly broke him financially and community service which nearly broke him spiritually.

Considered damaged goods in his prior universe, he was snatched up by St. Matt's at a fraction of what someone with his pedigree should have cost. Starting life anew in the humdrum, boring world of hospital finances, Greg accepted his sentence in purgatory. This was economics 101 for him. St. Matt's played it by the book in all matters when it came to the federal and state government. His job was to cross the T's, dot the I's, and meet with his parole officer once a month. No funny business. Cesari didn't like him, but guessed he probably wasn't a bad guy at heart. He just got caught up in the action of what everyone around him was doing.

Besides, Cesari doubted you could find a single person in the entire country who felt the federal government wasn't already getting too much of everybody else's money. In some ways, some people would consider Greg Polanski a modern-day Robin Hood. If it wasn't for the one-hundred-foot yacht the IRS confiscated, the ten thousand square foot mansion the IRS put up for public auction, the two Bentley convertibles they found in his garage, and the discovery of a nineteen-year-old bikini clad blonde lying on a chaise lounge doing lines of coke by his swimming pool, a lot of people might have considered him a real working man's hero. Greg had just finished reviewing the minutes of the last meeting and was about to start new business as Cesari poured himself coffee.

Greg said, "Cesari, I'm surprised to see you."

"You know I would never miss a budget meeting, Greg. It's too easy to get thrown under the bus if you're not here to defend yourself."

A polite chuckle from the others drifted across the table.

"I do know that, but we all heard about last night's extraordinary events. I assumed you'd be exhausted today, and when I heard you cancelled your office this morning..."

"You assumed incorrectly that I would be lying down somewhere hugging my pillow. Truth be told, I am wiped out, but I came in to check on my patient from last evening. I actually did forget about the meeting, but fortunately, Dr. Hong reminded me," he said and turned to Xi sitting across from him. "Thank you, Xi."

Xi Hong was first generation Chinese American who grew up speaking Mandarin, waving the American flag, and throwing darts at pictures of Chairman Mao. He hated commies, hippies, and Asian stereotypes. There was a poster on the wall in his office that read, *I don't know kung fu, I almost failed calculus, I drink gin, not tea, and I play golf, not fucking ping pong.* As chief of anesthesia, his job was to interface with the surgeons and nursing staff to insure a smoothly running and efficient operating room, and to this extent, he was largely successful. No easy task considering the colossal egos involved.

Xi replied, "No problem, Cesari. These meetings are so much more fun when you're around."

Greg cleared his throat and seemed uneasy. "Okay, then let's get on with it."

Cesari sensed something was wrong. The CFO had seemed full of confidence just a moment ago when Cesari had first entered the room but now suddenly seemed unsure of himself. With Vito's family and Emily Hoffman weighing heavily on his mind, Cesari couldn't even begin to contemplate any new calamity. But when Greg cleared his throat for a second time, he knew something was definitely off. For a guy that nearly found himself serving seven to ten years like his senior partners, you'd think he'd be dancing a jig every time he woke up a free man instead of hemming and hawing in front of a bunch of physicians with pasty complexions. Maybe the feds had found some new charges to bring against him? One never knew with the government. It was always best to stay under the radar with those guys. He smiled inwardly at that thought considering he was giving safe harbor to a young woman who had admitted to shooting a Secret Service agent.

Finally, Greg said, "As you all know, the hospital has been contemplating renovating the GI endoscopy suite."

Cesari didn't like the sound of that and interrupted him, "What do you mean contemplating? It's been a done deal for months."

"Yes, well…"

"Yes, well… what?"

"It's complicated."

"Complicated? I've been working on designs, meeting architects, and evaluating new purchase orders for almost half a year. We've even picked out colors for the patient bathrooms." He turned to the others. "Spanish white if anyone is interested."

Some more people giggled.

Greg took a deep breath and let it out slowly. "What I mean is that the board has unanimously decided to postpone those renovations for now."

A hushed murmur rose from the room. They knew this was Cesari's pet project and how hard he had been working on it. He was more than a little stunned by this news. This was his baby, and he had been nursing it along night and day for hours on end."

"Why?" he asked suspiciously.

Greg looked down as he slowly said, "Frankly, the board feels the money could be put to better use at this time."

The room went dead silent as everyone held their breath. Eventually, his voice dripping with sarcasm, Cesari said, "Do tell, Greg. We're all dying to hear. So where has the board decided to spend the GI department's ten million dollars?"

Sheepishly, Greg whispered, "The board thinks there will be a better return on our investment by expanding the OR to accommodate our burgeoning orthopedic surgery needs."

Cesari felt his chest tighten. Across the table, Xi's left eye twitched. There was no love lost between orthopedics and anesthesia. The anesthesiologists were viewed by the orthopods as indentured servants and in some cases slave labor. Xi himself had nearly come to blows with one of the ortho guys over his condescending and demeaning attitude. In fact, the orthopedic mental vision of things was that the entire medical and nursing staff existed for the sole purpose of providing them support. The amount of disrespect demonstrated by the orthopedic surgeons toward the rest of the medical community was reaching a fever pitch and this new development was sure to push the bad relations over the top.

"So that's what the board thinks, is it?" Cesari said slowly, starting to burn. "Is that why Arnie isn't here? He couldn't look me in the eye and tell me himself?"

"Arnie is interviewing prospective CEO's to take his place when he retires at the end of the year. His absence here in no way implies a sense of guilt or disapproval about this decision. He is fully supportive of the board's conclusion, and in due time, I'm sure he was planning on discussing the matter with you. It was a straight up business decision and nothing personal. The board recognizes the hard work and dedication of all the gastroenterologists on staff, particularly yourself.

This decision should in no way detract from the high esteem in which we hold you and your colleagues and the significant contributions you make to the wellbeing of the community. So please, there's no need to be angry."

"You think I'm angry? Greg, if I was angry, you'd already be on a stretcher headed toward the emergency room. I'm just confused. What suddenly changed in the board's mind?"

Greg paled a little and being a lawyer wondered if that was enough of a threat to warrant some type of legal action. He decided it wasn't. He also decided he didn't want to rock the boat with St. Matt's favorite son. Besides, Cesari had cleverly posed it as a hypothetical situation. Still, it was an incredibly inappropriate thing to say, but no one else raised any objection. Rumors of Cesari's mob connections and temperament had reached him almost immediately upon starting at St. Matt's, and although he was technically in charge of this meeting, he suddenly felt as if he were in the interrogation room of the Ninth Precinct, or more aptly, in the basement of an abandoned warehouse tethered to a metal pole. He unconsciously scanned the table for a rubber hose or a cattle prod.

Unnerved, he continued to speak even when common sense indicated he shouldn't have, "Let's face facts, Cesari. Orthopedic procedures bring in nearly ten times that of GI procedures. It's simple math, but if you want to cut right to the chase, I will. The new orthopedic surgeon, Dr. Bell, says he can double his volume if we build him a couple of new OR suites dedicated just to orthopedic procedures. He is also in the process of recruiting several of his colleagues in sports medicine at Mount Sinai to join us with their patients. I might as well let you know that as part of the deal, we're planning on dedicating a wing of the hospital just for orthopedic patients to recover and rehab. The feeling is that specialized nursing care postoperatively will improve outcomes and speed up turnover. It will be a public relations coup with the community. We're going to call that part of the hospital the Alexander Graham Bell center for excellence in orthopedics. At the rate he's performing total knees and hips, and with the anticipated increase in volume, I've calculated a twenty percent return on our investment in the first year alone."

Cesari was at first numb but then became hot. "So that's the way it is, Greg? Money talks and bullshit walks?"

"That's not what I'm saying at all. The board understands the need to increase the hospital's revenue stream, and quite frankly, when you crunch the numbers, GI just doesn't make the cut. You should be aware that Alexander was quite sensitive to the predicament we've placed you in. When we offered to take over one of your endo rooms on a temporary basis until his new suites are built he magnanimously declined feeling that would be a bridge too far."

"Alexander? So now you're on a first name basis with him. That's sweet, and that was very generous of him to leave me with a place to work. Maybe I should send him a thank you card. Let me make sure I fully understand. You, the board, and Arnie have decided that fixing teenagers' knees so they can keep playing soccer is more important than colon cancer?"

"That's not what I said."

"Maybe not in so many words, but it's the gist of it, nonetheless. Whose brilliant idea was this anyway? This doesn't sound like Arnie's style."

Looking like a guy who just jumped out of a plane and suddenly realized he forgot his parachute, Greg mumbled half-heartedly, "Like I said, it's simple math. Unfortunately, in the cold light of day, the revenue from GI doesn't compare to orthopedics, and as the CFO, I have a fiduciary responsibility to advise the hospital on how best to manage its money."

Cesari paused for a second before saying, "So you crunched some numbers and came up with GI gets a testicle removed? This is bullshit, and so is your definition of simple math. In the Bronx simple math is when a guy falls on a baseball bat and breaks his leg and the next day falls on the same baseball bat and breaks the other leg, how long will it take him to stop pissing off the guy holding the baseball bat?"

"I think you're overreacting."

"I disagree. Overreacting would be calling your parole officer and telling him I saw you smoking crack with a teen-age candy-striper in the hospital parking lot. Now that would be overreacting."

Xi started laughing. "Now that's the Cesari I know."

The CFO turned white at that. He didn't take the baseball bat story seriously, but anonymous calls to the parole board could ruin him.

He stammered, "Please don't encourage him Dr. Hong. This was a difficult decision for the board but one they felt they had to make."

"I bet it was," Cesari muttered. "Is there anything else you'd like to tell us? Perhaps you're giving my parking space away to one of the new guys? It's pretty close to the main entrance and we wouldn't want them to be late for their cases. Or maybe there'll be reserved seating in the cafeteria for orthopedics?"

Greg bit his lips and said, "You're not going to like this part either, so I'll just spit it out. In the interest of full disclosure, I should add that there are plans to upgrade a section of the cafeteria to accommodate the nutritional needs of the orthopedic surgeons. They are young and fit with high metabolic rates and considering their level of productivity we can't have them waiting in long lines for hot dogs and frozen pizza. Naturally, they'll need to dine in a comfortable and supportive atmosphere and not be exposed to the daily cacophony and grumbling that is the want of hospital employees. It would destroy their morale."

Cesari was dumbfounded. "They're going to have a private dining area?"

Xi wasn't laughing anymore. He was outraged and rose to his feet, shouting in Mandarin, "这是彻头彻尾的狗屎!" (*"This is total bullshit!"*)

Chapter 13

A few hours after that debacle of a budget meeting, Cesari walked into his apartment holding a large pizza, a bottle of red wine and a plastic bag with Emily's medications. He had called Vito several times, but each call had gone to voicemail. That wasn't surprising. Vito's dark side was rising, and storm clouds were gathering. He needed to be alone as he pondered his next move. Against whom was the question.

Tierney was still there which wasn't that surprising. It was close to five and Cesari guessed the detective didn't want to leave Emily alone. It was a good guess, but there was more. Cesari placed the pizza and wine down on the kitchen table and waved to Tierney and Emily in the living room. She was speaking to her parents on the burner phone Tierney had given her and the detective sat nearby reading a stack of papers piled up on the coffee table.

He put the bottles of mesalamine and 6-MP on the kitchen counter and Humira in the refrigerator. He was able to procure enough of her medications for at least the next thirty days. That should tide her over, he thought. Antibiotics and prednisone would be easy enough to obtain to get her through flare-ups if the need arose.

Sitting near Tierney he said, "I got a pepperoni pizza, if you're interested in staying for dinner."

Tierney said, "I might grab a slice on the way out. I have to check on my cat. Stonewall gets edgy when he doesn't see me for long periods of time."

Cesari grinned. Calling Stonewall a cat was an understatement. He was the size of a bobcat but not even half as cuddly. "I understand. Any new developments?"

In response, Tierney pointed at the stack of cards and letters on the coffee table. "They're love letters addressed to Claire. I found them in her suitcase. I've been reading and re-reading them all afternoon, hoping to pick up a clue. Help yourself, but I'm going to warn you. Most of them are X-rated and extremely graphic."

"Who are they from?"

"They weren't signed or postmarked."

"Not one of them?"

"Nope, not a one."

Emily hung up the phone. Tears streamed down her face. Cesari and Tierney waited for her to say something. Eventually, she asked, "Can I have a slice of pizza?"

Cesari replied, "Of course. I brought it for you."

"There's wine too if you're interested. Help yourself to whatever you want. There's a corkscrew in the drawer by the refrigerator."

She thanked him and sauntered off into the kitchen. Tierney said quietly, "It's been like that all afternoon."

"It's understandable."

Cesari began reading the cards and letters. There were about thirty in all. All hot and steamy but very neatly devoid of any incriminating details such as names or places to allow identification of the sender. Not even the slightest hint of who the writer was or how they knew Claire. What was very clear, however, was that whoever wrote the torrid cards and letters was hopelessly in love.

When he was finished, he looked over at Tierney, "Fascinating, and very possibly unrelated, but it's interesting that whoever it is was concerned about keeping his identity under wraps."

"I agree. So, we're either talking about a married man or someone important enough that a fling with a hot blonde secretary could potentially damage his career aspirations."

Cesari mulled that over. "You mean like perhaps she wasn't suitable enough for high-ranking cocktail parties or to make the rounds with him at Pennsylvania Avenue social functions."

Tierney nodded. "Exactly."

"And how does this tie-in with what happened?"

"I don't know. She was certainly leaving town in a huff because of it. She sounded deeply hurt by something that had happened. Some change in the relationship. Maybe the guy decided to break it off with her and she was leaving town rather than have to face him every day."

Emily returned to the living room with a glass of wine and half-eaten slice of pizza. She sat opposite them, folding her legs under her. Cesari asked, "Would you agree with that Emily? That Claire was emotionally distraught over a love interest and that's why she was leaving D.C.?"

"She was definitely bent out of shape over some guy. Why she would leave D.C. is another question. If some guy dumped all over me,

I'd be damned if I'd leave my job and my apartment to get away. You cry a little and then find someone else."

Cesari said, "I agree. Breaking up with someone doesn't usually lead to fleeing town in the middle of the night."

"Then why did she leave?" Tierney asked and then added, "You know, in the old days, women used to have to leave town all the time. Either to terminate a pregnancy without anyone knowing or to have the child without anyone knowing."

Cesari shook his head. "These aren't the old days, Detective. Women don't leave town anymore. I don't buy that one at all."

Emily said, "I don't buy it either."

Cesari sat back and crossed his legs. "Allow me a moment of speculation…"

Tierney interrupted, "You speculate while I grab a slice."

He stood and walked into the kitchen as Cesari continued, "Claire's dating somebody who is either married or climbing the ladder of power. They're going at it hot and heavy. This guy decides it's time to cut Claire loose. Maybe she was pushing him to make their relationship more permanent, and he now sees her as a liability. She gets upset and decides to leave town, maybe for just a short time to regroup after her dreams of marital bliss are dashed upon the rocks of reality."

"And a secret service agent killed her why, Cesari?" Tierney called from the kitchen.

"Maybe Mr. Important is way more important than we're thinking and didn't like the idea of Claire potentially going public with their relationship. Maybe he's the kind of guy who doesn't like loose ends."

The room went quiet for a minute as Tierney returned with a slice of pizza, sipping red wine. He said, "Do you realize how powerful a man would have to be to get a member of the Secret Service to do something like that, Cesari?"

"I said I was just speculating."

"Yes, you did."

"Can you get these cards and letters dusted for fingerprints without raising any alarms."

Tierney nodded. "I can do that. Too bad we don't have any prime suspects. I could do a handwriting analysis as well."

"No prime suspects?" asked Cesari. "How about Senator Taylor. She worked for him, didn't she? He's the one who asked Emily to drive Claire to the airport, didn't he? He's pretty important, isn't he? Everybody thinks he's going to be the next president."

"Take a deep breath, Cesari."

Emily said, "He's got a point. As ridiculous as it sounds, his footprint is all over this."

Tierney shook his head, "This is getting way out of control. We're jumping to all sorts of conclusions based upon flimsy circumstantial evidence. I couldn't even get a warrant based on any of this. Let's start with the fingerprints. I have no way of getting a sample of the senator's handwriting and if we start levelling accusations, everybody will know where Emily is."

Cesari said, "You could just go online and do a search for samples of the senator's cursive. Everything's online these days. He may have written a public note to thank someone or some group or responded to someone with a handwritten letter which was then published. No one has to know why you're doing it."

Tierney thought it over and said, "All right. I'll do that."

Emily said, "I need more wine."

She ambled back to the kitchen, and switching subjects, Cesari asked, "Have you heard about the result of the toxicology from last night?"

"Yes, I received a call earlier, but I was busy with everything going on here. It doesn't change a whole lot. We were pursuing it as a criminal investigation anyway and now we have confirmation of that. Who and why still remain wide open questions. I guess we'll go after the disgruntled worker angle a little harder now although the old lady and her son back in Sicily are still a possibility."

"I agree with that one," growled Vito from the entrance to the apartment, with a lit Camel dangling from one hand.

Cesari hadn't locked the door when he came in before and Vito stood there with Gerry Acquilano. Vito had a scowl on his face that could kill. They all looked at once at the sound of the booming, deep, menacing voice. Gerry closed the door and the two of them approached closer.

Tierney said, "Gianelli, you know something I don't?"

"Not yet, but I intend on finding out. Me and Gerry are going to Palermo to discuss the matter personally with Rosaria and Ernesto."

"Maybe you ought to cool off first, Gianelli," suggested Tierney.

Cesari added, "Maybe you should put the cigarette out first. Then come in, pour yourself a glass of wine and we can discuss it rationally. There's pizza on the table in the kitchen."

"There's nothing to discuss. Gerry get me a glass of wine and a slice of pizza, and here put my cigarette out with some tap water," Vito directed, handing the butt to his stooge. "Rosaria and Ernesto did this. The only thing left is for them to confess and face the consequences of their actions."

Emily asked, "Who are these guys?"

Tierney laughed. "You really should lock your doors, Cesari."

"They're friends of mine Emily, and there was a case of mass food poisoning at a restaurant in Manhattan where we were eating last night. Several of his family members became ill, and my friend here thinks he knows who did it," Cesari explained. "Vito say hello to Emily. Emily this is Vito, and the little guy is Gerry. He's Vito's… helper."

Vito glanced at Emily and then back at Cesari and Tierney. "What the hell's going on here?"

Tierney shook his head in frustration. He hadn't wanted to involve anybody else, but he should have anticipated Gianelli showing up eventually. He knew what good friends he and Cesari were. The flip side was that maybe it wasn't such a bad idea to bring Gianelli in the loop. He certainly knew how to keep a secret, and he knew how to evade law enforcement. He'd been doing that for years. Without doubt he and his men were armed and could handle themselves. Not a bad idea at all.

He said, "Sit down, Gianelli. We need to talk."

Chapter 14

Munoz was shaken to the core. She couldn't accept the notion that Mills was anything other than the victim of an unjustifiable attack. The idea that he was possibly the bad guy in all this was preposterous. Or was it? It was all she could think about. She thought about it in the Tysons Corner morgue where the coroner had already started the autopsy. He confirmed that the angle of the wound was upward and that he was either shot by a much shorter person or perhaps while leaning over to speak to someone who was sitting. The bullet had entered his throat just below the hyoid cartilage at a about a forty-five-degree angle and had probably found a new home in the back of Mill's brain. He would know more when he cut the skull open and found the bullet, but the size of the hole strongly suggested it was a small caliber round like a .22 or a 9mm, but definitely not a .45.

Munoz thought about it all the way to the Tysons Corner police station where Morehouse debriefed officer Bud Morrison in private while she went to collect Mills' cellphone and then went to the forensics' lab to see if they had positively identified the bullet found in the cement wall. They had. It was a standard .45 caliber ACP round, commercially available almost everywhere and matched the jacket found on the ground nearby.

They drove most of the way back to D.C. in silence as she continued to think about it. Eventually Morehouse asked, "Is something bothering you, Munoz?"

"Yes...I feel stupid for not considering the possibility that Mills' might have instigated the shooting."

"You shouldn't. Loyalty and trust of your fellow agents is built into your training. The same is true of the military, law enforcement, fire departments and a slew of other organizations. It would be impossible to function effectively if we didn't trust our comrades. It would be even worse if we couldn't count on their loyalty."

"But you thought about it."

"Initially I didn't want to, and it's still only one of several theories. Loyalty is good but what separates a good agent from a great agent is the ability to think laterally. All that glitters is not gold kind of thing. But the idea that an agent might be bent or freelancing should be given careful scrutiny when something untoward happens like last night."

"What do you really think?"

"I think I'm going to try my best to find out the truth, and in the process come up with a logical explanation for what happened that doesn't involve Mill's turning to the dark side. But if he did, then I'll have no choice but to hang him out to dry. I didn't tell you what I did to make you paranoid or angry at Mills. I told you because you're my second in command and I need you to think on a higher level."

"What about the others?"

"Like I said earlier. I want this compartmentalized. They have all the information they need to know to perform the tasks I assigned to them, and now so do you. My speculation that Mills' may have started the shooting last night stays between me and you."

He pulled into the Secret Service headquarters' parking garage and cut the engine when he reached his designated space. He said, "Bring Mills' phone to Dirk and tell him he has two hours to tell me everything that's on it. Then write up a preliminary report of the crime scene in Tysons Corner. No opinions. Just the facts. Then see how Ben is making out. I gave him a lot to do this morning. There were fifteen agents assigned to Taylor's security detail under Mills' command. Give him a hand getting their statements. I want you all in my office in three hours to review what we know so far. If anybody starts getting hypoglycemic, remind them where the vending machines are."

She seemed distant as they entered the building and passed through security. He said, "Munoz?"

"Sir, I was wondering if I should have cots brought in for the team to sleep on?"

"That would be a great idea except for one thing."

She waited…

"I don't anticipate anyone sleeping tonight."

She nodded and they parted ways. Morehouse went to the director's office and let himself in. Burke was sitting at his desk and looked up.

"What do you have for me, Grayson?"

"Bud Morrison is a diamond in the rough and was very eager to help. He'll keep the more sordid details under his hat for the time being. He made sure none of it was included in his initial report which he filled out personally. In return, I told him we've already started a background check on his son in anticipation of any future relationship with the Service. I was friendly but noncommittal. It seemed to satisfy him."

Burke grinned. "You're slick, Morehouse. What about anyone else who saw or knows about the gun?"

Morehouse returned the grin. "I learned from the best. Obviously, multiple people over there know but don't necessarily understand the significance. There's not much we can do about that. He'll do his best to keep it on the down low. In that regard, I have confidence in him. He seemed to have a tight grip on his men."

"Good."

"Anyway, preliminary results strongly suggest that Mills may well have fired first on the occupants of the car who then returned fire with deadly outcome. No witnesses have come forth saying they heard or saw anything. What, if any, was Mills' motive is entirely unknown. There was no contraband on his person or in his SUV. We're examining his phone, his bank accounts and his apartment as we speak. We have warrants out to the phone companies and are tapping into our sources at the FBI. We're in the process of getting statements from Mills' team. There's a lot of ground to cover. After I leave here, I was going to call the senator. I wanted to have some facts under my belt first."

"Don't bother. We're meeting the senator and his chief of staff for cocktails and dinner at 8:00 p.m. at the Old Ebbits Grill. Rufus Youngblood called me this morning. He wasn't happy that the FBI was leading the investigation. He's concerned that things could spiral out of control in the middle of an election year. I told him that we had no choice because of jurisdiction, but that we were all over it too. He wasn't satisfied that we were all over it. He said the senator wanted to hear the details in person from me, not my flunky, so brace yourself for some major arrogance, D.C. style."

"Rufus Youngblood called me your flunky?"

Burke nodded. "He claims he was quoting the senator, but I don't believe him. He should be fun to work with if they manage to win the White House."

Morehouse frowned. "I can't wait. Why don't they want to come here for a sit down? That would be better than taking a chance of being seen by the press."

"Not from their point of view. There could only be one reason why they would come here whereas they could always claim the Ebbits Grill was a straightforward social get together and that we didn't discuss anything more serious than vacation plans. He doesn't want the FBI thinking they can call him in for a meeting too. They've reserved a private room away from prying eyes. This guy Rufus is smart."

Morehouse contemplated that for a bit, weighing the pros and cons. "We'll have to get there early and sweep the room for listening devices and cameras."

"Naturally, and they know that. Just make sure our guys are discreet. There's no point in alerting the press. Anyway, there was a bright side to the call. While I had him on the line, I asked him if he knew if Mills had a significant other. I figured since they were pals in the SEALs, he might know. He told me Mills did indeed have a girlfriend over in Dupont Circle. He gave me a name and address. He only had that information as an emergency contact for Mills. He never met the girl. Apparently, he and Mills weren't close on that level."

"Did anyone reach out to her yet?"

Burke nodded. "I was saving the best for last. The phone number Youngblood gave me was no longer in service, so I sent an agent out to the address to bring her in, but she wasn't home. We assumed she might be at work. An hour after that I received a call from someone at the CIA telling me that she was off limits, but not to worry. She had nothing to do with it."

"She works for the CIA?" Morehouse asked incredulously. "Who was it who called?"

"He wouldn't say. Said it was unimportant. The call traced back to Langley but that was as far as I could get. Apparently, she has top level clearance. Anyway, I explained that we really needed to talk to her concerning an ongoing criminal investigation and that I really didn't give a crap about her spook status."

"You said that?"

"I did."

"How'd he react?"

"He hung up and an hour after that I received a call from the White House Chief of Staff telling me to use more sensitivity in dealing with the other agencies. Maureen gave me a whole speech about catching more flies with honey than vinegar."

"Did you learn your lesson?"

"You tell me. While you were in Tysons Corner playing footsie with Bud Morrison, I ordered a team to go back to her apartment, kick the door in, and bring her here in handcuffs. If she wasn't home they were to ransack her apartment as if she was the only child of Osama Bin Laden and today was September 12, 2001."

Morehouse chuckled softly, "Where is she now?"

"That's just it. She's gone. When they arrived, the apartment was completely vacated as if no one had ever lived there, not even a scrap of toilet paper to wipe your ass with."

Morehouse whistled. "Do we know anything about her?"

"Just what I told you. Youngblood said he never met her, and really couldn't even be sure that Mills was still seeing her. He said her first name was Rosemarie but couldn't recall the last name. He only knew her first name because he wrote it down next to the contact info."

"This is unbelievable," Morehouse said incredulously.

"You're telling me?"

"Did Mills know the woman worked for the CIA?"

"That's the fifty-million-dollar question. Rufus Youngblood didn't, but I already don't like the smell of this."

"Did the guy from the CIA say anything about her?"

"He didn't even acknowledge her existence. Never said her name or even implied that he knew we were talking about a woman. He simply said that whoever it was we were looking to talk to at that particular address was involved in matters of national security and was unavailable on a permanent basis."

"Damn..."

"You got that right. By the way, any word on the identity of the guy in the car?"

"Not yet, but I should be hearing something later today about the cellphones. Plus, we're collecting all the security tapes from every, traffic light, gas station and 7 Eleven in Tysons Corner for review. This kind of stuff will take some time, especially if we're going to keep it in house with a small team."

"I understand, but we need to keep this as low key as possible. Even more so now that we know Mills was cavorting with spies."

"What do you think that's all about?"

"I don't know but I don't like it."

"Maybe it's unrelated. She could just be an analyst or an office worker. The CIA are pretty touchy about their people being in the spotlight."

"Give me a break, Morehouse," Burke retorted. "One of our guys goes rogue in the middle of the night and now we find out he's been screwing a chick from the CIA who's suddenly gone to ground, and you think it's unrelated. You probably think Lee Harvey Oswald acted alone too."

"Just playing devil's advocate, boss."

Chapter 15

The nondescript four door sedan pulled into Lansdale at 8:00 p.m. and parked in the shadow of an ancient Norway spruce halfway down the block from the house. Rosemarie had stolen the car, switched the plates and planned to dump it somewhere appropriate on the way back. It was quite dark out, with residual clouds from the recent foul weather obscuring the moonlight. She had opted to follow up on the only lead she had which led her to the family home of Emily Hoffman. The lights were on, and it seemed like an ordinary night on this tree lined suburban patch of ordinary, U.S.A. There was a two-car garage but both bays were closed. She knew dad was a cop and mom was a nurse. Fred and Kathy. There would be firearms in the house and she needed to be careful. Emily's car was nowhere in sight, but it could be in the garage. She would wait until the lights went out and they went to bed.

But that's not what happened. At 8:30 p.m. one of the garage doors cranked open and a beat up red pickup backed out. There was a man driving and he was alone. She presumed it was Emily's father. This was good and bad. Good, because she'd rather not have to confront a cop, and bad because she had hoped to catch the whole family at once. She watched as his taillights pulled away in the distance and then made her decision. If Emily was inside, there would never be a better time. She didn't know how long he would be away. If this was just a quick run to the grocery store, he could return relatively quickly. She had to act fast and estimated she would have no more than thirty minutes. But for someone like her, that was plenty of time.

She cut the engine and stepped out of the car. In her over-sized bag, she hid an Uzi with a thirty round magazine and a spare. It was an additional ten pounds of weight, but she was used to it. Outside the vehicle, the humidity was stifling, and she took a moment to acclimate to it. She had disguised her appearance with a broad brimmed hat, silk scarf, and lightly tinted sunglasses. The most any casual observer would say was that she seemed to be a little oddly dressed for the night, but if asked to describe her in greater detail, they would be at a loss for words. Five feet four inches, maybe a little taller. White, maybe light-skinned Hispanic. Short, dirty blonde hair, maybe. Hard to say with the hat and scarf. Thin, but not skinny. That was it, and that was only if they were paying attention. In her experience, that was almost never the case.

The apparel was already causing her to perspire, and she hoped the house was air conditioned. She glanced in all directions and made a bee line toward the open garage door. Inside, she looked around. There was another car parked there but it wasn't Emily's. She went over to the house entrance and tested the door. It was unlocked and she paused to listen. There was a television on inside. With one leather-gloved hand, she reached into her bag and took out the Uzi, attaching the silencer with the other. Once the silencer was screwed into place, she pulled the bolt back, chambering a round.

Taking a deep breath, she entered the Hoffman kitchen. Kathy Hoffman sat at the table sipping tea and watching a small TV which had been set up on the counter. The look of surprise on her face was indescribable as she dropped the cup, shattering it on the tiled floor. She wanted to scream, she wanted to run, she wanted to do something, but she could do none of those things. She was paralyzed with fear as she stared down the barrel of the automatic pistol loaded with 9mm ammunition aimed directly at her. The woman behind the gun put her index finger in front of her lips in the universal hush gesture. Kathy's mouth hung open in sheer disbelief at what was happening. She felt as if she were in a film noir murder mystery. The woman's bizarre appearance, the hat, the sunglasses, the leather gloves created a surreal atmosphere.

Rosemarie said, "Where's Emily?"

Kathy's lips quivered, her body trembled, and her mind raced. She decided to go with what she and Fred had rehearsed, and whispered, "We don't know. We haven't heard from her all day. We're very worried."

The lines came out easily enough and the woman hesitated and then asked, "Where's your husband?"

"He's upstairs in the bedroom," she lied. "He has a gun. He's a cop."

Kathy hadn't anticipated being alone if and when someone like this arrived. It never even crossed her mind that the woman might have been watching the house and seen Fred leave.

Rosemarie said, "You're lying, Kathy. That was a test. I saw him leave in the pickup. One more chance. Where's Emily?"

Kathy broke and started crying, then she started praying. The woman went over to the stove and felt the tea pot. It was warm but not hot, so she lit the burner. "I'd rather not do this the hard way, Kathy. It's up to you. Third degree burns can be extremely painful... and quite disfiguring."

The menacing tone in her voice convinced Kathy that the woman was deadly serious. In desperation, she jumped up and lunged for a knife on the kitchen counter, but she wasn't fast enough. The woman caught her by the hair and slapped her hard with the side of the Uzi. Kathy fell to the floor stunned and in pain, bleeding from a fresh gash under one eye. The woman pulled hard on her hair and Kathy howled as roots ripped from their follicles.

"That wasn't very nice, Kathy," Rosemarie hissed.

"Please don't hurt me. Emily left hours ago. She won't tell anybody. I promise you. She just wants to be left alone."

So Emily had come home. It was nice to have that confirmation. "Was Claire with Emily?"

Kathy nodded, weeping uncontrollably now. "Claire was dead," she whimpered. "She was murdered."

That was good news. "Where is Claire now and her belongings?"

"Gone, everything is gone. My husband is taking care of everything. That's why he's not here."

"There were a stack of letters and cards. What happened to them?"

"I don't know what you're talking about," Kathy stammered. "I really don't."

"Tell me where Emily is, Kathy. She has nothing to be afraid of. If she returns the letters and agrees to not tell anyone what happened, I won't hurt her. But I really need those letters back."

Sobbing and wanting to believe everything would be all right, Kathy said, "Do you promise?"

"I promise I won't hurt her if she agrees to keep quiet."

"How can I be sure?"

In a conciliatory tone, Rosemarie said, "You can't but why would I want to make things more complicated than they already are? Besides, once I have the letters you claim to not know anything about, then I will have no further interest in you or your family."

Kathy didn't respond to that, and the woman pressed the muzzle of the Uzi hard into the back of her head. "If you make this difficult for me, then I will be in a very bad mood when I finally do catch up with her. And after I'm done with her, I might still be so angry I may decide to come back here for you and your husband. Cooperate now and I'll be generous. All I want are the letters and to be reassured of her silence. Now which is it going to be?"

"She's in New York City," Kathy stammered. "…with a friend."

"What kind of friend?"

"An old friend of Fred's from the Marine Corps. He's a New York detective. His name is Robert Tierney."

Rosemarie didn't like that. Another cop to deal with. More guns. "Do you have an address?"

Kathy shook her head. "No, I don't."

"New York's a big place, Kathy."

"I'm sorry… I really don't know. Manhattan or Brooklyn, I think. Fred hadn't spoken to him in years and they both decided it would be best if we didn't know where she was going."

"Is that all, Kathy? And you'd better not lie."

"When Tierney came to pick up Emily, he was with another man. A Dr. John Cesari. He was Emily's doctor in New York when she was in college."

That was interesting. "Why does Emily need a doctor?"

"She has Crohn's disease."

"Is she ill right now?"

"No, but she's going to need medications."

Rosemarie was fascinated by this new development and wasn't sure how it would figure in. She glanced around and asked, "Anything else?"

Kathy shook her head and whispered, "I swear…"

"If I find out you lied to me, I will come back. Then you and your husband will suffer beyond imagination. Do you understand?"

"I'm not lying."

Rosemarie sighed. She was very well-schooled in the art of interrogation and felt she probably wouldn't get much more out of her. "All right. That wasn't so hard, was it? Let me help you up."

She assisted Kathy off the floor and back into her chair. Then she went over and turned the stove off. Turning back to Kathy, she raised the Uzi, aimed it, and pulled the trigger. The Uzi coughed, and relatively quietly, spit out three well-grouped rounds directly into Kathy's face. She and her chair flipped over backward onto the floor, dead on impact. Kathy stared up at the ceiling through lifeless eyes as blood oozed down the sides of her face pooling onto the white flooring.

The house wasn't very large, and Rosemarie searched it quickly, satisfying herself that Emily wasn't hiding under a bed or in a closet. She wasn't, but at least now the search was narrowing down and beginning to pick up traction. Granted, New York was an enormous and effective place to hide, but she had a name and almost unlimited resources on her side. She was certain Kathy was telling the truth. She judged her to be too naïve and frightened to be an effective liar.

What to do now though? She could wait for the husband to return and interrogate him as well. It would be nice to cross reference the information Kathy had told her, but her husband would probably be armed. Most cops were. She had the advantage of surprise, but still things might go awry in a hurry, and she didn't want to take a chance of a shootout. She finally concluded that she could always come back and have a chat with him if need be.

So after just under thirty minutes total in the house, she slipped out the same way she had come in. Breathless but satisfied, she started up the car and drove off. She abandoned the vehicle in downtown Philadelphia and took a cab to within a block of where she had parked her Range Rover. Once safely in transit to Manhattan, she called her contact in D.C.

"Find out everything you can on a New York City detective named Robert Tierney and a physician named John Cesari."

Chapter 16

Vito stared across the table at Emily. To her credit, she didn't blink and simply stared back. Cesari watched Tierney who was strumming his fingers on the table in front of him. They had moved from the living room to the kitchen. The pizza box and bottle of wine had been replaced by a pot of freshly brewed French roast. They each had a cup. Gerry was outside the apartment, standing guard. Now that they all were brought up to speed with each other's story, they were trying to decide what to do. Vito wanted to go to Sicily and beat a confession out of Ernesto and he wanted Cesari to go with him to act as a cultural liaison and a voice of reason to temper his steel. Emily was in extreme and imminent danger and needed as much support as could be mustered, and Vito could muster a lot.

"Who are you exactly?" asked Emily innocently.

Vito narrowed his eyes suspiciously as he replied, "I'm a legitimate businessman."

"What's that supposed to mean?" she persisted.

Cesari said, "What's important is that he can help us, Emily."

Tierney added, "Mr. Gianelli has access to certain resources that the type of people who may be looking for you won't know about."

"And why would a *legitimate* businessman like Mr. Gianelli want to help me?"

"Because deep down beneath his gruff exterior beats the heart of a marshmallow," grinned Cesari, thoroughly amused with his own wit and quickly added, "And Mr. Gianelli knows that if he helps us then I will help him with his Sicilian problem."

Vito grunted at that. "You'd better."

Emily looked even more confused and turned to Cesari. "What kind of a doctor are you anyway? I thought you were on the up and up."

He said, "I am on the up and up."

"So you say, but I'm beginning to wonder what lies deep down beneath your painfully cute exterior."

Tierney explained, "Emily, these two go way back. They've been friends since kindergarten."

"The first grade," corrected Vito.

"Yeah, well," continued Tierney. "They're closer than Siamese twins. For better or worse, they come as a package deal."

Emily nodded and looked at Cesari. "But why would you want to help me at all? Detective Tierney was friends with my father. That I can understand, but you're my doctor. Why would you risk your life?"

Cesari said, "Why not? I wasn't doing anything anyway."

She grinned, "I get it. You're an adrenaline junkie. All right. So now what?"

Vito said to Tierney. "I'll put a guy downstairs full time. No one gets in or out of the building without permission. I'll place a second guy across the street to back up the first guy. I can have anything you need brought right up to you. The real question is how long do you think this is going to go on?"

Tierney shook his head, "We've no idea. We don't even know what happened yet. All we know is what we just told you and what's been on the news which means we know next to nothing."

"Do I have to ask permission to go to the bathroom?" asked Emily sarcastically.

"Nothing changes from your point of view, Emily," Cesari said. "You're not a prisoner here, but the general consensus by everyone at this table is that it is not in your best interest to leave the building, at least not for the next few days."

"Can I stick my head out a window for fresh air?"

All three men simultaneously and emphatically said, "Absolutely not."

"Great," she muttered drolly. "I'm in witness protection indefinitely."

No one said anything. What could they say? She was right. The silence was deafening and when Vito's phone started bleating with a call, they all breathed a sigh of relief at the break in the mounting tension.

Vito put the device next to his ear. "What's up, Gerry? I'm busy."

He listened for a minute and said, "Slow down, Gerry. You're not making any sense. Hold on. I'm going to put you on speaker phone so Dr. Cesari can hear."

He pressed a button on the phone and placed it on the table. "Go ahead, Gerry. Repeat what you just told me."

Gerry was more agitated than was his usual. "There's a bunch of foreigners down here trying to go up to the apartment. They look like terrorists or maybe commies. I can't be sure. I'm certain one of them's with the Black Panthers. What a crew. Anyway, I got the drop on them and brought them into the vestibule so we're out of the public eye. You know, just in case I needed to plug one of them to keep the rest in line. One of them's gigantic too. He's bad news for sure. He's pretending to be scared. Another one's wearing a headpiece. He could have a bomb under it. I'm thinking this could be a suicide mission."

Cesari said, "Are you on drugs, Gerry? Ask the big guy his name?"

After a moment, Gerry said, "I can't understand him. He's still doing the crying routine."

Cesari suddenly realized what was happening and shouted, "Put your gun away, Gerry. They're my friends. I'm on the way down."

As he ran to the door, he called back to Vito, "Your boy is a maniac."

Bounding down the three flight of stairs, he was breathless when he arrived to find four of his friends from St. Matt's with their hands held high in the air and Gerry standing a healthy distance back with his .45 at his hip trained on them.

"Everybody put your hands down and relax. I'm sorry about this," Cesari said apologetically. He went over to Gerry and put his hand out. "Give me your piece."

"The hell I…"

Cesari raised his hand to slap him, but Gerry put his hands up in surrender. Cesari took the weapon, emptied the chamber, and dropped the clip to the floor. He tossed the disarmed weapon away where it bounced and clattered into a corner.

He said heatedly, "From now on, I don't want you carrying anything more powerful than a water pistol when you enter this building. Now start apologizing to my friends or the next sound you hear will be that of an ambulance siren coming to collect you."

Gerry glanced at the four men, saw the anger in Cesari's eyes, and said sheepishly, "Hey guys. I'm sorry about the misunderstanding."

The four men said nothing. They were anesthesiologists Cesari worked with every day in the OR at St. Matt's. They all specialized in pain management and were affectionately known as the pain killers. One of them was Jaskaran who provided the sedation for Vito's aunt when she had her endoscopy. He wore a blue traditional Sikh turban, and apparently was Gerry's suicide bomber. Standing next to him at nearly seven feet tall in dark rimmed eyeglasses was Parikh, also Indian but Hindu, and at the moment slightly teary eyed and trembling from the emotional trauma. To his right, straight from the budget committee meeting, was Xi, undoubtedly the commie Gerry so astutely unmasked. Xi was amongst other things, a committed conservative and lifetime member of the NRA, but hell, that could be a clever cover story. Then there was Jeremy Macallan, black with a thin mustache, fashionable red eyeglasses, sporting a sharp and very expensive looking paisley maroon smoking jacket with a gold silk cravat carrying a leather briefcase. He looked like he just stepped off his yacht. Clearly, a prime example of the latest trend in Black Panther chic as seen in Vogue, Esquire, and Ebony magazines.

Cesari went to Parikh and looked up at him. "You going to be okay?"

The big man nodded and in a pronounced Indian accent whispered, "Thank you, sir. I think so."

Cesari added, "C'mon upstairs. I have ice cream. It'll make you feel better."

Vito was on the staircase watching the proceedings. He said accusingly, "Fucking Gerry. It's always something with you."

"But boss, you said don't let nobody in what looks suspicious."

"Four well-dressed, intelligent guys look suspicious to you? You could have at least asked them who they were and what they wanted?"

"I did but I didn't believe them. They said they were doctors here to play poker. There wasn't any poker game going on, and look at the guy with the smoking jacket. Does he seem like a doctor to you? He looks like Hugh Heffner."

"Shut up, Gerry, and don't say another word." Vito barked and turned to Cesari questioningly.

Cesari shrugged. "With all that's been going on, I forgot I invited these guys over to play five card draw. Every couple of weeks we meet at each other's place to hang out and drink scotch. Tonight was my turn to host."

Vito looked hurt. "And you didn't invite me?"

"You're invited now. Let's go upstairs. I think Parikh needs some scotch."

Parikh said, "I would prefer ice cream if you don't mind. It will calm me down better. Do you have chocolate?"

"You got it, pal. Sprinkles too, and I'm very sorry."

Xi and the others crowded around Cesari. Xi demanded, "What's going on here, Cesari?"

"It's complicated and you deserve an explanation. Follow me and we'll have a drink while I run through it. Nice jacket, Jeremy. Is it safe to assume your briefcase is loaded with cigars?"

"Cubans," Jeremy replied.

"Cigars are okay, but cigarettes aren't?" Vito asked peevishly.

Cesari nodded. "That about sums it up."

"You got balls, Cesari."

"Yeah, two of them."

Jeremy interjected, "We need to talk about food. If you forgot about the game, you probably also forgot about food. You said you'd have something and we're starving."

"Damn, you're right. I completely forgot," Cesari said. "Hey, Gerry, how about you make amends and go get us something to eat."

"I don't work for you, Cesari."

Vito said, "Do what the doc says, or I'll murder you myself. And pick up your gun. You're a disgrace."

"Fine… What do you guys want?"

Cesari said, "Run down to the Second Avenue Deli and pick us up a bunch of hot pastrami sandwiches. And don't forget the pickles. On the way back stop at a liquor store and grab a couple of bottles of Johnnie Walker Blue."

"A couple of bottles? Hey, who's paying for this? That's a small fortune."

"You are, Gerry."

Gerry looked at Vito for support, but Vito said, "You heard him. This is your penance. Now get going."

Gerry was pissed and turned to leave, but not before Parikh launched a parting salvo at him. He called out mockingly, "Yes, get going and make it snappy, Gerry. I am very hungry."

The pain killers all chuckled at their friend's newly discovered courage. Jaskaran in particular was tickled and said, "Parikh, you're a tiger."

"Very much so, my friend."

Chapter 17

By 8:00 p.m. Deputy Director Morehouse knew a whole lot more than he did a few hours earlier. He knew that Claire Tompkins, a thirty-two-year-old secretary to Senator Taylor for the last three years had gone missing. Her phone had pinged off the cellphone tower in Tysons Corner near the underpass at about the same time Mills had been shot. She had left town in a hurry on some type of family emergency and was on her way to Dulles International Airport but never made her flight. Oddly, her family was unaware of the grave emergency that prompted Claire to take off. They didn't even know she was on the way. No one knew where Claire was. Her phone had stopped pinging somewhere on the outskirts of Philadelphia.

Morehouse mulled that over as he walked to the Old Ebbit Grill on 15th Street in the shadow of the White House and across from the Treasury building. It was Washington's oldest bar and restaurant and known for their oysters and raw bar. He was the first to arrive and settled in with a double Glenfiddich while he waited for the others.

So Claire Tompkins was hot to get out of D.C. for some reason. Rufus Youngblood might have the answer to that. The other bit of information that intrigued him was that the phone of a twenty-two-year-old intern named Emily Hoffman had pinged at the same time and location as Claire's. She worked for Senator McGuigan, whose office was literally down the hall from Taylor's. She hadn't shown up for work this morning and no one knew where she was although her phone was now pinging near Pittsburgh. What was the likelihood of that being a coincidence?

Morehouse was deeply dissatisfied at the way things were unfolding. He didn't like any of it. Mills' phone had a Rosemarie in the contact list with the same non-functioning number Youngblood had given them. He had someone trying to trace it back to its owner but had a sinking feeling that would lead nowhere. Otherwise the phone was clean without obvious suspicious messages. His apartment was clean too. The man led an orderly life, but he would have expected no less from a decorated SEAL. Interestingly, there were no photos of any women or any signs that one had spent any time there.

Morehouse sipped his scotch, took two manila folders out from his briefcase, and opened the files in front of him. They were Mills' and

Youngblood's service records in the SEALs, and he read them again for the second time. After thirty minutes, he put the folders away and ordered another scotch. He was half-way through when Director Burke, Senator Taylor, and Rufus Youngblood walked through the door to the private dining room. The Senator's security detail remained outside.

"Sorry we're late," said Burke. "But you seem to have figured out how to entertain yourself."

Burke nodded at the scotch glass as Morehouse stood to greet them. "This is Washington, boss. Waiting is part of the process. Good evening, Senator... Rufus."

They all sat down and ordered drinks and oysters. The Senator said, "Good evening, Deputy Director. Thank you for being patient. I was stuck in an Appropriations Committee meeting or should I say brawl?"

Rufus Youngblood grinned and nodded in Morehouse's direction as a way of acknowledging him. "Brawl is probably too kind a description."

The senator was a tall, wiry man in his early sixties. His full head of perfectly coiffed hair with silvery streaks and clean-cut looks made him appear very presidential. His voice was deep and booming. It made for great oratory.

The senator took charge of the meeting and added, "You know how it is working with politicians. They're like cranky children high on sugar. Anyway, thank you both for taking the time to meet with us... Let me start off by saying how much I appreciate all the hard work and dedication shown by your people every day. The tragic loss of a fine agent like Mills truly drives home the serious nature of your duty. I can't even begin to imagine how you both must feel right now. I only knew him for a short time, but he was a good man."

The man was a consummate politician, thought Morehouse. Burke responded with, "Yes, he was the very best, and thank you. We are dealing with the loss as best we can without letting it interfere with the ongoing nature of our responsibilities."

A waiter deposited a massive gin martini with three blue cheese stuffed olives in front of the senator, a beer in a tall pilsner glass in front of Rufus Youngblood, and Blantons, neat, in front of Burke. Morehouse stuck with his scotch. Two was enough. A second waiter set a platter down in the center of the table with four dozen assorted oysters, cocktail sauce, mignonette, and lemon wedges.

The senator said, "It's late. How about we just stick with an endless supply of oysters and martinis?"

"That's fine with me," affirmed Burke. Rufus Youngblood and Morehouse nodded their approval.

"Fine, let's dig in while we talk," Taylor said, grabbing an oyster. "Bring me up to speed on the investigation, Travis."

Leaving out the silencer and latex gloves, Burke summarized what they knew so far for the senator and his chief of staff, Rufus Youngblood as Morehouse listened dutifully.

When he was done the senator asked, "I don't mean to be mercenary, but can we be sure this has nothing to do with my campaign? He was the head of my security detail afterall."

Burke replied, "We're not sure of anything right now, but since you haven't even announced yet, I can't see how it possibly could."

Taylor snorted. "Anybody who lives or works within fifty miles of the beltway would know. It's imperative that we find out if this was an attack on me. If so, it could be meant as a warning. Have you considered that?"

"With all due respect senator, I don't see how this could have anything to do with your campaign but if you know something that I don't please enlighten me. For instance, have you received any threats recently in reference to your desire to run for president that I am unaware of?"

"No, I haven't."

Burke turned toward Rufus Youngblood, a hard looking fit guy just shy of six feet tall, and one hundred and ninety pounds of pure muscle in his mid-forties. Battle-hardened and inscrutable, he had the look of a Navy SEAL. They were strong and resilient, but their single biggest asset was their nearly superhuman levels of endurance.

Burke asked, "And you? Do you know of any threat against the senator's candidacy that perhaps you felt was unnecessary to burden him with?"

"No, of course not. I would never withhold information like that," replied Youngblood without hesitation.

"Okay, have there been any threats or crank calls in the last six months that we are unaware of? Anything at all?"

The senator and Rufus Youngblood shook their heads and Burke added, "And yet you seem to think Mills' death might be related to your campaign."

The senator responded with, "I never said that. I just want to make sure it isn't before we go into full blown damage control."

Burke said, "I understand… Gentlemen, this morning's tragic event has shaken us all up. I wish to reassure you that we are exploring any and all possibilities including the one you mentioned but we are still in the earliest stages of our investigation."

Rufus Youngblood asked, "What was Mills doing out there in the middle of the night?"

"That's not one hundred percent clear, but there is some evidence that he was performing an independent investigation of a previous case he had been involved with. Which case we don't know yet, but we think he was tracking down a lead on his own time and was possibly ambushed. The details of what happened are a bit sketchy."

"I hate to keep beating on this horse, Director Burke, but is there any chance whatsoever that what happened out there in Tysons Corner could tarnish the senator?"

There it was, Morehouse mused to himself. These two could give a rat's ass about Mills. Burke replied, "As I said, at this moment in time, I don't see any, but we will keep you appraised of developments."

The senator interjected. "What about the rest of Mills' team?"

"They will be kept in place for now and a new team leader will be assigned unless of course you have an objection to that."

Rufus Youngblood glanced at the senator and replied, "We have no objection. They're good people."

"I understand that you were good friends with Mills from your time in the SEALs," Burke said.

"I was his commanding officer for a whole year before I left for a career in politics. He was a good SEAL, but I wouldn't describe us as good friends. We were warriors. I respected him, and I'd like to think he reciprocated."

"On a personal level I wish to extend to you my sincerest condolences."

Rufus Youngblood said, "Thank you. Has anyone contacted his family?"

"Not yet. We've been in an uproar all day, but it was on my flunky's to do list."

The senator looked confused, and Rufus Youngblood cleared his throat at the rebuke, "I apologize for that remark, Director, and to you as well, Deputy Director," he said contritely. "As you can imagine, this has been a very stressful day."

The senator said, "I'm not sure what exactly happened but I would appreciate it if we all moved on without any further rancor. Remember, we're all on the same side."

"Well said, Senator," added Burke.

Morehouse said, "Water under the bridge, Rufus. No harm, no foul, and for the record, I've been called much worse... I'd like to ask you a few questions about Mills, seeing as you knew him in a very different light than the rest of us."

Youngblood glanced at the senator who suddenly stood anticipating that a conversation he didn't want to be part of was about to begin. He glanced at his watch, saying, "Time really does fly, gentlemen. I must go now, but Rufus will see to it that all your concerns are addressed."

Burke stood as well, "I'll walk you out, Senator."

"Thank you, Travis. I'd appreciate that. Better optics for anyone who might be watching."

And just like that, after only two martinis and a couple of dozen oysters, the senator was gone, leaving the flunkies to get down and dirty.

Morehouse didn't waste any time. "How about we start with Mills' girlfriend?"

"I already told the director all I know. I never met her. I can say that I never got the feeling from Mills that he was very serious about her."

"Why is that?"

"I don't know," he shrugged. "He never talked about her much. Why are you asking about her? What did she have to say about their relationship?"

"That's just it. She hasn't said anything. We can't seem to locate her. The address you gave us was an unoccupied apartment."

"Seriously?" asked Youngblood. "Who was it leased to?"

"According to the landlord, nobody. It hadn't been rented in over a year. Are you sure you got the address right?"

He thought it over for a minute and said, "To the best of my knowledge, yes."

"How long were they dating?"

"I don't know. Like I said, we weren't nearly as close as you might think given our background history. He didn't offer details and I didn't pry."

"Yet, you were close enough to request him to lead the senator's security detail."

"He was good at what he did."

"All right. Tell me about Mills in the SEALs. Were there any issues or behavioral problems that you recall. Maybe something that didn't warrant official reprimand but stuck in your gullet."

Youngblood sat back as the waiter cleared the table. When he left, he shook his head, "None at all. He was a great SEAL. It was an honor to serve with him."

"I've read your files. You both served in Iraq Part II after 9/11when we decided Saddam Hussein had to go."

"That's right."

"It said in your files that you and your team went behind enemy lines during the first days of military action to disrupt communications and seek out high value targets."

"If that's what it says, I won't deny it."

"You both received the Navy Cross for your efforts."

"That's also correct."

"You know what's interesting though?"

Youngblood sipped his beer. "What's that?"

Morehouse opened the manila folders containing the files and turned them for Youngblood to see. He said, "I've read and re-read your files. You both received the highest award the navy offers but I can't for the life of me figure out what exactly you did."

Youngblood looked down at the heavily redacted pages with black markers through at least sixty or seventy percent of the words. He grinned and said, "I guess that's classified."

Morehouse snorted. "Are you going to make me go to the Secretary of the Navy?"

"Good luck with that. What's it got to do with anything anyway? Unless you think Mills getting murdered in the middle of the night in Tysons Corner has something to do with ancient history."

"Maybe it does. There's way too much going on behind the scenes with Mills that I'm not happy with."

"Such as?"

"Did you know his girlfriend that you never met worked for the CIA?"

Youngblood looked surprised. Whether it was genuine or not was hard to say. Morehouse was rapidly getting the impression that Youngblood was as good a liar as any career politician. "No, I did not, and how do you know that if you couldn't find her?"

"Because we received a phone call from inside Langley telling us not to bother looking for her."

"Jesus..."

"New subject. What can you tell me about Claire Tompkins?"

"Beautiful woman. Very capable office worker."

"Is that all?"

"What else is there?"

"What was the family emergency in Miami she had to leave for?"

"I don't know. As I said, I don't pry into people's personal lives. I do my job and they do theirs. I prefer to leave the personal baggage at the door."

"Well, her phone pinged in Tyson's Corner in the same location and time of night that Mills was shot, and she never made her flight to Miami."

"That is interesting."

Chapter 18

Plumes of cigar smoke filled the room as Cesari dealt out another hand of five card draw from a brand-new deck. The remnants of once magnificent pastrami sandwiches sat in front of them, and they were working on the second bottle of Johnnie Walker Blue. A window fan hummed nearby straining to relieve the fumes out onto Sixth Avenue and a floor fan strobed back and forth to keep the air circulating. They used small ceramic cereal bowls as ash trays and steak knives as toothpicks. These were men the way men were supposed to be. Primitive beings with full bellies and slaked thirsts competing for dominance against other men on the modern battlefield. They picked up their cards and eyed each other warily. The seven of them squared off in preparation for the battle royale. Cesari, Tierney, Vito and the pain killers sat awkwardly around the small kitchen table while Emily hid in his bedroom from the smell of tobacco and the toxic levels of masculinity.

Tierney threw in a couple chips and said, "I'll raise fifty cents and hold."

The pain killers groaned and two of them folded immediately. Parikh said, "I will meet you, sir, and would enjoy the pleasure of two more cards, thank you."

No one knew what to make of this. As the night wore on, Parikh had revealed himself to be a master at bluffing and was now fifteen dollars ahead and picking up steam. Even worse, he smelled blood in the water.

Vito took three cards, Xi took two, Tierney took one. Cesari had a pair of jacks and dealt himself three cards after the others. To keep the game friendly and casual, all chips were valued the same at twenty-five cents and there was a ten-dollar limit per pot. No one would accuse them of being high rollers, but the idea was to smoke a robust cigar and enjoy a flavorful scotch. On a good night you might take home fifty bucks more than you came in with. On a really good night you'd walk out with a hundred big ones. On a great night you'd lose a hundred and not care because you were drunk.

"You know, Cesari," Tierney said staring into his hand. "I really should bust you for holding an illegal poker game and distributing contraband cigars."

Cesari grinned. "No need for acrimony, Detective. I'll slip you a few aces on the next deal and maybe you can just look the other way."

Tierney laughed. "That would work. Unfortunately, I'm going to have to make this my last hand. It's getting late and I have a lot to do including soothing my cat who's probably clawing up the curtains because I'm late. And I'm meeting first thing in the morning with the fingerprint guys."

Jaskaran asked, "Is there anything we can do to help?"

Despite Tierney's misgivings about the ever-expanding circle of people in the know, and because of the unusual circumstances they all found themselves in, Cesari elected to bring his friends into the fold.

Cesari said, "Not at the moment, but thanks. It certainly would be nice to have other places we can bring Emily just in case this apartment is no longer secure."

Tierney sighed, "Cesari's right but I'm concerned about this being the worst kept secret in history. This was supposed to be hush hush."

Xi said reassuringly, "We won't tell anyone. Besides, what would we say? We know where a fugitive from government assassins is hiding. We'd be in the psych ward before we finished the sentence."

Tierney snorted. He'd met Cesari's friends once before and liked them. Truth was that he felt comforted at having such trustworthy allies. He said, "Just remember, the walls have ears."

He then spread his hand onto the table revealing a mixed suit straight, Jack high. Cesari, Vito and Xi folded, and just as Tierney went to collect his loot, Parikh waved his finger and smiled.

"Not so fast, Mr. Detective, sir. I believe a full house beats a straight."

He spread his cards out for all to see, revealing three fives and two kings. Gleefully, he swept the chips into his already substantial pile.

Tierney shook his head, "How the hell does he do it? If the stakes weren't so low, I'd think you guys were scamming me. Well, it's been real fellas. I'll see you tomorrow, Cesari."

He stood to leave, and as he did, Jeremy proffered him a 60 ring Montecristo, saying, "It's yours if you stay for one more hand."

"Thanks, Macallan, but I hope this isn't a bribe."

Jeremy gave him a cat-eating grin. "Me? Bribe a cop? Never..."

This brought a chuckle from the others. Vito said, "I usually just hand him a suitcase full of cash."

More laughter.

Cesari said, "C'mon, detective. One more hand. I feel your luck is about to change."

Tierney hesitated, glanced at his watch and said, "That's easy for you to say, Cesari. I'm the one in the hole for seventeen dollars and fifty cents."

"Yeah, but you've been drinking two hundred and fifty dollars a bottle scotch all night and smoking cigars that cost way more than you lost."

Tierney seemed to relent and sat back down. "You guys are killing me. All right, one more hand, and give me that cigar."

****

"Okay, people, tell me what you have. Dirk, bring the team up to speed on the phone situation," Morehouse said.

It was close to midnight, and they were in a conference room in Secret Service headquarters reviewing what they knew. Dirk had tacked a map of the U.S. on the wall and there were empty boxes of Chinese food cluttering much of the table in front of them. Ben Forman and Angela Munoz sat with their legs crossed.

Dirk said, "In summary, Agent Mills' phone pinged in Tysons Corner off the same cell tower at the same time as did Claire Tompkins' and Emily Hoffman's phones. Claire Tompkins worked for Senator Taylor. Emily Hoffman was an intern for Senator McGuigan. Why their phones were all pinging at the same place at the same time is unknown, but it's too much of a fluke to ignore. We do know that Claire Tompkins was on her way to the airport to catch a flight to Miami where she reportedly had a family emergency. We now know that she did not have a family emergency at all, but her reasons for the hasty exit from D.C. remain unknown. Both her and Emily's phone pinged together all the way from D.C. leading me to conclude they were traveling together. Probably, Emily was driving her. Emily had a car registered in her name. Claire did not. Claire never made that flight. Her phone last pinged off a cell tower in Lansdale, Pennsylvania not too far from the family residence of Emily Hoffman. Emily's Hoffman's phone is still pinging and is now on its way to Chicago. I've tried calling both phones but there was no response. I've called Emily Hoffman's parents several times but again there was no response."

Dirk uncapped a magic marker and approached the map. "According to the phone trail, Agent Mills and the two women were in approximately the same vicinity at the same time. Agent Mills got shot and his phone remained in the same spot. The two women who were on the way to Dulles suddenly changed course and headed to Lansdale together. And now Emily is on the way to Chicago."

He drew a line from D.C. to Tysons Corner and then up to Pennsylvania. Munoz asked, "Why were they in Tysons Corner? The highway would have been a much faster way to reach the airport."

"I'm not sure," Dirk replied, furrowing his brow. "The weather was horrific last night and there were traffic delays. Perhaps, Emily decided to circumvent the tie up. Alternatively, it may have been something ordinary like a restroom stop. It's hard to say. But what's peculiar is that Mills' phone pinged along the exact same path until they converged near the underpass."

"And what's your conclusion?" queried Morehouse.

"Something happened in Tysons Corner that caused the women to reconsider their original plan and head off in a different direction and now one of them is off the grid."

"And Mills?"

Dirk hesitated before saying, "I'd rather not speculate, sir."

"Speak freely, agent. I insist," ordered the Deputy Director.

"One possible explanation for last night's events is that Agent Mills was following the women from D.C. and whatever happened in Tysons Corner frightened them sufficiently to run for cover. In fact, Emily Hoffman is still running."

"Claire Tompkins?"

"She was smart enough to destroy her phone."

"And why Lansdale?"

"It's where Emily Hoffman grew up and lived her whole life until six months ago. It represented security and comfort."

"Mommy and Daddy? Are you saying she ran home to Mommy and Daddy, Agent Bradbury?"

"I'm saying, sir, that if she was frightened, she may have gone to the one place she knew was safe."

"So what frightened her?"

"The women may have witnessed Agent Mills getting shot. I think they were in that underpass when it happened, and now they've gone to ground."

"So far, so good, but why were they all in that underpass together in the first place? What possessed them all to stop there?"

"That I can't say with any degree of certainty."

Morehouse turned to the others. "Anybody?"

"Was agent Mills following them or providing them escort?" offered Ben Forman who until that moment had been quiet.

"Escort?" repeated Morehouse. "If he was, he didn't tell anybody. Why would he do that anyway? He could have just offered to drive Claire to the airport himself. How about this… Maybe he wasn't following the women. Maybe he just happened to be there for as yet some unknown reason, but whatever prompted them to get off the highway also prompted him to do the same. And whatever caused the women to stop in the underpass also caused him to stop and then it all went sideways. I want everybody to think this through from every angle and possibility without prejudice. Everything is on the table. Maybe the women got off the highway because they were having car trouble. Did Mills recognize them or their car and decide that he could spare a few minutes to help them? Maybe a bad guy came along and Mills arrived just in time to take a bullet for them? I don't want anybody jumping to conclusions prematurely."

They all sat there thinking about that for a minute. Morehouse said, "Ben, what do the other agents on Taylor's detail have to say?"

"They liked Mills. He was competent and respected. They don't know why he was in Tysons Corner."

"What about his personal life?"

"His apartment was clean as was his cellphone and laptop. He kept to himself and was very professional at work. No illicit relationships that anyone knew of and no bad habits."

"What about this girlfriend, Rosemarie? Did anyone know her?"

He shook his head. "No one on the team even knew he had a girlfriend."

Morehouse thought about that for a minute and turned to Munoz. "Does that make sense to you?"

"Yes and no. It would all depend on his relationship with the members of the detail. Still, it does seem a little odd. You're with people day and night. Stuff like that usually comes out. However, if she worked for the CIA then he might have been tightlipped about her."

Morehouse nodded. "I'm not comfortable with it but it's not entirely out of the realm of possibility that he would keep his relationship quiet. Okay, we're going to shift gears a little. Dirk, I want you to focus on finding Claire Tompkins and Emily Hoffman. Call our field office in Chicago and have them track down her phone. If we get lucky, Claire might still be with her. Start digging on Claire and Emily's backgrounds. I want to know who they are and what the hell happened last night that scared them so much they took off like jack rabbits. Put out a bulletin to the local and state police where Emily's phone last pinged. Give them the make and license plate of her car and description of the young ladies. Ben, I want you to dig into Mills' background and his relationship to Youngblood. They were in the SEALs together and are highly decorated veterans. Much of their files are redacted, however. I'd like to know why. See what you can find out without creating a firestorm. I have no doubt you will meet fierce resistance. I want to know how fierce and from whom before I call in any chips at the DoD. Agent Munoz and I are going to work on who this Rosemarie woman is and why the CIA doesn't want us talking to her. Okay, everybody, let's go."

Dirk and Ben left the room leaving Munoz and Morehouse behind. He said, "The director and I had a lovely chat with Rufus Youngblood and Senator Taylor over scotch and oysters earlier. The senator didn't have a whole lot to add to our body of knowledge, but eventually, they left me and Rufus alone. That's when things got interesting."

"How so?"

"I'm not sure exactly. At times, Youngblood seemed on the up and up. Then there were moments when I was sure he was full of shit. For instance, he told me he didn't know what the big family emergency was that caused Claire to leave for Miami abruptly."

"That doesn't seem reasonable to you?"

"Not in the slightest. He's the senator's chief of staff. His job is to know stuff like that in case there's any blowback to the senator. And then there's Rosemarie… Don't you think it's strange that he's the only one who knew about her? And on top of that, claims he never met her."

Munoz mulled it over for a bit before saying, "Sure, a little but then again, maybe not. We're talking about hard men. Men who've seen combat. They may not behave socially the way others who haven't walked in their shoes might."

Morehouse nodded. "Maybe… Even stranger though was that he wasn't particularly alarmed when I told him someone from the CIA had intervened on her behalf."

Munoz said, "I see what you mean. If it's his job to stamp out fires, then the head of his Secret Service security detail dating someone in the CIA would be a big deal."

"Exactly, and the fact that she's suddenly disappeared didn't seem to bother him all that much either. I mean, he was taken back by the news but not overly concerned, sort of a tepid reaction, which in itself is surprising"

"I wonder what that means?"

"That's what we need to find out." Morehouse glanced at his watch. "It's getting late. Find the guys and tell them to do as much as they can, and then try to get some sleep. A lot of what I asked them to do can't be done in the middle of the night anyway and I want everybody fresh as daisies in the a.m., and that includes you."

"You're letting us go to sleep?"

He looked at her. "It's almost midnight, Munoz. Do I seem like a monster to you?"

"Fickle, perhaps," she laughed. "But I'll take it. I'm beat."

"You can go now, Munoz. We'll regroup here at seven sharp. Now, I have to call my wife and tell her how much I love her and miss her and can't live without her."

Munoz smiled. "That's so romantic."

"No, that's called being practical. I haven't spoken to her all day, and I don't want her throwing things at me when I walk through the door because she's been worried sick about me."

"You make love sound dangerous."

"It can be."

Chapter 19

At 3:00 a.m. Tierney's phone buzzed. He was staring at the three aces in his hand and chewing on the stub of a Monte Cristo. Vito, Cesari and Jaskaran were all that were left. Parikh was sleeping on one arm of Cesari's L-shaped sofa and Xi on the other. Jeremy had passed out at the table. He was snoring with one side of his face pressed into his chips.

It was Fred Hoffman on the phone and Tierney knew this couldn't be good. He threw his cards down and stepped away from the table. Fred was distraught, and with great urgency in his voice, said, "Bob, you need to get Emily out of there now. I don't know how much time you have."

"Slow down, Fred. What happened?"

Fred's voice was shaky and faltering from emotion. "They killed Kathy. I brought Claire's body to D.C. like we talked about. I just returned and found Kathy on the kitchen floor with three bullet wounds to the head."

Tierney was shocked and thoroughly alarmed. Everyone at the table picked up on his body language and were watching him intently. "Jesus… Fred, I'm so sorry… I don't know what to say. Can you tell me anything else?"

"No, only that she's dead."

Tierney took in a deep breath and exhaled loudly. His adrenaline was rushing and he was fully awake. "This is going to sound dumb, but how certain are you it's related?"

"Please Bob… What else could it be? A home invasion and nothing appears to have been stolen? Three well-grouped bullets to the face? Rigor mortis is already setting in, so they have a few hours head start."

"You're right, Fred. I was just thinking out loud. I'll get Emily out of New York. We have to assume Kathy gave them my name and Dr. Cesari's name. People this connected will already have our addresses. What are you going to do?"

"I haven't gotten that far. I've been too upset and now I'm scared half to death for Emily's sake."

"You should speak to Emily."

"I know… She's going to lose it."

"It can't be helped, Fred. I can't keep this from her. You're her father. It's best she hears it from you."

"Is she there?"

"She's in the bedroom sleeping. I'll get her. After you speak to her, we'll get moving and call you as soon as we settle in again."

Tierney glanced quickly at everyone and then went to the bedroom. Cesari instinctively stood to offer assistance. Everyone could feel the urgency as the tension in the once very relaxed room started to rise. They didn't know the details yet, but they got the gist that something really bad had just gone down and immediate action was required. Cesari and Jaskaran woke their friends. Vito called down to Gerry to keep his eyes open and stay on the alert.

Tierney gently woke Emily and handed her the phone. Fred broke the news as gently as he could, and they both wept quietly on their respective ends. Fred said, "We'll have time to mourn later, Emily. Now you must move fast and do whatever Bob and his friends advise. These bastards could be coming for you as we speak. Your mother would want you to be strong, Emily."

Sniffling she said, "I will be."

"Good... I love you, Emily. I have to go now."

Emily said goodbye and burst out bawling.

Tierney placed a comforting arm around her, and she buried her head into his chest sobbing. He said, "Emily, I can't even begin to tell you how sorry I am."

She didn't say anything.

"I know you're tired, but we have to keep moving. Get your things together and meet me in the living room. All right?"

She nodded. "What's going to happen?"

"I wish I knew," he answered truthfully.

Tierney returned to the living room where the others were waiting. He filled them in on the details and watched their incredulous expressions. A few hours ago this was just an amazing story but now it was real, and serious, and dangerous, and very close. And all of them were now involved. Previously exhausted faces were now on edge and hyper alert.

Vito said, "These people don't know me. Let's take her to my apartment in Little Italy. There's plenty of room, and I have heavy security there. No one can get in or out without permission or going through my private army. We can use my Escalade to transport her. It's fitted with bullet-proof glass."

Tierney nodded. "I think I'll take you up on that offer, Gianelli. For tonight anyway. Thanks."

Cesari said, "But there's the long-term picture we have to consider as well. If you think Emily's mother gave them our names, then they'll soon be looking for us, and anyone with half a brain and access to the internet will figure out who Vito is."

Tierney agreed. "You're right but it will buy us some time. I don't know who these people are, but I assume they would rather use stealth than cannons and tanks, so in the short run Gianelli's apartment will work. The question is for how long can we keep her there?"

"She's definitely not going to want to grow old hiding there," Cesari quipped. "And sooner or later she's going to want fresh air."

"Maybe she should leave the country?" suggested Jaskaran who had been listening with great interest.

Cesari thought about that. The situation was escalating rapidly. They had caught up with Emily's family much more quickly than anyone would have thought and had acted with extreme violence. It was hard to believe, but the United States was starting to suddenly feel very small. The government was plugged in to every aspect of daily life, and there were few places you could hide for very long. Going off grid wasn't nearly as easy as the movies would suggest.

"Where?" Cesari asked. "Canada, Mexico?"

Tierney wasn't sure if he liked this idea. He couldn't just leave the country to be with her, but he was worried that he had just become a liability. They could be tracking his phone and credit cards as they spoke. Besides, he needed to go to Fred. Her father was in danger too now that these people had declared all-out war on the Hoffman family.

Vito smiled.

Tierney said, "Spit it out, Gianelli."

"We can take her to Sicily."

Tierney looked at him. "Sicily?"

"Sure, I had business there anyway as I mentioned earlier. Me and Cesari can keep a close eye on her. We can kill two birds with one stone."

"You can't be serious? You're going to ground zero for the mafia to rough up some of your relations and possibly worse and you want to take Emily with you? No offense, Gianelli. I know your heart's in the right place but I'm not sure that's the smartest thing I ever heard. We're trying to hide Emily not get her mixed up in a mob war. What do you think, Cesari?"

Thinking it over for a minute, Cesari eventually said, "I don't know, Detective. The idea has some merit, and Emily's young enough that she could pass for my or Vito's daughter, so travelling together wouldn't raise any eyebrows. I can stay with Emily when Vito goes to discuss his problem with Rosaria and Ernesto."

Cesari glanced at Jaskaran. The pain killer was younger than him. He said, "Even better. Emily and Jaskaran are much closer in age. They could pass for a married couple."

Jaskaran raised his eyebrows. "You want me to come with you?"

Cesari said, "We'll need as many diversionary targets for the killers as possible."

"Thanks, Cesari," he laughed.

"Would you consider it? A married woman travelling with her husband will elicit much less unwanted attention than an attractive young woman travelling with her father might."

It didn't take Jaskaran long to decide. "I'm in. You only live once, right?"

Parikh said, "I am jealous, sir. Jaskaran gets to go on an adventure and I have to stay home to clean my house and whatever else my wife orders me to do."

"You can come if you want. In fact, you all can. The more the merrier. There's safety in numbers."

Parikh shook his head and peeked at his watch. "I am already in too much trouble for staying out this late. I must go home now and accept my punishment."

Xi nodded in agreement. He and Parikh were married with little kids. Xi said, "Parikh's right. My wife's pretty tolerant, but this was longer than any poker game we've ever had. She isn't going to be thrilled either. Look, if you need anything right here in Manhattan, just let me know, but I have to draw the line on international travel."

Jeremy had been very quiet taking it all in. He had a girlfriend, but it wasn't like they were tied at the hip. She had been known to let him off his leash once in a while.

Cesari asked, "What are you thinking, Jeremy?"

"I've always wanted to visit Sicily."

"That only leaves you, Detective."

"I'd love to, but Emily's father needs me right now, and I'm going to Lansdale. You keep Emily safe. Depending on the circumstances, I may try to catch up with you later."

****

After the emotional call concluded, Fred Hoffman looked around his kitchen trying to decide what to do. If he called the authorities and reported it as a home invasion gone bad, he would have to explain why he wasn't home and why it took him hours to discover Kathy's body. And he didn't have any good response to the question of where he might have been in the middle of the night. If he said he was home in bed sleeping when it happened, then it would beg the question of what kind of a home invasion didn't result in theft or finding a second person in the house? Then there was the issue of how believable would it sound that three shots were fired and he didn't wake up? Not very.

The other course of action would be to call the FBI directly and tell them the whole story. That Kathy was slain by operatives working for the government cleaning up a mess they created down in D.C. No one would believe him of course other than the shadowy killers themselves. In fact, many would want Emily brought to justice for murdering a Secret Service agent. Emily would never make it alive to trial if she were apprehended under these circumstance. No, he mused, the truth would have to be put on hold for the moment.

So what to do?

Looking at Kathy's body one last time, his heart sank and self-doubt and regret filled his soul. He should have taken her with him. She would still be alive if he had. Twenty-two years on the force and he had never been as shaken as he was right now. His gun was in its holster on his hip, and he thought about putting it up to the side of his temple.

But then he thought about Emily. She needed him now more than ever even though she couldn't be with him. A double blow like that would devastate her. Besides, it was the coward's way out. After a few minutes, an idea came to him. He walked to the front entrance of the house and let the front door swing wide and conspicuously open. He took the battery out and threw the burner phone into thick foundation bushes. Then he went down to their unfinished basement and placed his pistol on a shelf in the gun safe, leaving the door ajar. He looked around studying his options. There were several round steel structural support posts, and he touched one. This could work. He took his keys out from his pocket and threw them across the room where they slid along the cement slab into the far wall. Then he did the same with his real cellphone.

Wrapping his arms around one of the steel posts, he handcuffed his wrists together. If he didn't show up for work or call in, sooner or later somebody from the department would investigate. Hopefully, a neighbor would find the front door open a lot sooner than that. He braced himself that it could take a while, but he needed to lend authenticity to the story or some eager beaver D.A. would try to pin Kathy's death on him. Now for the hard part. If the home invaders were ruthless enough to pump three bullets into Kathy's head, then it would be unlikely that they would leave him unscathed.

He took in a deep breath, girded himself and swung his face as hard as he could into the steel pole. The shock of the impact rattled him. His knees buckled but he remained standing and shook it off. His face on that side was already starting to swell and he could wiggle a tooth loose. He focused and on the count of three, swung his face even harder than the first time. This time two teeth came loose, and he spit them out with blood and saliva. His eye began to swell shut and he knew he wouldn't be eating or speaking normally for a while. His thoughts were processing a little more slowly than before and he couldn't quite see straight. His legs were barely able to support him now and he wished Kathy was there to comfort him. The last blow resulted in a crunch as he broke his maxillary bone and slumped to the floor unconscious.

Chapter 20

Morehouse had barely taken the first sip of his first coffee at 6:30 a.m. when Agent Munoz barged into his office without knocking. Agents Bradbury and Forman were close behind. All three were excited about something.

Glancing at his watch, he said, "You're early. I said seven."

Munoz was breathless. "You haven't heard?"

"Haven't heard what?"

"They found Claire Tompkins' body this morning."

Morehouse perked up. "Where? When?"

"About an hour ago, behind the Lincoln Memorial wrapped in a tarp. Park maintenance called the D.C. police. They knew we were looking for her and called me. She'd been shot in the forehead. They identified her from her driver's license and congressional ID. Her bag was lying right next to her. Only her phone was missing. It doesn't look like a robbery or sexual assault."

"Has it hit the news yet?"

"Not that I can tell but it will."

Morehouse said, "What about Emily Hoffman?"

Dirk answered, "Nothing yet. One of our people found her phone taped to the bottom of a seat on an Amtrak train in Chicago. I tried calling the parents again but no luck."

"What do we know about the parents?"

"Mom's a nurse at Jefferson Hospital in Lansdale and her father's a police lieutenant in the same town."

"That's it?"

"Father was a corporal in the Marines for eight years, served with distinction in the Middle East. When he came out, he made the force in New York and served there for a while before moving to the Philadelphia area. Clean record."

Morehouse sipped his coffee. "I don't like this. Claire's phone last pinged in Lansdale with Emily's. Now Claire's back in D.C. dead and Emily's phone is taking a joy ride to Chicago. What does that mean to you, Munoz?"

"They were buying time. Somebody was after them and they knew it."

"I agree, but Claire got unlucky. Both women were fairly young and inexperienced in the ways of law enforcement, yet they pulled off a nifty trick with the phones. Do you think either one of them was capable of that?"

Agent Ben Forman offered, "Possibly, but certainly Emily's father would have known about our ability to track phones."

Dirk said, "So they panicked and went to Emily's house. Her father realizes that if they were being followed, they'd need to do something about the phones. Claire throws hers away and Emily tapes hers to a seat on a train bound for Chicago. Claire decides to come back to D.C. for some reason and runs right into her killer and Emily is where?"

Munoz said, "I'd like to add one more thing. Ordinary citizens can't track phones like that, so the father knew that the people coming for Emily had extraordinary resources."

Bradbury added, "That would be in line with them having witnessed Agent Mills' murder. Whoever shot him must also have been with the government or law enforcement. The women knew this and told her father. He put two and two together and realized that they could track the phones and by the same token he couldn't call law enforcement for help."

Morehouse said, "Okay, new plan. Dirk, go to the crime scene and morgue. Find out anything you can about Claire's death. Then get warrants and search both her and Emily's apartments or tag along with the FBI if they're already there. Call over to Tysons Corner and see if they have any blood or tissue from the crime scene or the bullet they found that we can match up to Claire Tompkins."

Dirk raised his eyebrows. "You think there's a possibility she was killed in Tysons Corner?"

"Something bad happened in that underpass in Tysons Corner, Dirk. So yeah, I think that's a possibility."

"And then what?" asked Dirk. "Emily drove her all the way to Philadelphia and then back to the Lincoln Memorial?"

"Unless you think Emily had the wherewithal to wrap Claire's body in a tarp she just happened to have lying around and then drop her off before driving back to Lansdale."

"Not possible according to the timing and placement of the phone pings, and why would she have held on to Claire's phone? Both phones pinged all the way to Lansdale. It doesn't make any sense. And if she drove all the way home with a dead body in her car, why would she then drive it back to D.C. a few hours later?"

Morehouse suddenly snapped his fingers. "Because she didn't drive it back."

"Then who did?"

"You're not a father yet, are you Dirk?"

Dirk shook his head.

Morehouse explained, "I think the father drove Claire's body back. Think about it. Suppose Emily drove all the way home with a dead body in her car and told her father, a former Marine and police lieutenant, that she got mixed up in a shootout with government agents or rogue law enforcement or people she mistakenly took for rogue law enforcement, and that they might be following her, there's no doubt he would do everything his cop instincts told him to do to ensure her safety while he sorted it out."

Munoz said, "Send her phone in one direction and she in another, and dump Claire's body as far away as possible."

Morehouse nodded. "The more I think about it, the more I'm convinced that's what happened. We need to consider that from his point of view, the threat to Emily's safety was real and imminent. He's a cop but right now he's thinking like a father. Maybe that's why they're not answering their phones. They don't know who might be listening and they certainly don't want to answer any potentially incriminating questions. Ben, you keep digging into Mills' background and his relationship to Youngblood. Also, see what you can find on Emily's parents. Where might Emily go to stay under the radar? The parents must have cellphones. See who they called in the last twenty-four hours."

"And me?" asked Munoz.

"We're going to Lansdale. I want to meet this Marine and see what he's all about." He turned to Dirk and Ben. "It's a three-hour ride. I expect you to call me on the way with updates. All right, everybody. Let's go. We're wasting time."

Munoz and Morehouse beat a path to the garage and were on the road minutes later. Munoz drove the Suburban while Morehouse called Director Burke. "Boss, have you heard the news?"

There was a loud sigh into the phone. "Yes, it's not every day a body shows up behind the Lincoln Memorial. What happened?"

"I don't know."

"Best guess, Grayson."

"She was killed in the underpass and the Hoffman girl wigged out and drove her all the way home to Lansdale. Her father's a cop and former Marine. He managed to get her off the grid at least temporarily through some clever misdirection. I think he may have brought the body back to D.C. in an attempt at even more subterfuge."

"Do you think it was Mills' who shot her?"

Morehouse shot Munoz a quick glance. They were rocketing up I-95 at ninety miles an hour with their lights flashing and she was paying full attention to the road. "That is the big question, isn't it?" he replied. "We'll know better if forensics can match any of her DNA with what was found in the underpass and on the bullet."

"Where are you now?"

"On the way to Emily Hoffman's family home outside of Philly to interview her parents. I have a feeling Emily's the only one who can tell us what really happened. Maybe I'll get lucky and find her hiding under her bed."

"The FBI?"

"I think I'm still one step ahead. As far as I can tell, they still don't know about Clair Tompkins and the Hoffman girl, and if they do, they haven't made a connection with Mills yet."

"Okay, let's just hope the girl's in one piece when you do find her."

"I know. I'm worried about that. Whatever she saw has probably got someone somewhere very uptight. You'll need to fill Youngblood and Senator Taylor in on Claire Tompkins so they can start their spin machine going. Two people from their camp getting murdered in one day is bound to make headlines."

"They're next on my to do list. I wanted to make sure you and I are on the same page. Okay, keep me posted."

Morehouse hung up and watched as Munoz inched the heavy vehicle upward toward a hundred miles an hour. They whizzed by cars and trucks as if they were all parked at a curb. At close to 9:30 a.m., they pulled off I-95 onto I-476 N. Thirty minutes from their destination, they picked up Philadelphia traffic and Munoz necessarily slowed her speed down appropriately. They were making good time.

Munoz said, "Any word from Ben or Dirk?"

"Not a peep yet... I'm not happy, Munoz, and I'm worried about this Hoffman girl."

"So am I... What possible motive could Mills have to kill Claire Tompkins?"

"I don't remember saying he did."

"It's on the table, isn't it?"

"Unfortunately, yes... A love affair gone wrong maybe? Maybe she decided to end it and he was one of those guys that doesn't take breakups well."

"You don't believe that?"

"It's possible."

"Sleeping with a protectee's secretary? That's pretty far out of bounds."

"So is murdering a woman because she rejects you, but it happens all the time. To be honest with you, it would be better all-around if we find out he snapped and acted alone."

"You mean in terms of damage control with the press?"

"Yes, we could always call it a murder suicide. Two ex-lovers, bad blood, tempers running hot. It all comes to a head on a rainy night in Tysons Corner. It has sort of a romantic feel to it."

"I doubt Claire Tompkins would agree with that."

"No, not at all. But I would rather not find out he was the tip of the spear for some whacko conspiracy that leads us to dark places. I can't even imagine the amount of harm that would do to the Service."

Persisting in this vein, Munoz said, "If Mills did shoot Claire, then it raises a somewhat fantastical possibility."

"You mean that perhaps it was the Hoffman girl who shot Mills?"

"Exactly... Last man standing kind of thing."

"Well, if she's still alive, we'll ask her. But we can't rule out the possibility that they were simply passive spectators in whatever went down."

They made a turn onto a tree lined street and saw multiple emergency vehicles in front of one particular house. There were two ambulances, a fire engine, six police cars and a multitude of curious citizens milling about. Munoz brought the Suburban to a gentle stop along the curb half a block from the scene.

Morehouse said, "Please don't tell me that's the Hoffman residence."

"All right, I won't tell you."

"Damn," he murmured under his breath. "So much for the, he-acted-alone, theory."

"Aren't we getting ahead of ourselves? Maybe somebody won the lottery and had a heart attack."

Morehouse smirked. "Let's go find out."

She cut the engine and they exited the vehicle. It was a balmy fifty-five degrees. Damp and overcast but decidedly not inclement. They made their way through the crowd to the front door of the home just as two EMTs wheeled out a stretcher with a zipped-up body bag to one of the waiting ambulances. Morehouse and Munoz watched them pass by and glanced at each other. Down the quiet road the first news van was arriving. They flashed their badges at the uniformed officer guarding the front door. He raised his eyebrows in surprise when he saw they were from the Secret Service and let them into the house.

The officer said, "You'll need to put on booties and gloves if you don't mind. There's a box just inside the doorway."

They nodded, donned the gear and entered the main living area. There were a myriad of police and forensics personnel snapping photos and collecting evidence. Most of the activity was coming from the kitchen. Blood splattering was easily visible on the floor, the table and the kitchen counters. A chair was overturned and a coffee cup had shattered. Morehouse introduced himself and Munoz to the officer taking pictures and another bagging shell casings.

Morehouse asked, "What happened?"

"We're not sure yet. Possible home invasion. A neighbor saw the front door flung wide open and found Mrs. Hoffman on the floor, dead with three bullets to the face, 9mm from the size of the entry wounds and the casings. There could have been some sort of struggle from the looks of things."

He pointed to a nine-inch chef's knife on the floor near the body. Morehouse nodded. "And the husband?"

The officer pointed to an open door and said, "He's in the basement. The medics are tending to him. Still alive but beaten pretty badly. The chief's down there with him."

Morehouse thanked him and went down the stairs with Munoz close behind. The cellar was unfinished with a cement slab for a floor and multiple metal support posts. The usual items could be found; furnace, hot water heater, storage shelves, peg boards, tools and an open gun safe. Fred Hoffman was lying on a gurney moaning incoherently as a medic applied a dressing and antibiotic ointment to his swollen and purple face. His left eye was completely closed like a prize fighter after twelve rounds, and Morehouse spotted a couple of teeth on the floor. The man in charge was a big beefy guy, a few years shy of sixty with clean-shaven, ruddy cheeks, a big belly, and no neck. His name was Sanders, George M. Sanders. The M was for Montgomery. He was the chief of the Lansdale police department, and he was pissed off.

Morehouse showed him his ID and said, "I heard about his wife. How is he?"

The chief replied angrily, "Pretty obvious, don't you think? Right now, he's concussed and babbling. He may have a skull fracture, and I'm not even sure he knows his wife is dead... What brings the Secret Service here, Deputy Director?"

"We wanted to speak to their daughter, Emily. She works for one of the senators and might have pertinent information regarding an inquiry of ours. She's gone missing though. We were hoping to find her here."

"Emily's gone missing?" the chief said, suddenly changing his tone as he became concerned for her safety. "How much more can go wrong for this poor family? Are you sure she's missing?"

Morehouse shook his head. "Not really, but she didn't show up for work yesterday and we've been unable to reach her by phone."

The chief looked puzzled. "Does the Deputy Director of the Secret Service always go out in the field himself to interview people? Must be a helluva case you're working on."

Morehouse smiled disarmingly, "I'm afraid I'm not at liberty to talk about it. Suffice it to say I'm a hands-on kind of guy. So, what do you think happened here?"

Getting back to the matter at hand, the chief rubbed his chin and said, "As far as we can tell, they were having tea in the kitchen when someone or multiple armed persons broke into the home for a smash and grab. The sequence of events isn't entirely clear but Fred was herded down here, handcuffed to the pole and worked over with a blunt instrument probably to get him to give them the combination to the safe. Whether the wife was killed before or after is uncertain. Time of her death is estimated between eight and ten last night."

Morehouse went over to the safe and peered inside. There were a half-dozen handguns, a scoped hunting rifle, an AR-15, and a couple of shotguns inside with lots of ammo. "They weren't looking for guns, I see."

"No," the chief concurred. "Fred kept a box with a few thousand in cash for emergencies down here. That's all they took."

"Was Fred able to tell you about the money?"

"No, but I knew about it. We've been friends for years. We talk."

"Is it possible they knew their assailants?"

"Possibly or somebody just took a lucky guess. A lot of people keep money hidden around the house for rainy days."

"Do they?"

"In my experience... Maybe it's just a cop thing."

One of the EMTs working on Fred Hoffman said, "We're ready to go, Chief. Anything you want to say to him?"

They all walked over to the stretcher where the chief touched his friend's hand and said, "We're going to find these sons of bitches, Fred, and they're going to pay for this. I promise you."

Fred was barely conscious and through his one good eye looked at the chief. He couldn't say anything, but he weakly squeezed the man's hand in acknowledgement.

As they started to wheel him away, heavy footsteps bounding down the stairs caught their attention. A man appeared sporting a crewcut, wearing a three-piece tweed suit, white shirt, solid red bowtie and carrying a brown bowler derby hat. He was quite the sight as he flew across the room to the stretcher and stared down at Fred Hoffman. He was noticeably distressed. The chief studied the newcomer who hadn't introduced himself.

Finally, the chief said, "And just who the fuck are you?"

The man flipped out his badge saying, "Detective Robert Tierney, NYPD."

Chapter 21

Vito owned the five-story building on the corner of Mulberry and Hester Street in Little Italy. The first floor he rented to the Caffe Napoli, famous for its home-made cannoli and extra rich coffees. The second floor was Vito's apartment complex. Five thousand square feet with six bedrooms, a gym, a sauna, a full bar, and most importantly firearms discreetly hidden from view in every room. He had passageways built to connect easily to every floor, the rooftop, and the restaurant below in case he needed quick and clandestine egress. In the basement there was a maze of tunnels leading to other buildings, including the parking garage on Mott Street where he kept his fleet of Cadillacs and SUVs. During the night he had mobilized a brigade of foot soldiers to guard the apartment. There were armed sentries at the street entrance, men in the hallway outside the apartment, men inside the apartment, and more men in cars on either end of the street leading to the apartment. There was always one SUV on standby in the garage with a driver at the ready. Needless to say, this was not a child friendly environment.

After the poker game had broken up the night before, the pain killers had gone their separate ways to sleep it off as much as they could, go to work exhausted and hungover, and where appropriate beg forgiveness from those who needed their forgiveness begged. Parikh was the only one who had the day off and no doubt would be cleaning the house to make amends with his wife. But since he was the big winner last night Cesari guessed he would be mopping the floors with a big smile on his face.

Emily was drained of all emotion. Fatigue and despair were setting in. She sat on a chair in Vito's kitchen with her back against the sink, staring blankly ahead as if she were in a coma. A thirty-year-old black woman with green almond shaped eyes, long dark hair and a stunning figure cut and dyed her hair. The woman was, Lorna, a makeup specialist and costume consultant on Broadway, as well as aspiring actress, and apparently a sometime employee of Vito's. From the way Vito greeted her that morning with a long kiss on the lips, Cesari surmised that they were or at least had been very good friends too at some point. Either that or mouth to mouth resuscitation between consenting adults was becoming a thing.

Cesari and Vito sipped espresso at the table watching with great curiosity the transformation taking place. It had been decided that Emily would travel to Sicily as Jaskaran's wife and now they were trying to make her look the part. Teresa, Enzo and Angelina were on their way to visit Sofia who was recuperating nicely at St. Matt's and would probably be discharged in a day or two. His cousins had seen what was going on with Emily but had decided not to pry. It was possible they didn't know who Vito really was or what he did for a living when they first met him, but the sight of all the armed security, hyper-vigilance, and now this, was a pretty good tip off that their American relation was a chip off the old Sicilian mafioso block.

After she finished with the hair, Lorna applied dabs of makeup and eyeliner. The effect was subtle but dramatic. She then held up a mirror and let Emily see her new self from multiple angles.

"I think you look great, Emily," Lorna said enthusiastically. "All we need is some authentic clothing which I'll pick up today and no one will ever know you weren't born and raised in India."

To that Emily rolled her eyes. "Great."

Vito added, "Great job, Lorna, but don't you think she should have the dot on the forehead thing?"

"You mean the bindi," she replied and then looked at Cesari. "You said the guy she's supposed to be married to is Sikh."

"I did," said Cesari.

Lorna turned back to Vito. "The bindi is a Hindu tradition, not Sikh, but I suppose it couldn't hurt."

"No, thank you," interjected Emily. "I'll survive without it."

"That settles that," said Lorna. "I'll be back early afternoon with the traditional wardrobe and some appropriate costume jewelry."

Vito walked Lorna to the door as Emily removed the plastic gown she was wearing and stood up. She asked, "Now what?"

Cesari replied, "We need to take some photos of you to have a new passport and driver's license made to support your new identity and appearance. It should only take a few minutes."

"I'm Emily Singh now?"

Cesari smiled disarmingly. "It has a good ring to it."

She sighed. "I suppose. Any updates from Detective Tierney about my father?"

Cesari shook his head. "He'll let us know as soon as he learns anything. In the meantime, we have to be patient. Too many calls could cause problems even with the burner phones."

Vito returned shortly with a white-haired pudgy guy in a rumpled suit holding a deluxe model digital camera with flash attachment. His name was Murray and he had been sitting in the hallway waiting for his turn. Murray was a man of many talents, but forging passports and high-quality phony identification was his main claim to fame in certain circles. His prices were outrageous, but Murray didn't do it for the money. It was a pride thing with him. He considered himself an artist no different from Michelangelo or Picasso. Vito introduced him and Murray got to work.

He studied the kitchen and then peeked in the living room, eventually saying, "The lighting is better in the other room. Would you mind?"

Vito nodded. "Sure thing. Lead the way, Murray."

They filed in and Murray said, "Please, young lady. Stand against the wall. Yes, right there, and no smiling."

He then took up position a few feet in front of her and snapped multiple photos, examined the results on the digital screen in back of the camera, and satisfied said, "Thank you, Emily."

Vito asked, "You need anything else?"

"Emily Singh, age twenty-eight, country of origin, U.S. I'll make sure the documents are a little beaten up and that the passport reflects several trips abroad."

"Sounds good."

"I'll have the passport and driver's license ready for you tomorrow morning."

"Thanks, Murray. I appreciate you doing such a rush job."

"No problem, and don't forget the cash. I'm behind on my alimony payments and I got a kid starting college."

Vito laughed. "I won't forget."

After he left, Emily asked, "I'm only twenty-two. Why is he making the passport say I'm twenty-eight?"

Cesari replied, "Just a little added confusion for anyone who might be tracking passports looking for a twenty-two-year-old. For the same reason, we toyed with the idea of making your country-of-origin India and giving you a green card. But we thought that might cause unnecessary scrutiny and complications especially since you don't speak Hindi or Punjabi which would raise eyebrows potentially leading to questions you'd be unable to answer. Same thing with your first name. For the sake of ease, we'll just leave you as Emily so there'll be less chance of you slipping up. For now you are Emily Singh, age twenty-eight, Indian ethnicity but born in Queens, New York, and a through and through American girl. You recently married Jaskaran Singh and are travelling to Sicily on your honeymoon. All the rest of your background and education stays the same."

She managed an unconvincing grin. "Am I really going to have to wear a sari?" she asked, referring to the traditional Indian women's fashionwear Lorna was purchasing for her.

"I'm not sure what Lorna had in mind in terms of attire, but I do know that there's more variety to Indian clothing than just saris. The short answer is it might be prudent to give the charade a one hundred percent effort if we want it to achieve its purpose. If they tracked you to your parent's home in less than a day's time, it's entirely possible they have the resources to watch airports. At this point it's better to be safe than sorry. Once we're in Sicily, you can wear whatever you want."

****

"Where are you?"

"In New York, tracking down a lead," replied Rosemarie.

"Did you hear the latest developments?"

"Yes."

"How on earth did Claire's body wind up behind the Lincoln Memorial?"

"I don't know."

Frustrated he asked. "And the Hoffman disaster in Lansdale. Was that you?"

"Some of it was, but something else happened. The husband wasn't home when I was there."

"He wasn't home?"

"No, the wife was alone."

"I don't understand. Someone came into the house after you and beat him half to death? Who would do that?"

"Once again, I don't know."

The man sighed deeply into the receiver. "How close are you?"

"If the mother was telling the truth and I believe she was, then I'm very close."

"All right, we need to wrap this up before people start connecting the dots."

She hung up the phone and glanced across the street at the apartment building. She double-checked the address and cut the engine to the second car she had stolen in as many days. She got out wearing the same coat, scarf, hat, and sunglasses she had worn at the Hoffman residence in Lansdale. Quickly she strode across Water St. in an up and coming section of Brooklyn Heights not too far from the Manhattan and Brooklyn Bridges. There was a video camera watching the door as she deftly and discreetly picked the lock and gained entrance. She was very good and to any casual observer, it appeared as if she were merely fumbling with her keys.

Once inside, she raced up the stairwell to the fourth floor, found the right apartment and again picked the lock. Before entering, however, she drew the Uzi from her bag and attached the silencer. When ready, she gently nudged the door inward and stepped inside. Her adrenalin pumped as it always did in these situations, but years of experience allowed her to keep her heart rate and breathing under control. She had been a one-woman tour de force for more than twenty years. Affectionately known inside the agency as the Widow Maker, she had eliminated more of her country's enemies than almost anyone on active duty. A certain number of her country's friends as well, she mused as she furtively made her way from room to room searching for her target.

It was a typical male apartment with spartan furnishings and only the barest of essential decorations. Except for a container of milk, a six-pack of beer, eggs, and an unopened pack of hotdogs in the refrigerator you could hardly tell anyone lived there at all. After going through all the rooms, she was disappointed at not finding anyone. Still, she knew Emily Hoffman had been here. She must have, but where was she now? And where were the damn letters?

She went through the apartment again with greater purpose. Pulling out and overturning drawers. Emptying closets and cabinets hunting for the missing items. It wasn't a very big place and after thirty minutes, it looked like a mini-tornado had ripped through it.

Deeply frustrated, she cleared a spot on the couch and sat down to map out what she should do next. Sitting there, she gained a different view of the apartment and for the first time noticed the furry thing hiding behind an armchair across from her. She had noticed the litter box in the kitchen but hadn't paid it much attention. Detective Tierney had a cat. For some inexplicable reason she found that incredibly amusing and smiled. Rosemarie, you're getting soft, she told herself.

"Here kitty, kitty," she called out gently.

Stonewall hesitated but slowly came out from his hiding place and jumped onto the coffee table in front of Rosemarie. She laughed out loud when she saw him up close and said, "Jesus Christ, what does he feed you? I've never seen a cat as fat as you. How did you manage to stay out of sight? I should put you out of your misery right now, kitty. God only knows how many thousands of dollars that'd save the detective on cat food alone."

Whether Stonewall understood the slurs or not wasn't entirely clear as he studied the human in front of him without expression, his tail swaying slowly and noncommittally back and forth. Encouraged by his approach and bolstered by her own excessive self-confidence she moved a little closer. She was fascinated by his size and curious, large yellow eyes. He appeared to be more like a small mountain lion rather than a house cat. She estimated he weighed at least thirty pounds, not an ounce under and probably more.

She reached out with her left hand to pet him and faster than lightning, and just as unpredictably, he grabbed her with his paws and bit her finger. She jumped up screaming and swearing. Stonewall freaked and leapt upward at her slashing her cheek deeply with his claws. She grabbed his tail and flung him backward across the coffee table where he landed on his feet and raced away to the bedroom. She picked up the Uzi and was about to follow through on her previous threat to the cat when the door opened, and an old man stood there holding a grocery bag.

He said, "Is everything all right? I heard someone yelling."

Pfft, pfft, pfft. Almost as a reflex, she fired three rounds into his chest, and watched him lurch backward, dropping his groceries. She ran to the body, scanned the hallway quickly for witnesses and dragged him and the spilled groceries into the apartment and out of sight. Cursing under her breath she made her escape back down to the street.

Stonewall would live to fight another day.

Chapter 22

"Thanks for having coffee with me, Detective."

They were sitting at a corner booth in a diner not too far from the Hoffman residence. It was an old-fashioned eatery with round swivel counter chairs, upholstered booths, and linoleum floors. The blue green fading paint job was particularly outmoded. The place needed a facelift, thought Tierney. But the coffee was good. Maybe not as good as a latte but decent.

He took a sip from the steaming ceramic mug, and said, "It's Bob, Chief Sanders. And anything I can do to help…"

"Thanks, and my friends call me Monty. So you're the famous Gunny Sergeant Tierney Fred was always talking about."

Tierney grinned. "That would be me."

"Well Fred spoke very highly of you and your time in the Corps. He told me you were very close back then."

"We were, and in fact, I still feel very close to him. The bonds men make in combat never really fade away."

Monty thought about that for a moment and then said, "Thank you for your service."

Tierney nodded his appreciation. "What can I do for you, Monty?"

"It's quite a coincidence you showing up here when you did. Don't you think?"

"Not really. Fred and I go way back as you know, and I've been meaning to drop by for some time."

The chief accepted that. "Were they expecting you?"

"Only in general terms. Today was a good day for me. I was off and figured to surprise him either at home or at work. Take him out to lunch or something."

The chief nodded some more. "That seems reasonable. Still, it's quite a coincidence."

"The world is filled with them, I find."

"When was the last time you saw the Hoffmans?"

"Ten years I think, maybe a little longer. Fred and I kept in touch by phone, albeit infrequently, sometimes just to catch up and sometimes to discuss police work. As you know, we didn't just serve together in the Marines but in the NYPD too, but then he got married and moved out here. After that, we just kind of drifted apart."

"So, you don't know anything that might be related to what happened here?"

Tierney shook his head. "No, we spoke the other day and he said everything was fine. He encouraged me to come for a visit. Once the idea got in my head, I couldn't shake it so here I am. Besides, it looks like a straightforward home invasion to me."

The chief made a humming sound. "Really?"

"Why do you say that?"

"I don't know. Maybe it's because of all the coincidences."

"I already told you why I'm here."

"Yes, you did, but you haven't asked me about the elephant in the living room? Surely you must be curious about the Secret Service being here also?"

"I learned a long time ago not to ask questions above my paygrade, Monty."

The chief grinned. "A very wise path to follow for most people, but from the way Fred described you, I find it hard to believe you're a bury your nose in the sand bureaucrat just biding his time until retirement."

"Okay, so why is the Deputy Director of the Secret Service here?"

"He said they're looking for Fred's daughter, Emily. She's part of some D.C. inquiry he wouldn't tell me about and that she's gone missing. They also coincidentally showed up here at the same time you did looking for her. You see my problem here, Bob?"

Tierney nodded and signaled the waitress for a refill on his coffee. "That's one heck of a coincidence for sure."

"I'll say… You know what else strikes me as strange?"

"I'm all ears, Monty."

"The Hoffman front door was unlocked. In fact, it was wide open. That's how Kathy's body was discovered. A neighbor walking her dog saw it and investigated. Whoever it was just walked in."

Tierney thought it over and shrugged. "Pretty careless for a cop, but we all get complacent from time to time."

"Indeed… And how about the fact that the robbers stole a couple of thousand in cash and left five thousand dollars in handguns and other weapons behind, Kathy's diamond ring on her finger, and all her jewelry in her bedroom?"

"No one said they were very bright."

The chief smiled. "Not bright at all."

"Maybe they were in a rush?" offered Tierney.

"They took the time to kill Kathy, torture Fred, and apparently make a cup of tea. Does that seem like they were in a rush to you?"

"There are some inconsistencies for sure."

"I'll say," grunted the chief. "And then you and the Secret Service show up and I'm supposed to believe it has nothing to do with what happened? I don't know about you, Bob, but I don't like it when people piss on my leg and then tell me it's raining. You may have been a good friend of Fred's back in the day, but he was my friend right here and now in the present. And that was my friend's wife lying on the floor with three bullet holes in her face. Are you going to tell me what's going on or are you just going to keep pissing on my leg? Because if you are then I might need to buy me an umbrella."

****

Morehouse dabbed his face with a napkin. It was twelve o'clock noon, and after they had left the Hoffman house, they decided to stop for Philly cheesesteak sandwiches before heading back to D.C. While making a mess in the Suburban, they decided to hash it out.

Munoz asked, "What do you make of all this?"

He shook his head in frustration. "I don't know. It's very sad."

"That's not what I meant."

"I know what you meant. You meant do I think this has anything to do with Agent Mills? I don't know for sure, but if it's not, it's one heck of a fluke. Don't you think?"

She nodded. "Way too much happenstance. My mind can't accept it being unrelated."

"Neither can mine… Let's agree for a minute that it's all related. If it is, we can rule out the Mills was an angry lover and acted alone angle. Clearly there are others involved. Emily sees and hears something the night Mills and Claire are murdered. She manages to narrowly escape and run home. The killers track her here, but she's not home. They kill mom but what was that with dad in the basement and why didn't they kill him too?"

"Maybe they assumed mom and dad knew where she was, and separated the couple figuring it would be easier to extricate information that way. Perhaps they killed mom as a way of instilling fear into the father."

"Or maybe mom went for that knife in the kitchen, and somebody got trigger happy. They beat the father until he was unconscious and figured they'd get no more out of him. Who knows? Maybe they thought he was dead when they left."

"So the question is; did mom and dad know where Emily is and did they give her up?"

"No, Munoz, the question is why was the safe wide open if these guys were looking for Emily? Because if it's the same people who did this, then it wasn't a robbery. And the other question is do they have Emily right now? Was she here in hiding and did they find her and take her with them? Maybe she came out when she heard all the shooting? Maybe that's why they left the father alive? Maybe she came out of hiding to save his life?"

"Wouldn't they just shoot her?"

"You would think, right? Unless there's some other reason they're searching for her so hard?"

"Other than being an eyewitness to murder?"

"Yes."

"Such as?"

"Let's take a stroll outside the box again, Munoz. The secretary for the most powerful senator in congress declares some sudden family emergency and takes off for Miami. She's murdered on the way to the airport along with the Secret Service agent assigned to protect that senator, but something goes wrong. Emily sees the whole thing and flees with Claire who's already dead. She comes home to mommy and daddy. Mom's a nurse, dad's a battle-hardened ex-Marine and a cop. The killer comes here to finish the job, but maybe Emily's not here? Or maybe she was but there was something else he was looking for that wasn't? Maybe he thought that something was in the safe. It wasn't. So he needs to keep her alive long enough for her to lead him to what he needs?"

"You're suggesting that Claire may have taken something of high value that needed to be retrieved at any cost and now Emily has it."

"It's possible that's what the killers may believe."

"Or maybe the killers found what they were looking for and Emily hasn't heard what happened yet. She might still be hiding somewhere, but what could Claire have taken?"

"That's a good question… Suppose it was something compromising to someone or several persons. That begs the question; was Mills primary goal to retrieve whatever it was? The other thing is that up until now, we've been assuming that Mills acted alone but there could have been another person with him that night. The one who dropped the gun perhaps? Maybe the same person who was here? Or was a different person sent to intercept the women in the underpass and Mills learned about the plan, and in fact, tried to rescue them?"

"You're trying to give Mills the benefit of the doubt."

"I have to."

"Well, you're doing a very good job of it. If I were on a jury, I'd be so confused, I'd have to acquit."

Morehouse took another bite of cheese steak sandwich and washed it down with a swallow of bottled water. "I'd love to stick around and interview the father, but that might raise eyebrows with the locals. And we don't know how long it will be before he'll be able talk to anyone. That is, if he'll ever be able to talk to anyone ever again."

"Speaking of the locals, should we have been a bit more forthright with the police chief? Fred Hoffman was his friend after all."

"Not a chance," Morehouse said, shaking his head decisively. "This situation is already getting too much publicity, and since we're not one hundred percent sure of any link, it would serve no purpose. The last thing we need is for an accusation to be splashed across the news that the death of a Secret Service agent in Tysons Corner was somehow linked to a home invasion and murder in the suburbs of Philadelphia. Besides, I want the chief to investigate this fully and without prejudice as if it was what it superficially appears to be, a robbery gone bad. Who knows? Maybe that's all it was."

He looked at Munoz for an extra moment and asked, "Are you going to finish that?"

Lost in thought, she didn't understand. "What?"

"Your sandwich? You've only eaten half."

She glanced down into her lap. "No, it was too big… Would you like it?"

"Only if you're not going to eat it."

"I'm not going to eat it."

"You're sure?"

She laughed. "Yes, I'm sure."

She wrapped it up and handed it to him.

He smiled. "Thanks."

Chapter 23

"Cesari, where are you?" Tierney asked, his voice straining with anxiety.

"At the hospital checking in on Vito's aunt."

"And Emily?"

"She's wrapped up tight and safe in Vito's apartment. Every entrance is guarded by armed men. It would be easier to get into Fort Knox. What's up? You sound stressed?"

"That's because I am stressed. I've got a problem. When I got home from Philly, I found a dead body in my living room and my apartment had been trashed."

Cesari whispered, "Jesus…"

"Exactly… The stiff was my neighbor. An old guy, never bothered anyone."

"What happened?"

"From the looks of things he must have interrupted whoever it was, and they overreacted with three bullet holes to his chest. These guys are plugged into the system deep, Cesari. I wouldn't go back to your apartment if you don't have to. My guess is that you're next on their to do list, but if you do go back, take six or seven of Vito's men with you."

"Roger that. What were they looking for besides Emily? The letters?"

"Probably… or they got pissed when they didn't find Emily and took it out on my furniture. I'm guessing my neighbor heard unusual sounds coming from my apartment and decided to check it out. Poor slob."

"I'll let the troops know to stay on high alert. How was Emily's father?"

"Not good. Somebody got to him before I arrived. He'd been beaten pretty badly, and was barely conscious. They were carting him off to the hospital just as I showed up. It's not clear yet what happened or how bad his condition is. Whatever you do, don't tell Emily. She's got enough going on."

"She's going to want to talk to him."

"I'll handle it. I'll tell her that he's being watched and is concerned that they can eavesdrop and maybe even trace his calls even though he's using a burner phone. There's no need to add to her depression right now."

"What do you make of all that?"

"I'm not sure, but the deputy director of the Secret Service was there as well as the police."

"The deputy director of the Secret Service? Wow. What did he want? They couldn't possibly know it was Emily who shot their guy."

"It's impossible to say what they know or don't know. The deputy director's name was Grayson Morehouse, and he was tight-lipped with me, but the police chief told me they were looking for Emily."

"Did he say why?"

"That's just it. The chief didn't really know. I think we have to assume it's about what happened to their agent, but I wouldn't trust any one of them right now. For all I know this guy came all the way from D.C. to finish the job. Who knows? Maybe he even sent someone to my apartment."

"Damn…"

"Shit's getting real, Cesari. When's the flight to Sicily?"

"Vito has a guy making Emily's new passport as we speak but it won't be ready until tomorrow morning. As soon as it arrives, we'll drive to Toronto where we have flights booked on Air Canada to Rome leaving at 10:00 p.m. From there we'll connect to Palermo. We didn't want to take a chance on using JFK or Newark."

"That makes sense, but that's a long day."

"You're not kidding. Toronto's an eight-hour drive from Manhattan, but hopefully we'll sleep well on the plane."

"Let's hope Vito's passport forger knows what he's doing, or it will be an even longer day."

"He does. He's been in the business thirty years."

There was a pause and after a minute Tierney said, "I know you're busy, Cesari, but I have a bit of a dilemma on my end."

Cesari understood right away what the detective was getting at. "The dead guy in your living room?"

"Yeah… As a cop, I've sent many people away for doing bad things. As a Marine, I've had to terminate the lives of others who were trying to terminate me, but I don't recall ever having to hide a body before. My instinct is to call it in, but if I do, there's no easy way of explaining things without drawing attention to Emily."

"I understand. Has he started to stink yet?"

"No, I don't think he's been dead more than a few hours. Rigor mortis hasn't set in yet and the blood is still pretty fresh. Why?"

"I don't like moving decomposing bodies. Does he have family?"

"He has a wife, but I don't think she realizes he's not coming home yet or else there would have been cops here."

"Too bad. If he lived alone, we could just have carried him back to his own apartment. How big is he?"

"Not very. Five seven, a hundred and sixty pounds if that."

"Let me finish up here and I'll come right over. Give me an hour."

Cesari hung up and walked into Sofia's hospital room. She was sitting up eating her lunch of roast turkey and steamed carrots. Enzo, Angelina and Teresa sat around her gabbing away in their Sicilian dialect, a language so different from the Italian taught in schools as to be nearly incomprehensible. Unbeknownst to many, Sicilian was as different from Italian as Portuguese was from Spanish.

He smiled and greeted them.

"And how's my patient doing today?" he asked beaming at Sofia.

After Teresa translated, Sofia grinned broadly and spoke a few words. Teresa said, "Mama say thanks to you and God, she feels well and that from now on you will be in her prayers."

Cesari said, "Tell her I said thank you and that her doctor plans to discharge her today."

They all seemed relieved to hear this good news.

He continued, addressing all of them. "Vito will send a car to pick everyone up later and bring you back to his apartment where you can stay for as long as you like. Unfortunately, Vito and I will be leaving early tomorrow morning and won't be back for a while. He's occupied today checking in on his business enterprises so he may not see you before we leave. He told me to tell you that he will see you all again soon and that his men have been instructed to take good care of you. He will pay for everything while you are here."

Vito had a hand in just about every illegal activity that existed in Lower Manhattan, and he was running around giving last minute instructions to his various crews before he left town. There was a strict chain of command and he wanted to make sure that operations continued to run in an orderly and lucrative fashion during his absence.

Teresa asked worriedly, "You go Sicilia to kill Ernesto?"

Cesari was taken aback by that and shook his head. "No, why would you think that?"

"Because that is what Vito tell me when he learn that mama was poisoned."

He let out a deep sigh. "Vito is very emotional right now, and sometimes he says things he doesn't necessarily mean. Yes, we are going to Sicily but not to kill anyone. We just want to talk with Ernesto and Rosaria."

Teresa said, "Just to talk is a good thing, because Ernesto has many cousins in Palermo. They would no like if you kill him."

Great, thought Cesari and replied, "Thanks for the warning. I'll let Vito know."

She gently touched his arm and added. "Ernesto no do this. Please, you must believe me. He is kind man."

There was something in her eyes that reached deeply into Cesari. For some reason he did believe her and said reassuringly, "I will do everything in my power to make sure that Vito doesn't act rashly, but I know him a long time. He needs to get this out of his system and find out the truth for himself. To be honest with you, it's not looking good for Ernesto and Rosaria. They had motive and it was his olive oil that made everyone ill."

"But I helped Enzo make the caponata. I taste everything. Why do I no get sick?" she protested.

He didn't know this, but it really didn't change anything. "I don't have an answer for that, but symptoms are dose dependent, and it's possible you didn't eat enough of the caponata. In addition, not every bottle of olive oil was contaminated so you may have just been lucky."

She looked skeptical at that so he added, "I will do all I can to protect Ernesto from a miscarriage of justice. But if he confesses, then I can't guarantee what's going to happen."

She thought about that and said, "I am coming to Sicily with you."

He stepped back. "No, you're not. Your family needs you here. Sofia isn't well enough to travel yet, and you're the only one who speaks English."

"And you don't speak Sicilian. How will you interrogate Ernesto? With clubs?"

She wasn't too far off the mark with that, but Cesari hadn't thought that part through. A miscommunication at this juncture could be fatal. For Ernesto anyway. As if reading his mind she said, "I will come with you and my family will stay in cousin Vito's apartment for a few days more until Sofia is well enough to return to Palermo. They will be fine for one or two days. They are in Little Italy. There are many Italian speaking people there."

She was right about that, and he and Vito really did need a translator. Plus, Cesari calculated, having Teresa present may help Vito to keep his temper in check. There was also the added benefit that travelling with a second woman as a companion to Emily would further confuse anybody attempting to track them. There were a lot of advantages and very little downside that Cesari could see.

He said, "All right. Have your bags packed and your passport ready to leave at six tomorrow morning. I'll buy your ticket later today."

Her eyes went wide with surprise that he had been so effortlessly swayed. "You are not like real Italian man. They no give in so easy."

He laughed softly. "Keep in mind, Teresa. In America, most men are neutered. It's mandatory after a certain age. Our women like us docile."

She seemed puzzled. "What mean neutered?"

"It means we do what we're told."

"Is good. Maybe we start neutering Italian men."

Chapter 24

"Hey, Cesari, slow down," Arnie said, "and watch your language. We're trying to make a good impression here."

Cesari and Parikh were sipping coffee in the hospital cafeteria when Arnie Goldstein and a guy in a suit walked in and joined them. The cafeteria had temporary partitions in place, effectively separating the room into two halves. The hospital had wasted no time in beginning the renovations to accommodate the orthopedic alimentary needs. The construction noise coming from that side of the room was thunderous.

Arnie was a seventy-year-old hematologist and current CEO of St. Matt's. He was pudgy and white haired and had never met a piece of pie that was unworthy of his attention. Cesari liked Arnie and they had been friends for years. The guy with him was fifty, black, equally pudgy and wearing a three-piece suit with a crisp white shirt and tie.

Cesari glanced at his watch. He had told Detective Tierney he'd meet him in an hour, and that was forty-five minutes ago. He took in a deep breath and let it out slowly. He had bumped into Parikh and decided a friendly cup of joe with his favorite Hindu was worth spending a few extra minutes. Neither one had expected the spectacle they were witnessing in the cafeteria and when Arnie arrived Cesari had unloaded on him, calling him a Benedict Arnold and orthopedic sycophant among other things.

Arnie let the insults fly over his head. He had bigger fish to fry at the moment. "If you're through, I'd like you to meet Clarence Sterling. He's interviewing to be the new CEO. As you know I plan on retiring at the end of the year. He's infectious disease by trade hailing from the Cleveland Clinic but he's had his fun in patient care and now wants out of clinical practice, so he went and got a master's in health and hospital administration in addition to his M.D. Dr. Sterling, please meet John Cesari, St. Matt's head of gastroenterology, medical director, and local hot head. Sitting next to him is one our finest anesthesiologists, Parikh Chowdhury."

The men shook hands and Cesari said, "Pleased to meet you Dr. Sterling."

"Clarence, please."

"And I am just Parikh, sir. Thank you, and I agree. It is most pleasureful to meet you."

Cesari said, "I go by Cesari. Don't ask me why. It's been like that for as long as I can remember."

"Well, Cesari. Your reputation precedes you. Arnie and just about everyone else I've met here speak very highly of you."

"Don't believe everything you hear around this place, Clarence. There are a lot of undercover agents for orthopedics working here."

Sterling laughed. "I'll keep that in mind. It was the same at the Cleveland Clinic. They're like locusts. They ravage everything in their path."

Arnie glared at Cesari. "It's not going to be that bad, Cesari."

"Are you serious, Arnie? Have you seen what's happening on the other side of that partition?"

"No, I haven't."

"Then let's take a peek together because I have."

Arnie stated emphatically, "I will not. This is childish."

Cesari stood despite Arnie's protestations. Parikh stood as well, and slowly Clarence rose to his feet, saying, "I'm kind of curious myself, Arnie."

Arnie sighed and they all walked over to the partition, pulling chairs with them, even Parikh. He was six feet, eleven inches tall but the top of the divider was still just out of his field of vision on tip toes. They climbed up on the chairs and rested their elbows on the top of the makeshift wall. Parikh had to avoid hitting his head against the ceiling. Looking down, they saw frenetic activity on the other side as an army of carpenters and electricians plied their trade reconstructing the dining area. Hardwood floors were being installed, chandeliers were dangling from the ceiling and a variety of other improvements were being attended to by industrious craftsmen. An Asian guy in a chef's hat and smock was shouting in Japanese at another worker as they were setting up a counter.

"Who's that guy?" asked Clarence.

Cesari smirked. "That's the sushi chef we just hired."

Clarence chuckled quietly and said, "What's going on over there?"

He pointed to where the workers had knocked down a wall and were installing a massive refrigeration unit. Cesari replied, "Not sure… It could be for the raw oyster bar they have planned, or possibly the gelato station."

Arnie groaned. "I didn't know anything about this."

Parikh said, "I like ice cream."

"That's not for us, Parikh," Cesari cautioned. "Sorry, friend, and I don't care that you didn't know Arnie. This isn't right, and you should have known. Next time read the fine print when that felon of a CFO asks you to sign off on something."

As they jawed back and forth, two very beautiful, very buxom, long-legged, young women strode into the construction area wearing short, tight skirts, high heels, big hair and massive hoop earrings. Their presence caused a stir and almost every worker including the sushi chef stopped to gape.

Parikh said, "Oh boy…"

Clarence said, "Damn…"

One of them saw the four doctors leaning on the partition and came over. She smiled and giggled, "Dr. Cesari. What a pleasant surprise."

Cesari blushed. "Hi Savannah. What are you doing here?"

"Bambi and I are interviewing for the new club opening here. Some doctor named Alexander was at the Kit Kat the other night and told us he was going to need cocktail waitresses and to drop by and check it out." She looked at Parikh, giving him a seductive smile. "Hey there, tall, dark, and handsome. You got a name?"

Parikh turned eight shades of crimson and stammered meekly, "My name is Parikh, madam."

Savannah purred demurely, and said to Cesari, "Ain't he adorable?"

Cesari said, "His wife thinks so."

Savannah turned slightly and said, "There he is. Got to go. See you sometime soon, I hope, Parikh. Ta, Cesari."

Dr. Alexander Graham Bell had entered from the other side of the construction area and waved to the girls. He was tall, buffed, and Nordic god-like in appearance like an orthopedic surgeon should look. The girls put on quite a show as they swayed and slinked one hip at a time through the sawdust in Bell's direction, leaving a wake of men on either side too confused to work. Arnie's eyes went wide, but he was too stunned to speak.

Clarence said, "Damn…"

Parikh asked, "How do you know the young lady, sir, may I respectfully ask?"

Cesari glanced at Clarence and Arnie. There was no easy answer. The Kit Kat was a gentlemen's club on Second Avenue owned by Vito. Although food and drink were available, the specialty of the house were the topless waitresses and sultry pole dancers. For the high rollers, luxurious rooms were available for private entertainment.

Cesari explained cagily, "The Kit Kat is a place I have lunch sometimes. She works there."

Parikh thought that over and then said, "I think I would very much like to have lunch with you there sometime."

Cesari cautioned, "As your friend, I think I should warn you that your wife might not approve."

Parikh replied, "Sir, in India there is an old Hindu saying passed on directly to the people from the god, Vishnu, himself. It goes like this. आपकी पत्नी को जो नहीं पता वह उसे चोट नहीं पहुंचाएगा।"

"I don't speak Hindi, Parikh."

Deadpanned, Parikh, explained, "It means, sir. What your wife doesn't know, won't hurt her."

Clarence laughed, "I'm on board with you guys. I'm in town for a couple of days and wouldn't mind a little R&R. That is, if three's not too much of a crowd."

Arnie stepped down from the chair. "I've seen enough, Cesari. You've made your point."

They all stepped down and faced each other. Parikh checked the time and said to Clarence, "I must go now. I am late for pain clinic. It was nice to meet you, sir."

He walked away, and with an amazing ability to compartmentalize, Arnie acted as if nothing at all had just happened, and said, "Clarence, me and a couple of board members are going out to dinner tonight to get to know each other. I was hoping you might consider joining us, Cesari."

Cesari decided to let it go for a moment. With everything else going on, the ortho fight would have to be put on hold. "I'm sorry, Arnie. I would have loved to Clarence, but I'm pressed for time. I'm leaving the country tomorrow and have a million things to do."

"Leaving the country?" asked Arnie, surprised. "Where to?"

"Italy…"

"Italy?" Arnie's voice rose an octave higher. "Why didn't I hear about this?"

"That's my fault, Arnie. I haven't had time to talk to you about it. A family member unexpectedly fell ill in the old country and I'd kind of like to meet him before he kicks the bucket."

"I didn't know you had relatives over there."

"Neither did I. It came as a surprise to me, Arnie. It's all kind of sudden. A distant cousin contacted me out of the blue, and told me I had an Uncle Giuseppe who is close to meeting his maker."

"Uncle Giuseppe? That's fascinating. How long are you going to be gone?"

"Not exactly sure, Arnie. At least a week, two at the most."

Clarence said, "I'm sorry to hear about your uncle's illness, Cesari. I hope he pulls through."

"Thank you, Clarence. As you can imagine I have a thousand different emotions surging through me right now. I didn't even know I had a relative over there until recently, and then I did, and then I find out he's dying."

Cesari didn't enjoy lying but once the task was placed before him, he embraced it with relish. It was easier to make up a story than to explain his relationship to Vito.

"Well I'm sorry to hear this, Cesari," said Arnie with great sympathy. "My heart goes out to you, pal. You take all the time you need, and when you get back, we'll clear up this little problem you're having with ortho."

"You're the best, Arnie. Well, I have to run. Nice to meet you, Clarence. I hope things work out for you. If you get the job, you'll be following in some pretty big footsteps."

"Thank you, Cesari. I think St. Matt's is a great place. Good luck in Italy."

As he turned to leave, Arnie admonished, "And you watch out for those Italian girls, Cesari. They get a good look at you, and you might not be coming home."

Cesari grinned. "I'll be careful, Arnie."

Arnie turned to Clarence. "There's a diner not too far from here that makes great apple pie. Do you like pie?"

Clarence replied enthusiastically, "Does a baby like to poop in his diapers?"

Not quite out of earshot, Cesari heard the comment and raised his eyebrows. Apparently, Clarence was a live one.

Chapter 25

Outside the hospital, Cesari walked a few blocks over to Greenwich Village and found an army surplus store where he purchased a heavy duty over-sized canvas duffel bag in army green, paid for it in cash and then hailed a cab over to Tierney's apartment. He texted Tierney that he was on the way, and when he arrived, found the door unlocked. Tierney was sitting on his sofa stroking the biggest house cat Cesari had ever seen. The place was a mess and although the detective had picked up the chairs and tables, the carnage was still very apparent, as was the corpse of the elderly neighbor lying on the rug with three bullet holes in his chest. Cesari closed the door behind him.

"They really tossed the place good," Cesari commented as he glanced around.

Tierney rose and Stonewall scampered away. "That's an understatement. Whoever it was threw a container of milk on the floor and smashed a beer bottle against the wall in the kitchen. I cleaned it up but it's going to take a while for the odor to go away."

"Do you give your cat steroids or just feed him too much?"

"Leave my cat alone. I thought you were here to help."

"I am. So what's your neighbor's name?"

"Porter Wellman. Nice guy or at least he was. Retired engineer. Lives three doors down. It's a damn shame, Cesari. Why can't a guy just die in his own bed anymore?"

"I don't have an answer for that one, Detective. Then again there are a lot of things I don't have answers for; like why do children get cancer or why do men hurt women?"

Tierney nodded. "Or why would anyone poison an entire restaurant?"

"Yeah, but hopefully, we'll find out the answer to that one soon enough."

"You really think it was that guy and his mother back in Sicily?"

"I find it hard to believe, and so would anyone else, but maybe that was the point."

"What's that you got there?" Tierney asked indicating the rolled-up canvas duffel bag Cesari was holding.

Cesari unfolded it and shook it out to full length. It was forty-eight inches long and had an opening of twenty inches on one end which pulled closed with a cord through a series of metal grommets.

"Porter should fit in here nicely."

Tierney looked at the duffel bag and then at the body on the floor. "And then what? The poor guy has a wife and maybe kids somewhere. We can't just make him disappear."

"I agree. We just don't want him found here. Are you parked nearby?"

"Two blocks away."

"Let's secure Porter in the bag and then you can get your car and pull it to the front of the building. I'll carry him downstairs and put him in the trunk. We can leave him somewhere and then call emergency services. It'll be heartbreaking for his wife, but I don't think there's any way around that whether he's found here or somewhere else."

"My thoughts exactly. All right, let's get started, but what if someone sees us coming down the stairs with him?"

"Not to worry. With the proper packaging, he'll look like a big bag of dirty laundry that needs washing. As a matter of fact, get some sheets and towels. I'll stuff them in on top of him so that they're readily visible to any casual observer. I'll carry him over my shoulder. No one will be the wiser."

"Proper packaging?"

"He's not that big. We'll fold him in half."

"Fold him in half? Humans aren't that flexible, Cesari."

"I didn't say we could do it without breaking a few bones."

"Jesus… This is my neighbor were talking about."

"We're also talking about prison for the both of us if we're caught."

They maneuvered the small man feet first into the opening of the duffel bag much the same way you might slip a pillowcase onto a pillow. When he was half way in, they bent him at the waist and tucked his head into the opening. Then they hoisted the bag upright and let him slide the rest of the way in. After they finished, they studied their handiwork. Cesari thought the body was bulging a little too conspicuously and pushed down hard onto the man's back until a cracking sound was heard and the bulge disappeared. Tierney winced in discomfort at the thought of having to eventually face the neighbor's wife if only to offer his condolences.

Cesari said, "All right. You get the car. I'll wait here for your call."

"Why don't we both carry him. It'll be easier."

"You're a little new at this, aren't you, Detective? Two grown men carrying one bag of laundry? Won't that seem a little odd? Just get the car and call me when you're ready. If you see something you don't like, we'll hang tight until the situation improves."

Tierney nodded assent and left the apartment. Ten minutes later, Cesari's phone buzzed. Tierney said, "I'm in front of the building. It's all quiet down here."

"Okay, here I come."

He hoisted the duffel bag onto his shoulder and felt a little like Santa Claus making a delivery without the benefit of reindeer. He grunted and strained as he carried the man down the stairs. Porter wasn't a big guy, but a hundred and sixty pounds of dead weight was still a hundred and sixty pounds.

At the bottom, he caught his breath and peered out the small window of the entrance. Tierney was standing by his four door Buick sedan with the trunk open. There was some light traffic and a pair of pedestrians across the street busily chatting away. He stepped out into the waning sunlight and walked quickly and uneventfully with his load, depositing Porter neatly into the trunk. Tierney closed the lid, and they got in.

As they drove off, Tierney asked, "Do you mind if I ask a pointed question, Cesari?"

"Isn't that what cops do?"

"Yes, it is. Let me just say one thing first. We've known each other for some time now and I guess some would say we're friends of sorts. I've come to respect you as a physician of the first order in your field. I've even been considering letting you do my first colonoscopy. My primary care doc has been busting my hump for months to get one. Hell, if he brings it up one more time, I may arrest him for harassment."

"So what's your question?"

"Just how many times have you done something like this? You know, hide a body, or misdirect a crime scene? I mean, you seem pretty natural at it."

Cesari grinned ever so slightly. "That's not the question you should be asking, Detective?"

"No? Then what is?"

"You should have asked how many times have I been the reason something like this had to be done?"

Tierney looked at him. "I'm pretty sure I don't want to ask that."

"I think we're going to get along."

Tierney snorted. "Where to?"

"Not far. There are plenty of places such as under the Brooklyn Bridge or an underpass of the F.D.R. drive or in a deserted alley on the East Side. Take your pick. Then we'll head over to my apartment and see if anyone has paid me a visit too. I need to pick up my passport and pack a bag. Vito was going to come over with some guys to provide security, but as long as I got you, I might as well enjoy the protection of New York's finest.

"I like the Brooklyn Bridge option. New York's finest owes you one, Cesari."

"And I plan on collecting that debt one day."

Darkness descended on them as they crossed the Brooklyn Bridge into Manhattan and turned off, winding their way around and down to the structure's foundation. Tierney checked his watch as they got out of the car, and Cesari scanned the area for unwanted company. They were alone. The only sound was traffic in the distance and the lazy lapping of the East River against the sides of the massive towers supporting the thousands of tons of steel and cement. The base of the Brooklyn Bridge was a very lonely place at night.

"It's kind of peaceful here," Cesari noted.

"This isn't a date, Cesari. Where are we going to put him?"

"Not too close to the water. We wouldn't him to get washed away. How many bodies you think were placed here like this over the years?"

"Are you kidding me with a question like that? What's gotten into you?"

"The Brooklyn bridge has always fascinated me."

Tierney opened the trunk and said, "I have to admit. It's a beautiful bit of architecture. Pretty old too. At least a hundred years, I think."

They each grabbed one end of the duffle bag and lifted Porter out of the trunk. Cesari said, "Older than that. It opened in 1883, thirteen years and change after they broke ground."

"1883? Geez, that's old. You're pretty smart, Cesari. I'm impressed."

They carried the body deep into the pitch-black recess directly under the center of the bridge above and gently laid it down far enough away from the water's edge that there was no chance of a high tide dragging it away.

"Don't be. I watch a lot of documentaries. What's really impressive though is that when construction began in 1870, there were no electric lights, telephones, jackhammers or cranes. Think about that for a minute. Almost fifteen thousand tons of steel and concrete assembled by hand."

They walked back to the car and got in. Tierney said, "It's a little hard to fathom. I bet the guy who designed it got a medal."

"Actually what he got was tetanus. His name was John A. Roebling. A month after his plans were accepted by the New York Bridge Company and three years before construction even began, he was standing on a pier examining locations for the Brooklyn tower site when his foot was crushed by an incoming ferry. He died seventeen days later from complications."

Tierney started the engine and looked over at Cesari, thoroughly chagrined. "What the fuck is wrong with you?"

"What do you mean?"

"I mean I'm in the middle of the worst day of my life and you had to tell me a depressing story like that."

"Forget I said anything."

CHAPTER 26

"I met a brick wall with Youngblood's and Mills' service records," Dirk said. "Nothing short of a presidential order will get us the skinny on them. I even received a call from someone at the DoD telling me to back off. The Rosemarie woman has disappeared into thin air. I went back to her apartment building and knocked on every door on her floor and came up empty. No one could tell me anything. The landlord is some holding company based out of Virginia. They tell me they never met the woman and that all the paperwork was done electronically and by mail. Everything they have on her is smoke and mirrors. She gave them the last name of Zelle. No one exists by the name of Rosemarie Zelle. They received a bank check every month and that's all they cared about. And forget about getting anything from the CIA. I was told to get a court order and then to stand in line."

Morehouse had reconvened with the team back in his office in D.C. He had expected that outcome and nodded. He sat back in his chair and mulled that over. "Zelle?" he mused. "What kind of name is that? It must have some significance?"

"It does. It's Dutch," explained Dirk. "When you do a simple internet search, the first thing that comes up is that it's the surname for Mata Hari, the famous spy for the Germans during World War I. Her given name was Margaretha Geertruida Zelle. Apparently, this Rosemarie person has a sense of humor."

Morehouse studied Dirk for a moment before saying, "I wonder if she realizes that they arrested Mata Hari and then executed her. But go on, Dirk. Tell me about Claire."

Dirk continued, "Large caliber round to the forehead. Came out the back of her head. The bullet recovered in Tyson's corner was too damaged to perform ballistics on so we can't be sure if it was fired from the gun recovered in the underpass. There wasn't enough DNA recovered from the cement wall or the bullet to analyze. On a slightly more depressing note although not unexpectedly, there were no fingerprints on the recovered pistol or any of the remaining bullets in the magazine."

"Great," said Morehouse wryly.

"Now for the good news," said Dirk with an equal volume of sarcasm. "We did recover the bullet from the base of Mill's brain. It was a .38 special."

Munoz said, "Now we know for sure the gun that was recovered wasn't the one used on Mills. That's something."

Morehouse agreed. "So somebody had a .38 on them. What does that tell us? Who uses .38 specials?"

"Not drug dealers or law enforcement," Munoz said. "It's not a weapon for someone who means business. At least not in the twenty-first century. It's more of a personal protection kind of piece. It won't stop a big guy."

"It stopped Mills, and he was a big guy," Morehouse argued.

Munoz countered, "Given the circumstances, I believe that was an extraordinarily lucky shot."

"Or extraordinarily unlucky for Mills," Morehouse said. "However, I agree with your explanation of who might carry a .38 with exception. A .38 can be a backup weapon or a throwaway piece for a dirty cop to plant on someone."

"Or for a father to give to his daughter to protect herself in a dangerous city," Munoz speculated out loud.

The room was quiet for a long minute as they all digested that possibility. Eventually Morehouse said, "For the sake of argument, let's say whoever fired that shot may not have been a professional actor and was possibly a civilian in the wrong place at the wrong time."

One by one, they all nodded. Morehouse turned to Ben. "What do you have?"

"A lot. The phone records have been very revealing. At about the time of the shooting in Tysons Corner, Emily Hoffman called her father. Four hours later and roughly about the time we think she made it to her home in Lansdale, her father dialed a Robert Tierney in New York."

Morehouse and Munoz glanced at each other with raised eyebrows. Morehouse said, "Let me guess… This Robert Tierney is a New York City detective."

Ben looked surprised. "You already know about him?"

"He was at the Hoffman house in Lansdale this morning. He identified himself as a friend of the family who was visiting to have lunch and catch up with the father."

"They're definitely friends," Ben added. "They served in the Marines together and in the NYPD. before Fred Hoffman moved to Lansdale."

"What else?"

"Shortly later, Detective Tierney made a call to a Dr. John Cesari."

"Who?"

"John Cesari. He's a gastroenterologist employed at St. Matt's Hospital in Lower Manhattan. It's not clear what his relationship is to Tierney, but Cesari is known to the Hoffman girl. According to her records, she has Crohn's disease and Cesari took care of her while she was in college in New York. His name was on a bunch of prescription medication bottles we found in her apartment."

The room fell into contemplative silence as they attempted to decipher the significance of that. Finally, Morehouse asked, "Do we know anything about this doctor?"

"This is where it gets interesting. Cesari's phone log indicates numerous calls to a Vito Gianelli, a well-established person of interest in the Manhattan underworld who has been linked to many assorted crimes and other notorious mob figures. He has even been arrested by Tierney in the past although they were never able to make the charges stick. Apparently, the guy's as slippery as an eel. Anyway, in the early hours of the next morning following the shooting of Mills, there was a flurry of calls between the three of them."

Morehouse struggled to make sense of this. With furrowed brow, he said slowly, "Okay, the floor's open for discussion. Does anybody have any idea what this means?"

Munoz said, "Fred Hoffman obviously called his friend, Tierney, for advice. They go way back and have bonds forged in battle. Once a Marine, always a Marine sort of stuff. He knows he can trust Tierney..."

"So Tierney advises his friend as best he can, but then Tierney calls the doctor, and the doctor calls the mobster. I don't see the connection."

"I don't know... Is it possible that Emily was hurt or wounded in the underpass, and they didn't want to bring her to a hospital, so they called the only doctor they knew on a personal level?"

Morehouse was skeptical. "Possibly, but a gastroenterologist? What's he going to do to help her? Last I heard colonoscopy doesn't do much for bullet wounds. And this Gianelli character. What on earth could he possibly bring to the table in a situation like this? Ben, have you got anything else?"

"Not yet."

"Dirk, I want you to figure out who these guys are and how they're related. There has to be some connection. I know you have a contact in the bureau. See how far you can push him without broadcasting our interest. This is our little secret for now, all right?"

Dirk replied, "Without making a formal request from our office to theirs, any information we get is going to be spotty and limited. My friend inside will only stick his neck out for me so far."

"I understand. Do the best you can. Right now, it behooves us to play it close to the vest. Okay then, I let you all off easy last night. There'll be no sleeping this time. Munoz, you and I are going to New York to talk to Tierney. We should get there by midnight. He's a big boy. He should still be up. Meanwhile, Ben, Dirk, call me with any news."

Morehouse's phone buzzed with a call from the director. "Yes, Travis."

"Are you in the building, Grayson?"

"Yes, why?"

"Swing by my office. Senator Taylor and his chief of staff, Rufus Youngblood are here and would like an update."

"Will do."

He hung up and said to Munoz, "I'll meet you down in the garage. The director has asked to see me. I don't know how long this will take but probably not too long."

"I'll get the engine warmed up."

Morehouse walked directly to Ed Burke's office and let himself in. The senator and Rufus Youngblood were seated and didn't rise to greet him. The hour was late and the mood was sullen.

Youngblood went right for the jugular. "You said you were going to keep us in the loop, Deputy Director. Instead, we're getting all our information from television."

"Even worse," snorted the senator, "The reporters have been lobbing conspiratorial bombs at me as I walk down the corridors of the

Capitol. I had asked you previously if there was going to be any fallout for my campaign and you reassured me…"

"That we didn't know," interjected the director.

"Well now we do," said Youngblood. "This is an unmitigated disaster. We need a rapid conclusion to this mess."

Morehouse wasn't in the mood. "It's not that simple."

"I'm not sure I agree with that, Deputy Director," explained the senator. "It's pretty obvious what happened."

"Is it?" asked Morehouse dryly.

Rufus Youngblood cocked his head, "Yes, it is. Agent Mills and Claire Tompkins were obviously having an affair and Claire decided to end it. Mills couldn't handle the rejection and went off the deep end. Murder-suicide. It happens all the time. The public can handle that. In fact, it's so damn mundane, they'll forget all about it in a couple of days."

Morehouse said drolly, "I'm afraid the facts don't fit that narrative."

The senator rose from his chair signaling an end to the meeting. "Then make them fit. God damn it."

With that, the senator stormed out of the room, slamming the door behind him for emphasis. Morehouse noted with great curiosity that Youngblood not only didn't follow his boss, but seemed unperturbed. Clearly the scene had been rehearsed.

After the senator left, Youngblood said calmly, "Mills' death was bad, but Claire's murder will be catastrophic to the senator's campaign if we don't figure out a way of bringing both calamities to a rapid and satisfactory conclusion. It's all the press want to talk about."

Burke sat back in his chair and clasped his hands. "So the truth be damned?"

"Truth, Director? Let's be serious here. This is Washington D.C. The last time the truth was spoken in this city, they were wearing powdered wigs and carrying muskets."

Morehouse said in reply, "Perhaps we should try better to emulate those founding fathers. They were prescient."

Youngblood stood to leave. "Then I suggest you buy a powdered wig and a musket, but if its prescience you want, then I ask you to consider your futures should the senator's election bid tank because of a lack of cooperation here at the Secret Service. President or not, he will remain one of the most powerful men in the country, and he has a long memory."

Chapter 27

Made cautious by the fiasco at Tierney's apartment, Rosemarie had decided to change tactics. It occurred to her that rushing headlong into Cesari's place might not be the most prudent course to take. It didn't help that the scratches on her face were deep enough to require bandages and her index finger had swollen to twice its normal size from the cat bite. Both wounds hurt like hell, and she knew she would have to get a tetanus shot and some antibiotics soon. Sitting in her car on Sixth Avenue a half a football field away and on the other side of the street from Cesari's apartment, she'd been waiting patiently for hours when Cesari and Tierney finally showed up. She crossed referenced their appearance with the photos on her phone she had received from D.C. for confirmation. It was them for sure and they were clearly on the alert. Through her binoculars, she could see them standing beneath a streetlight scanning in all directions before entering the building.

They had obviously been to Tierney's apartment, and she wondered how they had handled finding the dead man. She gave them a few minutes, glanced down at the Uzi between her legs, put the car into drive and pulled closer to the apartment. As she was about to get out of her car, a Cadillac SUV rushed by nearly knocking her side mirror off. It careened to an abrupt halt ten feet in front of her and three men got out. Two were the size of wooly mammoths and one appeared to be slightly larger than a dwarf. One of the big men ran into the building and the other two stood guard at the entrance. The shorter man was edgy and kept his hand inside his jacket nervously fingering a handgun. She memorized the license plate of the Escalade, restarted her own engine and pulled away to figure things out. Back in her original observation perch, she collected her thoughts. Who were these new players? Cop friends of Tierney's maybe? Private security?

She called D.C.

"Things have gotten complicated."

"You're telling me? The Secret Service is breathing fire down our necks. They're making inquiries into things we don't want them to. I just played my last ace to get them to back off, but this needs to end fast. What have you got?"

"I've got eyes on Tierney and Cesari. They're in Cesari's apartment in Greenwich Village, but they've got company in the form of armed security. I need you to run a plate."

She gave him the number and he said, "What's this about armed security?"

"Yes, at least three. Two outside and one inside. I don't know who they are. They could be friends of Tierney's, but they don't look like law enforcement or ex-military. It occurred to me that maybe they belong to Cesari, but that begs the question of who he really is? The mother told me he was Emily's doctor, but I need you to dig deeper. Maybe she meant he was a doctor as in maybe he's a fixer type of guy."

"Great... Is Emily in there?"

"I don't know, but I don't think so. I've been watching the apartment all day and there's been no sign of life. Even the lights were out until Cesari arrived with Tierney minutes ago."

"Where could she be?"

"Good question. They must have her holed up in a safe house."

"I'll run the plates and see what I can find on this guy, Cesari. I'm tapped into the FBI so I should be able to dig up his history, known associates, phone logs and credit card activity without too much difficulty. I want you to sit tight. We've had enough collateral damage for one night and don't need a firefight erupting in Greenwich Village. Understood?"

"Understood."

"You should also be aware that the Secret Service is stonewalling me."

"Meaning what exactly?"

"Meaning they know more than they're letting on." The voice on the line paused a beat and then added, "I think you need help."

She unconsciously glanced in the mirror at her bandaged face and then down at her swollen finger before responding, "I've never needed help before."

"You've never fucked up before," came the flat retort. "This was supposed to be a surgical strike against two defenseless women, but in case you haven't noticed, there are bodies scattered up and down the northeast corridor. And now you tell me there are goons with weapons standing outside a doctor's apartment."

She didn't try to defend herself against the rebuke. Unfortunately, it was a fairly accurate assessment.

The voice said, "I'm sending Booker up there."

Booker P. Crisp was Force Recon. She had been his handler in Iraq and Afghanistan until his discharge. In a world where killing and mayhem had been normalized, he enjoyed it a bit too much, and was eventually deemed unstable by a military psychiatrist. Unfortunately for the psychiatrist, Booker disagreed with that assessment and broke the man's neck before being hauled away in handcuffs. Rather than go to trial and have Booker potentially expose all the unsavory things he had done on behalf of Uncle Sam, he was decommissioned and whisked away with a tidy pension to keep him quiet. However, he was very talented and was quickly snapped up by the country's covert services. He was the hammer brought in when stealth failed.

"Booker?" she practically gasped. "He's an unmitigated psychopath. If anybody could make this situation worse, it's him."

"He's tried and tested, and you've worked with him before. Besides, he's available and pretty close by, and I think it's safe to say that we've lost the element of surprise. Last I heard from him, he was in Connecticut. I'll brief him now. He'll arrive in a few hours. Just make sure he stays on his medications."

The phone clicked off and she quietly groaned. Glancing back at the apartment, she let out a deep sigh. If only she could get to Emily and finish the job, she could spare herself the Booker experience. But to go into the apartment with both barrels blazing, lighting up the Manhattan skyline like it was the Fourth of July would very likely be a counterproductive, possibly fatal mistake, especially if Emily wasn't there. She resigned herself and waited, her mind wandering to a different time and a different battle.

Booker P. Crisp was as unbalanced a human being as she had ever known. He had told her once that he loved being at war because it was the only time a black man like him could kill a white man and get a medal for it. When she had pointed out that he wasn't black, he pulled a knife on her and called her a racist bitch.

Of course, it might have been the wording of it that triggered the response. She had actually said, "Hey Vanilla Ice, just because you like black men in thongs doesn't mean you're black, you dumb fuck." If it wasn't for Mills intervening at gunpoint, she might have had her throat cut on a mountain outside of Kabul. But that was nothing compared to the time, in a deliberate attempt to goad him into a rage, she had called him by his middle name, Percival, in front of the other men. She smiled to herself at the memory. He had frothed at the mouth and had to be gang tackled by four Marines to prevent him from getting at her. It always amused her at how some men were so easily manipulated.

Such was the nature of the team she had assembled. But despite Booker's sometimes tenuous grip on reality, and extremely low threshold to see red, they had been highly successful. As their CIA handler, she identified the targets, assembled the intel and coordinated their attacks. She was fluent in all the various spoken tongues of Afghanistan including Dari and Pashto and thanks to her Afghan mother looked the part. She'd been embedded in the region for over a year playing the role of a grieving widow whose husband had been martyred by the great Satan that was America. It wasn't all fun and candy. She'd been sexually assaulted three times and had to flee for her life on more than one occasion because she had killed her would be paramour and the Taliban were coming for her brandishing torches and pitchforks. Life could be difficult for a woman in America, but that God forsaken place was downright hell on earth when it came to women's rights.

After the draw-down, she found herself floundering at a desk job in Langley, analyzing mile high stacks of paperwork in a cubicle hoping to find the slightest crumbs of a threat against the U.S. and then passing those crumbs on to someone higher up the food chain. That's where he found her and offered her the job of reassembling the team, only now the stakes were so much higher. No less than the presidency of the United States of God damn America itself. Oorah, semper me and all that bullshit. She and the others had jumped down the rabbit hole at the chance to relive their glory days and up until now it had been a walk in the park. Mostly just tracking down people unfriendly to their guy and discrediting them. Most people in Washington had a skeleton or two in their closet they didn't want exposed. And if it wasn't there already, they would place it there. The key was making sure it never got back to the principal. Once in a while physical coercion was necessary, but she had yearned for the real thing, and had jumped at the leash when the Claire and Emily project had arrived. And now it was a shit show. Oh well, she thought. Be careful what you wish for.

She looked up at Cesari's window. Round one to you, Doctor. But now it was game on, asshole.

****

"I'm sorry I'm late, Cesari, but it looks like I didn't miss anything."

They stood in Cesari's living room. Tierney said, "Better late than never, Gianelli. You're lucky though. It doesn't look like anything's amiss here. Cesari, go finish packing while Gianelli pours me a scotch."

Cesari said, "There's at least a glass or two of the Johnnie Walker Blue left from the poker game. I'll be quick and pack light. If I need anything, I'll pick it up over there."

Vito poured Tierney and himself the scotch, emptying the bottle and they sat at the kitchen table. Vito said, "Cesari told me what happened at your apartment."

"Yeah, it was pretty bad. My cat was an emotional wreck when I arrived."

Vito sipped his scotch. "What do you think?"

"I think they're not going to stop until they get what they want."

"Which is?"

"Emily dead and those love letters."

"Speaking of the letters. Any word on the fingerprints?"

"Not yet. I didn't request a high priority on them. I didn't want to attract attention to the fact that I'm working on a high-profile case no one else knows about. I slid them through the back door to a friend of mine. It'll be a couple of days."

Vito nodded. "When are you going to tell the girl about what happened to her father?"

"I'm not. Not now anyway. Not until she's safely out of the country. If I tell her now, she'll go running straight to her father's bedside. We can't have that. For all we know, he was left alive for the sole purpose of drawing her out into the open."

"Poor kid."

"I can think of better ways of spending my youth."

"Are you going to come see her before we leave for Toronto?"

"That's a negative, Gianelli. I'd rather not lie to her face about her father. It's hard enough being evasive on the phone. I'll call her before you leave. Besides, I have a lot to do here figuring out what's going on. First order of business is to go back to Lansdale and see how her father is doing. Hopefully, he'll be able to give me a hint as to what happened to him and his wife."

"Any word on his condition?"

"When I last called the nurses said he was improving, but they weren't allowed to give me any more information because of privacy rules."

"Let's hope for the best."

"Thanks... As soon as you figure out where you're going to stay in Palermo let me know."

"I can let you know right now. We're going to stay at my cousin Teresa's apartment. I've been there. There's plenty of room. You planning on visiting?"

"You never know. It wouldn't be the first time the Marines had to rescue Americans on foreign soil."

Vito grinned. "She lives at number 8 Via Orologio, on the third floor, two blocks from the Piazza Verdi."

When Tierney didn't attempt to write the address down Vito asked, "You going to remember that?"

"Number 8, Via Orologio, third floor, two blocks from the Piazza Verdi. Yeah, I'll remember it."

Cesari emerged from his bedroom with a duffle bag as they were finishing their drinks. He said, "I'm glad to see you two guys getting along for a change."

Tierney grinned. "I'm sure it will be a short-lived truce, but for the time being I'm very grateful to the both of you."

The men rose and left the apartment. Downstairs, Cesari and Vito piled into the Cadillac with Gerry and Vito's other guy. Tierney left for other parts in his Buick. Vito opened the window and lit a cigarette.

Cesari admonished him. "I thought you were trying to quit those things."

Vito blew a puff out the window. "Leave me alone. I'm under stress. Besides, I saw you smoke two cigars at the poker game."

Cesari snorted. "Fine, knock yourself out. See if I care."

With all that was going on, no one noticed the car following them.

Chapter 28

Detective Robert B. Tierney entered his apartment at close to midnight, and in a day filled with surprises, he was once more taken aback. Sitting on his couch was Deputy Director Morehouse of the Secret Service and on a club chair next to him was Special Agent Munoz, gently stroking Stonewall's head while the cat cooed affectionately.

He closed the door behind him and said, "You'd better be careful, Agent Munoz. Stonewall doesn't like it when women break his heart... You two have had a long day. All the way from D.C. to the Hoffman house in Lansdale and now to my apartment. I'm starting to think that whatever's happening is over my paygrade."

Morehouse and Munoz stood. The Deputy Director said, "I'll get right to it, Detective. I don't know if you've seen the news but one of our agents was shot and killed in an underpass in Tysons Corner last night."

"Tysons Corner? I'm sorry to hear that, but I hope you realize you're in Brooklyn right now."

Morehouse continued unfazed, "Emily Hoffman, the daughter of your friends, Fred and Kathy, is a congressional intern. We have reason to believe she was in that underpass at the time of the shooting, and we'd like to ask her what happened, but we've been having trouble locating her."

"What's this got to do with me?"

"We'd really appreciate your cooperation, Detective. We know that Fred Hoffman called you early on the morning after the shooting, and then you showed up at the house within hours after he and his wife are attacked. That's quite a coincidence."

"People keep saying that to me."

"Look at it from our point of view. We're simply tracking down leads like you would. Just routine procedure."

Tierney said, "Is breaking and entering someone's apartment at midnight routine procedure at the Secret Service?"

Morehouse grinned. "Your door was unlocked, Detective. If I were you, I'd be more careful."

"Bullshit, and even if it was, you still don't have the right to come inside. A man's home is his castle."

"Not true. I heard someone or thing in distress so like a devoted officer of the law I investigated. Turns out it was your cat in need of cuddling."

Despite his fatigue and ire, Tierney found himself smiling at that. Finally, he eased up a bit. "I'll admit that does sound like Stonewall."

"May we have a chat like grownups, Detective?" asked Morehouse.

"If I say no?"

"Then agent Munoz will be instructed to place handcuffs on you."

"For what?"

"In case you haven't noticed there's a large blood stain on your nice wood floor and carpet and overwhelming evidence that some type of physical altercation took place here. Unless you're going to tell me that you cut yourself shaving and knocked over all of your furniture as you stumbled into the kitchen looking for a bandage, this looks very much like a crime scene. That's just for starters. I could follow that one up with obstructing the ongoing investigation of the murder of a Secret Service agent."

"I don't know what you're talking about."

Morehouse scowled. "Please don't challenge my intelligence, Detective."

Tierney sighed in resignation. "How about I put on a pot of coffee? I'm beat, and we can talk just as well in the kitchen."

They moved into the kitchen and Tierney filled a carafe with water and measured out some coffee from a can. Munoz and Morehouse sat at the table watching him.

Munoz asked, "So what happened? It looks like a tornado came swirling through here."

Tierney decided to lay his cards on the table, and replied, "You should have seen it before I cleaned up, but to answer your question, I wish I knew. I came home and there it was, a dead body in my living room and the place ransacked like someone was looking for a treasure map."

Morehouse appreciated the candor. "Who was the victim?"

"A neighbor. He lived three doors down."

"What happened next?"

Tierney sat down and said, "You don't want to know. Besides, it's your turn."

"My turn? I think you're confused, Detective. We're the ones asking the questions."

"I get that, but you know how it is in this business. There's always a little quid pro quo. I give you something and you give me something. So why don't you tell me what you really want. Because I suspect you know more about what happened in my apartment than I do."

Morehouse glanced at Munoz, nodding his head ever so slightly. She said, "As the Deputy Director told you, we're looking for Emily Hoffman. We believe she has information that is pertinent to our investigation into the death of one of our agents in D.C. We know for a fact that Emily called her father at the time of the agent's death, then travelled to her family home in Lansdale. We know that Emily's father called you just before she went missing, and just before the attack at the Hoffman residence. Let's face facts, Detective, only a simpleton would accept the story that you just coincidentally happened to drop by at the Hoffman house hours after the mother was murdered and the father beaten. Fred Hoffman enlisted you to protect his daughter, and that is exactly what we believe you are doing. So if you really do care about her safety, we need you to turn her over to us."

They let that sink in for a minute. Tierney said, "Aren't you leaving out a few important details?"

"Such as?"

"Why would Fred feel the need to protect his daughter and from whom?"

Morehouse said, "Detective, I know what you're implying so let's cut to the chase. Special Agent Mills was in the underpass that night at the same time as Emily and her co-worker Claire Tompkins. Claire's dead, agent Mills is dead. Mills was an exemplary agent without a single blemish on his service record. We're just trying to sort out what happened without prematurely casting aspersions on anyone's character or reputations. If you know something that I don't then lay it on me straight."

"The problem I have Deputy Director is that I can't be sure I can trust you," Tierney stated dryly and then added, "In fact, I'm pretty sure

I don't. How do I know you're not the ones who killed Emily's mother and my neighbor?"

"Don't be ridiculous, Detective. I'm the Deputy Director of the Secret Service. If you want, you can call the Director himself for confirmation of that. It's late, but I can reach him."

Tierney suddenly stood, drew his Glock from his shoulder holster and trained it on them. Munoz's eyes went wide, and Morehouse's jaw dropped.

Morehouse said, "This is just a guess, but this may be the dumbest thing you've ever done, Detective."

Tierney smirked, "Not by a long shot, but then again you don't know me that well. Now both of you place your hands on the table where I can see them."

Munoz interjected in a calming tone, "Detective, if we wanted to harm you, you wouldn't have walked in on us playing with your cat."

Undeterred, Tierney said, "I said hands on the table and no sudden moves, all right? I'm tired and a little on edge."

They put their hands on the table in plain sight as Tierney went behind them and deftly relieved them of their weapons and cellphones. He placed all the items in the sink and faced them again.

"Now let me tell you both a story. A young woman was driving her friend to the airport and was pulled over by a Secret Service agent in a desolate part of Tysons Corner. Without provocation, the agent shot the friend in cold blood and was about to do the same to the young woman. Unbeknownst to the agent, the young woman was armed and returned fire. Ever since, people have been trying to kill her. So desperate are they to end her life, they murdered her mother, beat her father half to death and came all the way to this apartment looking for her and inadvertently murdered my neighbor. I didn't mention this before, but my neighbor had a tight grouping of three small caliber rounds in him just like Emily's mother. I don't know about you, but that sounds very professional. Now you two show up and think I'm going to turn her over to you just because you asked nicely. Do I look like I was born yesterday? Something stinks and it stinks real bad. Furthermore, the stench is coming right from the Secret Service."

Morehouse frowned. "I can see how you might think that.... Is that what Emily told you? About what happened in the underpass?"

Tierney nodded. "It is."

"I didn't know that. We've been working on the assumption that there might have been others involved."

"You mean you've been hoping there was another explanation. Well, there wasn't anyone else there that night. So the question is why was Mills sent to assassinate those women and why are they still after Emily?"

"I honestly don't know, but we want to find out as badly if not more so than you. But pointing a gun at the Deputy Director of the Secret Service isn't going to help your cause."

"Probably not, but you're obviously a smart guy and can see my dilemma."

Morehouse nodded. "I do although the list of reasons why I might have to arrest you just got a lot longer. I'm not sure how I can convince you we're on the same side. If Mills was bad, then I want him to burn. But we have to prove that what you said is actually what happened, and that's why we need Emily."

"Maybe you need proof, but I don't. Emily's word is good enough for me. I'm afraid I've been in the swamp too long, Deputy Director. It tends to make a guy cynical. The military, the police, it's all the same. When a scandal comes everybody does their best to cover it up, and when that doesn't work, they try to whitewash it, and when all else fails you bury it along with any witnesses. You may not have ordered Mills to murder anyone, but I know one thing for certain. The best way for you to make sure this thing goes away would be to silence Emily."

Tierney reached behind his back and returned with a pair of metal handcuffs. He tossed them across the table at Morehouse. "Cuff your right hand to Munoz's right hand so your facing each other."

Morehouse nodded and did as instructed. Restrained in such an awkward fashion, their movements would be severely restricted, thus reducing the risk of a coordinated attack. Nonetheless, Tierney did not intend on taking any chances and sat opposite them with his pistol aimed in their direction. He took out his cellphone and called Cesari.

"You're not going to believe this, but I have two Secret Service agents in my apartment looking for Emily."

"And....?"

"They say they're the good guys but there's no way of being sure of that or if there are more of them crawling around."

"What do you think we should do?"

"I'm going to babysit them, but I think you guys should start moving."

"Got it. Call you when we land."

"Roger that. Although the next time you see me, I may be wearing an orange jumpsuit."

He hung up the phone and Morehouse said, "That last part was quite prophetic."

Tierney grinned. "Relax, Deputy Director, it's going to be a long night."

Morehouse sighed. "Fine, but why'd you bring us into the kitchen? The sofa was more comfortable."

"Because I really did want a cup of coffee."

Chapter 29

Cesari mobilized everyone and within an hour they were ready to go. Vito asked, "What about your friends, Jaskaran and Jeremy?"

"I'll call them when we're on the way. They can meet us in Toronto."

Teresa and Emily stood at the kitchen table wearing jeans and sneakers, drinking coffee, and trying to wake up. Vito had sent Gerry to the garage to warm up the Escalade. They were all travelling very light with one carry-on each.

"Vito, ask your guys on Mulberry and Mott Streets if they see anything suspicious. Tierney said there might be other agents sniffing around."

A minute later, with the phone next to his ear, Vito said, "There's a white Ford Taurus about a half block away on Mulberry Street with a man and woman talking."

Cesari glanced at his watch. It was 1:30 a.m. "Just sitting? How long have they been there?"

Vito spoke to his guy and said, "They're just sitting and talking. He's not sure how long they've been there. What do you think?"

"I think we should get out of here, but I'd like to get a better look at them first. Can your guys get close enough to take a few pictures without alarming them? Just in case we run into them again."

Vito rolled his eyes. "Cesari, give me a break. My guys aren't the subtle types. And it's the middle of the night. Who wouldn't be alarmed at someone approaching their car snapping photos? Besides, why do you need to see them?"

Cesari thought it over. It was probably nothing anyway. "You're right. I'm getting paranoid."

"Of course, I'm right, but if it helps. My guy downstairs says that he can see them pretty clearly. They're white, in their late thirties, early forties. The woman has short blonde hair and has a bandage on one side of her face. The guy is bald and has a full beard."

"That's pretty good. I thought you said your guys weren't subtle."

"They're not but that doesn't mean they're blind. Whoever it is isn't making any attempt to hide so that goes against them being anything but what they seem. So if you're happy now with that information, we should go, before someone really bad shows up."

They walked through Vito's specially built underground passageway from his apartment facing Mulberry Street to the parking garage facing Mott Street where the Escalade was already fired up and waiting with Gerry driving and another guy riding shotgun. When he was really trying to be evasive from prying eyes, Vito would have a car pull up to the front of his apartment and have a stand-in disguised in a trench coat with turned up collar and a turned down broad brimmed fedora hustle out the doorway surrounded by security. The body-double would quickly make it into the back of the car and then speed away. After the feds followed the car, he would make a leisurely exit from the garage on the other side of the block. He found it immensely amusing that after years of pulling the same trick, no one ever figured it out.

The Escalade easily fit the six passengers in relative comfort, and they settled in for the drive, the women in the way back, with Vito and Cesari in the middle row. As the car turned onto the West Side highway aiming north for the thruway, Cesari was already mulling over the next phase. Getting Emily safely out of the country was one thing, but then what? Was she going to live on the run forever? Worse, she didn't even know why.

Not good.

He pulled out his phone and called Jeremy. They were all supposed to meet at Vito's place at the crack of dawn and they needed to be updated on the sudden change of plans.

"Sorry to wake you, Jeremy, but there's been a development, and we're on the move. We'll catch up with you in Toronto. Let Jaskaran know. Whatever you do, don't come looking for us at Vito's apartment. It may be under surveillance. We'll talk more later."

Sleepily, Jeremy replied, "Got it. I'll call Jaskaran now. See you soon, Cesari."

Cesari clicked off and turned back to Emily and Teresa. "How are you two holding up?"

Emily looked glumly at him and said, "I'm just fine and dandy."

"I understand, Emily. We'll get through this."

"Why would anybody want to kill me?"

Cesari replied sympathetically, "I really don't know, but we're working on it."

"This so surreal. The Secret Service is trying to murder me, and my salvation is the guy who did my last colonoscopy. I feel like I'm trapped inside a nightmare, and I can't wake myself up."

Cesari nodded. "I wish I could say something to make you feel better."

With unexpected anger, Emily spat, "You can tell me my mother is still alive and that this is all just a fucking sick joke."

When he didn't say anything, Teresa placed an arm around Emily in an attempt to comfort her. Vito had told Teresa earlier about Emily's predicament. He felt he had no choice but to involve her if they were going to travel together.

Teresa said, "I am sorry, Emily. I didn't know your mama, but I am sure she was a good person. I one hundred percent believe that she is in a better place and watching you right now this very minute. If she could talk to you, I know she would say to be strong and always remember how much she love you."

Emily buried her face into Teresa's shoulder and started to sob.

****

Rosemarie said, "Go ahead. You're on speaker phone. I got Booker here. So what's the scoop on the Escalade?"

"It's registered to a Vito Gianelli. He's some type of mob thug there in Manhattan. The feds have a file on him."

"The mob?" asked Rosemarie incredulously. "What the hell is going on here?"

"It's not entirely clear, but my source tells me that Tierney, Gianelli and Cesari are, for want of a better word, friends."

"You have got to be kidding?"

"No, I'm not. I think Fred Hoffman asked Tierney for help to hide Emily. He turned around and asked Cesari for help. Cesari then recruited Gianelli. And now we have a freak show on our hands. Do you still have eyes on the SUV?"

"No, the driver dropped off Cesari and a big, ugly guy at the front entrance to an apartment building on Mulberry Street. The

Escalade took off after that presumably to some nearby garage. There are two guards standing out in front of the building, and more on either end of the block. I'm assuming there are probably others inside as well. Handguns are a given, but we can't rule out the possibility of them having heavier ordinance. There's no way of storming the place under these conditions."

The voice on the line reluctantly agreed. "That's probably the safe house where they have Emily."

Rosemarie asked, "I agree, but why would Tierney ask Cesari for help in the first place?"

"Two reasons possibly. First, I've found out that Emily Hoffman has Crohn's disease and Cesari is or was her doctor when she lived in New York. It's possible she might be sick. Second, the big, ugly guy you saw is probably Gianelli. According to the FBI, Cesari is a lifelong friend of Gianelli. Whereas Tierney may have felt a certain reluctance to directly enlist the aid of someone of Gianelli's ill repute, Cesari would have had no such qualms."

"This is unbelievable. Well, I don't see how we're going to get into the building without an artillery barrage."

"You may not have to. There's a new wrinkle. I think they're planning on leaving the country. I started tracking all of their credit cards and included Gianelli's when you gave me the license plate number to his SUV. Interestingly, within the last twenty-four hours, he purchased seven tickets to Rome, Italy, leaving tonight at 10:00 p.m. on Air Canada out of Pearson International Airport in Toronto. From Rome they are connecting onward to Palermo. What are the odds of that being unrelated? I think Gianelli is helping Cesari and Tierney get the girl out of the country."

"Tierney, Cesari, Gianelli and Emily Hoffman make four. Who are the other three?"

"I don't know. Security maybe. I'll know more if I can get someone to discreetly tap into the Air Canada passenger log."

"Are the feds going to notify the Canadian authorities and have them detained?"

"And tell them what exactly? That they don't like Dr. Cesari or his friends and would like to prevent them from traveling to Europe? They don't even know who Cesari is or what his involvement is. They can't do anything about him leaving the country. Besides my guy inside, tells me the feds are spinning in the wind on this one."

"Don't they want to talk to the Hoffman girl?"

"Right now the FBI is not only clueless about Emily Hoffman but Claire Tompkins as well. They haven't connected either woman to the death of Mills yet, only the Secret Service has and they're not volunteering any information. They want to reach the finish line first in order to save face and to be in control of spin. The attack on the Hoffman family is being handled by the Lansdale police as a local matter for the moment, and they don't feel the need to involve the feds."

Rosemarie asked, "Okay, they're going to Italy. Now what?"

"They have a flight out of Toronto tonight, so they'll have to come out and either drive, take a train, or a plane. One way or another they'll have to surface. There should be plenty of opportunities between here and there."

"And the letters?"

"Naturally, we'd love to have them returned or destroyed, but they take a back seat. Without Emily Hoffman around to tell everyone what really happened, we can defuse them if we have to."

"It's not going to be pretty. In fact, it's going to be as messy as it gets. We can't just walk up to her and pop her in the head anymore. She's surrounded by bodyguards now."

There was quiet on the other end for a minute before he continued, "You're right...Here's an idea. Drive to Pearson International Airport and wait for them there. We know which airline, flight, and time of departure. You know them but they don't know you. Sooner or later she'll need to use the bathroom. That'll be your chance."

"That could work...possibly. I'll never get a weapon through security, but I suppose if I could get her alone, I could break her neck or strangle her."

"That's the spirit."

"And if she doesn't use the bathroom or the opportunity doesn't arise? I hope you don't think I'm going to try anything in the middle of a busy airport in a foreign country with cameras every ten feet and hundreds of witnesses."

"You're no fun anymore, Rosemarie. I'll get you and Booker on that plane with them if it comes to it. Just make sure you both have your passports. You'll get firearms after you land in Sicily. It'll be easier than dealing with customs, and the last thing you to want to do is to trigger a background check."

Rosemarie checked the time and started the engine. "We're on the way, but you better make sure she's on that plane."

"Trust me. I have an instinct about this. It's too damn convenient."

"Fine."

Chapter 30

They arrived in Toronto at 9:30 a.m. and crashed at an inexpensive motel, slept most of the day, and then grabbed dinner at a pub near the airport. Check-in at Air Canada went smoothly, and heading through security, they decided to split into two groups to be less conspicuous. To any observer, Jaskaran and Emily, Vito and Teresa appeared to be two couples traveling together, and Cesari, Jeremy and Gerry Acquilano were three friends vacationing in Europe. At 9:00 p.m. they took seats in the waiting area of the departure gate as their plane was being cleaned, fueled and readied. It looked to be a full to capacity flight from the number of people Cesari saw milling about. Vito, Teresa, and Jaskaran were chatting four rows away. Emily sat quietly by Jaskaran's side. She looked the part, he thought. Vito's makeup artist had done a superb job transforming her into a young Sikh wife. From the darker toned cosmetics, haircut, contact lenses, and traditional clothes, no one would even think twice about her ethnicity.

That illusion was bolstered by Jaskaran's presence next to her. He wore a business suit and his enormous fluffy beard flowed down over his tie. He outdid himself with today's choice of turbans. At work, he generally wore a modest one in subdued colors. Today, he was making a statement and wore a bright red dastar with an ornamental brooch in the center. While it did bring attention to him, his broad smile, affable mannerism, and relaxed attitude easily disarmed onlookers. Even better was that although he was American through and through having been born and raised in Queens, New York, he feigned a pronounced stereotypical Indian accent and sounded a little like he was performing a comedy club routine. He was every cliché about Indian immigrants and more, and appeared to be thoroughly enjoying the schtick.

Cesari was impressed at how well everyone was playing their part. You could never tell by looking at them that there was a powder keg of anxiety, tension and fear lying just below the surface. Even Gerry had risen to the occasion. Vito had decided to bring him along as an all-around go-to guy and troubleshooter. Gerry had a lot of flaws, but he also had a lot of strengths. One of them was that because of his size, people frequently didn't take him seriously as a threat and often overlooked his presence. That was a big mistake and more than a few of

Vito's enemies had discovered their error too late. His other big positive was a relentless determination to please Vito. He would move heaven and earth, day or night, to get the job done for his boss. While this unbridled enthusiasm sometimes led to misguided judgement, overall it worked to Vito's advantage and so here he was. It also worked to Cesari's advantage as Vito had given Gerry clear instructions that when Cesari told him to do something he'd better act as if the word came from Vito himself. Cesari had given Gerry a small test and sent him to buy coffee for everyone. Everyone but Emily. It was decided that under no circumstances was she to leave the safety of the herd, including bathroom breaks. Therefore no coffee or other beverages for her until after they boarded.

Noticing Cesari's pensive mood, Jeremy asked, "Is everything all right?"

Cesari nodded. "Almost too good. I don't like it when things go this smoothly. The only glitch is that we won't have any firearms with us when we land, but we'll figure something out."

"Italy doesn't allow people to bring legal handguns into the country?"

"That's the glitch. We don't have any legal weapons. Vito, me, and Gerry are ex-felons and can't legally own a handgun. And you and Jaskaran don't own any, unless you've been holding back on me?"

"No, we don't…. Take a step back. You're an ex-felon?"

"It's a long story. How about I save it for another day, but I didn't murder anyone. Several years ago, I told a little white lie to a federal officer. I was trying to protect a friend and got the book thrown at me."

"I'm sorry to hear that."

"And I'm sorry to say it, but it is what it is."

"On a lighter note, Jaskaran is cracking me up."

Cesari grinned. " Me too. He's really getting into it."

"Parikh told me they're turning the cafeteria into a nightclub for the orthopedic surgeons."

"That's mostly accurate. Dr. Alexander Graham Bell is wasting no time in leaving his mark on St. Matt's. Did you have a chance to see it?"

"Not yet, but I heard they're planning on calling it either Bar Alexander or Bar Bell. They're leaning toward Bar Bell because he's really into weightlifting big time. Word is that he uses steroids."

Cesari shook his head in amazement. "I have no doubt. I wonder if Dr. Bell is from the south. Then they could call the club, The Graham Cracker."

Jeremy laughed. "I like that."

"When we return, we'll sneak over there, and I'll buy you a martini."

"Parikh also said we might be able to get lap dances there."

Now it was Cesari's turn to laugh. "I think Parikh has an overactive imagination."

"On a more serious note, what's the plan when we get to Palermo?"

"Right now it's day to day. Personally, I can't believe we made it this far. Whoever is after Emily, made it all the way to Tierney's apartment. I hate to be paranoid, but for all I know they're watching us now."

Unconsciously, Jeremy scanned around the terminal. "I guess we wouldn't know them by their appearance?"

"I doubt that very much. These are U.S. minted professional hitmen, Jeremy, not Koran waving jihadists or skinheads with swastikas carved into their foreheads."

Gerry returned and handed Cesari and Jeremy black coffees. Cesari said, "Thanks, Gerry."

Gerry sat next to Cesari. "No problem. Vito says I should do whatever you say, so's that's what I do."

"That's a good plan, Gerry. Are you looking forward to seeing Sicily?"

"No, not really. My people are from Calabria. I always thought my first trip back to the old country ought's to have been where my grandparents are from. Not to the place they hated."

Cesari was surprised. "Why did they hate Sicily?"

"They always said that Sicilians weren't real Italians, and that Sicily was nothing but a rock that broke off from Africa and floated north." He leaned over and said to Jeremy, "No offense meant. I'm sure Africa is a beautiful country."

Jeremy smiled. He was gradually getting used to Gerry. He responded, "None taken. The more of your people we get out of my continent the better."

Cesari nearly snorted coffee out of his nose at the comment. He loved Jeremy's droll wit. "Okay, boys. Enough with the tribalism."

****

Rosemarie and Booker sat together at the gate across from Vito and Cesari giving them a clear view. They had arrived an hour earlier and set up surveillance. The arrival of the eclectic, harmless group headed by Cesari and Gianelli had momentarily thrown them into confusion. Neither of the two women fit Emily's description and the accompanying men were as far from a personal protection squad as you could get.

She called her guy in D.C. for an update. "I see Cesari and Gianelli, but not Tierney or the girl. Are you sure she's on this flight?"

"I can't be sure of anything but why else would they be taking off for Italy on such short notice? It makes no sense otherwise."

"It looks like some sort of group holiday from where I'm sitting. Other than Gianelli, I don't see anybody that would even remotely qualify as hired muscle. What's taking you so long to find the passenger list?"

"Are you serious? May I remind you that Canada is still a foreign country. I can't just demand to see their flight registries. We need to offer them credible evidence of a threat to our or their national security or that they are giving safe harbor to a fugitive. I can't do either without tipping our hand, and the last thing we want is for the FBI to suddenly decide they want Emily for themselves. Look around. Are you certain you don't see her there?"

Rosemarie glanced at the photo of Emily she had on her phone. Then she searched the waiting area again with special attention to Cesari and Gianelli's travelling companions.

Eventually, she replied, "Cesari's with two men. One is short, black, and well-dressed, looks like a professor or something. The other is a middle-aged midget with a sour puss. When the killing starts, I'll throw him in for free. I'll take pictures and send them to you to identify. Gianelli is with a loquacious Indian guy in a turban and two women, about Emily's age but neither look anything like this photo you gave me. One of them is definitely Indian. She's with the turban. The other could be Gianelli's younger sister. The similarity is that strong, but trust me, I don't mean that as a compliment to her."

"Could Emily be disguised?"

"I guess that's always a possibility," she glanced down at the picture again, "but it would have to be one hell of a disguise. Seriously these two chicks are about the right height and build but don't bear the slightest resemblance to the photo, and one of them has a mustache. I don't know any woman that would do that deliberately even in the face of certain death."

"Anybody go for a potty break? You could get a closer look."

"No, they're sitting tight, and the waiting area is packed. For the record, they all look very relaxed, like nothing's going on. They either have nerves of steel or are consummate actors."

Booker grabbed the phone unexpectedly and in a deep guttural voice, whispered, "Sir, I can take both women out without a problem...mission accomplished."

"Booker, don't do anything until Rosemarie tells you to unless you want to wind up back in a straitjacket eating spiders off a cement floor like when I found you. Now return the phone to Rosemarie."

She wrestled the phone back and said, "They're going to board in ten minutes... Plan?"

"I hate to say it, but Booker may be right about taking both women out. At this point, what's one more body? For now, just stay with them and I'll stay on Tierney. Remember the golden rule, when in doubt, shoot first and ask questions later. You'll be in a country where the police spend ninety-percent of their day on break and the other ten percent having cappuccino. Combine that with a top-heavy bureaucracy and lax border security and you should have no trouble getting out if the shit hits the fan so apply your justice liberally."

"Understood."

She clicked off and turned to her companion who appeared to be engaged in conversation with no one in particular. She asked, "Who are you talking to, Booker?"

"You don't want to know," he growled.

"Okay, but promise me one thing."

"What's that?"

"If the person you're speaking with talks back, you'll tell me right away."

"What if he orders me not to tell you?"

"Then you'll both be in straitjackets. Now promise me."

"I promise you."

"You promise me what?"

"I promise you, ma'am."

Chapter 31

Tierney filled the two martini glasses to the brim with Hendrick's, plopped an olive in each, and placed one on the coffee table in front of Stonewall. He then sat back holding his glass with one hand and his gun with the other. Stonewall sniffed the gin, purred approvingly, and lapped up some of his martini.

Tierney said, "Good cat."

Morehouse and Munoz stared at Stonewall. Morehouse said, "Your cat drinks martinis?"

"Only when I'm out of scotch. Now where was I?"

"Iraq, your second tour," offered Morehouse.

"That's right. And so there I was. Alone on the wrong side of Baghdad with Corporal Hoffman ten feet away unconscious and bleeding like a stuck pig from a bullet wound in his leg. I was down to my last two clips of ammo, one grenade and my knife. Our patrol got ambushed and the Humvee was a fiery, smoking mess from an RPG. Two of my men died in the attack. It was a miracle that Fred and I survived. I had singlehandedly held them off for over two hours, and just as the Iraqis were about to launch a final assault on our position, two Apache helicopters came bursting in over the horizon. This was followed shortly by a column of armored vehicles to extract us. I'm not a hundred percent sure what happened next because one of the rockets from the choppers came a little too close and knocked me off my feet. You have to keep in mind the bad guys were only about half a city block away and back then this shit wasn't an exact science the way it is today. Anyway, the next day I woke up in an army hospital with my head bandaged, my arm in a sling, and a catheter in my dick draining bloody urine. I won the silver star for my trouble, but do you know what the only thing I really cared about was?"

Morehouse shook his head and sighed. They'd been held against their will for almost twenty-four hours, and it was now almost 10:00 p.m. the next night. He was sitting on one end of Tierney's living room sofa and Munoz was lying down on the other end with her feet pressed against his thigh. His right wrist was now handcuffed to her left ankle. Tierney sat opposite them most of the night with his cocked pistol trained on Morehouse's chest. They'd been treated civilly, with plenty of coffee, toast, eggs and a seemingly endless supply of pop tarts and war stories. Bathroom breaks were awkward but manageable. Sleep was nearly impossible, and they simply dozed for ten to fifteen minutes at a time. Tierney hadn't slept at all. They were all exhausted and getting a little ripe.

Morehouse said, "I'll bite. What was the only thing you really cared about, Detective?"

"You would think that as a young virile marine full of piss and vinegar my main concern would have been the functionality of my reproductive organ or my weapon of mass adoration as I liked to call it. But no, not a chance. All I cared about was whether my friend, Fred Hoffman, was alive or not. Are you starting to get the picture about me and Fred, Deputy Director?"

Morehouse nodded. "I am. So what's the plan, Detective? Are we prisoners of war?"

Tierney grinned. "Not at all, and I'm saddened you feel that way. I consider you an honored guest."

Thirty minutes later and knee deep into a story about a whorehouse in Kabul he frequented, Tierney's phone buzzed with a text from Cesari that they had boarded the plane uneventfully and were taxiing for takeoff. He smiled, put the device away and studied his captives. It was time to face the piper, he mused. Raising his pistol in the air, he dropped the magazine to the floor and emptied the chamber. Placing the weapon on the coffee table, he then took the handcuff keys out of his pocket and freed the Secret Service agents. Before they could fully register what was happening, Tierney got on his knees facing away from them and clasped his hands together behind his head.

Morehouse and Munoz glanced at each other completely astonished at the proceedings. As the night had worn on, they had fluctuated in their opinions about their future and whether or not Detective Robert Tierney was mentally unstable. Munoz stood and stretched as Morehouse wasted no time in cuffing Tierney who offered no resistance.

After he was done, Morehouse helped Tierney to his feet and asked, "Would you like to say anything, Detective?"

"Sir, Gunnery Sergeant Robert B. Tierney. United States Marine Corps. 158-54-2203. Sir."

****

 The massive double decker airbus had taken off smoothly and reached its cruising altitude of thirty-five thousand feet in just under twenty minutes. It was truly an amazing demonstration of just how far the human race had come. Nearly three quarters of a football field long, it weighed over one million tons at take-off and could carry over five hundred passengers, dwarfing all its competitors. When Vito purchased the tickets, there were only four first class seats left so he, Jaskaran, Teresa and Emily travelled in comfort on the upper level while Jeremy, Cesari and Gerry sat in the very back row of the economy class below. Once everybody had settled in and the lights went out, Cesari closed his eyes and dozed for a couple of hours until he was woken by the sounds of Gerry snoring and drooling on his shoulder. Jeremy was sound asleep. Cesari pushed Gerry back into his own seat, yawned, and thought about a cocktail, but cancelled that notion in favor of a cup of black coffee, if he could find one. He had missed the initial beverage service but had no doubt he would find something to his satisfaction. Overhead was a digital flight tracker indicating they were somewhere over the north Atlantic just south of Iceland. He glanced at his watch. Not quite halfway there. He unbuckled, stood and stretched. Behind their row of seats were two bathrooms, one which was an extra-large handicapped accessible room, and not a lot else. It would make a great place to hang out with his coffee. He didn't like sitting for long periods.

 The lower deck was divided into four sections by flight attendant stations, galleys, and plenty of bathrooms. In the front of the plane was the staircase to the upper level and he decided to wander up there to see what Vito was up to. Meandering forward through the very next grouping of seats something caught his attention, and he slowed to study the sleeping figures more carefully. It was a man and a woman. The woman had a bandage covering one side of her face and her left hand. The man was big and bald with a full beard, a hard-looking guy for sure. They were only two rows in front of the flight attendant station. There were a lot of things Cesari didn't believe in. One was Santa Claus, another was the Lee Harvey Oswald acted alone bullshit, but mostly he didn't believe in coincidences.

He digested the implication and kept moving onward to the galley at the very front end of the plane where he was greeted by a pleasant group of flight attendants who poured him a cup of hot albeit stale coffee. He sipped the steaming liquid and was about to walk up the stairs to first class when he was met with stiff resistance from a young flight attendant half his height and about a third his weight with a heavy French accent. She bristled at the notion of letting someone from the lower classes disturb the peaceful slumbers of her well-to-do passengers. Apparently, the lessons of the French revolution had been lost on her. However, when he identified himself as Vito's personal physician and that he had life-saving medication which needed to be administered urgently, the young woman relented. As he passed by however, she gave him a superbly dubious look which suggested to Cesari that she didn't believe a word of it, but felt that such an imaginative cock and bull story deserved to be rewarded.

Vito was stretched out in an aisle seat with Teresa on his right toward the center. Jaskaran lay in the aisle seat across from him with Emily on his left by the window. They were all fully reclined and asleep. Cesari nudged Vito several times until he reluctantly woke.

"Cesari, what's up?" he asked groggily.

"I think we have a problem. Come with me."

Vito brought his seat up, slipped his shoes on and followed Cesari down to the kitchen where he also grabbed a cup of coffee. Vito said, "Have you ever been on one of these mega-planes before?"

"No, why?"

"There's a full bar up there with a bartender."

"I didn't know that. I'm glad you're enjoying yourself."

"So what's the problem that you woke me up for?"

"Remember the descriptions your guy gave you of the people in the car parked on Mulberry Street."

"Yeah, a blonde with a bandage on her face and a big guy, hard-looking, bald with a beard."

"Good, now let's walk down to my seat in the back of the plane. Keep your eyes peeled to the left. I'll nudge you when it's time."

Cesari walked behind him and when they reached the section in question, he poked Vito in the back, and they slowed to get a good look.

Satisfied, they regrouped in the back of the plane by the bathrooms. As they passed by, they saw Jeremy still sleeping and Gerry yawning and looking drowsy. He didn't notice them walk by in the dark cabin.

Alone, Vito said, "I see what you mean, Cesari. It could be them. They fit the description anyway."

"Exactly... We have a problem."

"What do you want to do?"

"Not sure yet. We still have four hours to go so there's plenty of time to think about it."

"Do you think they're Secret Service?"

"Don't know and don't care. If they were the good guys, they wouldn't be stalking us. They would have announced who they are and what their purpose was. If they were the good guys, and wanted to speak to us about a legitimate concern, they never would have let us board a plane to a foreign country."

"Valid points. What do you think happened to her face?"

"I don't know. Her hand is injured too."

"I saw that. You think they're the ones leaving bodies all over the place?"

"That's hard to say. They could have lots of friends."

Vito nodded. "Hopefully, not on this plane."

"I agree with that... Boy, these guys got some major pull. How could they have known we'd be on this flight? That's the reason I had you buy all the tickets. I thought they wouldn't know you."

"They must have figured out our relationship and tracked my credit card activity."

"I guess, but if they figured out we were on this flight, do you think they also figured out we bought Emily a ticket using a false identity?"

"We should probably assume the worst."

"Yeah, but what to do? Have you ever killed someone on a plane?"

Vito snorted. "You're a riot, Cesari, but no, it's never come up. Besides, we're not talking about one person, we're talking about two."

"Still, eliminating one of them would increase our chances of survival by fifty percent."

"Or get us thrown into an Italian prison the minute we land."

"There's that if you want to be negative."

"Cesari, you can't be serious. We don't even know who they are."

"If I find out who they are, would that make you happy?"

"Okay, for the sake of argument, let's pretend they're the bad guys and they're following us with the intent of harming Emily and whoever gets in their way. What do you propose to do?"

"I need to think about it."

"While you think about it, I'll check on Gerry. It's not a good idea leaving him alone too long."

"You do that, but don't say anything about this yet. There's no need to get a guy with a hair trigger like him wound up without a plan."

"Understood."

Vito walked to Gerry's seat and Cesari lingered there, thinking things through. Although he had been flippant about it with Vito, it didn't sit well with him to take the life of someone he didn't know and who's intentions he wasn't certain. But what were the odds of two people sitting vigil in front of Vito's apartment just hours ago in Manhattan, now appearing on this particular jet with them? A million to one? A billion to one? A trillion to one, more likely.

He found himself studying the bathroom door while he contemplated the problem at hand. Specifically, he was staring at the green vacant message beneath the metal lavatory sign. Stepping closer, he noticed the metal lavatory sign was slightly askew. Just enough to appear as if it were about to lift upward. He reached out with his hand and pulled gently on it, and to his surprise, it did lift upward. He glanced in both directions as if he had done something wrong. Beneath the metal sign was a small button that appeared amenable to being slid along a track. Filled with curiosity, he slid the button all the way to one side, listened to the lock engage and watched the vacant message turn to occupied. He pushed the button back to its starting position and the message returned to vacant. It must be an emergency release latch for kids who lock themselves in or people who become ill or unconscious, he concluded.

Now that was interesting.

CHAPTER 32

Cesari wandered around the lower level checking every bathroom and found that they all had the same safety feature, including the oversized handicap bathroom at the very rear of that level. Then he sized up the situation, weighing pros and cons. The bathrooms in the way back of the plane were the most isolated and would serve his purpose best. If he could lure one of them back there, it just might work. There were a lot of risks, however. Other passengers or flight attendants showing up at the wrong time was the big one. His opponent might not go down so easily and put up a noisy struggle was another. But the big problem was getting them back there in the first place. From where they were sitting, the nearest bathrooms were two rows to their rear. They would have to bypass those to the desired ones further on toward the back of the plane where Cesari's seat was. On the other hand, if he changed the vacant messages of the bathrooms nearest them to occupied, they would wait a while and then naturally move to the next nearest restroom. That could work, but he would need help.

He found Vito talking to Gerry and Jeremy who were both now wide awake, and he brought them all to the back of the plane. "Okay, guys. We have a situation. There are bogeys on board with us."

He explained what he knew and both Jeremy and Gerry nodded. Jeremy asked, "But you're not a hundred percent certain?"

"No, but it's a hundred percent possible, and I intend on finding out for sure."

Cesari then filled them in on the secret lavatory release button he discovered and ran his plan by them, "There are two of them. A man and a woman. If we wait for them to use the rest rooms, we can funnel them down to the handicap bathroom back here by turning all the bathroom messages to occupied except for that one."

Vito said, "That's a hell of a plan, Cesari. You're going to kill someone taking a leak on an international flight?"

"No, I'm going to interrogate someone and neutralize the threat is all. We need to stand by the bathrooms nearest to their section and when we see them rise, we change the messages to occupied. After they move past, you change the message back to vacant so other passengers can access them."

"What if it's the woman who goes to the bathroom first?" asked Jeremy. "I don't like the idea of assaulting a woman in a restroom. It will make for really bad press if you're wrong. Besides, she might just be travelling with the guy as a cover to make him look less suspicious. Big guys traveling alone always make people nervous."

Cesari thought about that for a minute before replying, "Sound logic, Jeremy, but I think you're being a little too chauvinistic in regard to the woman. In my experience, women can be every bit as dangerous as men, and she may be part and parcel to several recent vicious homicides although I'll grant you we don't know that for a fact."

"Not knowing that for a fact is a big deal in my book. I can't condone harming her if we don't really know that she's done anything wrong."

Cesari acquiesced, "Okay, Macallan, you've made your point, and I hope your quaint chivalry doesn't get us all killed. The woman gets a pass, but not the bald guy. He's an asshole. I can sense it a mile away. I'm like a dog when it comes to this stuff. Maybe he's not here to kill us but he's done something in his past that he needs a beating for. I'd bet money on it. He's got that look… If the woman gets up first, just let her do her thing. We'll focus on the guy for now."

"It's settled. We focus on the guy. Then what?" asked Vito.

"If we get lucky and things go as planned, he'll come down here to find an unoccupied restroom which will be the larger handicap bathroom. Once he enters and settles in, I'll unlock the door and follow him."

Vito shook his head. "Just like that? And what if he puts up a fight?"

"I'll have the element of surprise. If I move fast, there shouldn't be much resistance."

"This is the most ridiculous idea you've ever had, Cesari. You're going to get us all tasered by the air marshals."

"I don't know about that," Jeremy offered. "It could work, but it would probably help if we created a distraction up front to occupy the flight attendants and passengers. We can't take a chance on anyone coming back here looking for coffee."

"That's not a bad idea," Cesari agreed. "What did you have in mind?"

Gerry gushed with excitement. "I could start a fight with someone. Just pick some random mope and slug him in the kisser. Then a quick knee to the nuts. That'll get everybody's attention."

Vito slapped him in the back of the head. "No, Gerry. Don't attack anybody. Understand? Aside from the possibility that there might be air marshals on the plane, there could be other passengers who feel compelled to intervene. You could start a riot, and we don't want that."

Gerry nodded.

Vito said more firmly, "Tell me you understand."

"I understand, boss."

"I appreciate your enthusiasm, Gerry, but we need a certain amount of finesse here," Cesari explained. "It'll work better."

Jeremy said, "How about this? After the guy passes to the rear bathrooms, I could go to the front of their section and pretend to fall and hurt my knee. Lots of groaning in pretend pain. I'll writhe around like I'm dying. Everyone will focus on me."

Cesari was impressed. "Macallan, you never cease to amaze me. I love that idea."

Jeremy beamed. "Glad I can help. What are you going to do with him once you get him alone is the question?"

"I don't know yet, but I'll think of something. Okay, battle stations. We're going to have to be patient. Vito and I need to stay out of sight for as long as possible. We have to assume that if they're following us that they know what we look like. I'll hang here and keep civilians away as best I can. Gerry and Jeremy, you two monitor the bathrooms on either side of the aisle from them and use your discretion. Vito will point the guy out to you and then return here to back me up. We'll be watching and waiting for you to signal us. Let's go."

Vito returned several minutes later and leaned against the bathroom door facing Cesari. "You're one hundred percent insane. Did you know that?"

Ignoring the barb, Cesari focused in on Vito's wing-tip dress shoes. "Are those Allen Edmonds?"

Vito looked down. "My shoes?"

"Are there any other kind of Allen Edmonds?"

"Yeah, they're Allen Edmonds. Seven hundred bucks a pair. Why?"

"I just had an idea. Give me one of your shoes."

"Why would I do that?"

"Because I'm wearing light weight shoes with rubber soles. Your shoes look like they would make a great billy club."

"You're going to bludgeon the guy with my shoe?"

"I could strangle him with my belt but that could get messy."

"Great. Now I get to stand here all night with my shoes off?"

"I only need one shoe."

Vito rolled his eyes, stepped out of his shoes, and handed over one of them. Cesari took it and weighed it in his hands. "Damn you have big feet. What are these, size fourteens? How do you wear these things? They're so heavy."

"They're well made. Supposedly, with proper care they'll last a lifetime."

Cesari tapped the heel and was impressed. "This is perfect. It's hard like a rock."

"For the record, this is a terrible idea."

"If you have a better one, I'm all ears."

"You realize of course that he may not have to use the bathroom and we'll be standing here all night for nothing."

"The thought crossed my mind."

"Can I at least go back to first class and get us a couple of cocktails?"

Cesari laughed. "Sure, why not? As long as you don't mind walking there in your bare feet."

An hour later, they were bored sitting on the floor on either side of the fuselage watching Gerry and Jeremy as they played with the bathroom signage depending on who approached. Vito's rocks glass was empty by his side. Cesari hadn't touched his scotch. Several passengers had stepped over them and used the bathrooms, but this was clearly a less frequented area of the plane. The unexpected popping in and out of flight attendants presented some challenges, but did not occur frequently enough for them to be overly concerned.

Suddenly, Cesari stood up. "Look alive, Vito, and get out of sight. Gerry just signaled me. The bald guy is coming down my side. Jeremy's heading up his side to begin the distraction."

Vito leapt to his feet and ducked forward into hiding. Cesari flipped the message to occupied on the door of the non-handicap bathroom and made sure the message read vacant on the handicap bathroom before joining Vito in hiding in the aisle opposite the one the man was traveling down.

It took longer than expected, and Cesari presumed the man probably stopped at the restroom nearest him and waited a few minutes before frustration set in and he decided to move on to the next nearest lavatory. In all, he arrived just over five minutes after Gerry's signal.

He was a big, mean looking guy in his early forties weighing in at around two hundred and forty pounds, with a shaved, not naturally bald head, a full beard and sideburns. He was well-built, muscular and rough around the edges. Cesari hoped he was right about this guy's past because things were about to get ugly. He must have had an urgent situation going on because he went right up to the occupied bathroom, pushed on the door, and became very annoyed when it didn't open. Realizing his error, he moved to the handicap bathroom, checked the sign and went in.

Cesari whispered to Vito, "Keep people out of here for a few minutes. Tell them you have friends with some type of GI bug and they're very sick in the restrooms and that it could be a while. Warn them that they could be contagious."

Vito nodded and Cesari walked up to the handicap bathroom, a size fourteen Allen Edmonds, classic wing tip in hand. In front of the door he collected himself and counted to ten. The sounds of a commotion filtered down to him from further up the plane and he smiled. Jeremy had sprung into action. He then gently lifted the metal lavatory plate and even more gently slid the button along its path. Once the vacant sign engaged, he rammed the door open forcefully and burst in. The guy was seated with his pants down around his ankles staring at his cellphone. The look of surprise on his face was indescribable as Cesari slammed the heel of Vito's shoe down on his forehead using all the force he could muster in the small confines of the room. Stunned but not out, the guy instinctively tried to kick out but was hampered by his awkward position. The second shot to his head, made his eyes roll upward and drop his phone, but he still had some fight left in him and attempted to punch Cesari in the groin.

Despite the man's great strength, the concussive effect of successive head blows made his counterattack weak and lacking steam. Still, Cesari winced as he whacked him again in the same spot and watched him slump to the side unconscious with an apricot sized lump rapidly developing on his head. Cesari closed the door behind him, picked up the cellphone and searched the guy quickly for ID. He found his wallet and passport in his pockets and scanned them. Booker P. Crisp. American, aged forty-two. Lots of airtime to the middle east and back. He had a veteran's ID card indicating he had been in the Marines, and his driver's license was registered in Washington D.C. The phone screen had turned off but Cesari pressed the man's limp fingertips against it until one of the prints gained him access.

There were numerous calls to a woman named Rosemarie and to a guy named Rufus, both of whom had D.C. area codes. Cesari next went through the guy's text messages and held his breath as he saw photos of Emily, Tierney, Vito and himself sent by the guy called Rufus.

Bingo!

Cesari entered the numbers into his own phone and then got to work. He didn't want this guy waking up and coming after him. Not being sure if he was left-handed or right handed, he snapped both of his thumbs causing the guy to groan but not wake up. Cesari thought that should keep him busy and certainly would make aiming a gun difficult. For good measure, Cesari gave him one last whack to the head to ensure that he wouldn't regain consciousness until the plane landed and because he just plain didn't like him. Maybe it was the beard? When he was done, Cesari poked his head out of the bathroom and Vito gave him the all clear sign. He exited and re-engaged the occupied sign. He had been in there less than five minutes. Not bad, he thought.

Vito said, "No problems on this end. Your pal, Jeremy, should go to Hollywood. He's got nearly the entire flight crew and half the passengers gathered round him. I only had to deal with one sleepy passenger and a curious flight attendant who was okay with the sick friend story. How'd it go in there?"

"Guilty as charged. He's ex-military from D.C. and had pictures of all of us on his phone."

"Damn... Is he dead?"

"No, but I slowed him down quite a bit. He's going to have a hell of a headache when he wakes up. I doubt he'll even remember what his last meal was. I took his passport for good measure. Even if he's able to walk off the plane, he won't be going far. I wish I could stick around and see what happens."

Cesari held the passport up for Vito to see.

"Damn, Cesari. Remind me not to piss you off. So we just leave him here with the occupied sign on?"

"Yeah, when the plane begins its final descent we'll need to change it back though. The flight attendants will be checking to make sure no one's in the lavatories during the landing, and if no one responds when they knock, they'll open the door and we'll be stuck in Italian airport hell."

"And if he wakes up before that?"

"One step at a time…"

"Fine, and the woman?"

"I don't think we need to do anything with her. She'll be occupied trying to figure out what happened to her friend, and besides, we know who she is now. The playing field has just levelled a little bit."

"The hunted have just become the hunters. Is that it?"

"Something like that."

As they returned to their seats, there was a tall guy with an athletic build helping Jeremy to his feet while a half dozen flight attendants watched.

Cesari signaled him that the show was over, and he pushed the guy away, growling with disdain, "Take your stinking paws off me you damn dirty ape."

Vito and Cesari glanced at each other. Vito said, "That sounded familiar."

Cesari laughed. "It should. He stole that line from the original, *Planet of the Apes*, movie."

"This guy, Macallan, is hysterical."

Chapter 33

"Robert B. Tierney, Gunnery Sergeant, United States Marine Corps. 158-54-2203."

Travis Burke, Grayson Morehouse, and Rufus Youngblood stood outside the interrogation room in the basement of Secret Service headquarters staring through the one-way glass. Inside was Detective Robert Tierney handcuffed to the table being interrogated by Angela Munoz. They had each taken a turn at him without coming away with anything more than a headache and a strong desire to reach across the table and throttle the cop.

Youngblood hissed through clenched teeth, "I swear to God. If he says that one more time, I'm going to waterboard him."

Burke said, "Take it easy, Rufus. You're not even supposed to be here, and if it wasn't for the extreme sensitivity of the situation and the impact it may have on the senator's political ambitions, you wouldn't be."

"I understand that, Travis, and thank you. The senator and I appreciate being granted this courtesy."

"Good, then no more talk about waterboarding an American citizen in the middle of Pennsylvania Avenue, even in jest.

Morehouse added dryly, "Besides, Rufus, I get the feeling Tierney might like it."

Burke asked speculatively, "Is he not well mentally? Perhaps we should bring in a psychiatrist?"

"I think he's just fine upstairs," commented Morehouse. "He knows exactly what he's doing."

"You think so?" chimed in Youngblood. "He's been in there eight hours and every question he answers with his name, rank and serial number. Given the severity of the charges he's facing, that doesn't seem entirely normal to me."

"He's a combat vet, Rufus, just like you," said Morehouse. "In his mind, he's at war, and we're the enemy."

Burke didn't look happy. "What do we do? Charge him? Turn him over to the FBI? We can't keep him here indefinitely?"

Youngblood snorted. "Do you really want this exploding all over the front page?"

"I have to agree with Rufus on that one," Morehouse agreed reluctantly. "Tierney knows everything and suspects even more. If we turn him over to the FBI for obstruction, conspiracy, harboring a fugitive, accomplice to murder or whatever, it will be a public relations nightmare. Every sordid detail we've been trying to contain will spread like metastatic cancer in an immunodeficient patient. We'll be roasted from one end of Washington to the other. The repercussions would be cataclysmic."

Youngblood was way more practical in his assessment. "And the senator's campaign will sink like the Titanic."

Burke shook his head in exasperation. "You can't expect me to just let him go. For God's sake, he kidnapped the Deputy Director of the Secret Service and held him at gunpoint."

"No one understands that better than me," Morehouse said. "But I honestly don't believe he had anything to do with Mills' or Claire's death. From his perspective, he's just trying to protect the daughter of a good friend from bad actors. The problem here is he thinks we're the bad actors. Can you imagine the firestorm if the media caught wind of that angle?"

"I can see that. He's David and we're Goliath. Jesus Christ, Grayson. This is getting more complicated by the minute."

"That it is, boss, but if we release him, he may take that as a sign of good faith which could potentially earn us his cooperation."

"You can't be serious?"

Rufus furrowed his brow in thought before saying, "I don't know, Travis. The idea has some merit. Since we're all in agreement that Tierney is more or less an innocent bystander, it may be to our advantage to let him run free and see where he takes us."

The director gave Rufus an incredulous look. "You too? Since when did Tierney become an innocent bystander? Two minutes ago you were talking about waterboarding him."

Rufus shrugged. "I've cooled off a little. Let's think about it. He's a cop and knows exactly the kind of hell we can bring down on him. He's obviously made up his mind he doesn't care what happens to him personally. Upon reflection, trying some honey instead of vinegar could work in this instance."

Morehouse said, "I agree. We're not going to get anywhere with him here and if we don't charge him, allow him access to legal counsel, or hand him over to the FBI soon, we could be charged with violating his civil rights."

Burke snorted derisively at that but softened his stance. "Fine, get him out of here, but put someone on him. I know you're spread thin, Grayson, but don't let him out of your sight."

Morehouse walked into the interrogation room with Munoz and Tierney. He held a plastic bin which he emptied onto the table in front of Tierney. His cellphone, wallet, badge, gun, belt, and loose change spilled out. Angela Munoz looked up in surprise.

As he released him from the handcuffs, Morehouse said to Tierney, "It's your lucky day, Detective. The director and I have decided we have more important things to do."

Tierney rubbed his wrist and tried not to look shocked. "Just like that?"

"Don't look a gift horse in the mouth, Tierney. Agent Munoz, join me in escorting the detective out of the building"

As Tierney walked through the front door, Morehouse pointed. "Union Station is in that direction. It's a healthy walk or a short cab ride. The Secret Service appreciates your cooperation, Detective, and thank you for all you've done for your country."

Tierney stifled back a laugh and walked briskly away. Once he was out of sight, Morehouse filled Munoz in on the Tierney saga.

"By the time, he buys his ticket and catches his train, it will take him at least five or six hours to reach his apartment. You and Ben can get there in three. I want you on him like a glove, Munoz. I want to know every move he makes, everywhere he goes, and everyone he talks to. If he goes into a public restroom, you send Ben in there with him."

"What if he doesn't return to Brooklyn?"

"He has to. He has that martini drinking cat, remember? He'll go there first to check on it and to make arrangements for boarding it somewhere if he plans on travelling. Given the state of his apartment, he can't just call someone to come in and cat sit."

She nodded. "And what if he takes off, as in tries to run?"

"I'm giving you wide latitude to use your discretion. Make sure you and Ben are loaded for bear. I don't think the detective is a bad guy but there are some really nasty people lurking in the background."

After she left, Morehouse summoned Dirk to his office. Ten minutes later, he asked, "What have you got for me, Dirk?"

Dirk said, "A lot but I'm not sure how it factors in. Less than two hours ago a friend of mine at the FBI who I've been massaging for information told me a co-worker was just called on the carpet for clandestinely running credit cards without authorization."

Morehouse was interested. "Continue, Dirk."

"Apparently, he was tracking Tierney's, Cesari's and even that mobster Gianelli's credit cards. No one over there knows why. He's been suspended pending an investigation. Apparently, he was freelancing and hasn't given up who he was working for yet."

Morehouse mulled that over for a minute. "Somebody must have made the connection between them and the Hoffman's, but who and why didn't they want anybody to know? So what did this agent find out?"

"Not a whole lot other than Gianelli purchased a bunch of plane tickets to Italy which left out of Toronto last night."

"Italy?"

"He landed in Rome an hour ago and is in route to Palermo as we speak."

"Who is he travelling with?"

"I called Air Canada. The guy I spoke with said he couldn't release the passenger list without a court order, but he did allow me to play twenty questions."

"Twenty questions?"

"Yeah, I say a name and he says yes or no. Gianelli and Cesari were on the plane, but not Emily Hoffman. I asked twice about her. In addition, I was able to find out that Gianelli has travelled back and forth to Sicily several times in the last couple of months. He's part owner in a new Sicilian restaurant in Manhattan and it may have something to do with that."

"I don't like the smell of this."

"You're going to like this even less. On a lark, I threw out another name just to see what would happen."

"And?"

"Rosemarie Zelle was on that flight as well."

Deputy Director Morehouse raised his eyebrows in astonishment. "Why is Mata Hari travelling with Gianelli and Cesari to Italy?"

Dirk shook his head. "I don't know."

Morehouse considered it for a long moment and then snapped his fingers. "Dirk, you find that guy in the FBI who was suspended and beat it out him who he was working for. Threaten him, cajole him, promise him amnesty, promise him death, promise him anything but get that name. It looks like we're going to Palermo."

Ben said, "What are you thinking?"

"I think Emily Hoffman is planning on having calamari overlooking the Mediterranean tonight, and I think Mata Hari is planning on putting a bullet in her brain while she does."

"But Emily's not even on the plane," argued Dirk.

"The hell she isn't."

****

The airbus 380 had touched down and disembarked most of its passengers by the time Rosemarie spotted Booker staggering down one of the aisles in a state of total dishevelment. He had finally woken up and staggered out of the bathroom not knowing or remembering anything that had happened. He had a purple lump on his head and both his thumbs were broken and swollen. His shirt was hanging out of his pants, and he was babbling. Rosemarie gathered him up and explained to the flight staff that he was prone to falling because of a medication he was on. Secretly, she was alarmed. They had been discovered. The flight crew helped Booker into a wheelchair, and she whisked him away.

Cesari was on the immigration line with the others and watched her from a safe distance as she maneuvered the big man in the wheelchair trying to decide what to do with him. They would never let him board the plane to Palermo like that and would demand he seek immediate medical attention. Even better, once the authorities realized he didn't have a passport, the shitstorm would begin in earnest. It was time to have some fun, but first things first. He walked over to the nearest trash can and tossed Booker's passport, wallet, and phone inside. He then took out his own phone, and dialed the number of the woman called Rosemarie and hoped it was her.

It was and she picked up immediately. "Who is this?"

He hung up. He just wanted confirmation as to who she was. Next he dialed the man called Rufus. It was 7:00 a.m. back in the states.

"Who is this?"

"Is this Rufus?"

"Who wants to know?"

"A friend with an international calling plan and a burner phone which I'm going to dispose of as soon as I end the call so don't bother trying to trace it."

"What do you want?"

"Who are you? CIA? NSA? Some sort of third-party black-ops asshat?"

"You don't know jack so cut it out. We don't care about you. Give up the girl and go in peace."

"That simple?"

"That simple."

"I think you should call Rosemarie. She and Booker are having some problems getting through customs. You really should consider hiring better quality people."

Then he hung up and watched as Rosemarie's phone buzzed almost immediately. She spoke animatedly, clearly frustrated at being on the wrong end of an operation gone sideways. As he reached the head of the line at immigration, he lost sight of her and pondered what would happen next if he were in her shoes. She and Rufus, whoever he was, would be pissed. She and Booker would miss the flight to Palermo but depending on who they worked for the situation could be potentially remedied without too much effort. If Rufus had pull, which Cesari was sure he did, he would contact the state department or the embassy and reissue Booker his passport. The question was would Rosemarie abandon Booker here in the airport and continue her pursuit of them alone. He thought that abandoning Booker would be a supremely bad idea. With a severe concussion, there would be no telling what he would say or who he would say it to. She would stay with him, he concluded, but not for long. Cesari estimated he would have no more than twenty-four hours before the bad guys were back on their trail, hotter than ever and now thirsting for revenge.

He sent a quick text to Tierney, committed the number to memory, and collected everyone's phones. Including his own, he tossed them all into the nearest trash can. He was concerned that if they could track the number he had been using, they might also be able to track the numbers of anyone he may have called or who may have called him. Maybe he was giving the other side too much credit. He didn't know. But the price of a few phones for added security seemed worth it. Once he had a new phone, he would reach out to Tierney to keep him in the loop. He knew the man would be worried sick if they suddenly went radio silent for a prolonged period.

An hour later, he was sipping prosecco on the short flight from Rome to Palermo watching the land mass of mother Sicilia come into view. Cesari was a forward viewing animal. He always had been. The past is the past. He never dwelt on things and had never been overly sentimental about his Sicilian roots. In his mind, his grandparents had left that island because they hadn't been treated well. They were poor uneducated farmers subjected to the whims of greedy landlords, corrupt politicians, nasty mafiosi and a host of other social parasites that plagued the average man. Why on earth would he be soppy about his family having fled poverty, crime and political oppression? But now that he was about to touch down in the land of his forefathers, he was beginning to feel a little tingly. He couldn't help it. Despite everything it felt like he was coming home, and he was starting to feel pretty good about it.

He turned to Jeremy and clinked his champagne flute with his. "You did a great job back there on the plane with your distraction."

"Thanks, but I think you did an even better job."

"Who was that big guy you did the, *take your dirty ape hands off me,* routine on?"

"He was an orthopedic surgeon on vacation. They found him in first class having a sloe gin fizz with his stripper girlfriend."

Cesari stared at him. "How did you know his girlfriend's a stripper?"

"I just assumed."

Chapter 34

Morehouse said, "We have a leak, Travis."

"What do you mean?"

"Somebody knew about the Gianelli, Cesari and Tierney connection and was doing a private investigation. A low-level agent at the FBI was caught running their credit cards without a warrant or specific authorization. The agent has been suspended, but as far as I know, no one at the bureau is aware of the connection between them and Mills, so he was freelancing. What I'm really concerned about is that the information could only have come from one of our people."

Burke clucked unhappily. "Not good. Do we know who or what prompted this agent at the FBI to perform such a task? He must have known that what he was doing was illegal."

"I'm sure the what was money or promises of career advancement, The who I'm working on. I sent Dirk over to his apartment to have a serious chat with him. I didn't want to get involved directly."

"That was smart. Is the leak someone on your team?"

"It could be anyone. An accidently dropped word here or there or a careless statement in the bathroom or at the water cooler. Perhaps a nosy co-worker with big ears, but I'm having the conference rooms, offices, and vehicles swept for listening devices just in case we have a bigger problem. We've retired all of our phones and laptops for new ones. In this day and age, it's almost impossible keep out determined prying eyes and ears."

Burke sighed. "Jesus... I'm getting tired of all the bull, Grayson."

Morehouse nodded sympathetically. "I hear you, boss."

"What do you think?"

"It could be someone inside the FBI itself who caught wind of our investigation heading in a different direction than theirs and decided to take independent action to see if we were on to something before sounding the alarm with his superiors."

"Or?"

"Or we've made someone very nervous. So nervous in fact that they've already sent someone to Italy to check things out."

"This Rosemarie Zelle spook?"

"Yes..."

"How is it the bad guys knew about this before we did?"

"I take full responsibility for that. I authorized my team to work discreetly in the background gleaning as much information as we could from the bureau without creating a buzz. To run the credit cards of three seemingly uninvolved citizens would have required accessing bureau assets and raising red flags. And had we gone through the backdoor, there would have been a shitstorm if we were exposed."

"Like the one that's about to take place with this suspended agent?"

"Exactly, so we decided to play it low key like a fly on the wall, but knowing we couldn't run down every lead the way we would have liked."

"Fine, and Emily Hoffman?"

"I think Emily Hoffman was on that plane under an assumed identity being protected by Cesari and Gianelli. I think that's the reason Tierney kept me and Munoz hostage all night in his apartment. He was buying them time to get to Toronto to catch their flight. And I think Rosemarie Zelle was sent to Italy to murder Emily."

"How sure are you she was on that plane?"

"I've never been more sure of anything in my life."

Burke took in a deep breath and exhaled slowly before saying, "And now you want to go to Italy to rescue Emily Hoffman?"

"Yes, I do."

"By yourself?"

"I was thinking of taking Agent Munoz with me. She's tailing Tierney right now, but she has backup."

Director Burke strummed his fingers on his desktop deep in thought. "I can't let you take Munoz. That would be way out of bounds for me to authorize an agent of her level and experience to pursue a murder suspect, and a CIA operative, no matter how evil, outside the borders of the United States. It could ruin her career before it even got off the ground."

Morehouse nodded. "I understand. Then I'll go alone."

"No, I'll accompany you. You'll need a wing man, and there's no better way to finish an illustrious career than with a great big bang and a high-profile collar. It'll do me good to get out in the field and will protect you from repercussions. I ordered you on this mission and accept full responsibility should it end disastrously. You had absolutely no choice, understand?"

Morehouse was stunned, relieved, and thrilled at the same time. "Let's give them hell, boss."

****

Teresa had a third floor, three-bedroom apartment in the heart of bustling downtown Palermo off a narrow side street. Nearby was the Teatro Massimo, Italy's largest and by far grandest opera house, built to honor King Victor Emanuel II who unified Italy in 1861 through a combination of politics and military might. Bringing the then Pope Pius IX to heel was slightly more difficult as he was used to running things his way in and around Rome. He excommunicated Victor Emanuel and defiantly declared himself a prisoner of the Vatican after Victor Emanuel's forces marched triumphantly into Rome in 1870. Fortunately for Victor Emanuel's eternal soul, the excommunication was lifted years later, shortly before his death.

Once they had settled in, Emily went to her bedroom to clean up from the long flight. Cesari said, "All right, Emily gets a bedroom, Teresa gets a bedroom, Jeremy and Jaskaran, can flip a coin over who gets the third bedroom. The loser gets the sofa. Vito and I will get a room at the closest hotel."

"Where does that leave me?" asked Gerry.

Vito said, "The floor carpet looks pretty cozy. Maybe Teresa can get you a pillow and a blanket."

Teresa said with a touch more sympathy, "The leather chair next to the sofa can fully recline and is quite comfortable. I've slept on it often."

Cesari added, "No sleeping until we say, Gerry. We still have a lot to do. For now, this is the plan. Jaskaran and Jeremy, I want you to stay with Emily in the apartment. Gerry, you hang in the lobby or just outside the building. There's a bench downstairs you can sit on. You all know who's looking for us; a really big guy, bald with two broken thumbs and a lump on his forehead, and a woman, five feet four inches tall, with short blonde hair and a bandage on her face. We can't be sure there aren't others, so be alert. Vito, Teresa, and I are heading out to procure weapons and phones. We'll need her to guide us around. In the meanwhile, everybody lay low."

Jaskaran who was staring into an empty refrigerator, asked, "Would it be all right if I went out for groceries? Supplies are a little low."

Teresa said, "I am sorry for the no food. We have been gone from Sicily now almost one week and were planning on being away longer. There is dried pasta and canned tomatoes in cabinets, wine, and also espresso."

She walked to one of the overhead cabinets and opened the door revealing a variety of canned and boxed products. She then pointed to lower cabinets and drawers saying, "Pots and pans are below, but there are many grocery stores and markets within walking distance if you desire."

Cesari thought about it and said, "I think it would be okay if you went out for some fresh produce... You in the mood to do some cooking?"

"Lamb vindaloo is comfort food where I come from. I thought it might work here."

"Ahh, I see," said Teresa. "There are multiple Indian shops and markets maybe ten-minute walk from here on Via Roma. It is our version Little India, and you will find excellent products there."

"All right everyone, stay alert," said Cesari. "See you all in a couple of hours."

Cesari, Vito, and Teresa went to the basement of the apartment building where Teresa had her car garaged while Gerry assumed his position in the front foyer and Jaskaran went shopping.

Teresa drove a five-year-old military green Fiat Panda 4x4 hatchback, Italy's version of a sub-compact SUV. It was a little over half the length and three quarters the width of a Suburban. When you're used to driving big cars on big highways, the Panda seemed tiny, but in a city like Palermo where all the roads were narrow, all the cars were small, motorcycles harassed you in every direction and traffic laws were just a suggestion, it didn't take long for the Panda to grow in stature and feel like a tank.

Cesari sat in the back, Vito scrunched his bulk into the passenger seat, and Teresa stepped on the gas heading toward the Brancaccio district five kilometers away. The Brancaccio neighborhood was Palermo's equivalent to an L.A. barrio, Chicago's Southside or one of Paris's no-go zones. It was an area of poverty and anger nurtured by crime and drugs. The police more or less stayed out of it as long as the animals stayed in their cages. But should the violence and rapine seep out of the borders of the Brancaccio into greater Palermo, the men in riot gear armed with cannisters of tear gas and rubber bullets would swoop in and harshly bust skulls until order was restored. Then would follow weeks of rounding up and harassing, rightly or wrongly, local mafiosi who governed the Brancaccio until the crime lords convinced the local government they would better control their enclave. This was the last remaining stronghold in Palermo of the ever weakening cosa nostra in Sicily.

Once inside the Brancaccio, the scenery changed dramatically, starting with graffiti everywhere and the sudden appearance of the homeless congregating in alleys. The streets were littered with debris and rubbish. Boarded up windows and storefronts attested to the desolation and hopelessness to which the area had sunk. If it wasn't for the palm trees and baroque styled architecture, the scene resembled any inner city anywhere. Not quite as severe and bombed out as a Detroit ghetto, this was a place where drugs poured in and money flowed out. Prostitutes either launched or ended their careers here. Anything and everything was for sale. The insanity of it all was that the cash that fueled the many vices came from the outside. Visitors like them from the more affluent parts of the city who came in to pick up whatever it was they needed to get a thrill and then drove off again as fast as they could.

They were relatively safe because even in this primitive world there were rules. Number one rule was don't kill the golden goose. It would scare off other customers and bring the police in on them like hornets. Rule number two was don't make a lot of noise. Their business was best performed in the shadows. Rule number three was a deal was a deal. Once prices were agreed upon there was no turning back or negotiating.

Pulling her car to the curb, Teresa said, "We are here."

Chapter 35

"This place doesn't look too bad to me," commented Vito.

Teresa was apprehensive, her eyes darting nervously in every direction. It was late afternoon, and the sun, although still high in the sky, had begun its arc downward. Traffic was light at this time of the day and would pick up dramatically once dark descended. They had been sitting in the Panda for thirty minutes and no one had approached, but they could all feel unseen eyes on them, assessing them, speculating. Another hour passed and the waning sun glimmered weakly as it kissed them good night over the horizon.

Cars began piling into the neighborhood, some stopping ahead and some behind. Others ventured deeper into the territory seeking less trafficked areas. Street walkers appeared out of thin air approaching vehicles and negotiating transactions. Drug runners tapped on car windows to take orders. Money exchanged hands and little plastic bags were handed over. It was all very peaceful and orderly. Deeper in the district, brothels specializing in S&M, illegal gambling and much darker vices thrived. The sex trade was alive and well in this part of the world.

A swarthy character in jeans and a tee shirt sauntered up to their car and Vito rolled down his window. He was thirty, emaciated with bad teeth and even worse breath. He said something in Sicilian and Teresa leaned over to translate.

Vito said, "Tell him we're not here for drugs or girls. We need guns."

Teresa spoke to the guy in her native tongue and said, "He say guns are expensive. Bring lots of trouble to Brancaccio."

Vito nodded. "Tell him I have plenty of money and if I get angry the Brancaccio will have even more trouble."

The guys eyes went wide as she translated the warning, but he calmly replied and then walked away. Teresa said, "He needs to talk over with boss."

Five minutes later, the guy came back and said something to Teresa. She said, "He wants five thousand euros, and he will bring weapons."

Vito snapped at the guy with Teresa translating. "You want five thousand euros for what? I have a right to know what I'm paying for."

"He say, 'This is how we do in Brancaccio. You no like, then go Walmart.'"

Vito asked, "There are Walmarts here?"

Teresa shook her head. "No, he is be sarcastic."

Vito's features darkened and he got out of the car. Cesari followed without being asked. Together they towered over the man, Vito a full head taller and at least a hundred pounds heavier. He stared the guy down with a menacing scowl and then retrieved a thick envelope from his suitcoat. He counted out twenty-five one hundred-dollar bills in crisp new American currency.

He handed it to the guy and said, "Teresa tell him half now and half when I see the guns. And I don't care that it's not in euros. Take it or leave it."

The guy rolled his eyes but accepted the money and walked away. They waited ten full minutes before three different men came back. One was as large as Vito, another slightly less so. The third was average sized but wiry and nasty looking. The original guy was nowhere to be seen. These three were better dressed and kept. The smaller guy held a brown paper shopping bag. The bigger men were obviously muscle. They stood to the side.

The guy with the bag stepped up to Vito and sized him up. He spoke broken English and said, "The Brancaccio is no a very good place to cause the trouble."

If the guy was attempting to intimidate Vito, he had failed miserably. Vito said contemptuously, "Who the fuck are you and where's the guy who took my money?"

"I am Bernardo and this is my quartiere."

Vito wasn't impressed. "Teresa. Please translate for me so there's no chance of a misunderstanding… Tell Bernardo that I didn't come here to make trouble. I came here to make a purchase. Now, he either has my merchandise or he doesn't. If he doesn't then I suggest he refund my money or I'm going to ram my foot up his guinea ass."

Teresa hesitated and let out an audible groan but translated anyway. All three of the goons registered surprise and then anger but no one came at him or pulled out a weapon. Bernardo held Vito's gaze for a few seconds and then handed the bag to him. Vito took it and looked inside.

There was a partially rusted, old Colt revolver with a worn black walnut grip and six bullets, an even older .32 caliber Walther PPK with one eight-round clip, and a sawed off over under twelve gauge with five shells. Vito shook his head and looked at the guy.

"If this is a joke, I'm not laughing. You expect five thousand dollars for this crap? C'mon… I need more than three bullshit weapons like this or at least some more ammo."

Bernardo glanced at his companions and started to laugh. Then he turned back to Vito. "Where do you think you are? At NRA convention in Texas? This is Palermo. Is good deal. As you say before, take or leave, but if you leave then you leave twenty-five hundred dollars poorer as compensation for all the aggravation you have caused."

While they haggled, Cesari noticed two guys crossing the street toward the driver's side door of the Panda. Both held baseball bats. Teresa didn't see them because she was leaning over to Vito's open window to help translate. Clearly, that couldn't be good. He cleared his throat and said, "Vito, pay the guy and let's go."

Bernardo sneered. "Your friend is smart man. You should listen to him."

Vito glanced over his shoulder, saw the men coming and understood. Negotiations were over. He reached into his jacket and came out with another twenty-five hundred dollars. Bernardo counted it out and said nothing. He just turned around and walked back to the hole from whence he came. The two guys with the bats saw the deal conclude to their boss's satisfaction, stopped in the center of the street, and slowly melted back into the shadows.

Cesari and Vito got back in the car and Teresa sped off, breathing hard from fear and excitement. As they reentered civilization, Vito said, "What an asshole that guy was."

Teresa looked at Vito with her eyes wide. "You are pazzo, cugino. You could have gotten us all killed."

He replied, "That would have drawn a lot of attention which you said they don't like to do."

"No, of course not, but they do so all the time anyway. Especially Bernardo. He don't care about anything. I never like him. He is sadist."

Vito gave her a look of surprise. "You know that sleazebag?"

"Of course. Everybody knows everybody in Palermo. Besides, he is Ernesto's cousin."

"You've got to be kidding?"

"I no kid. They are very close. Bernardo no like if you hurt Ernesto."

"I'll keep that in mind."

Cesari added, "I think we should go get some phones and then stop at a hardware store."

Vito glanced over his shoulder at him. "Why a hardware store?"

"I'd rather have a crowbar than a rusted old pistol."

****

Dirk entered the apartment building and took a deep breath, rehearsing in his mind what he would say. Agent Timothy Bragg was a twenty-eight-year-old analyst with the Bureau four years and apparently in good standing. Single, middle of his class at Quantico, he had never been in the field although he had applied several times. When he got caught illegally tracing the credit cards, he at first acted like he had no idea what they were talking about but the overwhelming evidence of his digital footprint caused him to change tactics and he soon decided to not say anything to anyone other than he was working alone on an anonymous tip. This raised eyebrows even more and he was suspended without pay pending an internal investigation. The idea was to give him a few days to cool his heels and stew in his own juices until he came clean because no one understood why he was interested in Gianelli, Cesari and Tierney. No one knew that Tierney had been in the basement of Secret Services headquarters all night.

Dirk was fascinated by Bragg's reluctance to come forward on what he was doing and whom he was doing it for. It was possible that Bragg wasn't given any background or context on the relationship of the three names. In fact, that was probably very likely, but certainly he didn't expect anyone to believe that he pulled three random names out of his ass to spy on. Which begged the question of who was he protecting? Someone who could make or break his career was the only conclusion Dirk could come to. A suspension, a slap on the wrist, a possible warning in his file would be better than total career annihilation.

Taking the elevator up to the tenth floor, he found the apartment, rang the buzzer and rapped on the door several times. No one answered. It was 10:00 a.m. He might have gone out for coffee or to consult with an attorney. Maybe he was jogging? But Dirk didn't like the feel of it. He had tried calling but Bragg didn't answer and all the calls went to voicemail, and now this. What did it mean? Was the guy hiding under his bed? Did he bolt for some reason? Why would he do that? He was in trouble for sure but nothing that wasn't survivable, Dirk thought. Especially for a guy in good standing. Certainly, he wasn't looking at anything prosecutable.

Dirk tested the knob and to his surprise it wasn't locked. The handle turned gently, and Dirk pushed the door open. He scanned the empty apartment as much as he could from his vantage point before stepping over the threshold into uncharted waters. He called out but no one answered. The question now was had he just broken the law himself? That was an interesting constitutional vagary. He didn't break anything and if he didn't take anything just exactly what law did he break? It wasn't as if there was a no trespassing sign on the front door. That last thought caused him to crack a quiet grin. He was getting good at sleuthing.

Closing the door behind him, he looked around the empty living room and kitchen. Not a whole lot going on here which was to be expected in a bachelor's apartment. There was a rowing machine facing a window and a large flat screen TV juxtaposed to the sofa. On the kitchen table was an open bottle of pinot noir and a wine glass three quarters filled. Dirk took long strides toward the closed bedroom door and gently knocked on it.

No answer.

He turned the knob and the door swung inward with a low creaking sound. Lying under the sheets on the queen-sized bed was agent Timothy Bragg peacefully at rest with his eyes closed. Except he wasn't resting. He was dead. Or was he? His skin was white and cold and there was a half empty bottle of Jack Daniels on his night stand next to a mostly empty bottle of pills. The smell of booze was everywhere.

Dirk picked up the unlabeled bottle and studied the remaining pills. There were several pills left. He took one out and held it up to the light.

Fentanyl 200 mcg.

Bragg was a drug addict? Dirk took the man's pulse. It was weak and thready but still there. He leaned close to the man's face and felt the hint of a breath. He was still alive. Dirk took a few seconds to think it over. Something didn't feel right at all. Who opens a bottle of pinot noir, pours himself a glass, doesn't drink it and then goes straight to the bedroom to overdose with a bottle of whiskey and fentanyl?

Dirk suddenly felt very cold as his heart pounded and his mind raced. He reached for his cellphone not sure whether he should dial 911 or the Deputy Director. If he didn't engage the authorities immediately then he really would have stepped over the line. Making his decision, he hit the buttons, and as the line rang, he felt a sharp pain in the back of his head causing him to fall forward over agent Bragg's comatose form.

Unconscious, his phone slipped from his hand just as someone answered, "Emergency services, how can we help you?"

Chapter 36

Rufus Youngblood picked up Dirk's phone with a gloved hand and disguising his voice, spoke to the emergency dispatcher, "Everything's all right. The call was made in error. I'm sorry for the inconvenience."

He listened for a moment and responded, "Yes, I'm quite certain. Thank you. I'll be more careful next time."

Rufus disconnected the line and placed the phone in his pocket as he looked at Dirk lying on the bed. What to do? He hadn't anticipated being interrupted like this and kicked himself for not locking the door when he arrived. He knew Bragg was upset and that was to be expected. Who wouldn't be? No one ever expects to get caught, but he had managed to keep him calm and had come over to plan strategy with him to bolster his courage. In one pocket, he had ten thousand dollars in cash as an incentive for him to keep quiet and in his other pocket he had the fentanyl, purchased easily on the streets, just in case he judged Bragg a poor risk.

He had found Bragg in a state of near frantic anxiety, trying to calm himself with wine in the middle of the morning. His nerves were frayed so badly, he was shaking as he filled his glass. Rufus had decided to act quickly and decisively, herding the man at gunpoint into his own bedroom and force feeding him the bottle of illicit fentanyl. Bragg hadn't revealed who had solicited his help tracking Gianelli and Cesari's credit cards but that would only be a matter of time. Sooner or later, Bragg would have come to the realization that Rufus wasn't going to come to his rescue. He simply couldn't do that without the whole thing unraveling and then to save his own skin, Bragg would spill his guts. Bragg had become a loose end that needed tidying up. He had barely got the man under the sheets when he heard the sound of Dirk entering the apartment and calling out.

Watching from a crack in the bathroom door, he had hoped Dirk would simply hightail it out of there, but Dirk had chosen the higher road and dialed EMS. He hadn't wanted to hurt Dirk, but he couldn't afford to be trapped there waiting for an ambulance. Now he studied the situation through fresh eyes, as always, trying to determine if he could somehow turn events to his advantage.

After a moment or two, it occurred to him that the scene presented some possibilities for subterfuge. If he arranged things just right, he could keep them spinning their wheels for weeks, months and maybe forever. Of course, there was no circumstance in which agent Bragg could come out of this alive, but Dirk Bradbury could. He may wish he hadn't though because he was about to be thrust into black-ops hell.

He searched Dirk for his service pistol, and found a Glock 19, fully loaded and ready to go. Then he placed a pillow over Bragg's chest and pressed the barrel hard into it just about where his heart was and pulled the trigger. The bang was loud though muffled by the pillow. Bragg's body lurched and fell back limp with a final shudder. As the smell of cordite filled the confined area, blood oozed from the wound, seeping out onto the burnt pillowcase.

Rufus picked up the fentanyl bottle and placed it in his pocket as the new plan began to emerge. Initially, he thought to make it look like a disgraced agent committed suicide rather than face the music. Granted, committing suicide over an illegal credit card search seemed extreme, but one never knew what was going on in the heart and mind of a high-strung young man whose career trajectory had just taken a turn for the worse. Everyone knew the youth of today had no coping skills. This new theatric was highly appealing.

There was a reading chair in the bedroom and Rufus hoisted Dirk's unconscious body into it, sitting him up as best he could. Dirk groaned and stirred slightly. Rufus didn't want him waking up too soon and thought about how best to manage that. Another blow to the head and it would be obvious that Dirk was the victim and not the aggressor. Then he had an idea and went to the bathroom, returning with a glass of water.

Gently shaking Dirk, he called his name as if he were waking him for the school bus. After several attempts, Dirk gradually responded with eyes barely fluttering open and then closing. Good enough, Rufus thought and reached into his pocket for the remaining fentanyl pills. There were six left. Twelve hundred mcg all at once should knock out a non-addict for hours, maybe even put him in a coma. Hell, it might even kill him. Rufus smiled. It was a risk he was willing to take.

He shook Dirk again and said, "Open your mouth, Dirk."

Semiconscious, Dirk obeyed the command and Rufus slipped the little pills in and raised the glass of water to his mouth. "Dirk, take a sip and swallow. Okay?"

Dirk sipped weakly, coughed, and gagged a little but swallowed the pills. He slumped back into the chair and closed his eyes. Rufus watched for a full ten minutes until he was satisfied that he wasn't going anywhere fast. He was wearing latex gloves and although he wasn't worried about leaving his own prints, he was concerned that he may have smeared Dirk's and he didn't want to leave any doubt in anyone's mind about who shot who. So he pressed the Glock into Dirk's hand, rolled it around and then placed it on the floor by the side of the chair. As a last measure, he placed the empty fentanyl bottle in Dirk's pocket along with the envelope containing the ten thousand dollars.

Rufus was delighted at his work. He could just see the D.C. police and FBI losing it over this. An FBI analyst gets suspended for wrongdoing and before the investigation even begins, he's murdered by a drug addled Secret Service agent found with a wad of unexplained cash on him. The possibilities were endless. Assuming he lived, Dirk would deny it all, but it was his gun with his prints on it and fentanyl in his blood stream. And then there was the cash… True, he had a bump on his head, but no one would care about that.

As he left the apartment, Rufus dialed 911again using Dirk's phone. This time, when the dispatcher answered, Rufus pretended to be hysterical. Despondently, he cried almost unintelligibly into the receiver, "I've done something terribly wrong."

After babbling the address of where he was, he hung up and thought things over. Timothy Bragg was no longer a problem, and it was now time for Detective Tierney. He would be a bit more challenging than Bragg, and possibly messier, but that's why he was paid the big ones. He didn't like the idea of taking down a fellow combat veteran, but Tierney had invited this on himself. Gunny Tierney was screwing with things he knew he shouldn't be and just wouldn't let go. He sensed that long after the dust had settled Tierney would still be raising Cain about it, and that couldn't be allowed. The detective needed a long-term solution.

He glanced at his watch. He could be in Manhattan by sundown, take care of Tierney and catch the next flight out of JFK to help Rosemarie and Booker. Those two had fucked up royally in sunny Italy and now he had to go there to make things right. His adrenaline was flowing. It felt good to be on a hell-raising mission again. The quiet combat in the halls of congress was much too tame for him.

****

Tierney peeked out from the side of his window at the Ford Taurus parked on the street below. Angela Munoz and another agent he didn't recognize had been watching his apartment all day and it was starting to piss him off. They had even followed him to the supermarket earlier when he purchased ammonia and other cleaning products to wash the bloodstains off his floor. They were either lousy at surveillance or they wanted him to know they were there as a form of clumsy intimidation. He wasn't sure. The Secret Service's main function was to protect important people and their families, most notable of course was the president of the United States. After that, they investigated cyber and financial crimes with a little bit of this and a little bit of that thrown in. Clandestine monitoring of suspects probably wasn't very high in their training, but this was less than subtle even for the unskilled. Still, he was grateful they had let him go even though he knew it was only because they hoped he would lead them straight to Emily. He had fully expected to be charged with numerous crimes and handed over to the FBI. To be walking around a free man was a perk he hadn't expected. He was also thoroughly relieved that Emily had made it out of the country safely, but remained apprehensive at a cryptic text he had received from Cesari when they had arrived in Rome.

Landed safely but we had company. Dealing with it.

What the fuck did that mean? When he tried to text back and call, there was no response. In fact, no one was answering their phones. He didn't like that and had fretted about it most of the afternoon. While he mused, his own phone rang. It was an unknown number from Philadelphia. He decided to answer and was glad he did. It was Fred Hoffman calling from his hospital bed in Lansdale.

"Gunny, you all right?" Fred Hoffman whispered, his voice weak and hoarse.

"I'm good, Fred. You had us all worried."

"Never mind me. How's Emily?"

"She's safe Fred."

"Are you with her?"

"No, I didn't think that would be wise. They're watching me, but I have good people with her."

"Don't tell me where. I'm so doped up with pain meds I'd tell anybody anything. And don't come here to visit me. The doctors tell me I'm going to be okay. Whatever it is you're doing to protect Emily, keep doing it. I don't need to know the details. Reassure her that I'm okay and I'm thinking about her. Right now, all I need to know is that you're doing everything in your power to keep my daughter safe."

"I am and I will, Fred."

"Then I can mourn my wife in peace. When this is all over, we'll have a beer, Gunny. Just like in Baghdad."

"You got it, Fred."

Tierney hung up and sat down on his sofa, resting his head back, staring at the ceiling. His best friend's daughter's life had been placed squarely in his hands and he had no idea what was going on except for the ambiguous message from Cesari. He was very uncomfortable with sitting on the sideline waiting. Suddenly he leapt to his feet, went to his bedroom, found his passport, and threw some toiletries and a change of clothes into a small duffle bag. He thought about bringing his handgun in a secure lockbox, but decided that he wasn't familiar enough with Italian law and might get into a hassle with customs. Not wanting to risk an interaction with Italian authorities, he decided to leave his weapon.

He found Stonewall's pet carrier and packaged him inside. Letting out a deep breath, he felt better. Inaction was never his strong suit. For better or for worse, he decided that if somebody was going to hurt Emily, they were going to have to go through him first, and it wasn't going to be pretty. Armed or unarmed, he was nearly equally proficient at killing. His adrenaline flowing, he sprinted down the staircase and across the street with Stonewall and his duffle bag. Munoz rolled down her window as he approached, staring at him and the cat in utter confusion.

He came to a halt three feet from the side of the car. Munoz asked, "Can I help you, Detective?"

"Are you one of the good guys, Munoz?"

"Of course, I am. We all are. It's what we've been trying to tell you. Where are you going with Stonewall?"

"As long as I'm not under arrest, I decided to take Stonewall on a much-needed vacation."

She looked surprised. "Where?"

"I haven't decided yet. I might just flip a coin when I get to the airport, but here's the thing. There are a lot of bad guys out there and some of them are looking for me. Right now, I haven't been charged with a crime, and your boss told me I was free to go. I haven't made any threats against one of your protectees and as far as I know I'm not suspected of any financial crimes, and yet here you are following me."

"You're very observant, Detective. Once again, how may I help you?"

"I'm thinking that your right to tail me is on extremely shaky legal grounds, and certainly you would have no jurisdiction outside the country."

"Maybe you should leave our legal rights up to the DOJ if it ever comes up."

Tierney nodded and smiled thinly. "Far be it for me to question how the Secret Service operates, but I will tell you how I operate. Once I'm outside the borders of the U.S. I might start thinking that anyone stalking me should be considered one of the bad guys. Does that make sense? I'm only telling you because I kind of like you and wouldn't want you to get hurt."

"Are you threatening the Secret Service, Detective?"

"Not at all. I'm trying to be nice by letting you know how I think. Granted, I have a fair amount of PTSD superimposed on natural paranoia. But if you combine that with recurring night terrors and an occasionally flimsy grip on reality, I can sometimes be a handful, if you know what I mean?"

Munoz stared at him and blinked. "Thanks for the head's up."

"Good, now would you mind giving me a ride to JFK?"

"You can't be serious?"

"Why not? You're going to follow me there anyway, aren't you?"

Chapter 37

After their shopping spree in the Brancaccio, they returned to Teresa's apartment to distribute the new cellphones and weapons. Vito saw Gerry in the lobby and gave him the sawed-off shotgun admonishing him to keep it out of sight in the shopping bag. In the apartment, they were greeted by the strong aroma of lamb in a curry sauce. Vito went off with Teresa to call Ernesto and arrange a meeting with him and Rosaria while Cesari entered the kitchen.

He found Emily sipping wine with Jeremy at the table. They had found a deck of playing cards and appeared to be engrossed in a hand of gin rummy. But nothing could have prepared him for the sight at the stove. Jaskaran was sautéing zucchini in olive oil with a wooden spoon. He was wearing an old-fashioned khaki military uniform of the Punjabi army that probably hadn't seen the light of day since the British Empire controlled half the world. Complementing the outfit were leather boots with leg wrappings, a shoulder strap with an empty pistol holder, a foot long curved blade in a scabbard tucked through his belt and a massive saffron colored turban, easily twice the size of anything Cesari had ever seen him wear. He looked about eight feet tall in it. His beard was fluffed out to maximum effect, and he was grinning from ear to ear.

Cesari's jaw dropped as he studied his friend from top to bottom. Eventually he said, "I assume there's some explanation?"

Emily smiled. "I think he looks great."

Jaskaran explained, "I was shopping for groceries when I came across this Indian store that specialized in traditional clothing and ceremonial costumes. Since we're at war, I thought I'd look the part. More importantly, if Emily wears the clothes we got for her and I wear this, we'll definitely pass for an authentic Indian couple."

Cesari nodded. "More like an Indian couple going to a Halloween party, don't you think? Won't you attract a lot of attention with that outfit?"

Jaskaran laughed. "Very funny, Cesari, but that's the idea. Hide in plain sight. This way Emily and I can go outside once in a while or else she's going to go stir crazy. Sure, it will seem a little curious to people, but no one will expect someone in hiding to run around like this."

"Maybe... I'm not sure I'm one hundred percent on board with this plan, but I agree with Emily. You do look great. So what are you supposed to be?"

Jaskaran clicked his heels, snapped to attention and saluted. "Sir, I am no longer Jaskaran Singh M.D., pain management doctor extraordinaire and slave of the American empire's healthcare system. I am now Major Jaskaran Singh of the 36th Sikh Regiment of the British Indian Army, hero of the Battle of Saragarhi and the slayer of many muslims. Long live Queen Victoria!"

Emily clapped. Jeremy guffawed, "He's been doing that all afternoon."

Cesari grinned. "Excellent, but you may want to drop the slayer of many Muslims thing. This is Palermo. Muslims have been here a lot longer than Indians. Nice turban by the way. I love the color."

"I knew you would. In Hindi, it is called Kesari with a K. I thought you could relate to that since you're Cesari with a C."

"You're killing me, Jaskaran," Cesari laughed. "Is the knife real?"

"Yes, it is called a kirpan which is a traditional Sikh blade. Every Sikh has one. Usually they're just ceremonial but this one is real and very deadly."

He unsheathed the long-curved knife and presented it to Cesari who examined it carefully, gingerly testing its sharpness. "Damn, Jaskaran, you could hurt someone with this."

"I thought that's the idea."

He handed the knife back and said, "Yes, it is... I have some handguns for you guys just in case the knife isn't sufficient. They're not the greatest but they'll slow someone down well enough."

He handed Jeremy the Walther PPK and Jaskaran the Colt .45 saying, "The cowboy gun should fit right into your holster, Jaskaran. And, Jeremy, the Walther is James Bond's preferred pistol. I can picture you in your smoking jacket, holding a dry vodka martini in one hand and the Walther in the other."

The two men took their respective weapons and examined them. Jeremy astutely asked, "Is this all the ammo we get?"

"Unfortunately, yes. So, there won't be any practice sessions."

Jeremy studied his piece suspiciously, "How do you know it even works? It looks ancient."

"It is ancient, but it's all we have."

"Great…"

"At least you have a gun. All I have is a crowbar, but hopefully we won't need anything."

"You think?" said Emily. "They followed us all the way to Rome. They must know we're in Sicily."

"I think that's safe to assume, but they don't know where nor do they know that we haven't moved yet again to some other exotic place. Sicily may have just been a port in the storm. For all anybody knows, we're already halfway to Istanbul."

She nodded. "I hope."

Cesari concurred. "Hope is a good thing, but a solid plan is better."

"And we have a solid plan?"

"I'm working on it."

Jaskaran took a cast iron pot out of the oven and said, "Lamb vindaloo anyone?"

****

Munoz was in a quandary as to what to do. Morehouse wasn't answering his phone and she assumed he was enroute to Italy and had his phone turned off. She had dropped Tierney off at JFK because she didn't see any reason not to, and what better way to keep an eye on him? She knew exactly where he was and now she knew exactly where he was going. Exiting the car, he had made a bee line for the Alitalia counter without being particularly secretive about it.

After he purchased his ticket, he walked right up to her and said, "See you in Palermo, Munoz, but remember what I said about my PTSD."

She had figured that's where he was heading before he even said anything. Apparently, anybody who was anybody was going there. But after he had disappeared through security, a very peculiar thing happened. Rufus Youngblood, the chief of staff for Senator Taylor, came rushing through the terminal and up to the same Alitalia counter. He was so preoccupied with whatever mission he was on, he failed to notice Munoz standing there with her mouth open in astonishment. Quickly recovering, she blended into a crowd of people and observed him purchase a ticket and then wander off to security check-in. She had no doubt that he had just booked the same flight as Tierney, but why? Why was he even in New York? This was turning into an amazing evening. Did Tierney know Rufus was coming along? Did Rufus know Tierney was on that flight? Interesting questions.

Her phone rang. It was Elaine Monroe, Chief Operating Officer and acting director of the Secret Service in the absence of the Director and Deputy Director. "Agent Munoz, have you heard?"

"No ma'am. Heard what?"

"Dirk Bradbury is under arrest for murder and is now recovering from a fentanyl overdose at Georgetown University Medical Center. The paramedics got to him just in time and were able to revive him with Narcan."

Munoz gasped, "I don't understand."

"Well I need you to start understanding quickly. I just got off the phone with the director of the FBI and the D.C. police chief. Dirk is being charged with shooting an FBI agent in the heart in the said agent's bedroom. The director and deputy director can't be reached at the moment, but I do know you were working with Dirk on an assignment. I need you to come in immediately and brief me as to what that assignment was and how that could have led Dirk to the apartment of a suspended analyst."

"But…"

"No buts, Munoz," the acting director interrupted with startling clarity. "You are to come in immediately. Do you understand?"

"Yes, ma'am. I'm in New York City. It will take me four hours minimum."

"Why are you in New York?"

"It was part of the assignment Dirk and I were working on."

"I see… You have four hours, Munoz, and then I want to know what's going on. Just to be crystal clear because I know it's late, I don't care what time it is when you arrive. You are to seek me out the minute you arrive."

Munoz clicked off in horror. Her heart was pounding. What the hell happened to Dirk? Why would he shoot anyone? And fentanyl? That was illogical. She had known him since the academy. He was as strait-laced as they came. She couldn't just run back to D.C. and spill her guts, but what choice did she have? Until the director and the deputy director landed and were back online, Elaine Monroe was her direct superior, and she had just given her a very direct and unequivocal command.

She left the terminal and got in the car with Ben, instructing him to drive back to Secret Service headquarters in D.C. Pulling away from the curb, Ben asked, "Did you find out where Tierney's going?"

"He actually told me himself. He's going to Palermo."

"He told you? Just like that?"

"Walked right up to me and showed me his boarding pass."

"Boy, he's got a pair."

"Extra large, it seems. He also read me the riot act again about following him."

"Damn…"

"I'm not concerned. I read people very well. Deep down, he's a boy scout. He wouldn't hurt me."

"Still…"

Changing the subject, she asked, "Ben, did Elaine Monroe call you today?"

He furrowed his brow, puzzled. "No, why would she?"

That was interesting. So, she didn't know Ben was part of the team. That was good. "I was just curious. You know, with everyone out of town, I thought she might have checked in."

"Well, she didn't, and I'd rather keep it that way. Things are dicey enough."

"They've actually gotten a bit dicier."

"How's that?"

She filled him on what had happened to Dirk, and he whistled, "Jesus, that doesn't make sense."

"There's more… What would you say if I told you that I just saw Rufus Youngblood back there at JFK and that he bought a ticket to Italy less than thirty minutes after Tierney?"

"I'd say that's a rather odd thing for him to do."

"I agree, but that's exactly what I saw."

"What's it mean?"

She thought about it for a moment and then let out a deep breath. "Well, Ben, I think it means it's time for the baby birds to leave the nest."

He looked at her confused. "Meaning?"

"I need you to drive me to my apartment in Logan Circle so I can pick up my passport and then I need a ride to Reagan International Airport."

"You're going to Sicily."

It wasn't a question. She nodded and added, "Then, I need you to forget all about it. Think you can do that?"

"Am I putting my career on the line for you, Munoz?"

"No, you're putting your career on the line for cocktails and a steak dinner at Morton's when I get back."

He laughed. "Any wine I want?"

"Sky's the limit."

"Okay, Munoz. You got yourself a mole."

Chapter 38

They arrived at the villa at shortly after 8:00 p.m. Ernesto was a hair shorter than Cesari and roughly the same age and build. His dark hair and features spoke of a mixed genetic background from centuries of various warring factions slugging it out for control of the island and then being supplanted by the next invading horde. First were the Greeks, followed by the Romans, the Ottomans, the Moors of North Africa, the Spanish, the Normans, the Germans of the Holy Roman Empire, Napoleon. Even the Vikings managed to touch ground in Sicily. It was truly a melting pot of civilizations. Due to the almost constant surge of invaders Sicilians had developed a gene for stoicism over the centuries which allowed them to endure the suffering and abuse of thousands of years of being under the heel of others. They knew that time was on their side and that all they had to do was wait it out and eventually the conquerors would be the conquered.

The wrought iron gate at the entrance to the home was about five hundred years old and the path leading to the house was long, narrow, unpaved, and not amenable to vehicular traffic. So they parked outside the gate and hoofed it the rest of the way with lanterns strategically placed here and there for light. Ernesto was waiting for them outside, dressed casually in jeans and a short-sleeved shirt. He greeted them cordially speaking through Teresa who acted as interpreter. He had wanted to meet in the morning, but Vito had insisted. He was chomping at the bit.

Rosaria stood a few feet behind in the open doorway of the brick and stucco porch. She was still wearing a black dress and veil in mourning over the loss of her son, Enzo, to that hussy, Angelina. Rosaria was diminutive in stature but full of mean and Cesari had no doubt now that he met her, who ruled this hacienda. But such was the Sicilian way. On pedestals to either side of the doorway were large elegant, hand-painted ceramic heads, easily a foot in height and just slightly less wide. From the top of the hollowed-out heads sprung herbs and flowers. One of the heads was of a beautiful fair skinned woman and the other was a dark-complexioned bearded man wearing a turban and sporting a gold earring on one side. After meeting Rosaria, Cesari stopped to stare at the unusual planter boxes.

As Vito walked on ahead with Ernesto and Rosaria into the house, Cesari lingered and asked Teresa, "What's the significance of these heads?"

"Ah, the heads," she explained. "We have been much busy since arriving in Palermo but if you pay attention you will see them all over Sicily. The legend say that during the time of the Moor domination in Sicily, there lived a beautiful girl in the heart of Palermo who loved to take care of plants on her balcony. One day she was noticed by a Moor who fell in love with her. The man told her of his feelings and the two were overwhelmed by desire. When the girl found out that her lover would soon travel back to the East, where his wife and children were waiting for him, she became crazy mad with jealousy. The girl killed the Moor while he sleep, and in a fit of savagery, she cut off his head and used it as a vase in which she planted a basil plant. The girl watered the plant with her tears, and as time went by, the basil grew luxuriantly. When her neighbors saw how beautiful her basil grew, they immediately ordered ceramic vases with the same features as the Moor's head. That's how the beautiful girl started a tradition that is still in use to this day."

Cesari blinked. "You're kidding?"

"No, is true story," she giggled. "And is good lesson for Sicilian men not to betray their lovers."

"I'll bet it is."

After the lesson in local folklore, they joined the others in the living room. Cesari glanced around at the mixture of rustic and antique décor. The carpets were faded, and the walls needed a fresh coat of paint, but the furniture was in great shape. Vases filled with floral arrangements, busts of famous people, and a marble fireplace accented the quiet sophistication of the room dominated by an eighteenth-century pianoforte in one corner. Ernesto and Rosaria were obviously doing very well. Whether they could be considered rich or not was another question. A lot of the things he saw could have been inherited and not earned. It was hard to tell. What was obvious was that they were hardworking people who benefitted from the fruits of their labor. When Cesari shook Ernesto's hand he noted his grip was strong and his skin rough and calloused like a man who labored all day. Cesari immediately developed a positive impression of the man.

They sat down, with Rosaria in the center of the sofa, and Teresa and Ernesto on either side in a protective posture. Cesari and Vito sat opposite them in Queen Anne high backed armchairs. There was wine and a charcuterie board on a coffee table. Ernesto poured everybody some of his very own vintage and then raised his glass in a toast to everyone's good health.

The civilities performed, Ernesto spoke in Sicilian to Vito with Teresa translating, "How may I help you, my friend?"

Vito sipped his wine and sat forward in his chair. "Can I presume that you know about the unfortunate events back in New York?"

Ernesto nodded, visibly saddened. "Yes, bad news travels very quickly."

Vito concurred. "Yes, it does. A lot of people are speculating as to who may have been responsible. Some are saying that it may have been you."

After Teresa finished speaking. Ernesto raised his eyebrows in shock, but before he could say anything, Rosaria lifted her veil and said angrily, "How dare you enter our home and make such an accusation against my son? The tragedy in New York was God's way of showing his displeasure for that unholy union."

"Please, Mama," Ernesto said soothingly. "You know how weak your heart is. Let me handle this."

Teresa was having a hard time keeping up but did her best. Vito countered with, "I didn't accuse anybody of anything. I simply relayed to you what some people are thinking. You didn't want Angelina to marry your brother and suddenly everybody gets poisoned. See my point?"

Defiantly, yet with great composure, Ernesto denied the implication, "No, I emphatically do not see your point. I would never do anything to hurt my brother or Angelina. And personally, I did not disapprove of their marriage. It was out of respect for my mama that I did not attend the opening of the restaurant and celebration of their engagement. I told you this the last time we met."

Vito swallowed a piece of soppressata, and his eyes narrowed, "Yeah, but a lot has happened since then. How do you explain that the poison was found in a bottle of your olive oil that you sent as a gift?"

Ernesto looked confused as Teresa translated. He replied, "I did not know this and I have no explanation, but I no do. If you came here to find out if I would bring harm to my brother or Angelina, then you have traveled a great distance for nothing. Never would that happen."

Vito sat back a little seeming to relent at Ernesto's fiery defense and sincerity. After a moment's consideration he turned to Rosaria. "What about you, Rosaria? You're the one who seems the most bitter about Angelina and Enzo. Did you do it?"

In response to that, Rosaria rose off the couch to full height, all four feet eleven inches of her. She ran the fingers of her right hand under her chin and flicked them out at Vito, spitting venom at the same time.

"Vaffanculo."

Teresa didn't bother to translate that as Rosaria stormed out of the room, steam coming out of both ears. Ernesto stood to follow and said, "You have greatly upset my mama and hurt her feelings. She is a delicate woman. I think you should leave now. Maybe you feel justified in coming to my home like this because a great wrong has been done, but you have made things worse by committing another wrong."

They all stood, and Vito said calmly and completely unimpressed by Rosaria's temper tantrum, "Ernesto, I don't give a rat's ass about mama's feelings. My aunt Sofia, Teresa's mother, almost died a few days ago and a boatload of my cousins were made violently ill by a bottle of poisoned olive oil sent by you to Enzo's restaurant. I have no intention of leaving Palermo until I find out who's responsible. Right now, you and she are the only ones who had motive to spoil the wedding. And I would like to point out that your mama never answered my question. Now go find your mama and tell her I need a response before I go anywhere."

"Enough!" shouted Ernesto, his face turning purple with rage. "You will leave at once."

"Or what?" snarled Vito.

"Or else your friends in America will wonder why you never came home," barked a new voice.

They all turned to see Bernardo and the two big goons from the Brancaccio emerge from an adjoining room where they had been listening and waiting for the right moment. Apparently, that moment had arrived. The two big guys carried metal softball bats, and Bernardo held a Benelli semi-automatic twelve gauge aimed directly at Vito.

Unfazed, Vito grinned. "Bernardo, I had a feeling we'd see you again." Then he turned to Ernesto who had paled at the sudden turn of events. "You snake in the grass. You called this dirtbag here. If this was supposed to convince me of you and your mother's innocence, then I suggest you try again."

Teresa translated as fast as she could through gasps, tears and outright fear that was starting to overwhelm her. Cesari kicked himself for leaving his crowbar in the Fiat out by the gate. Ernesto held up his hands, "I no call Bernardo. I no call anyone. Please Bernardo. No bloodshed in my home."

"I would never dishonor your home in such a way, cousin. That is, unless this brutta bestia continues to disrespect you and my aunt Rosaria." He waved the Benelli at Vito. "Are you going to continue to disrespect my cousin in his own home, brutta bestia?"

Vito looked searchingly at Teresa. "What's a brutta bestia?"

Teresa sighed. "It means ugly beast. I am sorry but you ask."

Vito shook his head, "No problem. Tell him cheap insults ain't going to solve our problem here."

Bernardo replied by taking a step closer with the shotgun and said menacingly, "Maybe this help to solve problem."

He nodded at the two goons who walked up to either side of Vito. The one closest to Cesari wound up for a shot at Vito's right knee while the other waited his turn. Before goon one could unwind Cesari lunged at him, catching him by surprise and tipping him off balance into the nose of the Benelli changing its trajectory. The sudden action caused Bernardo to reflexively fire the weapon which was now pointing at the other goon's ankle. The close-range explosion was deafening, and goon number two's ankle disintegrated in a trail of blood and bone fragments. He fell to the floor screaming in pain. His now detached foot stayed in its shoe in the same spot with blood spurting from the remaining stump of a leg as the man continued to wail in agony. Vito grabbed the hot barrel, gave Bernardo a right cross and wrenched the Benelli free while Cesari delivered a blistering array of right and left jabs, hooks and uppercuts to the first guy that would have earned him praise in any boxing gym. The larger man dropped the bat and staggered backward onto the floor dazed.

Cesari stepped back to catch his breath and Vito pointed the gun at Bernardo. "I suggest you use your belt as a tourniquet on your friend's leg before he bleeds to death."

He turned back to Ernesto and Teresa who both stood there, slack jawed in shock. Blood had sprayed onto everything including their clothes and faces. He said, "I'm only going to say this one more time, Teresa. Tell him to go find his mama and make her answer my question or I'm going to empty this shot gun into that beautiful pianoforte over there."

****

Rufus Youngblood couldn't believe his luck. He had missed Tierney at his apartment in Manhattan and had no idea where to find him so he decided to proceed onward to Sicily as planned, thinking he could always finish his business with the detective at a later date. And just like that the man walks past him on an effin' Boeing 777 on his way to the bathroom. He was fairly certain Tierney hadn't seen him in the darkened cabin. Absolutely incredible. What was that saying? Oh yeah… good things happened to good people. He ducked low in his seat and made himself as small as he could considering his bulky frame. Tierney had only met him the one time in the interrogation room of the Secret Service, and he doubted he would remember him but there was no point in taking chances. He was practically giddy over his good fortune. Tierney would lead him right to the Hoffman girl and then he would take care of the both of them.

Chapter 39

The Fiat sped down the road away from Ernesto's home just as the ambulance arrived with its flashing lights and screaming sirens. Vito's visit to his new relations had left the place in an uproar. Cesari drove while Vito puffed away angrily at an unfiltered Camel in the passenger seat. Teresa was trembling from shock in the back seat next to the newly acquired Benelli shotgun which Vito commandeered as a spoil of war along with another five shells he found in Bernardo's pockets. He also found on Bernardo the five thousand dollars he had paid him earlier in addition to five hundred euros. All in all, it wasn't that bad of a night.

Cesari said, "I know you're pissed off, but can I speak without you taking my head off?"

Vito growled, "Go ahead."

"First of all, I hope you realize we have a new problem."

"Please," he scoffed. "They're not going to call the police."

"I agree. They'll say it was some sort of accidental discharge of a firearm."

Teresa added. "No one will believe, but because they are mafia everyone will pretend to believe."

Cesari nodded. "That's how I see it. The problem is even though Bernardo is a small fish, he probably has big fish friends. They're not going to like hearing what happened tonight to one of their own. You know how that works, and you can only imagine how Bernardo is going to embellish the story."

Teresa was dabbing at a bloodstain on her shirt. "That is correct. You have just started war with mafia. They will come for us."

"I can't worry about that right now," Vito said. "I have bigger problems. Ernesto and Rosaria are lying. I can feel it in my bones. Besides, we wouldn't be at war with anyone if Bernardo and his pals hadn't come jumping out of the shadows with guns and bats."

Cesari exhaled slowly. "Take a step back. I don't agree that Rosaria and Ernesto are lying. You pointed a loaded shotgun right at an eighty-year-old woman with a heart condition and she told you to go fuck yourself, for the second time tonight I might add. Ernesto swore up and down that they didn't do it, and I could tell from the look on his face when you confronted him that he was telling the truth."

While the goon lay bleeding on the floor, Ernesto had brought his mother back to the living room to be interrogated. Once she stopped shrieking at the sight of the wounded man bleeding out on her rug, Vito ordered her to confess at gunpoint, but she adamantly refused. Not a particularly nice way to treat your soon to be aunt-in-law, but Vito was pretty wound up after Bernardo's ambush which he blamed on Ernesto and Rosaria though both vehemently denied having arranged it. Cesari had narrowly managed to wrest the Benelli away from his enraged friend and convince him there was no benefit in shooting anyone else.

"If they didn't do it then who did?" demanded Vito.

"Just because I don't know doesn't mean they're guilty. You get that part, right?"

Vito flicked the stub of his cigarette out the window and sighed. "I guess. So now what?"

"You came here to find out if Rosaria and Ernesto poisoned your family. Unless some other compelling evidence comes to light, I would have to say they didn't. Remember, the only way this was going to work was if they confessed. That didn't happen and considering the circumstances I believe them. Either that or Rosaria's got balls of steel. So now we focus on protecting Emily and keeping out of sight of Bernardo's friends which brings us to the next subject. Does Bernardo know where you live, Teresa?"

"If he doesn't already, all he has to do is ask Rosaria. I am pretty sure she will not hesitate to tell him after tonight. You did not need to call her old witch, cugino. Was unnecessary."

"Maybe... I was upset... and I'm sorry about the trouble we've caused you, Teresa," Vito said, suddenly understanding the predicament they put her in.

"Still, Bernardo won't blame you for tonight, will he?" asked Cesari.

Vito interjected, "Don't be stupid, Cesari. These are lowlife gutter rats. Of course, they'll blame her. At a minimum, they'll try to use her to get to us. Which means if we leave her alone in her apartment, then she'll really be exposed."

"I don't suppose a heartfelt apology would help?" Cesari said jokingly.

Teresa managed a weak laugh. "I doubt it. Is best to stay as far away as possible from Bernardo and Rosaria, probably forever. Sicilians have long memories. Have held vendettas lasting generations over much less than what happened tonight."

Vito said, "I need a drink. Any place we can get a Manhattan or a martini, Teresa? Wine isn't going to cut it right now."

"In two blocks make left on Via Castello just past traffic light. There is trattoria with American style cocktails. I know very well."

"What about food?"

"Of course they have food, very good food, but we just had lamb vindaloo a few hours ago."

"The lamb was pretty good, but I worked up quite an appetite since then. How about you, Cesari?"

"I think a Manhattan would hit the spot right now."

"Maybe a plate of calamari too?"

Cesari grinned. "You're preaching to the choir now, brother. Big loaf of bread and extra virgin olive oil… yummy."

"And eggplant rollatini… Can we get eggplant rollatini there, Teresa?"

Teresa was appalled. "How can you both think about food after what just happened?"

Cesari replied, "We're always hungry, Teresa. Besides, we've been in Sicily one whole day and all we've had is Indian food. We need to try something Sicilian."

She thought about it and said, "Then you need to try the caponata di pesce spada alla palermitana. It is a famous dish of Palermo. It is regular caponata with chunks of fried swordfish. I make at home often. Is very delicious."

Vito turned around to her. "I'd like to conserve my cash for emergencies. Does this place take American Express?"

"Probably, but if not, we can always use Mr. Benelli. His credit is good everywhere."

Vito laughed, "Now I know for a fact we're related."

Several minutes later, Cesari parked the car, and they entered the restaurant. They were seated at a small table in the crowded dining room and ordered the caponata, calamari and rollatini to share along with a couple of Bulleit bourbon Manhattans and red wine for Teresa. Cesari glanced at his watch. It was 10:00 p.m. Vito took the time to call Gerry just to check in. While he did that Cesari bounced around in his head a few thoughts that didn't seem to add up about all the recent proceedings. He felt like he was given a puzzle that was missing a few pieces.

"Quite a busy place," he commented to Teresa.

"Oh yes, a local hot spot as you say. This is restaurant where Enzo first train as chef. Learn many things here. I was waitress here at the time. Was many years ago."

"How very interesting. Was Angelina also a waitress here? Is that how she and Enzo got together romantically?"

She shook her head. "No, at that time, she was away in Roma. She study at university to be social worker. Then she stay there a few more years to work at big hospital. But she already know Enzo. Our families know each other long time although she and Enzo hadn't seen each other for quite a few years. When she finally return to Palermo to work at hospital here, she come to visit me at restaurant and then she see Enzo again. He was dating someone else at the time. Eventually, they fall in love."

"That's sweet."

"Yes, when he see Angelina after all those years, he forget about everything else."

The drinks came and Vito hung up his phone. Cesari asked, "All quiet on the western front?"

"For now, anyway. I told Gerry to hit the hay. He was passing out on his feet from jet lag. They should be all right."

"You're a good boss, Vito."

"Damn straight."

"Modest too."

Vito raised his glass, took a sip, and then smiled. "Hey, this isn't too shabby."

The food came and they dug in. Vito and Cesari approved. Angelina not so much. Cesari asked, "Is the food not to your satisfaction, Teresa?"

"The calamari is good, I admit, but could be better. The rollatini not bad. The caponata needs more olive oil and perhaps a pinch more sugar to balance the acidity of the vinegar, and maybe a teaspoon more capers. I make all the time. My mama taught me the right way to make caponata as a young girl. I even show to Enzo how to make."

"That's right," Cesari said. "I remember you said you helped make the caponata that night at the restaurant."

She nodded. "Yes, it was much fun to be in kitchen with Enzo again."

"Did you used to help him here too?"

She laughed. "Help him? I taught him everything. He would have been fired if it wasn't for me teaching him how to cook after restaurant close down at night."

"Well, I don't know about the finer points of caponata," joined Vito. "But I think this is delicious."

"Is not bad, just not great."

Cesari smiled. "You have high standards."

"Only animals don't care about what they put in their mouths, Doctor… or who they let in their beds."

Cesari nodded and wondered. There was something, some vibe he was appreciating for the first time.

He said, "I'll keep that in mind."

Chapter 40

By noon the next day, Deputy Director Morehouse had checked into the Hotel Garibaldi with Director Travis Burke. Both men were road weary and had decided to grab an espresso and a pastry at the Antico Caffé Spinnato a block away in a pedestrian walkway. They were still shaking the cobwebs off as they sipped espresso at an outdoor table when Morehouse's phone rang.

"Munoz, is everything all right?" He glanced at the Bulova on his wrist that his wife had given him for a birthday present. "It's barely 6:00 a.m. there."

"I'm not there. I'm in Palermo. At the airport, actually, in line waiting for a rental car. I just deplaned twenty minutes ago. There's been a development."

Morehouse stood and walked away from the table to converse more privately. He was suddenly very concerned. "What are you talking about?"

"Tierney's in Sicily. Something happened and he had the sudden urge to come here. I don't know what, but that's not all. Rufus Youngblood took the same flight as Tierney."

"Rufus Youngblood? Why on earth is here?"

"I don't know but I saw him purchase the ticket and then go through security at JFK so..." She let out a deep breath before continuing, "I made an executive decision to follow them. I know I had no authority to do so, but it was way too coincidental for me to ignore."

"Do you have a visual on them?"

"No, I had to go back to D.C. to get my passport, so I'm a few hours behind."

"This doesn't make any sense. Are they travelling together?"

"I don't know. My instinct tells me they're not. They may not even know the other was on the plane."

"Damn... Okay, Munoz, what's done is done. Find your way to the Hotel Garibaldi and check in. I'll catch up with you later. If you need to shut your eyes for a few minutes, now's the time. I'm with the director having coffee. He'll be interested to hear all this."

"Before I go, there's more."

She filled him in on Dirk's arrest and the acting director's insistence on debriefing her as well as her direct insubordination.

Morehouse said, "What do you think happened to Dirk?"

"I haven't the faintest idea other than there's no way he murdered anyone. Nor is he a drug addict."

"I agree... He was framed... By who? And why?"

"Again, I don't know, but I've already scanned the press reports from Washington. A firestorm has been ignited. I'm surprised you and the Director haven't already heard."

"We haven't been on the ground that long ourselves. Okay, go to the hotel. As soon as you're able, text me your room number. Meanwhile, I'll brief the Director. I will also call acting director Monroe and have her stand down where you're concerned. You're on special assignment under my direct supervision. That's all she needs to know. I don't plan on telling her you're in Palermo, only that I need you in the field."

He clicked off and returned to the table where he found Burke on the phone as well. He sat and signaled the waiter for another espresso. By the time it arrived, Burke finished his call and placed the phone on the table.

Morehouse was about to relay all that he and Munoz talked about but was preempted by the Director who said, "I just got off the phone with Rufus Youngblood. He says Dirk Bradbury murdered some FBI analyst named Timothy Bragg for unknown reasons and was found at the scene unconscious from a fentanyl overdose. He wanted to know if I was aware of this which of course I wasn't. Were you?"

At the mention of Rufus Youngblood's name, Morehouse suddenly became cautious and decided to hold back what he knew. He feigned surprise and replied, "No, this is the first I'm hearing of this. There must be some misunderstanding. I sent Dirk to interview Timothy Bragg. Apparently Bragg had been suspended over performing an unauthorized background and credit card search of Tierney, Gianelli and Cesari. I wanted Dirk to find out why he was doing that and on whose behalf. He would have no reason to harm Bragg unless Bragg tried to harm him first."

"The whole thing seems preposterous, but the agent Dirk supposedly murdered was in bed naked and unarmed when the police arrived. Rufus is with the D.C. police as we speak gathering information so he can determine the ramifications for the senator, but clearly this isn't good.

"Rufus is with the D.C. police right now?"

Burke nodded. "As of five minutes ago when I was talking to him. He's got some issues, I admit, but he's Johnny on the spot when you need him. That's for sure. He'll try to spin the story as best he can in our favor, but of course, it's in his best interest to do so. I'm just glad he's on our side."

Morehouse sipped his espresso and nodded. "Me too."

Something was terribly wrong. Either Munoz was lying about Youngblood, or Youngblood was lying to the Director or Burke was lying to him. The notion that Munoz was lying made absolutely no sense. Or maybe not. Was she the leak feeding information on their investigation to the outside? Had she been turned? On a scale of one to ten, he rated that possibility a zero, but still… Would Youngblood so blatantly lie to the Director about his whereabouts and why would he do so? That didn't make any sense either. And then there was the Director. Did he know Youngblood was in Palermo and was lying about it? That didn't add up either. He could see no gain for anyone in any of it. Morehouse was suddenly feeling all alone in the world.

His thoughts were interrupted by Burke. "What are you thinking about, Grayson?"

He looked at the man. "I think I'd like to have another piece of cassata."

"I second that emotion."

"I was also thinking that it might behoove us to check-in with the U.S. Consulate here in Palermo as well as the police. Italy has pretty strict gun laws and even stricter carry laws. We got through their customs okay because of our credentials, but walking around Palermo armed could be a different kind of problem. I'd hate to have some SWAT team pounce on me because some local do-gooder spotted my shoulder holster."

"You want to walk into the consulate and the local police station and tell them what exactly?"

"Our version of the truth. That we're here on a clandestine investigation concerning a protectee for whom we've received credible evidence of a threat. As a common-sense precaution we need to be armed. They don't need to know the details. What more evidence of the severity of the situation could anyone want than the presence of the number one and number two guys at the Secret Service?"

"I can see several downsides to that. First of all, before we even leave the building, the Consul General will likely call his boss, the Ambassador in Rome, to alert him of our presence, and he'd have every right to do so even if we stress the need for secrecy. The ambassador is a political animal and may get on the hotline to D.C. to find out the dirt on what's going on. If that happens, we might as well wire the story back to the Washington Post ourselves. Then, there's the local police, or Polizia Municipale as they're known. They're not going to be comfortable with the American Secret Service running around their town with guns. They're going to bump it up to the Carabinieri who are the military branch of the Italian police. It's a little different here in Italy than back in the States. The Carabinieri are going to take a potential threat to an American protectee and our presence here a whole lot more seriously, and are going to want a whole lot more information than we're willing to provide. If you don't want SWAT teams breathing down your neck, then you definitely don't want those guys involved. They'll likely show up in armored cars."

Morehouse was depressed. "Then what do we do?"

"I say we wing it, and hope for the best. We can always explain away the guns if it comes to it, but I don't see the need to broadcast it beforehand. Alternatively, if you're worried that's too much of a risk, we can leave our weapons secured in our rooms. When we find Emily and determine the need, we can always go back and retrieve them."

"I like that option even less. That's like walking around with your pants down around your ankles."

"I thought you would see it that way. It's settled then. We search for Emily armed and ready to do battle. The only thing we need to figure out is how to get to the girl before they do."

"I'm working on it."

****

Tierney walked through the Piazza Verdi with Stonewall in a harness trotting well-behaved at his side. He had been wandering around Palermo for hours since landing. It was a sunny afternoon, and after a while they sat down on a bench, admiring the magnificent façade of the

Teatro Massimo. As he fed Stonewall by hand, an occasional passerby would stop and comment on Stonewall's size and ferocious appearance. Tierney didn't understand most of it but was surprised at how many people spoke at least a smattering of intelligible English. It was obvious that most of them felt Stonewall belonged in a zoo.

And maybe he did.

Twenty years ago, he had found Stonewall as a kitten in the rubble of a remote village in Afghanistan during his last tour. Abandoned by his mother and starving, there was something about the little ball of fluff that appealed to Tierney's gentler side and so he adopted him. But the cat grew and grew and soon he realized that he was no ordinary house cat. Although he had never DNA tested him, it was his considered opinion after much research that Stonewall was some sort of hybrid of a Persian with an Eastern Lynx. His face, coat and tail were all Persian, but his teeth, claws and size were all Lynx, and he tipped the scales at thirty-five pounds. Unlike most cats, Stonewall was trainable and obeyed commands. Their bond was unbreakable, and Tierney had discovered early on that Stonewall was different from other felines, not just in size but in nature. He seemed to understand loyalty and pack behavior and on more than one occasion had acted as an early warning beacon when bad guys approached.

Given his unusual nature Tierney had gone to the Marine canine instructors and put Stonewall through his paces. He astounded everyone not only with his ability to learn but also with his desire to do so and had come through with flying colors. He could sniff out C4 and sense enemy combatants long before they could do harm. Soon, he became the constant companion of Tierney and his squad and accompanied them on combat missions deep inside enemy territory. He was also ferociously protective of Tierney and had been given the rank of attack cat first class by Tierney and his men.

Tierney had learned to trust Stonewall's instincts and even though he was nearing the latter stage of his life expectancy, he was still a force to be reckoned with, showing almost no signs of his age. Tierney had read that in captivity some Eastern Lynx had lived up to twenty-five years or longer. Stonewall seemed on target for at least that. Ever since they deplaned, however, Stonewall had been agitated and Tierney couldn't understand why. He alternately growled and purred and paced in his carry-crate. When he let him out, he whipped around in all directions searching for something or someone who wasn't there. Trusting the cat, Tierney decided to hang out in the piazza rather than proceed directly to Teresa's apartment, potentially leading some malcontent there. They had sat and paced most of the afternoon. At the moment, Stonewall was calm lying across Tierney's lap, but Tierney didn't like the feel of it.

He would wait until Cesari called. The doctor had either turned off his phone for a good reason or had to get a new one, but sooner or later he would check-in. Tierney was confident of that. Meanwhile, he would sit and talk with Stonewall or feed the pigeons. There were many coffee shops or bars as they called them in Italy and a plethora of places to eat. He could always find a hotel, but he liked it where he was. Wide open and visually interesting. Maybe if he was patient long enough whatever it was that was bothering Stonewall would reveal itself. Maybe Cesari would never call.

Maybe he was dead.

Tierney looked down at the cat and said, "What do you think, Stonewall? Do you think Cesari is dead?"

The cat said nothing, and Tierney continued, "I agree. He's too resilient. You know, if he had the slightest modicum of self-discipline, he might have made a good Marine. He doesn't take orders too well either now that I think of it."

Stonewall suddenly snapped to attention with his paws on Tierney's shoulders. His body stiffened and the hairs on his back stood up as he stared at something across the street from the piazza. Tierney glanced around and then focused on the outdoor tables of a particular café. There were many people walking back and forth both in the piazza and on the sidewalk in front of the café, but something caught Tierney's attention. A woman sitting alone had abruptly angled away from them. She wore a broad-brimmed hat, sunglasses and had a bandage on one side of her face.

Stonewall snarled ferociously just as a text from Cesari finally arrived.

CHAPTER 41

The next day, Cesari heeded Teresa's advice and avoided going back to Ernesto's house. He didn't see any point in having a second confrontation with the family. In his mind, Vito had already done enough damage there to last two lifetimes, and no amount of apologizing was going to fix it. But he had questions that needed to be answered, so he told everyone he wanted to scout out the neighborhood better and then went back to the trattoria they had eaten at the previous night. Vito and Teresa were holed up in the apartment hoping against hope that Bernardo would possibly drop the matter. There was always the chance that Bernardo would be too ashamed to tell his boss what really happened, and may just stick to the accidental discharge story to save face.

Vito lived in that world, and understood the many emotions that were now going through Bernardo's mind. Hate, anger, desire for revenge had to be balanced with the appearance of being incompetent and weak which translated to useless, which meant expendable. It would be difficult enough to explain how one of his men shot off his own foot but that would be easier than telling everyone that two unarmed Americans overpowered the three of them, stole his brand new Benelli, robbed him of all his money, and beat the crap out of them in the middle of his cousin's living room.

After three glasses of wine and a good night's sleep, Emily was in a decidedly better mood. Cesari suggested that if she was willing to stay in character as an Indian woman on holiday with her new husband, he didn't see any reason why she couldn't get some fresh air. Excited at the prospect of stretching her legs and briefly putting her troubles behind her, she wiggled herself into a brightly colored sari and asked Jaskaran and Jeremy to go sightseeing. They were delighted to accommodate her, especially Jaskaran, who loved his new army uniform and the swagger it came with. Since open carry was strictly prohibited in Italy, and the Colt was illegal anyway, he slipped the weapon under his huge turban and secured it in place where it rested comfortably on the nest made by his curled up long hair. Watching him, Cesari thought the turban was large enough that he could probably fit a machine gun up there. Then Jaskaran tucked the kirpan into his trousers so that the handle was barely visible. Jeremy pocketed the small PPK and the pain killers were ready to rumble.

At the trattoria, Cesari had a late lunch of spaghetti alla cacio e pepe, a traditional Roman dish but popular throughout Italy for its simplicity and extraordinary flavors. Made simply with extra virgin olive oil, a healthy dose of Romano cheese, an overdose of freshly ground black pepper and served with a garnish of freshly cut lemon wedges, the dish was a prime example of how less can be more in the culinary world. Sipping his wine, he made small talk with almost every waiter and waitress that passed by. Progressing up the food chain through the waitstaff, the manager, the chef, and eventually the owner who came out to converse with the gregarious and affable American interested in all things Sicilian. Pasquale DiGiovanni was in his sixties, portly and happy, and was delighted to chit chat in broken English about Palermo and its people. He and his family had owned and operated Trattoria Il Posto for over thirty years. A fountain of information, he sat opposite Cesari, poured himself a glass of wine and signaled the waiter to bring out a trifecta of fresh sardines; marinated, fried, and stuffed with crab meat and breadcrumbs and then fried.

Cesari loosened his belt, and they sat there for the next two hours sharing stories, gossip and old wives tales as they sampled almost every appetizer on the menu. Finally, after his second cannoli and third espresso Cesari raised his hands in surrender. The man laughed and when Cesari asked for the bill was politely told that it was on the house, but he did allow Cesari to leave a healthy tip for the outstanding meal, pleasant company and impeccable service. Afterward, Cesari staggered to the sidewalk nearly comatose from the carb load and thought he would never eat another bite again.

Outside the fresh air revived him, and jolted back to reality, he realized he had neglected to tell Tierney about his new phone. The man would be worried sick especially after that last text he'd sent him with its clear implication. It took him a moment to remember Tierney's number, but he did, plugged it into his device and promptly corrected the omission as he got into the Panda. The alacrity of the response from Tierney startled him as did the message itself. Tierney was in Palermo and potentially in trouble. The text was brief and terse without explanation. He told Cesari not to call, just come to the Piazza Verdi and find him.

Cesari drove there immediately and parked the Fiat on the street. He spotted Tierney on a bench fifty yards away and walked briskly in his direction. When he was within a few feet, Stonewall glanced up at him and purred.

Tierney said, "Sit down next to Stonewall and pretend to make small talk."

He sat down on the bench and stroked Stonewall gently. "Who needs to pretend? Are you going to tell me why you're in Palermo?"

"Maybe I missed you? Now pay attention. We've got a bogey at three o'clock sitting at an outdoor table across the street about fifty feet from here. She's the woman with the hat and sunglasses on the phone."

Cesari casually stretched and glanced obliquely in that direction catching the woman out of the corner of one eye. He returned to his position and without looking at Tierney directly said, "Shit..."

"You know her?"

"Her name's Rosemarie. She was on the plane, but before that she was staked outside Vito's apartment. I thought we lost her in Rome."

"Was she the company you mentioned in your text?"

"Yes, and she was with a big guy named Booker, bald with a beard, ex-military. How'd you pick her up?"

"I didn't. Stonewall did, and I'm not quite sure how he does it. He loses his shit whenever there's any kind of a threat nearby. I didn't want to bring her to the apartment, so I've been sitting here all afternoon."

Cesari stared at Stonewall. "Good cat. Did you see anybody else? I neutralized the guy on the plane but that was only temporary."

"I haven't seen anyone else, and I've been looking hard. You neutralized the guy on the plane? What's that supposed to mean?"

"It means that if I don't tell you the details you can't testify against me in court."

Tierney grinned. "You're a pisser, Cesari. You neutralized the guy on the plane," he repeated shaking his head. "I can't believe what I'm hearing. You expect me to believe that you took action against an ex-military bad guy in mid-flight at thirty-thousand feet?"

"More like thirty-five thousand feet, but yeah, you got the picture. He's got a lump on his head the size of an apricot and two broken thumbs. With a couple of aspirin and some splints, he could be right back in the game although he should be easy to spot. The good news is that he's probably still trying to figure out what year it is."

"Well, I haven't seen anyone that fits that description but that doesn't mean anything with all these people and cars. He could be inside a store or a restaurant staring at us right now."

"And there's a third guy out there somewhere too. When I took out Booker, I scanned his phone real quick and came across a series of texts concerning Emily between him, Rosemarie, and another guy called Rufus. There were pictures of all of us on his phone."

Tierney looked at him curiously. "Rufus? Does he have a last name?"

Cesari shook his head. "No, all it said on the phone was Rufus. Why?"

"I was interviewed by a guy called Rufus Youngblood yesterday morning at Secret Service headquarters in D.C. He identified himself as the chief of staff for Senator Taylor."

"You've been busy, Detective."

"That's why I'm here. Things are getting hot, and I didn't feel comfortable sitting on the bench."

"What do you think?"

"I'm fifty years old and you know how many times I've met someone named Rufus?"

Cesari shook his head but didn't say anything.

"Not counting yesterday, never…"

"Quite a coincidence, I agree."

"There's a lot of that going around lately. Anyway, we'll save that for another day. So the big question is how do we get from here to the apartment without bringing your girlfriend, Rosemarie, along for the ride?"

"No, the big question is how did she latch onto you so quickly? You just arrived a few hours ago and there she is. These people have eyes everywhere it seems."

Tierney nodded. "You're right about that. Someone must have known I was on that flight here and tipped her off."

"Certainly appears that way."

Tierney mulled that over and then groaned. "Not good, Cesari. The only person who knew my itinerary was a Secret Service agent named Munoz who was assigned to tail me back in New York. She had me convinced she was one of the good guys, and I almost led them right to Emily."

"Water under the bridge, Detective. Don't beat yourself up. Thank goodness you brought Stonewall."

Tierney was fuming. "God damn spooks. I never met one who wouldn't lie to his own mother for no good reason, but now I'm really pissed. I warned agent Munoz what would happen if I decided she was on the wrong side."

"First order of business is to shake this Rosemarie character and whoever else might be with her."

"Do you think she's the one who killed my neighbor?"

"I have no idea. I don't know anything about her except that every time I turn around, she's standing right there."

"Maybe I should just go to a hotel and not run the risk of anyone following us to Emily."

Cesari shrugged. "Too late for that. They already know me, and if there's more than one of them, they'll split up and follow us individually."

"Great. So I fucked up royally. Is that what you're saying?"

"No, what I'm saying is that there's strength in numbers, and I'd prefer to have you with us when the shit hits the fan rather than sitting in some hotel bar sipping expensive scotch without me. Besides, we have guns, and if you want to start comparing notes about who fucked up the most, wait until you hear what happened to me and Vito last night. I'm pretty sure we'll win the door prize for stupidity. There's probably a hit squad of local mafia looking for us as we speak."

Tierney cracked a smile despite his bad mood. "You pissed off the locals that bad in less than twenty-for hours? That's got to be some sort of record, and what do you mean you have guns? How is that possible?"

"Detective, this isn't the JV team."

"Apparently not."

"I'm glad we settled that. Now package up Stonewall in his crate and let's take a walk."

"Where are we going?"

"To the house that Giuseppe Verdi built."

CHAPTER 42

Morehouse walked down the hallway and knocked on the door. Munoz opened it and let him in. They were on the seventh floor of the Hotel Garibaldi. Munoz had just recently showered, and her hair was still wet. She was dressed in jeans and a casual top.

Bypassing the usual banter, Morehouse got right to the point. "We have a problem."

"Another one?" she replied dryly.

"Yes, another one. You told me Rufus Youngblood boarded a plane to Sicily last night. No less than five minutes later, the Director told me he had just spoken to Rufus, and he was in D.C. talking to the police about Dirk."

She looked puzzled. "I don't understand."

"Somebody's lying about where Rufus is, and I don't like it."

"I hope you don't think it's me."

"I do not or else I wouldn't be telling you all this. After we spoke, I called Elaine Monroe to get her off your back. Then I called Ben Forman and asked him to find Youngblood on some trumped up pretext. Youngblood it turns out is out of town and no one knows where he is. He was told that it might be a couple of days before he was available again."

"Then he is here."

"I believe so, but I can't prove it, and neither can you. All we have are our gut feelings for the moment. The question is, if he is here why did he lie to Burke about it, and if he didn't lie to Burke, then why did Burke lie to me?"

They stared at each other for a long moment in thought before she said, "I think the better question is why would Youngblood desire to be in Sicily at all? I would think that as the senator's number one man, he would want to stay as clear from all of this as possible."

"I agree with that. There's no upside for him or the senator if he were caught in the eye of the storm should this thing go sour."

"And if he were here, there's even less reason for the director to lie about it to you. We're all on the same side."

He stared at her for a moment. "Unless we're all not on the same side, Munoz."

"What are you saying?"

"I'm not saying anything…yet. But until I can come to some point of clarity as to what's going on, I would prefer you to stay in the background and act as my backup."

"You don't want the director to know I'm here?"

"No, I don't."

"That's a tall order."

"It's not an order. It's a request, and if you don't feel comfortable with it, he's in room 1002. You can go there right now and announce your presence. Before you do that, let me fill you in on a few other details so that you can make a more informed decision." Morehouse cleared his throat and continued, "Agent Mills didn't just murder Claire Tompkins. He assassinated her. The weapon that was found by his side in that underpass had a military grade silencer attached to it and he was wearing latex gloves. We kept that out of the press for obvious reasons."

Munoz digested that for a minute. "So there was never any doubt about Mills' intentions."

He shook his head. "No, not really. I was trying to give him the benefit of the doubt as we investigated, hoping to uncover some other possible reason for the events of that night."

"When did you decide there was no other explanation?"

"When Detective Tierney told us what Emily went through that night, and what she told him. There was no way she would or could have made that up."

"And how does that relate to here and now?"

"Let's connect the dots. Rufus Youngblood and Mills were highly decorated SEALs together in Iraq and Afghanistan. They both received the Navy Cross and numerous other medals and citations, yet both their military records are so highly redacted as to be nearly useless in terms of trying to figure why they won any awards at all."

"Which means?"

"It could only mean black ops missions, search and destroy, assassinations, terror campaigns, torture. You name it. The things no one can ever talk about in the light of day. Things we ask our men in uniform to do and then get in front of a camera and condemn the other side for doing the same thing. This Rosemarie is a certified CIA operative and obviously very good at what she does. The only way I can tie her in to all of this is if she was in Iraq and Afghanistan with Mills and Youngblood during their time of service. Perhaps she was in deep cover. Soldiers don't get to pick their targets or their missions. She may have been their handler back in the day, and somehow, they kept up their relationship afterward."

Munoz sat down on the edge of the bed suddenly emotionally exhausted. "Please continue... Why kill Claire and Emily?"

"That part's obvious. Youngblood is on the fast track up riding on the coat tails of Senator Taylor's popularity. If Taylor wins the White House, Youngblood is sitting pretty as being the next White House Chief of Staff and God knows what else. Not bad for a non-com. I'm betting that an aggressive and self-confident guy like him wouldn't let much stand in his way."

"And Claire was in his way?"

"It's certainly starting to look that way. Try to imagine a randy, middle-aged senator sowing what remains of his wild oats in a lustful dalliance with his beautiful secretary. Suddenly, it dawns on him that she's a potential stumbling block in his race for the oval office. And then the light bulb goes off and he realizes that his right-hand man knows how to fix problems like this."

Munoz thought she was going to puke and turned white. "You can't be serious. You think Senator Taylor ordered this?"

"No, guys like that never implicate themselves that directly. I think he simply nodded in Youngblood's direction to take care of the problem. It's the only possible reason I can think of for Rufus to be here in Palermo. Things are spiraling out of his control, and he needs to make sure the job gets finished."

"You don't think he trusts that woman we're calling Mata Hari to finish it for him?"

"Too much has happened, and I think he doesn't want to take any more chances. Plus, Mata Hari may have called for backup. Emily's not alone anymore. She has Gianelli, Cesari and now Tierney protecting her."

"That would explain why he lied to the director about his presence here. It simply cannot be explained in any other way. But that would mean the director wasn't lying."

"Not necessarily. I told Burke right before we left D.C. that I believed there was a leak. He didn't seem all that surprised or outraged. Then when I said I was thinking of bringing you with me to Palermo to search for Emily Hoffman he immediately shot that down and offered to come himself which I didn't really question until now. Upon reflection, it seems a fairly big step for the Director of the Secret Service to take, unless…"

Finishing his sentence, Munoz said in a hushed voice, "Unless he wanted to make sure you didn't find Emily Hoffman."

"I don't know that for a fact, but it's a possibility."

She shook her head in disbelief. "I can't accept this."

"I get that too, but until I'm certain about what's happening, I'd rather be cautious than be on the receiving end of a nine-millimeter. Look, I've never known the director to be anything other than what he appears, but an element of doubt has just entered the equation. We're in a foreign country hunting for assassins and fugitives alike. No one knows we're here or why. A misplaced bullet would be all it would take, and then you'd be on your own."

"Maybe you should alert the authorities and the consulate for backup."

"I brought that up already with Burke and he emphatically said no."

"Why?"

"He was concerned about the political fallout, and he had a point."

"Unless he had another motive. If the authorities are involved and something happens to you, it would be that much harder to explain away. It would be better if no one knew you were here at all."

"Now who's the paranoid one, Munoz?"

"I can't even believe we're having this discussion."

"Neither can I, but I need some time to sort this out. No one knows you're here and that presents us with an opportunity. You can work behind the scenes objectively. All I'm asking is for you to give me twenty-four hours of your time. If nothing pans out then you can either bail out and go back to the States, no harm no foul, or come out of the shadows and join me and Burke."

"What is it exactly you want me to do?"

"Tail me and the director. Watch us and more importantly, see who else might be watching us."

"Like Rufus Youngblood."

"Or Mata Hari… Do you have your service weapon?"

"Yes, of course, but for the record, we don't know what Mata Hari looks like."

"I didn't say this was going to be easy, and remember to keep your weapon out of sight. Just because they let you into the country with it doesn't mean they're going to appreciate you walking around scaring their citizens with it, and you really don't want to spend hours and maybe even days explaining yourself to the Carabinieri."

She took a deep breath and let it out slowly. "Understood."

"You with me, Munoz?"

"I guess I'm on board."

"I'm glad because I need you."

"You do make a compelling if flawed argument, but I'm not convinced the director is guilty of anything."

"I never said he was… The director and I are heading out for a quick dinner down the block from here at a place called Ristorante Quattroventi. After that we're going to start canvassing all the hotels, boarding houses and hostels in Palermo to see if Emily showed up at one of them. The plan is to go at it all night or until we drop from exhaustion. Be discreet, and stay in the shadows."

"Every hotel? You have your work cut out for you."

"So do you."

"What kind of car are you driving?"

"We aren't. We didn't rent one. Neither one of us is familiar with Palermo and figured we'd waste too much time driving, parking and just trying to find every hotel in this city. Burke has arranged for a private driver to pick us up after dinner and drive us around."

****

"Where are they going?" Rufus asked. He was parked in a rented Mercedes about a hundred yards away with a pair of binoculars conferencing with Booker and Rosemarie.

"It looks like they're heading into the theatre," replied Rosemarie.

"With the cat? What are they up to?"

"I don't know."

"Do you think they made you?"

"I don't think so. They're far enough away and there are hordes of people and constant traffic interfering with their view. The cat gave me a bit of start earlier, but he calmed down."

"Stop with the cat already. It's just a fluke that he looked in your direction. There's no way in hell he recognized you and they don't do things like that anyway. A fly probably landed on his nose and got him riled up."

"That's no ordinary cat, though I agree with you in principle."

Rufus said, "Booker, do you have eyes on them?"

"I do," came the rumbling throaty reply. He had a headache from the beating he received on the plane and had trouble manipulating his phone with his broken thumbs which he hid inside a windbreaker when not in use. He could barely contain his rage. Compounding the matter was that he was forced to shave his beard to change his appearance and wear a hat to disguise the ugly bruise Cesari had inflicted on his skull.

"And?" asked Rufus patiently, understanding the man's mental prowess, never really on high octane to begin with, was now working short a few cylinders from the concussion.

"They're coming my way," Booker hissed. "But it doesn't make any sense. Cesari parked his car on the other side of the piazza. I saw him. It was a Fiat Panda."

Rufus was impressed. That was a good pickup for a guy who had double-vision a couple of hours ago. He said, "It doesn't matter, just back off and out of sight. Give them space. We don't want a confrontation right now, all right? You're justifiably angry. I understand that but there will be time for payback later. Right now, we need them to lead us to the Hoffman girl. So do not, I repeat, do not make contact. In fact, I think you should duck around to the back of the theatre in case they try to slip out that way. Rosemarie and I have the front and the sides covered pretty well."

When Booker didn't reply quickly, Rufus added, "Tell me that you understand."

The reluctant response came slowly, "I understand."

"Good… Rosemarie, you stay put. I'll call the big guy."

CHAPTER 43

Inside the entrance to the Teatro Massimo, Cesari surveyed his surroundings in awe. It was a magnificent architectural achievement and a just tribute to the great artists, performers and composers of Italy. Opera, he thought would always stand out as mankind's single greatest accomplishment that helped decisively separate him from the beasts of the jungle.

He scanned around and saw many people walking around gaping at the impressive marble columns, sky high frescoed ceilings and artwork on the walls. There were no obvious threats, so he doubled back to the entrance and peeked out the front door. Rosemarie was now closer to half a football field away but still sitting nonchalantly at the table.

Tierney placed the pet carrier on the floor. He was a strong man but carrying a thirty-five-pound cat all day was starting to take its toll. He stared over Cesari's shoulder and said, "She hasn't budged."

"No, she hasn't. I guess that's a good sign."

"She must have seen us walk here, right?"

"Unless she didn't even know we were there. Maybe she just serendipitously stopped there for a cappuccino."

Tierney wasn't that optimistic. "Give me a break, Cesari."

"I know. I'm a glass half full kind of guy, but why didn't she follow us inside?"

"Maybe she figures we'll have to come out again sooner or later and she'll just wait it out."

"That's a possibility. Let's see if there's another way out of this place."

As they whispered, an old woman who worked in the theatre came up to them from behind and said something in Italian. They both turned around abruptly. She was pointing at the pet carrier with Stonewall and gesticulating animatedly. Clearly, she was telling them that animals weren't allowed in the theatre and that they would have to leave.

Cesari nodded, and asked in terrible part Italian, part English if there was another way out. She got the gist and pointed to the back of the opera house past the stage. From what Cesari could gather, there was an entrance toward the rear for maintenance, supplies, and equipment drop off, but she raised her hand and waved her index finger back and forth in front of their faces, indicating that they weren't allowed back there.

Thinking quickly on his feet, Tierney reached into his pocket and came out with his gold detective badge. He showed it to her and using the only word of Italian he knew besides espresso, said, "Polizia…"

The woman backed away, suddenly very concerned about what may or may not be going on right here in her little fiefdom. Cesari and Tierney didn't wait for an invitation or for her to get on the phone to call for instructions. They zipped by her into the main performance area and along the red carpeted floor to the stage, bypassing the music pit and practicing ensemble who were in the midst of tuning their instruments. They circled around the stage and entered the bowels of the theatre passing stagehands, musicians and singers alike gearing up for a dress rehearsal. They found an exit that led to the outside, and emerged unscathed, and as far as they could tell unseen into a small well-paved parking lot, presumably for the employees, vendors, and maintenance crews.

Cesari said, "I have a car parked about a hundred yards from here but it's toward the front of the piazza. Rosemarie might see us. It would be smarter just to walk to the apartment rather than drive. It's only a few blocks away from here, and I can always come back later to pick up the car."

"Lead the way Cesari, but let me put Stonewall back in his harness first. My shoulder is screaming in pain from carrying him."

"Have you thought about putting him on a diet?"

"What are you talking about? He's all muscle."

Cesari laughed. It wasn't the first time he had ribbed Tierney about his cat. "If you say so, Detective, but I still think it would be wise to limit him to one cannoli a day."

Once in the harness, they strode in the direction of Teresa's apartment warily keeping an eye out for tails, but feeling confident that they had eluded Rosemarie. To be extra safe, Cesari took a circuitous route and circled around the same block twice, stopping for an espresso to give him time to hunt for the hunters. The fifteen-minute walk took nearly forty minutes, but they eventually arrived safely at their destination.

In the apartment, everyone looked up surprised and excited at the newcomer's presence and eagerly pressed him for the story behind this sudden change of plans. They were all in awe of Stonewall who ran around the apartment like he owned it.

Tierney turned to Emily and said, "I spoke to your father right before I left, Emily. He's doing very well, and told me to tell you how much he loves you. For security reasons, he still wants you to maintain radio silence for a little while longer."

Tearful, she hugged the Detective who stood there somewhat uncomfortable with the sudden display of emotion. She said, "Thank you."

"You look great in a sari," he noted.

Grinning, she said, "Meet my husband, Major Jaskaran Singh of her majesty's 36th Sikh Regiment of the British Indian Army."

Jaskaran stepped forward still fully decked out in his uniform, clicked his heels and bowed stiffly. "At your service, Detective. I see you have met my new bride."

Tierney laughed. "You guys are killing me, but I have to admit, the outfits are very convincing."

****

"We've got them now, Rufus," Booker whispered into his phone. "That Cesari's a slick bastard though with all that doubling back crap. Plus, they left their car at the piazza. That was clever of them to hoof it."

Booker had picked them up coming out of the rear of the theatre and notified his compatriots. They had then rotated following from behind alternating with moving up ahead with the Mercedes staying about a block away at all times. They had struck gold once they saw them enter the apartment building on Via Orologio.

Rufus said, "I agree, but not clever enough. They weren't counting on three of us tailing them at once, and leaving the Fiat back there was a mistake. The first thing I'm going to do is disable it."

"All right, we know that Cesari and Tierney are staying here but how can we be certain about the Hoffman girl?" asked Rosemarie.

"We can't, so we'll just stake them out for the time being. There's plenty of cafés and restaurants to hang out in without being conspicuous, but Rosemarie, I think they made you. That's why they slipped out the backside of the Teatro Massimo. That bandage on your face is a dead giveaway. Cesari probably saw you on the plane and recognized you in the piazza… or maybe it really was the cat. Either way, you have to do something about that."

"What do you want me to do? The wound is bad enough on its own merit, and I think it may be infected."

"Are you on antibiotics?"

"Yes."

Rufus mulled it over. "I got an idea. There's a strong Arab cultural influence here in Palermo. We should be able to find a shop selling hijabs and veils. That would cover the bandage and not look out of place."

Rosemarie bristled at first but then sighed, "Fine, I'll get one."

"Good… Booker you keep eyes on the building. Rosemarie and I are going to procure weapons, and then I need to find an Italian who doesn't care too much about the law."

"That shouldn't be too hard. People here aren't all that different from anywhere else. Have you ever been to Palermo before?" Rosemarie asked.

"No, you?"

"Several times. There's a district called the Brancaccio not too far from here. It's a wide-open wild west kind of place. You can pretty much get anything you want there. It's mostly a mob run neighborhood dealing primarily in drugs and whores but most people there will be open to suggestion if there's profit in it. We can get weapons there, but it may not be the kind of firepower you're interested in. There isn't a big gun culture here like back home, so we might have to settle for shotguns and revolvers. Old school stuff. In Italy when someone needs to be killed, a twelve gauge or a knife will do the job just as well as a Sig Sauer or an AR-15 and for a whole lot less cost."

"I'm not sure I like that. It's bad enough to be outnumbered but even worse to be outgunned."

"It might be the only option we have."

"What do they have against guns here anyway?"

"Nothing really, but the average person here doesn't necessarily feel the need to own firearms whether for recreation or personal protection."

"That's great. Another country filled with sheeple."

"I wouldn't go that far. You don't want to rile up the Italians especially the Sicilian branch. They do have gun stores here with modern firearms for enthusiasts, but you can't just walk in and buy a brand-new Beretta like you're at gun show in rural Georgia."

"Why not?"

She looked at him as if he were daft and said slowly, "Because there are strict gun control laws here and it takes months and years to wade through the permit process and as a foreigner you would never be granted a permit anyway."

He smiled. "That's not what I meant. Let's go to the Brancaccio first. Then we'll work our way up to a gun store. Booker, you remain here, and remember to stay out of sight."

"What if I see the girl and the opportunity presents itself? I think I should take action."

"What are you going to do? Strangle her in the middle of the street? Look how busy this place is with pedestrians. And if she does show up, she's not going to be alone. I don't want this to turn into a street brawl. The last thing we need is to be hauled into some police station for disturbing the peace. No, wait until we have real weapons and a plan. Besides, I have to deal with another situation first. There are some loose ends running around Palermo that need to be dealt with."

Rosemarie said, "What kind of loose ends?"

"The kind that need to be dealt with."

"I don't mean to be disrespectful, but shouldn't we know what's going on? We're all in this up to our eyeballs."

Rufus thought about it. She was right, and they were going to be involved one way or another. He said, "The Director and Deputy Director of the Secret Service are here in Palermo looking for Emily Hoffman."

Booker muttered, "Shit..."

Rosemarie scowled, "You weren't going to tell us?"

"Relax, I have a plan."

"Did you hear that, Booker? He has a plan," she said derisively. "How many agents do they have with them?"

"It's just the two of them as far as I know, but like I said, I have a plan."

"As far as you know? Don't you think this changes things a bit?"

"No, nothing changes at all... Look, they haven't found the Hoffman girl yet and we have, okay? That gives us the advantage, and I'm going to make sure they don't have a chance to become a problem."

"I can't wait to hear this."

Chapter 44

As dusk approached, Morehouse and Burke left the hotel to have dinner. Less than a mile away, Rufus and Rosemarie pulled the shiny silver rental Mercedes into the Brancaccio and parked. They got out and leaned against the passenger side observing and making mental notes, more or less routine behavior for seasoned veterans. They were letting the expensive car act as a beacon, broadcasting to all who were listening that wealth had just arrived and wished to be shared. Rufus held an attaché case in one hand and toyed with the five-inch stiletto in his pocket with the other. He had picked one up for himself and one for Rosemarie from a street vendor for thirty euros each. Stringent on guns but equally relaxed on knives, Palermo was a city of many paradoxes.

In five minutes time, a skanky twenty-year old with bad teeth and hair approached them glancing warily in every direction as if not certain he was being drawn into a trap. He stopped six feet away and stared at them carefully.

Finally he said in broken English, "Are you in need of something?"

Rufus assessed the kid as a flunky and nodded. "I need to speak to your boss."

"American?"

Ignoring the question, Rufus took a step forward, and said, "Are you deaf? Get your boss."

"He is in meeting. Tell me what you want."

Rufus raised the suitcase and flipped the lid open for the young man to see its contents. There were stacks of euros in tens, twenties and fifties filling the case, totaling fifty-thousand in all. The kid's eyes went wide and his jaw dropped.

Rufus closed the case and said, "I already told you what I want. If you don't turn around without another word and get him, I'm going to use your face like a speed bag."

The kid hesitated briefly, then turned around and disappeared into a dark alley. A minute later, three men slowly emerged from the shadows. Two were very large and they flanked an average sized guy in the middle who was obviously in charge. The two big guys were in dress pants and black turtlenecks. The boss was in his mid-thirties, swarthy and clean shaven wearing a dress shirt and pants.

He stopped several feet away and studied Rufus and Rosemarie a bit before saying, "I am boss, so speak…"

Rufus said, "I need your assistance, and it may take several hours of your time, but I'll make it worth your while."

"Is this joke? My time isn't for sale. You want girl. I have girl. You want drugs, I have drugs. Those are your choices."

"How about guns? You have guns?"

He nodded. "I have guns, but very expensive."

"Do you have a couple of Beretta 92FS's, Heckler & Koch P30L's or Sig Sauer .357's? Because if you don't then I need your help in getting them. I'm not interested in rusty shotguns and old revolvers."

Rufus opened the suitcase again, placing the money on display for the newcomers, but this time he took out a thousand euros and offered it the one in charge, saying, "Go ahead. Take it. It's yours just for listening to what I have to say. If you're not interested after I'm done, you keep the money. No strings attached."

The man looked greedily at the little bundle of happiness in front of him and then slowly reeled it in. He handed it to one of his henchman and then said, "What is to stop me from just taking the rest of the money from you?"

Rufus smiled. He knew that was coming. "Because, paesano, the woman standing next to me has killed more men with her bare hands than you have hair on your testicles."

The guy involuntarily took a step back and reappraised Rosemarie who didn't say or do anything. He said defensively, "Why are you Americans always in such bad mood?"

"Because you pecker heads in these third world shitholes are always fucking with us."

"It was joke is all. Bernardo make the joke."

Rufus exhaled slowly and continued, "My mistake… Well, I'm glad we got that out of the way. Now, I just handed you a thousand euros. Will you at least listen to what I have to say?"

"Yes, I listen."

"Good… I want you to come with us to a gun store and act as a translator so I can purchase a real gun. If you do that, I'll give you another nine thousand euros. Then, I'll need you to act as a taxi driver and pick up some very special friends for me. That will earn you an additional five thousand euros. That's a total of fifteen thousand euros for a couple of hours of your time."

"That's all you want me to do?"

"That's all."

"What about my men?"

"They stay here. I just need you."

The man's eyes narrowed, and he looked at them suspiciously. "How can I trust you?"

"You have a point. How about I leave half the money I promised with your men and give you the other half when we're done."

"You leave half with my men?"

"Yes, and you get the other half when we return. As I said, if you're not interested you still get to keep the thousand I already gave you."

The guy mulled it over for a while, his lust for money slowly overwhelming his instinctive fear of these strangers who had so brazenly entered his slice of paradise. Rosemarie opened the rear door of the Mercedes and stood there waiting. He wavered a moment and then nodded. Rufus counted out the euros and handed it to him, and he in turn handed it to his men. Giving last minute instructions to them, he returned and entered the rear of the Mercedes.

As Rufus stepped on the gas, he looked in his rearview mirror at the man sitting impassively in the back. "What's your name?"

"I am Bernardo."

"Hello, Bernardo. I'm Rufus and this is Rosemarie."

"Is pleasure, I am sure."

"So where is the nearest gun store?"

"Is Armeria di Carlo. Number 13, Via Zara. Is maybe one kilometer from here. Stay on Via Roma and I tell you when turn, but hurry. She close in less than one hour."

"Are there any security cameras in this store?"

He thought about it. "I am no sure of this. Perhaps... Is small store, mom and pop, as you say in America."

They arrived fifteen minutes before closing time and parked right in front of the gun shop. They all went in and were greeted by a balding middle-aged guy in dark pants, a white shirt with a button-down collar, and blue striped tie who looked like he was getting ready to go home for a nice big bowl of pasta con sarde. He wore a holster on his hip with a Beretta M9 secured in it. There was no one else in the store. Bernardo and Rufus went to talk to the guy while Rosemarie looked around. Rufus laid his attaché case on the glass countertop in full view of the man, as he casually scanned around searching for security cameras. He spotted two, one staring straight at him over the entrance to a back room and the other blinking from the side wall catching a panoramic view of things. It was a small store but had plenty of what he needed.

Bernardo introduced them. "This is Carlo. Is his store."

Rufus smiled affably. "Tell him I need three Beretta 92FS's with two fifteen round clips for each and two boxes of 9mm parabellums."

Carlo glanced at his watch as Bernardo translated. Bernardo said, "He say he can show you guns, but needs to see your purchase authorization... your license or permit, in order to sell to you."

"Of course," Rufus replied. "Tell him I'm just browsing today to compare prices. If I decide to buy, I'll return tomorrow with my permit."

Carlo was satisfied with that and moved to get a Beretta. As he did, Rosemarie went over to the entrance and turned the deadbolt without anyone noticing. Then she came up behind Rufus and whispered, "I don't think there's anyone else here."

Rufus nodded but didn't say anything. Carlo returned with one Beretta and placed it on the counter saying something in Sicilian. Bernardo translated, "Is nine hundred euros, but he will give to you for eight."

"That's very generous of him."

Rufus opened his attaché case, showed Carlo the money and said, "I will give him two thousand euros per gun and an extra thousand euros to overlook the fact that I don't actually have a permit."

After Bernardo translated, the man looked horrified and shook his head. "He say is much illegal and he will get in trouble... big trouble."

"Tell him I will double the price. Four thousand euros per gun and two thousand for his trouble. That's fourteen thousand euros. Hell, let's round it up to fifteen thousand euros. It's an easier number to work with. He can always report the guns stolen if he's concerned about the inventory discrepancy."

Bernardo translated and then turned to Rufus. "I tell him and also I add that it is very good deal. He should take."

Carlo didn't agree and pointed at the door, jabbering angrily at Bernardo who said, "He say we must leave now or he will call police."

In one smooth fast motion, Rufus reached over, grabbed the man's tie and yanked him forward hard so that his head was lying almost on Rufus's side of the counter. With his other hand, Rufus deftly pulled out the stiletto, flicked it open and placed the point near Carlo's right eye, paralyzing him into inaction. At the same time, Rosemarie leapt over the counter, got behind Carlo and removed his pistol from its holder. She flipped the safety and pressed the muzzle into the small of his back.

Rufus said, "Bernardo, tell him not to move or he'll never see out of this eye again."

Surprised by the fluidity of the team effort, Bernardo kept his cool. "He will not move. Too frightened. He say please don't kill. He has family."

"Just tell him to stay calm and keep his hands on the counter. Tell him I know he has a panic button somewhere and if he moves his hands or his feet without permission, he will die very quickly. Then ask him if there are any other employees hiding around here." asked Rufus.

"He understand and no move. Only one other worker, Giacomo, but he send home early because store no busy today."

"Good... Rosemarie, collect what we need and then go into the backroom and grab the DVD from the security camera recorder."

Rosemarie collected the weapons and ammunition and then went into the back room, quickly returning with the DVD. Propelling herself over the counter, she landed on her feet next to Rufus.

Rufus said, "Tell him that if I see anything about this in the news tomorrow, I will come back and plunge this knife so far into his eye it will come out the back of his head. Then I will find his family and do the same thing to all of them."

Rufus waited for the translation, and as the man began to tremble and shake his head in denial, said, "Now tell him I'm going to leave him five thousand euros to cover the cost of the pistols and any medical bills."

Carlo looked up and said something. Bernardo said, "He say what medical bills?"

Rufus took one of the guns from Rosemarie and slammed Carlo in the head with the butt. Carlo's eyes rolled up and Rufus shoved him back across the counter where he tumbled to the floor, unconscious.

Rufus said, "All right, let's go."

Bernardo protested, "Wait… You can't leave him alive. He will call police when he wake up."

"Maybe he will or maybe he won't. He may be too scared which is what I'm counting on. That's why I'm leaving him the money. It will help console him. I know it's a calculated risk, but if we kill him, then the police will definitely be involved, and I really don't want to be the subject of a city-wide manhunt."

Bernardo shook his head disapprovingly, "Men like this are unpredictable. In a few days, he may regain his courage."

"By then, we'll be long gone, but we can talk about it more in the car."

They hurriedly left the store and piled into the Mercedes. Rufus turned the ignition and said, "What kind of a place is this anyway? That was pretty lax security for a gun store. Don't they have any crime in Palermo?"

"Plenty of crime, but not here," Bernardo replied from the back seat. "This is protected store."

"Protected?"

"Mafia… Carlo pay for protection so he not have to worry about be rob like this."

Rosemarie laughed at the irony. "Boy, is he going to be pissed off when he wakes up. He may even want a refund on his protection payments."

Rufus was mildly concerned. "Are there going to be people coming after us?"

Bernardo said flatly, "As you say, maybe or maybe no. I hope not because they will be after me too. This place is off limits. Which is why I think we should have kill him, but he don't know me, so probably be okay."

"If you knew this was a protected store, why did you bring us here and not to another one?"

"Because you tell Bernardo you want to buy weapons, not steal them."

Rufus chuckled softly. "You're right, Bernardo. That's exactly what I said. Shame on me."

As they pulled away from the curb, Bernardo was very quiet, so Rufus asked, "Is everything alright, Bernardo? You seem perturbed?"

"Bernardo just curious. We make deal for Bernardo to translate to buy guns, but you steal guns. Bernardo is wondering if Bernardo should get more money."

"That's an interesting thought, but look at it my way, I gave the man five thousand euros for his pistols. So money was exchanged for the weapons. Technically, that was a kind of transaction. In America, we would call this a real gray zone."

"What is gray zone?"

"It's when a situation occurs, but it's not totally clear what just happened, and whether it is legitimate or not, or whether it is acceptable or not. Does that make sense?"

Bernardo digested that for a moment, and seemed to accept it. He asked, "Now what we do?"

As they pulled away from the curb, Rufus said, "Now we get Rosemarie a hijab and a veil."

"I hope this does not involve any more gray zones."

"I'm afraid that it's too late for questions like that, Bernardo, but I'm a fair man. I'm willing to give you all the remaining money in my briefcase, but the price for that is no more questions. That's a total of forty-five-thousand euros for a couple of hours of your time. That's not a bad payoff, but I'm serious, no more questions. Does that sound reasonable so far?"

Learning rapidly to be wary of Rufus's gilded invitations, Bernardo hesitated. Eventually, he said, "What is catch?"

Rufus was amused. The man had just asked another question even though he was told not to. Normally, he would have responded to that with a 9mm to the forehead, but he needed Bernardo for the moment, so he let it pass. "Do you have access to an SUV or some other type of large vehicle?"

Having already witnessed what he presumed was just a small taste of what this man, Rufus, was capable of should he be denied, Bernardo was getting a sinking feeling in his stomach that whatever hole he was digging may already be too deep to get out of. Even worse, they had all the guns.

He cleared his throat and said, "I have van back in Brancaccio for transport of merchandise and people."

"Excellent… Call your boys and tell them I need at least one of them and the van. Rosemarie, I'm going to meet up with Booker. You know what to do after that."

"I think Bernardo and I are going to get along just fine."

CHAPTER 45

They sat in Teresa's living room sipping wine and plotting their next move. Cesari said, "I hate to be the bearer of bad news, but they're here in Palermo, and it will only be a matter of time before they find us."

"How is that possible?" asked Emily frustrated. She had a great morning walking around with Jaskaran and Jeremy and now reality had come crashing down around her.

Tierney said, "I don't know, but they were in Piazza Verdi just a few blocks from here. They knew exactly when I'd be arriving too which is a bad sign."

Emily was becoming increasingly more despondent. "How could they know that?"

"That's a good question, Emily, and I suspect there are still people in the Secret Service who want to close the loop as far as your concerned."

"But I don't even know what I've done?"

"You didn't do anything," explained Vito. "You witnessed something that wasn't supposed to be witnessed."

"So they won't be satisfied until I'm dead?"

Tierney said, "That's not going to happen as long as I have breath in me, Emily. You're the reason I joined the Marines and you're the reason I became a cop, to protect the innocent and to defend America against all its enemies both foreign and domestic. I think it's safe to say these asshats fall under the domestic category. Well these guys have declared war against Emily Hoffman, United States citizen, which means they have declared war on me and all my fellow countrymen."

In spontaneous response, they all raised their glasses in unity. Tierney toasted the group. "Brave, gorgeous, intelligent and incredibly sexy...but enough about me, here's to you."

The tribute brought a riptide of laughter to the otherwise somber gathering. Even Emily found it amusing, and asked, "Is that how Marines get ready for battle?"

"It's how I get ready."

Cesari felt it was time to get serious. "Okay, they're in Palermo and even worse, they're in our general vicinity."

Vito said, "As much as I like it here, we need to relocate."

Tierney agreed. "Anybody have an opinion?"

Jaskaran and Jeremy nodded. Jeremy said, "Within Palermo, another city in Sicily, or off the island altogether?"

Teresa added, "Taormina is beautiful place. Is resort town on the eastern side of Sicily three-hour ride from here, and not too far from Messina which is very close to mainland. If we need to leave Sicily in hurry, we can always take ferry from Messina and be in Calabria one hour. Also Taormina is filled with tourists. We will blend in very well."

Cesari said, "It sounds as good as any other place. If they find us there, we'll just keep moving."

"Forever?" asked Emily. "Or just until the money runs out?"

Tierney grinned. "Don't worry about money, Emily. I have a full Marine pension, and every time Cesari does a colonoscopy, it's like robbing a bank. And let's not forget Gianelli who basically prints his own money in his basement. The way I see it, they'll run out of bullets before we run out of cash."

Emily didn't find that very reassuring, but kept her thoughts to herself. For every one's sake, she was trying hard not to be negative.

Cesari cleared his throat, and said, "Perhaps we should focus on the matter at hand. Teresa, would you mind helping me rent a car. There's too many of us to fit in your Panda."

Gerry said, "Wouldn't it make sense to at least keep one guy here? If they're watching us, he could guard the front door and keep up the illusion that everybody's still inside while everyone slips out the back."

"Are you volunteering, Gerry?" asked Vito.

"That I am, boss."

"You're just dying to shoot someone, aren't you?"

"I've got an itch that needs to be scratched, boss."

Vito laughed. "Fucking Gerry. You're going to be the death of me one of these days, but I have to admit your plan makes sense. It should buy us some time, but you have to understand, rain or shine, you're on your own. You murder someone and get arrested, I can't just come back and bail you out."

"Understood, boss."

"Okay, we'll take off as soon as we get a second car."

Teresa said, "Is too late to rent car. We have to wait until morning."

"Not acceptable," advised Tierney. "Our best chance is to leave under cover of night. That's basic operating procedure if we think they might have surveillance on us."

Cesari said, "The Panda seats five. Without Gerry, we have seven, but we can lap up."

Vito scoffed. "I hope you don't think I'm going on a three-hour ride with Tierney on my lap?"

"If I stay behind with Gerry, that's only six to fit in the Panda," offered Jeremy. "I can always rent a car in the morning and catch up to you. That is, if Gerry doesn't mind having a black guy back him up."

Gerry grinned. "I'm beginning to think the black guy is the only one around here with any balls."

"It still leaves us with one too many people," persisted Teresa. "Lapping up as you say is no so easy in a Fiat. Maybe for a small child but not for an adult."

Cesari said, "I'll stay behind too, but first I'll go get the Panda. I left it by the Piazza Verdi."

"I don't think that's a good idea," Tierney said. "They know you. If they're watching, they might follow and even decide it's time to start picking us off one or two at a time."

Vito said, "But they know all of us."

"Some better than others," mused Cesari. "They were waiting for Tierney, and the guy on the plane had all of our pictures on his phone... Well, not everyone's. They didn't have Jaskaran's, Gerry's or Jeremy's photos."

"Or mine," chimed in Teresa. "They are not seeking me. I could walk down to the piazza and get my car. It is not that late and there will be many people out and about, even some of my neighbors."

Vito thought about it for a moment and said, "There's no need for you to go Teresa. We have three healthy guys that can do it. Isn't that right, guys?"

The three in question murmured their consent. Teresa smiled, appreciating her cousin's protectiveness. "Even if they manage to navigate their way back here at night, which is a big if with all the one-way streets and dead ends, they will never be able to park in the garage. Parking in Palermo is an art unto itself. Each car is separated only by millimeters from the others. Parking like that with a stick shift takes years of practice."

Cesari concurred, "I can attest to that. I drove the Panda today. I feel like I lost three years on my life."

"Besides," added Teresa. "I need to get out even for a little bit. I have been cooped up all day."

Vito relented. "I guess it's pretty low risk, but you're not going alone."

Gerry stepped forward. "I got this covered, Vito. I won't let nuttin' happen to the lady."

"I appreciate the offer, Gerry, but you're not the most subtle guy. You're going to have to sit this one out."

Jaskaran said, "They're not looking for me. I'll go with her. This uniform I'm wearing will throw anyone off the scent anyway."

"I think that's a good idea," agreed Cesari.

Vito nodded approvingly. "I agree."

"I think you're making a mistake, boss. I can handle things better than him. I'm a pro," protested Gerry.

"That's enough, Gerry," admonished Vito. "If we send you, we might as well hang a flashing neon light outside the entrance."

"Maybe I should go with them?" suggested Jeremy. You know, the more the merrier."

Vito took a moment to consider that before saying, "Thanks, Jeremy, but I think this is one of those situations where two's company and three's a crowd. A young couple taking a stroll for some night air will seem very natural and will potentially blend in better." He turned to Jaskaran and Teresa. "Especially if you two play it up a bit by walking arm in arm and appearing intimate. But don't forget she's my cousin, Jaskaran, so don't play it up too much… You still have the Colt in your turban?"

Jaskaran shook his head. "No, I took it out when we returned to the apartment earlier… Damn thing weighs a ton."

"Well, put it back up there and maybe the knife too. Will they both fit?"

"Are you kidding? I could fit an arsenal up there."

Vito took a deep breath and let it out slowly. "Be careful. Stick with the crowds. Any sign of trouble, duck into a restaurant or a café and call me."

Teresa said, "What could go wrong? It is only a few blocks walk and I have a big, strong man with me."

Vito walked up to her and held her hands. "Are you sure you want to do this?"

"Yes, of course. It will be fine. I am more worry about Bernardo and his friends."

****

Burke was on the phone with the concierge at the hotel as Morehouse paid the bill for dinner. Morehouse was frustrated. He had hoped to have a quick meal and move on to the first hotel on the list he had made up, but the driver was delayed, and it felt like dinner had dragged on forever. Burke hung up and turned to his colleague.

"The driver's on the way. He'll be here in ten minutes. The concierge apologized. He misunderstood what I had said about needing someone to drive us all night. It took him a while, but he fixed it. They're sending a husband and wife team so one can spell the other as needed should they become fatigued as the night drags on."

"I can't wait to see the bill for this," Morehouse said dryly.

"You're right about that, but it beats trying to figure out this town on our own. This city is a maze of disorganized streets with no particular theme to the layout, but I'm glad I'll be long retired before any house committee decides to look into our expense account for this."

Morehouse grimaced. If things went as planned and Burke retired when he said he would, then he would be the one on the hot seat if it ever came to it while the former director was sipping pina coladas on some Caribbean island.

He said, "Thanks, boss."

"No problem… If it's any consolation, you have my permission to throw me under the bus when the time comes… So what's on the agenda?"

"We'll hit the four and five-star hotels first. My thinking is that they'll feel more comfortable with high end places because they might have a better chance of finding people who are fluent in English. I realize that my logic could be faulty on that for several reasons, but we have to start somewhere, and I suspect Gianelli is a bit of an Al Capone wannabe with a taste for the high life. Same for Cesari. I can't believe that a gastroenterologist is going to want to slum it for anybody. He's probably still trying to figure out how he got dragged into this mess when he could be chasing some sexy nurse around the operating room."

"I agree, but they have Tierney with them now. He's a Marine and a cop. He may feel very uncomfortable in a five-star hotel. The guy's used to sleeping on the ground with scorpions biting his ass and AK47 rounds flying overhead. Did you read his combat record? He's an effin' hero."

Morehouse bit his lip. How did Burke know Tierney was here? Keeping this question to himself, he nodded. "I did, and as I said, we have to begin somewhere. I thought we'd start at the Excelsior Palace downtown. It's a Hilton owned property and considered one of the best hotels in Palermo."

"Then lead the way. I think our car just arrived. There's a silver Mercedes outside with some guy standing by it holding a sign with my name on it."

Morehouse turned around and saw a dark complexioned, medium build, neatly dressed man through the window. They stood up and left the restaurant. Outside, Burke indicated to the guy who they were, and the man opened the rear door for them with Morehouse entering first and sliding over behind the driver's seat. Once Burke was in, the guy scooted over to the driver's side door. There was a woman in a black Hijab and veil in the passenger seat. She stared straight ahead and made no motion to greet them.

Once the driver was buckled up, he started the engine and adjusted himself. He smiled at them in the rearview mirror and said, "Is please to meet you. Where we go?"

Morehouse said, "As you may have heard, we're looking for a friend who's on vacation and for some reason can't be reached by phone. There's an emergency back home with her family and we need to find her urgently. All we know is that she's here in Palermo."

"Is no problem, Signori. We will take care of everything. You just sit back and relax. If need anything, just to ask."

"Okay, then take us to the Excelsior Palace on Via della Liberta."

"A beautiful hotel. I take you there quick. I know short cut. I know where all hotels are in Palermo. I have drive car many years now."

Burke looked triumphantly at Morehouse as if vindicated by the decision to hire a professional driver. Morehouse nodded his approval.

"I guess you were right."

"You mean again?"

Morehouse grinned and then said to the driver, "You never told us your name."

"I am Bernardo."

CHAPTER 46

Munoz watched from her rented subcompact. There was something very strange happening. The man and the woman who drove the Mercedes had arrived fifteen minutes earlier and had idled down the block from where Burke and the director were eating dinner. She knew that because she was parked down the same block. The expensive car had caught her eye when it pulled right in front of her to the curb. The woman got out of the car, walked into a small grocery store and came out with a panini. She had blonde hair and a bandage on her face. She ate her sandwich standing outside the car and when she finished her meal, she balled up her napkin and threw it to the sidewalk without making any attempt to find a trash can. Right before she entered the car, she donned a hijab and veil in full view of everyone on the sidewalk. How strange. No muslim woman would do that. Even stranger was when the same vehicle drove an additional two hundred feet forward and picked up Burke and Morehouse. Munoz didn't like that at all. Every instinct she had was firing on all cylinders.

****

Rufus gave Booker one of the Berettas and then sat across the street from him. They were doing their best to cross cover both the entrance to the apartment building and the parking garage next to it. At 10:00 p.m., they saw a strangely dressed Indian man and a slender woman exit the building arm in arm appearing intimate in the way they comported themselves. The woman might have been Indian or Sicilian it was hard to say. The man was tall and broad-shouldered and appeared even taller because of the massive turban on his head. The military uniform he wore was bizarre and eccentric to say the least, the kind that hadn't been worn in over a hundred years. They strode casually beneath the streetlights and appeared happily unconcerned.

Booker whispered into his phone, "What do you think?"

Rufus replied, "I don't know. There's more than one apartment in the building so it's hard to say." He glanced at the photos on his phone. "Neither one fit the descriptions we have, but when you were in the airport in Toronto, Rosemarie said there was another woman and an Indian guy with a turban. Do you recall that?"

"I don't recall even being in Toronto except in the vaguest way."

"But you remember it was Cesari who clobbered you on the plane?"

"Like it was yesterday."

"It was yesterday, Booker."

"Whatever... That's the way concussions work, Rufus. You remember some things and not others. When the bathroom door opened on the plane, I saw Cesari clearly. I just didn't have time to react."

"Fine... I say we follow these two. There's something fishy about them. They could be going for the car, not that it will do them any good since I slashed all four tires, but it would be nice to know what they're up to."

"You or me? Somebody should stay here."

"I'll tail them. You stay put, and call me if anyone else comes out of the building."

Rufus gave them a half block head start and then picked up the trail as they strolled nonchalantly along Via Orologio in the direction of the Teatro Massimo. The man was cool, but the woman nervously darted her gaze behind her and to the side several times, confirming in Rufus's mind that he had made the right decision. She was wary about something that was for sure. He smiled and his heart rate picked up a beat knowing that the chase was on. It was always thrilling to track your quarry whether it was in some backwater village or midtown Manhattan. He picked up his phone and dialed Bernardo's man waiting in the van by the disabled Fiat. He didn't know this guy, but his task was simple. Rufus had employed locals many times in his various exploits around the globe, and he assessed that if anybody should be able to handle a simple kidnapping then it should be the Sicilian mob.

"Tullio, we're on the way. Keep an eye out for an Indian man and a woman. You can't miss them. The guy is dressed in some sort of military uniform with a huge turban. I'm about a half block behind. If they go to the Fiat, we grab them."

Rufus had to repeat himself twice because of Tullio's limited command of English, but finally Tullio said, "Is understood. Indian man, big turban, and small woman."

The dark side streets made it easy to follow them unseen in the shadows. They were moving deliberately slowly so as not to appear uneasy, but it was their measured pace which confirmed the covert nature of their purpose. They didn't stop to grab an espresso, an aperitif, a gelato, or simply to enjoy the moment the way two lovers would. Theirs' was an inexorable push forward toward their ultimate destination and they didn't want to waste time with banalities.

They came to the Piazza Verdi and seemed relieved to have made it that far unscathed. All they had to do now was cross to the other side where the green Panda was waiting. Parked in front of the Fiat was a nondescript white van, the kind one saw every day in cities delivering flowers or catering parties. The back doors were open and there was a man leaning forward adjusting his cargo. There were quite a few people in the piazza and in the cafés lining it on all sides. It was the sense of normalcy all around they found reassuring as they picked up their pace.

Reaching the Panda, they abruptly halted just a few feet away, and gawked in surprise and confusion at the flat tires. They both approached closely, stooping to get a better look, trying to understand. Absorbed as they were in bewilderment, they didn't see Rufus race up behind them or Tullio suddenly turn in their direction. Teresa was closest, and Tullio literally picked her up and threw her into the back of the van where she hit her head and was momentarily dazed. Almost simultaneously, Rufus jammed the muzzle of the Beretta hard into the back of Jaskaran's head.

As threatening as he could, Rufus hissed, "Listen to me carefully, Mahatma Ghandi. Get into the van now or I'll blow your brains out right here."

Jaskaran felt the sting of the cold, hard steel and saw no alternative but to comply, and just like that, in barely more than ten seconds both he and Teresa were in the back of the van. Rufus got in with them and sat opposite with the Beretta as Tullio quickly closed the doors and jumped into the driver's seat. As far as snatches went, that was textbook perfect. The van lurched forward as it pulled away from the curb. Maybe somebody saw but no one reacted.

Rufus stared hard at his captives. "You speak English?"

They both nodded and Rufus added, "Sit on your hands and don't move. I don't say things twice. Understand?"

Too stunned and frightened to offer any resistance, they readily complied. They didn't know who he was, but they knew what he was. He was a trained killer, and he had the upper hand. Once they were positioned to his satisfaction, Rufus reached out and frisked them both for weapons. He relieved them of their cellphones and sat back.

Rufus said, "Let me start by saying that you better not fuck with me. I've killed many men who were highly trained killers themselves, and I'd have no more reluctance to end your life than I would a cockroach. But I won't just kill you. I'll put a hole in your ankle, then your elbow and then I'll cut out an eye and let you bleed to death in excruciating agony. Now I know you two are helping Cesari and Tierney hide the Hoffman girl. You first," he said, waving the gun at Jaskaran. "Who are you?"

Jaskaran broke out into a sweat. There was no point in lying. "My name is Jaskaran Singh and I'm an anesthesiologist. Cesari's my friend. We work together back in New York."

"An anesthesiologist? You've got to be kidding? So what's with the outfit?"

"It's a costume I bought here when we landed. You know, a disguise."

"Not bad. You have no military training?"

"None."

"Why are you helping Cesari?"

"It seemed like the right thing to do," he stuttered.

"I'll bet you're rethinking that right now." Without waiting for a response, Rufus turned slightly, and pointed the Beretta at Teresa causing her to catch her breath. "Your turn."

"My name is Teresa Tartarone. Vito is my cousin. I am let him use my apartment for to hide the girl."

"Vito? As in Vito Gianelli?"

She nodded. "Yes."

"So Gianelli's your cousin? Now that is interesting. Did you know he's a mobster or is that just kind of routine stuff with you guineas?"

She didn't say anything to that, and he let it slide.

He continued, "Where were you two going just now that you needed a car?"

They glanced at each other in momentary hesitation and Rufus pulled the trigger. The explosion caused them to flinch as smoke and burnt gunpowder filled the air. The round tore through the side of the van in between Teresa and Jaskaran whose ears rang in pain. Teresa began to tremble and cry.

Rufus said calmly, "I won't miss next time."

Jaskaran said, "We were going to Taormina. We didn't think it was safe for Emily here anymore."

"You were right about that. Who else is in the apartment and what kind of weapons do they have?"

Jaskaran was more or less forthright in his account leaving out as much as he thought he could without the misinformation being too obvious. He very noticeably didn't mention the weapons hidden in his turban.

When he was done, Rufus thought it over for a minute and then said to Teresa, "Taormina? Isn't that where Mount Etna is?"

Teresa regained her composure and nodded. "Yes, is maybe twenty or thirty kilometers away."

Rufus seemed genuinely curious when he asked, "It's still active isn't it?"

"Yes, is one of most active volcanoes in world. Erupt all the time."

Rufus was quiet as he contemplated that. After a minute, he came to some sort of conclusion and smiled.

Handing Teresa her cellphone, he said, "Call your cousin."

Shaking, she dialed the number and when Vito answered she started bawling uncontrollably into the receiver. Rufus grabbed the phone back and spoke, "Is this Gianelli?"

"Yeah... Who's this and what have you done to Teresa?"

"We'll get to all that... I'm told that you're on your way to Taormina. You may want to reconsider that."

"Why?"

"I have a proposition for you."

"I'm listening."

"Your cousin for the Hoffman girl, and don't bother denying you have her."

"You're going to regret this, asshole."

CHAPTER 47

"Where's Morehouse and Burke?" Rufus asked.

Rosemarie replied, "They're inside the Excelsior talking to the night manager. We're parked outside. What's up?"

"Change of plans… We have two hostages now. One of them is Gianelli's cousin, a woman named Teresa Tartarone. That's her apartment they've been hiding in. The other is a doctor friend of Cesari's who thought protecting Emily Hoffman would be a great adventure. Gianelli's willing to cough up the Hoffman girl in exchange for the two of them."

"Gianelli had a cousin here? Interesting, so that's why they chose Sicily. You trust him?"

"Of course not. There are six people still in the apartment and they're armed. I'm not a hundred percent sure I can count on Booker. His heart's in the right place but his mental faculties aren't quite where they ought to be. And Bernardo's guy is great for show, but I don't know how he'll react in a crisis so I need you."

"What should I do with Morehouse and Burke? I thought the idea was to keep them off the trail for as long as possible, and if that didn't work, then use the Beretta."

"Can't be helped. I can't go up against six-armed people by myself with Booker the way he is and a non-English speaking leg-breaker who may or may not run at the first hint of personal danger… Maybe you can just leave them there. It'll take them a while before they figure out they've been abandoned, and it's unlikely they'll be able to get another car until morning."

"They could take taxis around all night."

"I suppose, but what are the odds they'll figure out the Hoffman girl is holed up at Gianelli's cousin's apartment before morning?"

"Are you serious? They have a lot of resources at their disposal which I'm sure are working overtime right now, and they know the Hoffman girl is here. It will only be a matter of time before they sort out Gianelli's family connections. The machine is slow but not entirely stupid. Someone is eventually going to ask the obvious question of why they chose to hide Emily in Palermo? Then it will just be a quick phone call to our pals here in the Secret Service. At least that's the way I see it."

"I think you're giving them too much credit. I didn't even know Gianelli had a cousin here until thirty minutes ago, but I agree, there is that possibility."

"I just don't think it's a good idea to underestimate your opponents," counseled Rosemarie.

Rufus thought on that for a minute before adding, "Then bring them along."

"Bring them along? On what pretext?"

"On the pretext that you have a 9mm cannon and you're willing to use it."

One hundred feet away inside the Excelsior, Morehouse and Burke were disappointed and frustrated as they questioned the night manager and his assistant. They flashed their credentials which impressed the men who spoke English fairly well. They had no problem looking for Emily, Gianelli and Cesari's names in the registry but came up empty. The problem remained that they could have registered under false names and paid cash. At a nice hotel such as the Excelsior, you would think a passport or proper identification was required, and technically it was, but human nature was frail, and the manger admitted that on occasion the staff misbehaved and let an individual slip in under the wire for the right amount of compensation. Compounding that was the hopeless romanticism of the Italian people. If the man or woman at the desk thought that a young woman was hiding from a dangerous boyfriend or husband, they may well have looked the other way. There was no way of knowing for sure if that had happened.

While they tried to figure it out, Morehouse received a text from Munoz requesting that he call her urgently. Becoming concerned, he excused himself from the room and stepped out into the lobby.

"Bad timing, Munoz. What is it?"

"I'm sorry. I didn't know what to do and I didn't want to talk to you while you were driving, but there's something wrong."

"What? And make it quick."

"There's something off with that woman in the car with you."

"Such as?"

"I don't think she's really Muslim. Before they picked you up, I saw her standing on the street eating a panini without the hijab or veil. She put them on in full view of everyone and then got into the car."

Morehouse said skeptically, "Is that it?"

Munoz hesitated. "You don't think that's significant?"

"For what? Do you think all Muslim women love wearing that stuff? Or even believe in it?"

With some hesitancy, she replied, "Probably not…"

"That's right. That's as naïve as believing all women love to wear bras or all Orthodox Jews love to wear yarmulkes or all Catholics love to go to church every Sunday just to kneel, stand, sit and repeat for an hour while chanting two-thousand-year-old prayers. People do things they're accustomed to and because society or their tribe hammers it into them that they have to. It doesn't mean they like it and wouldn't mind a little break from the ritual once in a while."

"So you're not concerned?"

"Based solely on that…no. Look, I have to go. A long phone call is going to appear suspicious, but I'll keep what you said under advisement."

He clicked off and contemplated the conversation for a moment, thought better about cavalierly blowing off Munoz's concern and ducked into a nearby restroom. Removing his shoulder holster, he threw it away, and placed his Glock in the small of his back. On the way out, he glanced in the mirror and wondered if he was getting carried away. Then he joined Burke who was finishing up with the manager. They thanked the man and said good night.

Outside, Burke said, "Well, that was a waste of time."

"Not totally… I agree that they may have checked in under an assumed name, but it's still more likely that they didn't in my opinion. I say we stay the course."

Burke nodded. "Agreed… What was the phone call about?"

"My wife… We're remodeling the kitchen, and she wanted to know if the budget we decided on was hard and fast or just a suggestion."

Burke laughed. "Women are always shifting the goal posts."

"Isn't that the truth."

They got in the Mercedes in the same position as before, with Morehouse seated behind Bernardo, who stepped on the accelerator. As the vehicle heaved forward, Morehouse, used his left hand to reach discreetly behind his back and deftly retrieve his pistol. He placed it on the seat cushion next to him on his left side, between his leg and the door, hidden under cover of his suit jacket. Watching the woman in the hijab carefully, he suddenly didn't like what he saw.

****

Vito paced back and forth, his fists clenched, his face red and contorted with primal rage. It was several minutes, before he was able to control himself. Everyone sat and watched in silence, waiting for the storm to blow over. Eventually, he sat down and surveyed the room.

He said, "They got Teresa and Jaskaran. I don't know the details of how, but they got them."

"Who is he?"

"He said his name didn't matter. All that was important was that I listen carefully. He said if I ever want to see Teresa or Jaskaran alive again, we would have to give him Emily. He wants us to go to the Mount Etna National Park for the exchange, and that if we brought weapons or didn't do exactly like we were told, all that we would get were two headless corpses."

The room was very quiet at the news. Emily wept and ran into the bedroom, overwhelmed with guilt that all that was happening was because of her.

Cesari asked, "What did you say?"

"I agreed of course, just to buy time, but get this. We don't even have a car. They slashed all the tires on the Fiat."

Cesari glanced at his watch. "When are they expecting us to get there?"

"He gave me an hour to acquire a vehicle, three and half hours to drive there and thirty minutes for gas and breaks. So five hours starting now, and that's only if we get the lead out. For every ten minutes we're late, he's going to cut one of their fingers off."

"Jesus, it's almost eleven. How are we supposed to find a car at this hour, let alone one that will fit us all?"

"I think that's the idea, Cesari. He knows there are six of us and he's trying to thin the herd."

Tierney had been listening carefully, making calculations in his head. He said, "Which means he's either alone or doesn't have a whole lot of troops with him. I guess that's the silver lining here."

They were encouraged by that assessment. Vito said, "I'm not sure what to do with Emily. There's no way we're going to hand her off to anybody, but if we show up without her, then he's certainly going to kill Jaskaran and Teresa."

Tierney looked downtrodden. He had been in hostage negotiations many times. Not showing up with Emily at the exchange was a nonstarter and guaranteed Teresa's death. He said, "I hate this, but you're right. I'll talk to Emily and explain the situation, but the decision has to be hers."

"I'm coming with you," Emily said reappearing in the living room. "If I don't show up, they'll kill two good people who were trying to help me. How am I supposed to live with that? And then they're still going to come after me, right?"

Tierney nodded grimly. "Undoubtedly…"

Vito said, "Gerry, let's get moving. We have an hour to jack a car that will fit us all."

"As long as collateral damage isn't an issue, we'll get it done, but may I speak freely, boss?"

Vito narrowed his eyes and looked as dangerous as a human being possibly could. "Don't say it, Gerry."

"You should've sent me."

Chapter 48

Just under an hour later at close to midnight, they were loading onto a yellow short bus Gerry and Vito heisted from a nearby elementary school parking lot. It was less than half the length of a standard school bus and looked more like a very large jeep with a wheelchair lift and a large retractable stop sign. Gerry sat in the captain's chair and seemed quite proud of himself. It seated six comfortably and had plenty of room to accommodate several wheelchairs. Once they were buckled in, Gerry took off.

Cesari shook his head. "You've got to be kidding… This is a new low for you, Vito. Stealing a school bus for disabled children."

"I only had an hour, Cesari. I'd like to see you do better. Besides, it's Saturday. There's no school today."

They stopped at a gas station on the outskirts of Palermo and then settled in for the journey. It was an older bus, and the suspension system needed some work causing them to bounce along uncomfortably. It was not conducive to sleep, but their adrenaline was so high it was doubtful that anyone of them could have slept in a king bed snuggled under the covers with a white noise machine droning in the background and an empty bottle of scotch on the night table.

Mostly they sat there staring ahead anxiously wondering what was going to happen once they got to Etna. The gloves were off now and there was a solid chance some of them might not make it home alive. Tierney was the only one in the group who had any real combat experience, and hopefully more than enough to compensate for the rest of their inadequacies. Vito and Gerry had a fairly in depth understanding of gang warfare, but this wasn't gang warfare. Cesari had helped Vito out from time to time with his nefarious affairs and was not a total rookie when it came to hostile engagements. Jeremy and Emily, however, were total nubes, and they both looked like frightened rabbits. Stonewall was the only one who didn't seem to have a care in the world as he slept in his crate oblivious to the machinations of men.

****

Morehouse knew something was wrong the minute he entered the car. The woman's eyes kept roaming furtively to the rear-view mirror where she could see him. There was something about the veil and hijab that just didn't seem natural on her. He wondered about the gauze underneath the veil. Did Bernardo beat her? Then there was Bernardo. He was a tad too friendly considering the late hour. Since they left the Excelsior Palace, they'd been driving nearly thirty minutes. Their next destination on the list was the Grand Hotel et des Palmes on Via Roma which should have been approximately a ten-minute drive from the Excelsior give or take. Bernardo had taken a circuitous route because he said there was heavy traffic due to construction in that area. But now they were on the E 90 highway speeding eastward with the lights of the city behind them. Bernardo said they were leaving Palermo for a short period and then would circle back to reenter it at a point that would bypass the construction. Burke seemed unperturbed and stared straight ahead.

Morehouse asked, "How much longer, Bernardo? We have a long night ahead of us."

"Five minutes and we reach the next exit. We take that, cross over highway and head back. I am sorry for delay. It can no be helped. Back in city, we might as well walk, traffic so bad."

Burke said, "I know it's frustrating, Grayson, but don't work yourself up. We'll get there. I'm going to close my eyes for a minute. Maybe you should do the same? Like you said, it's going to be a long night."

Morehouse responded agreeably, "You're right. A five-minute power nap sounds mighty appealing at the moment. I'm exhausted. Wake me up when we get there."

"And vice versa."

The director barely uttered the words when he closed his eyes and drifted off. Morehouse shifted his body a little trying to get comfortable but actually positioned himself to better access his gun. His eyelids shuttered down most of the way but not completely as he watched the rearview mirror through the slitted view. There it was again. The woman's eyes bearing down on him. Only this time the look wasn't casual or curious. It was predatory.

Something was about to happen.

He pretended to doze and even feigned snoring. Eventually, her gaze returned to the road ahead. He fingered his pistol, and wondered if he was the victim of an overactive imagination. A few minutes later, he knew he wasn't. The car passed by the next turnoff without slowing down and suddenly he knew he was a prisoner. The only question that lingered was who in the car were his captors. Bernardo? The woman next to him who by this time Morehouse realized wasn't Bernardo's wife?

Burke?

God, he hated that idea. He had looked up to the man for so many years. He simply couldn't wrap his head around it. The only way to be sure was to wait it out and see what happened. He hoped Munoz was keeping pace with them. She might be his only hope if things went badly. If he pulled out his gun now, he would never know for certain whose side Burke was on and would probably get killed for his effort. He needed them to make the first move. With that in mind, he pretended to fall into a deep sleep, completely relaxed his body and began breathing in a steady, rhythmic pattern. He wasn't sure how long he could keep the pretense up but there was a lot at stake.

Forty-five minutes later, he felt the car slow and change direction. Stealing a quick glance, he saw that they had left E 90 and turned onto highway A19, a lonely road meandering across the middle of Sicily toward the eastern coast. He had never been there but knew that Palermo was on the western tip of the triangular shaped island. They had been travelling east along the coast on E 90 and now were heading southeast. There were about a million places they could be going, but the big ones were Agrigento on the southern coast and Catania or Siragusa on the east coast. He couldn't even vaguely imagine why they were going to any of these places, but it didn't bode well. It was also clear that as long as he pretended to sleep, they didn't feel the need to use force or violence on him which made sense. If a captive offered no resistance, why waste energy and ammunition?

Sooner or later however when he woke, they would spring into action. They would anticipate that he would realize what had happened and try to pre-empt any counter measures he might try. He had no doubt they must be armed, and they would in all likelihood expect that he would be also. He needed to be exceedingly careful at this juncture. They would be tired from the late hour and on edge.

Morehouse let another thirty minutes pass before yawning and stretching. He thought waiting any longer would seem unrealistic. Afterall, how long could a grown man sleep sitting up in a moving car without being drugged. Groggily, he looked around. Burke was still dozing. He glanced at his watch. It was 2:00 a.m. The woman was watching him.

Acting confused and drowsy, he asked, "Where are we?"

Burke woke up and also yawned. "Grayson, I think we overslept."

"Apparently… Hey Bernardo, where are we?" he asked again.

"We are to see the sights of bella Sicilia, Signore."

Morehouse looked out the window into the night as if not understanding, but when he turned back, he saw the dark menacing barrel of a Beretta staring directly at him. Rosemarie tore off her veil and said, "Relax, Deputy Director."

Burke said angrily, "What the hell's going on here?"

Rosemarie hissed, "Shut up, Director Burke, and you just might make it out of here alive. Hands up and then don't move. Both of you."

After they raised their hands, she turned fully around on her knees. Reaching over her seat, she opened Morehouse's jacket and seemed surprised and even a bit confused. Waving the Beretta in his face, she demanded, "Where's your gun?"

"I left it in my room at the hotel."

"Grayson, please don't be a hero," whispered Burke.

"I'm not. I left it in the hotel safe. After our conversation about the risks of carrying illegal weapons in Palermo, I decided not to take it."

Rosemarie didn't believe him and did a quick, awkward frisk in the dark, clumsily patting him down with her Beretta firmly pressed into his forehead. His gun was just far enough away that she missed it when she ran her hand along his thigh. She finished with a firm squeeze of his crotch and then stared at him incredulously. Almost as an afterthought, she turned her attention to Burke and relieved him of the Glock in his shoulder holster. She appeared to relax, and sat back partially turned with the muzzle of her pistol trained unwaveringly on Morehouse.

She said, "Everybody sit tight. We still have a ways to go."

"Where are we going?" asked Morehouse.

"For a walk in a park."

"May I ask who you are and what you want?"

"No, you may not."

Burke said, "If you're after ransom money, let me assure you that will never happen. The United States government doesn't negotiate with terrorists or kidnappers."

She smirked. "Then you're very lucky that's not what I'm after. Now, no more questions."

"Why not?" asked Morehouse. "You have the gun. What's the harm in answering a few questions? Like you said, we have a ways to go. We'll be bored to tears by the time we get there."

Rosemarie was amused. "Is this what they call maintaining control in hostage rescue training?"

"No, it's called trying to understand why anyone would be stupid enough to kidnap the Director and Deputy Director of the Secret Service?"

Burke was horrified at Morehouse's tone. "Grayson, have you gone mad? This woman's a killer. Please forgive him, we've both been under a lot of stress."

Morehouse saw a window of opportunity and decided to jump through it. "Speak for yourself, Travis. I've never felt better. The least this bitch can do is tell us her name."

His bad attitude threw her off balance, and she unconsciously glanced at Burke and then back again at Morehouse. The look was brief, but Morehouse caught it.

She hesitated, smiled, and then lied, "My name is Margaretha. Does that make you feel better?"

He had her off script now and pressed harder. "No, it doesn't. If you're going to kill me then the least you can do is tell me your whole name."

"Fine… My full name is Margaretha Geertruida Zelle."

"Grayson, why are you provoking her? No good can come of it," scolded Burke.

The woman nodded smugly. "You should listen to your friend, Deputy Director. He's trying to save your life."

"What happened to your face?" Morehouse asked, determined to goad her. "Was dinner late and Bernardo slapped you around?"

Burke was beside himself. "Grayson, I'm ordering you to stand down. You're going to get us both killed."

Morehouse stared at her. "Go ahead, Margaretha. Kill us both, but do me a favor and start with the director. I'd like to see that."

The woman raised her eyebrows in surprise. Morehouse was now fully out on a limb. Burke was aghast and getting agitated. "How dare you," he shouted. "You're insane. This woman's a bonafide psychopath. Don't test her patience. Please ignore him, Ro... Margaretha."

Bingo!

He shook the tree and look at what fell out. Morehouse slid his hand imperceptibly toward his Glock. "Margaretha Geertruida Zelle," he said. "You don't seem very surprised by her name, Travis."

"Who cares what her name is?"

"I do, because the last woman with that name died on October 15, 1917."

"What's that supposed to mean?"

"It means that this is the famous Rosemarie who's been wreaking havoc on our investigation. Rosemarie, a.k.a. Rosemarie Zelle, a.k.a. Margaretha Geertruida Zelle, a.k.a. Mata Hari, a.k.a. only God and her mother know her real name. We've been looking for you, darling."

She stopped smiling. Ever the professional, and having lived most of her life in the shadows, she wasn't thrilled at being unmasked even by some worm she was about to squash. Morehouse, on the other hand, was thoroughly pleased with himself. He had pressed all her buttons with good result.

Her features darkened. "You better make him stop, Travis. Deal or no deal, I'll end him now, painfully."

Burke became ashen, but before he could reply, Morehouse fired his Glock into Rosemarie's face, hitting her just above the bridge of her nose. She fell backward dead, and Bernardo involuntarily jerked, temporarily losing control of the car. The smell of cordite filled the cabin and Burke jumped back into his chair in shock. Bernardo braked hard and swerved back but overcompensated and the car skidded and swung around making a full circle before coming to a full stop facing the wrong way, nearly tipping over in the process. Breathing hard, Bernardo was still trying to figure out what had just happened when Morehouse jabbed him in the back of the head with his pistol.

"Are you armed?" Morehouse demanded.

"No, signore. The woman would not let me have weapon. I am prisoner just like you."

"I bet. Now turn the car around and pull off to the side of the road so I can frisk you."

By the time Bernardo, finished that maneuver and stopped the car, Munoz pulled up behind them. Morehouse leaned over the driver's seat and did a quick search of Bernardo for a weapon. Satisfied he was unarmed, Morehouse sat back in his seat.

Burke said, "What's happening, Grayson?"

"All in due time, Travis."

Munoz got out of her car and came over to the passenger side to avoid any oncoming traffic which was minimal at 3:00 a.m. She had seen the car suddenly spin around and come to a screeching halt, and now she saw Rosemarie's body and flinched. Burke rolled down his window in complete surprise.

"Munoz, what are you doing here?" he asked, stunned by the sudden turn of events.

Morehouse said, "I'll explain in a minute, Travis. Right now, we have to save the life of an innocent young woman. Munoz, would you mind dragging the corpse out of the car and joining us, but retrieve her cellphone and any ID she may have on her first. Also, there are two handguns floating around up front there that need to be secured."

Burke said, "Yes, please pass me my Glock."

Morehouse said, "No, Travis, for the moment I think it best that you remain unarmed."

Burke was rattled. "I don't understand."

"I'm pretty sure you do. Now hand me your cellphone. I'm really not in the mood for anymore bullshit. I'm done being reasonable with unreasonable people."

"Grayson, have you lost your mind?"

"That's a distinct possibility. Afterall, I just shot a CIA spook in the forehead in the middle of the night in the middle of a foreign country where I have no business being. That sounds pretty crazy to me. Does that sound crazy to you, Munoz?"

Munoz was examining the multiple ID's and passports she had found on Rosemarie. Without looking up, she said, "Very much so."

CHAPTER 49

"Keep driving, Bernardo," Morehouse ordered.

Bernardo was sweating profusely from fear and anxiety. "Please, Signore, you must believe me. I am victim too. The woman she has the gun and order Bernardo to drive so Bernardo drive. She was very bad person. Bernardo no like."

"I do believe you, Bernardo, but now I have the gun so start driving."

Trying to suppress the heart attack he felt coming on, Bernardo put the Mercedes in gear, and steered the car back onto the road. He stammered, "Same destination as before?"

"Which was?"

"Mount Etna National Park, l'entrata sud… the south entrance. Meet others in parking lot of Bar Silvestri near crater."

"Sure, why not?"

Munoz kept her gun trained on Bernardo while Morehouse held his Glock pointed at the director. With his free hand, Morehouse examined Burke's and Rosemarie's cellphones. After studying them for a few minutes, he turned to Burke and shook his head.

"I'm not going to sugarcoat this, Travis. I'm disappointed in you."

"You're making a huge mistake, Grayson."

"How can you say that? These cellphone messages damn you to hell. You've been on the wrong side of this since the beginning."

"You're a damn fool, Grayson," Burke said defiantly. "You're misinterpreting all the data in front of you."

"Feel free to enlighten me. The whole time I've been investigating the death of Agent Mills and the murder of Claire Tompkins, you've been in almost daily communication with Rufus Youngblood trying to prevent me from finding out the truth. This whole kidnapping tonight was orchestrated by him with your knowledge. The last thing Rufus texted you was that he was very close to neutralizing Emily Hoffman. How can you possibly call that a misinterpretation?"

"Listen to me, Grayson. I haven't been able to say anything before now, but I've been engaged in a mole hunt for months. We've had blowback on multiple fronts across several agencies for over a year and a half, and I've been working with the FBI and CIA trying to figure out what was going on. We knew someone or some persons had gone rogue, but we didn't know who or to what extent. We also knew it had to be one of our own but what we didn't expect was that several agents from different agencies were working together. What we found was that these people were looking to turn someone high up the food chain, and with the approval of the president himself, I volunteered. These people aren't stupid, and I had to go deep. They've been wiring me payments to offshore accounts closely monitored by the IRS and the FBI of course which you can verify when we return to the States. They're tracking the money trail. It's all on the up and up. I feed them information, little bits at a time, nothing major. Certainly nothing that would cause a catastrophe but enough to get them to trust me. Everything I've given them had to be approved by a committee made up of members handpicked from our intelligence communities. So far, we've been moderately successful, and at the same time deeply frustrated. Mills' death was their first big mistake, but we managed to turn it in our favor."

Burke paused to take a breath as Morehouse and Munoz listened in shocked incredulity. This was one hell of a pill he expected them to swallow. The man was entertaining if not believable. Yet, he was opening the door to some degree of doubt. Morehouse could see it in Munoz's eyes. She wanted to believe him.

"So there's a snake in the garden and you're a hero," mused Morehouse. "Is that what you're telling me?"

"I was just doing my job."

"Why did they send Mills to kill Claire? Was she having an affair with the senator?"

He shook his head. "No, she wasn't, and I don't know yet why Mills was sent to kill Claire, but I've been able to glean from my sources that she knew something about the senator that would have been very damaging to his presidential bid. I don't know what exactly, but I've been getting warmer every day. Apparently, it's very important to these people that the senator wins the election next fall."

"Is the senator involved? Is he in charge?"

Burke shook his head again. "No, definitely not. That part I'm sure about. He never would have ordered Claire's death no matter how badly it might have affected his ambitions. He's true blue all the way through."

"Yeah, but he's surrounded by unscrupulous toadies who would do almost anything to further their own interests. Doesn't that say something about his character? You know what they say. Lie with dogs and wake with fleas."

"You're not being fair, Grayson. Washington's a cesspool. Everybody's covered in sewage. You get what you get. You know that. A guy running for office in our country doesn't hire boy scouts. He hires people who get results."

"So how did you turn Mills' death to your favor?" asked Morehouse.

"Mills, Youngblood, and the now deceased Rosemarie are the only bad apples I've been able to identify beyond a shadow of a doubt. Mills' death sent a shockwave through their group and rattled their cage. They've been getting more and more desperate to silence the Hoffman girl as time goes on. They're not the kind of organization that likes to leave loose ends. In their frenzy to bring this to a conclusion they're starting to make mistakes. Murdering Emily's mother and Tierney's neighbor was sloppy as hell, and Rufus coming here was another huge mistake. He's put himself in an untenable position... You're probably wondering why I didn't tell you Rufus was here, but it was for the same reason I didn't tell you anything else. If I broke their trust and they found out, all the undercover work I've done would have been for naught and every one of them would have disappeared back into the muck from which they came."

"And you were just going to let them kill Emily so you could catch them red-handed?"

"Of course not, but I needed to let them think I was. There's a Mr. Big behind all of this, Grayson. He's the guy we want, not the small fry. I couldn't have you interfering in the process and scaring off their boss. My intel indicates he's here in Sicily supervising things personally. There's never been a better opportunity for us than this. Although I had one eye on my ultimate objective of capturing the big fish, I always planned on saving Emily. Your coming here threw a monkey wrench in the works because they didn't have one hundred percent confidence that I could control you. That's why they sent Rosemarie to mind us. She was their guarantee that you didn't do anything unexpected. We were supposed to lead you on a wild goose chase all night while they tracked down Emily, but something happened, and they changed their plans."

"So you knew that was Rosemarie?"

"Of course I did. I had never met her, but Rufus told me he was sending her to keep an eye on you. That's why I kept telling you not to provoke her. I knew she was a homicidal maniac with a hair trigger and the best assassin we ever fielded although you're not so bad yourself. How'd you pull that off anyway?"

Morehouse made a show of waving his gun at Burke. "Easy with the psyops, Travis. We're way too early for flattery. Just sit back and answer a few more questions."

"Ask away… Now that it's out in the open, I have nothing to hide."

"Why did Rosemarie tell me her name was Margaretha? What was the point?"

"The woman's been a covert operative for nearly twenty-five years, Grayson. Lying was a way of life for her. She couldn't have told the truth even if she wanted to. Look at what Munoz found on her body; three driver's licenses and two passports all under different names. Hell, I don't even know her real name. I doubt anybody does at this point."

"And her relationship to Mills and Youngblood?"

"She was their intelligence liaison in Iraq and Afghanistan. She worked deep cover, embedded in hot spots. From what I found out, she was part Afghan herself through her mother who married a GI. She was fluent in Pashto and Dari, and grew up hating the Taliban and extremists in general. Apparently, they didn't treat her mother too well when she was a young woman and Rosemarie held a grudge against them that lasted a lifetime. The CIA picked up on this resentment when she was an undergraduate at Stanford and recruited her right out of college. Anyway, as you guessed, Mills and Youngblood ran black-ops with her during their tours over there, and I guess they never stopped working together only now it was for profit, not patriotism."

Morehouse sighed. "Okay, why were they taking us to Mount Etna?"

"I have no idea. Sorry, but they don't tell me everything. They very much believe in compartmentalization. But if you want me to guess, then I would say that they have Emily or are about to apprehend her. Burying her six feet under the lava on Mount Etna would be as good as dumping her in a New Jersey landfill. No one would ever find her."

"He is right about that, Signore," offered Bernardo who had been listening intently to the conversation hoping to find a way out of his predicament. "Crateri Silvestri is great place for to get rid of body. Especially now she is deserted."

Everyone turned their attention to him. "Deserted? You mean because of the late hour?" asked Morehouse.

Bernardo saw an opening to ingratiate himself with the new players and took it. "No, is because this part of park Etna she has been closed to public for more than two months. Scientists say to have observed increased volcanic activity in crater and are worry she may go boom. They make park she close."

"Seriously?"

"I very serious. There have been the smoke coming out center with tiny bits of lava. We see on TV."

"Well, this is just grand. Isn't this just grand, Munoz? We're going to an active volcano site."

"It's definitely grand," she replied sarcastically.

"How are going to get up there if it's closed off?" Morehouse continued.

"We go around or take down barriers. Is no too difficult. If people want to do stupid thing in Italy, we no get too excited like in America. Too many people in world anyway."

"Great... Speaking of going up. Just how high is Crateri Silvestri? Are we going to freeze to death up there?"

"No, no, Signore," Bernardo said, "Etna has many crateri. The very active ones are much high, and can only be reach by hiking many hours, but Silvestri is no more than nineteen hundred meters, six thousand of feet. Like-a-your Denver in Colorado. No too cold this time of year, 15 Centigrado or 60 Fahrenheit during day, 10 Centigrado at night and of course, a little windy. I have to been there many times. Is popular tourist destination and usually very safe."

"Thank you, Bernardo. I think I understand better."

"You let Bernardo live, yes?"

"If Bernardo continues to behave like he has been I see no reason to hurt him."

Bernardo flashed a toothy grin into the rearview mirror and Morehouse made a mental note not to trust the slimy prick. He turned his attention back to Burke. "Okay, that makes sense. There's nothing like a desolate volcano in a foreign country to commit a murder, but what's the point of bringing me here? I'd be a witness."

"This day trip to Etna is hot off the presses for me, and I haven't had a chance to thoroughly digest it. Etna's a big place. They might just want you somewhere they knew they could easily reach out and touch you, but I'll be honest, it's possible that they haven't decided what to do with you. I would also hazard a guess that their boss is somewhere nearby, and their level of paranoia just went up a few notches."

"Fine... What did Rosemarie mean by deal or no deal, I'll end him here?"

Burke sighed, "For what it's worth, I made them promise not to hurt you."

"How very reassuring," Morehouse said drolly. "And you thought they would keep their word while they were burying a twenty-two-year old girl on the side of a volcano."

"I was doing the best I could to keep things together. Look, Grayson, I know this is a lot for you to absorb, but you're asking me to explain how murderous traitors think. I can't, but if there was a chance that I could identify or capture Mr. Big then I had to take it, and if there's a chance, I could save Emily then I would take that too."

"And I'm supposed to believe this after all the lies and deceptions? Why did you even let me come to Sicily? You could have ordered me to stay in D.C."

"I couldn't order you to stay in the States because I knew that I had to come to Sicily myself for Mr. Big. How would that have looked? So I made a difficult choice to place you in harm's way while at the same time trying to protect you."

Morehouse felt himself caving. Everything he said was so damn logical. "Who killed the FBI analyst and framed Dirk?"

"Just a guess, but probably Rufus. It has his fingerprints all over it."

Morehouse turned to Munoz. "What do you think, Angela?"

She had the kind of look on her face that said she'd rather be on a beach somewhere drowning in rum, or anywhere but here right now.

The idea that a man she respected and looked up to almost as much as her father might be a treasonous dog was too much for her.

"I want to believe him."

"I know you do. So do I. It's a shame I can't confirm any of this before we reach our destination, Travis. Is it safe to say that no one will acknowledge what you say you're doing?"

"Not via phone call in the middle of the night from Italy. Definitely not. That's the nature of covert operations. No one admits to anything except possibly in person in a lead-lined, soundproofed room," Burke said. "I understand your reticence, but there has to be some way I can convince you I'm telling the truth before it's too late for Emily."

Morehouse considered that for a long minute before saying, "Perhaps, there is."

Bernardo turned off the highway and merged onto a smaller road where they saw the first sign for the park. He turned to Munoz, saying, "We enter parco soon. No much longer from here."

Morehouse asked, "Bernardo, how difficult is it to find our way to the crater from this point?"

"No difficult. We just follow road. She make many turns. Big sign at top. No miss."

Morehouse glanced out the windows in all directions and made a snap decision. "Stop the car, Bernardo. Then get out and bring the keys with you. Munoz, I want you to drive, but meet me in the back by the trunk first, and bring the guns."

Burke said wryly, "I guess I'm not invited to this meeting."

"I'm afraid not, Travis."

In the rear of the Mercedes, Morehouse took the keys from Bernardo, popped open the trunk and said, "Get in, Bernardo."

Bernardo was frightened. "But you say you no kill me."

"I won't but I need you safely out of the way. Now get in before you make me do something almost equally unpleasant."

As Bernardo tucked himself into the trunk, Morehouse leaned toward Munoz and whispered, "Give me Burke's gun."

Chapter 50

With Gerry at the helm, the short bus chugged along SP 92 making its arduous ascent up the east side of Mount Etna toward Crateri Silvestri. Eventually they reached the level ground of a plateau just thirty feet below the ridge line of the summit and entered the visitor's parking lot. Gerry had no problem circumnavigating the temporary obstacles that had been set up by the local government to secure the area and simply drove around them. With the only light coming from a full moon, the black, barren, mountainous landscape seemed like an alien planet. The lot was empty save for two other vehicles idling nonchalantly about one hundred feet apart from each other. One was a white delivery van closest to the crater and the other was a silver Mercedes. It was too dark, and they were too far away to see who was in either vehicle. It almost didn't matter. For the moment, they were preoccupied staring out the windows at the ominous outline of the crater silhouetted in the background. Readily visible even in the gloom was a wide well-worn path leading to the top.

The restaurant and gift shop were closed, and the entire place had the feeling of abandonment. From the warning signs that lined the highway, Cesari was able to pick up on the fact that this area was closed to the public because of recent seismic activity. Confirmation of this was just a stone's throw away as there could easily be seen gentle plumes of smoke wafting eerily upward from the center of the crater which hadn't been active since the late nineteenth century.

This just kept getting better and better, thought Cesari.

Gerry stopped the bus an equal distance from both of the other vehicles and together they formed the points of a triangle. Cesari wondered what the significance of the spacing implied. Everyone in the school bus had gathered toward the front and nervously looked out the windshield.

Tierney said, "What do you think this means?"

"I don't know," replied Cesari.

Vito observed, "It means there are more of them than we thought."

"Fine, but why are they spread out like that?" asked Cesari.

"Maybe they don't trust each other any more than we do," suggested Jeremy.

"Or maybe they're trying to target us with crossfire if it came down to it," concluded Tierney. "Damn… Now that I think about it. That's what it has to be."

Nobody was happy with that thought. It made too much sense. Cesari said, "Let's not be too negative about this. We have weapons too, so unless they intend on taking casualties themselves, I doubt they're going to open fire on us for no reason."

Vito wasn't as convinced. "We have a sawed-off shotgun, a .32 caliber pistol and a twelve-gauge Benelli loaded with birdshot. We couldn't even reach them from here except by pure luck. For all we know they have rifles. This could be plain suicide."

"That's why we're not going to make this easy for them. They want Emily above all else, and she's the last thing they're going to get. As long as she stays in the bus, she has a chance."

"That's not how hostage exchanges work, Cesari," scoffed Tierney. "Both sides have to show up with their prisoners."

Cesari thought about that and said, "Fair enough, but we'll make a human shield around her at all times. And we make it clear that we have enough firepower to retaliate should they break the deal."

Jeremy asked, "How do we do that?"

"Me, Tierney and Vito will form a human shield around Emily when we exit the bus. Gerry, I want you to stay in the driver's seat and when we go outside you turn the brights on to blind them from getting a bead on Emily or us for that matter. Jeremy, you crack a window open and very visibly stick the muzzle of the Benelli out in their direction. They won't know it's a shotgun with bird shot. They'll have to assume it's a rifle. That alone will be a deterrent to hostilities. Vito, you take the sawed-off from Gerry, and Detective, you take the .32 from Jeremy. You keep them in plain sight so they know we can hit back from multiple points."

"What about you?" asked Vito.

In response, Cesari, held up his shiny new crowbar that he had purchased their first night in Palermo. "It's time to christen this baby."

Vito's phone rang.

****

"We have a problem, Rufus," explained Burke.

They had just arrived and were sitting in the Mercedes with their lights on so Rufus couldn't see Munoz in the driver's seat. "What kind of a problem and why isn't Rosemarie answering her phone?"

"That's the problem. Rosemarie's dead. Morehouse played us. He figured it all out and got the drop on her, and now she's lying in a ditch on the side of the road somewhere between Palermo and here with a bullet in her brain."

"What about Bernardo?"

"He's still driving but unarmed. He's switched sides anyway and is scared out of his mind. He won't even step out of the car."

"And Morehouse?"

"Sitting next to me with the muzzle of his Glock pressed into my side. He wants to talk."

"Put him on."

Burke handed his phone to Morehouse who really did have his Glock pointed at the Director. "Good evening, Rufus. Funny meeting you here."

"Hysterical…. I knew eventually we'd be where we are now. I was getting a little tired of the cat and mouse anyway. What do you want?"

"I want Emily Hoffman and I'm told you have her. I'll trade you Burke for her."

Rufus laughed into the phone. "The joke's on you. I don't have her, at least not yet. We're waiting for her to show up so can we trade her for Gianelli's cousin."

Taken aback by this, Morehouse glanced out the front of the car and saw a slow moving small yellow school bus appear at the other end of the parking lot.

"That's them now," said Rufus. "You didn't know Gianelli had a cousin here? C'mon Morehouse, you're behind the times. They were hiding Emily in her apartment back in Palermo."

"It doesn't change anything. Burke for Emily. That's a good deal. Together you two have a chance. I bring him back to the States under arrest and he's going to take everyone down with him."

Rufus was quiet for a moment thinking about that as the school bus pulled to a stop. "If I give you Emily, I might be on the run for the rest of my life. Burke gets to go back to his life. He was about to retire anyway. It's your word against his. Even if someone did believe you, you can't possibly think they'll act on it. They'll brush it under the rug and let him ride off into the sunset. I'll be left holding the bag for all of it."

"Think about it, Rufus. Emily doesn't know anything other than a Secret Service agent tried to kill her. She's never even heard of you. After everything she's been through, she just wants to go home. Her testimony won't even make sense to anyone. They'll just log it away along with the millions of other anti-government conspiracy theories. You don't think anyone's going to want to make a big deal of this in an election year, do you? You've been in Washington too long to believe that."

"Is it the same for you, Morehouse? Are you going to just let go of it? What about Tierney? He doesn't seem like the kind of guy that just lets go of things. Then there's this asshole Gianelli? I just kidnapped his cousin and threatened to kill her. I doubt that a guy like him is going to easily forget about that. He's already threatened me with retribution."

"We can work out the details, Rufus. I just want to protect Emily Hoffman. She's been traumatized enough. I'd even be willing to go so far as to say if you don't try to harm her and let us walk away, then I'd be willing to turn the other cheek so long as you promise to retire from politics. Quid pro quo, Rufus. I can't just let you storm into the White House next year. I'm sure you can understand that?"

"I can see your point on that, and I'd be willing to consider a deal so long as there was some display of good faith on your part."

"Such as?"

"Give me Burke, and I'd consider that evidence that I can trust you to keep your word."

"Just like that you want me to turn over my only ace?"

"You want the Hoffman girl or not? I'm facing enemies on all sides right now. I need some reassurance, or I'll just start blasting away at the school bus and hope I hit something."

"There's no need for that. I'll bring Burke out, but you're both finished in Washington. I hope I'm making myself clear. There won't be any comebacks from this even if I have to put you down myself."

"Understood... You bring him over here and I'll call Gianelli with instructions. We'll make all the exchanges at once so I can get out of here in a timely fashion."

"I'll bring him to the center of the triangle the vehicles are making."

"Fine, and I'll bring the cousin."

Morehouse ended the call and turned to Burke. "Now's your chance to prove yourself, Travis. If Gianelli's agreeable, we're going to do a three-way hostage exchange, and you're going to be at the center of it."

"You think they're going to give up Emily after everything they've done to protect her?"

"Hopefully, they'll trust us enough to see that there isn't much of a choice."

Burke wasn't very optimistic. "I have a feeling it's going to be like the O.K. Corral out there."

"He's got a point," Munoz said with a worried look on her face. "Hostage exchanges like this can go bad in a hurry."

Morehouse ignored that and looked at Burke. "Get out of the car and meet me in the back. Munoz, you're our backup, but if things get hot, I'm giving you wide latitude to use your discretion and high-tail it out of here if you think it's the right thing to do. You might be the only one left to tell the tale."

By the trunk, Morehouse got behind Burke, lifted the other man's suit jacket and shoved the director's own Glock inside the waistband in the small of his back. When he was done, he took out his own gun and faced the director saying, "I believe this means I trust you."

"Thank you, Grayson. You won't regret it."

"That's what I'm hoping. Okay, it's a simple plan. We'll march over there with you in front as if you're my prisoner and then we'll play it by ear, but I'm guessing all eyes will be on me. As soon as you can, make your move and I'll follow your lead. It would be nice to take prisoners, but I'm not married to the idea."

"My sentiments exactly."

"It's good to have you back, Travis."

Chapter 51

Cesari stepped off the school bus flanked by Tierney and Vito with their weapons in plain view. Emily coolly followed behind a few paces nearly hidden from sight by the bulk of the big men. A quick glance back revealed the barrel of the Benelli poking out from an open window. Tension was thick in the air. Cesari was in the middle as they moved forward. It had been decided to let him do the talking. Tierney and Vito were hot under the collar and itching for a fight. Not a good way to begin negotiations they had all agreed. Cesari held the crowbar at his side as if this was going to be a street brawl between warring gangs facing off on Gun Hill Road in the Bronx. In some ways, the scene was reminiscent of West Side Story.

With the crater in the distance, Cesari observed several people come out of the van. On either side of Teresa and Jaskaran were two large men, both were lean and hard. The one to the left wore a dark pin-striped suit and appeared to be in charge from the way he comported himself. The other man, greater in size, seemed very familiar, and as he studied his face, Cesari realized this was the asshole he had beaten senseless on the plane. The one named Booker. He had shaved his beard, and wore a hat, but it was definitely him. Directly behind Jaskaran and Teresa was a slob of a human being, wearing sweatpants and a warmup jacket. Not an ounce under three hundred and fifty pounds, he carried a baseball bat. Cesari recognized him too. He was one of Bernardo's guys. He had seen him in the Brancaccio and again at Ernesto's house. He had pummeled him too.

What the hell was he doing here? It was starting to feel like a reunion of everybody Cesari had slapped around since leaving Manhattan. Even more surprising was the sight walking over from the Mercedes. Two men in suits and ties, one in front and one behind holding a pistol. The one in front held his hands up in the air like a prisoner.

Ten feet from the bus, Cesari said, "Emily, you stay here. At the first sign of trouble, run back to the bus and stay down."

She stopped in her tracks, and although she had rehearsed in her mind everything that was happening, nothing could have prepared her for the adrenaline rush she was now experiencing leading to a pounding pulse, quick respirations, and sweating. The overwhelming desire to run had to be forcefully suppressed as was the desire to curl up into a ball and start crying. One hundred feet away and closing the gap were men whose stated purpose was to kill her. She wanted to scream, curse, but most of all she wanted to be with her parents one last time.

Gerry was told to stay in the bus with the engine running just in case they needed to make a quick exit. He was also to act as backup to Jeremy. Should the shooting start and Jeremy got hit, Gerry's job was to man the Benelli. However, watching Emily trembling, standing there all alone, he was overwhelmed with sympathy. He got off of the bus, came up to her and held her in his arms. This unexpected act of compassion from someone who seemed so incapable of such a response moved the entire group and forged their resolve. They would all lay down their lives today for Emily Hoffman if need be. It was a romantic notion, and at the same time, a very soothing, calming one. If one had to die, it may as well be for a good cause. And what better cause than to protect an innocent life?

The three groups converged and at about twenty-five-feet, Cesar announced, "That's far enough."

He picked that distance for several reasons. It was dark but they could now see each other quite clearly in the ambient light. They were also close enough to hear each other easily with slightly raised voices, but could still converse privately amongst themselves without being overheard. Most importantly, except for Vito holding the sawed-off, everyone was armed with handguns which, in such poor lighting, would be highly inaccurate at that range except for the most proficient of marksmen.

Rufus pointed his Beretta at Teresa, and glaring at Cesari said, "And just who the hell are you?"

"Cesari… John Cesari. Who are you?"

Rufus snorted. "Dr. Cesari. It's about time we met… Tierney knows who I am."

"That's Rufus Youngblood. He's Senator Taylor's chief of staff. He interviewed me in Washington with those two over there," explained Tierney. "The one with his hands up is Director Travis Burke of the Secret Service and the one holding the pistol on him is Deputy Director Grayson Morehouse."

They turned their attention to the two Secret Service agents. Cesari said, "What's going on over here? Your friends don't seem like they're getting along."

Rufus said, "The prisoner exchange just got a little more complicated. The director is of much higher value to me than Emily Hoffman, so I've agreed to give them Emily in exchange for him."

Cesari said, "You should have consulted with us first. Don't you think?"

"We're all grown-ups here, Cesari. The whole point of this gathering is to negotiate a settlement to everyone's satisfaction. The good news for your side is that Deputy Director Morehouse doesn't want to hurt Emily the way I do."

"That's a matter of opinion from where I'm standing." Then shifting his gaze back to Burke with his hands in the air, Cesari asked, "What did he do wrong?"

Rufus found that amusing and replied, "The worse thing anyone can do in our profession… He got caught."

"So just how do you envision this happening?"

"I need Director Burke before I do anything. I already told that to the Deputy Director. Once I have him, I'll march Gianelli's cousin and your friend over to you while you send Emily to Deputy Director Morehouse. By the way, I can fully vouch for Morehouse's integrity. Whatever you may be thinking, let me reassure you that he is definitely one of the good guys."

"I'm sure I'll sleep better knowing that," Cesari said cynically. "What happens if we don't agree?"

"Do you see that sloth standing behind your friend? His name is Tullio. He doesn't speak much English, but he understands basic human commands. Sort of like a dog. I wouldn't trust him with a gun but he's very good with blunt objects like the baseball bat he's holding. So if I say, Tullio, break the Indian guy's knees, he'll do it without any compunction whatsoever. Would you like a demonstration?"

"That won't be necessary…"

There was a low-pitched rumbling sound and the ground beneath them shook slightly. Instinctively, everyone looked down. It lasted less than five seconds and all was calm again.

Vito said, "Shit… What was that?"

"I guess Etna really is flaring up," Tierney commented.

Rufus called over. "Maybe we should get this show on the road?"

"Hold on," said Cesari. "We agree in principle to the terms, but we need some clarification on what happens next. Let's start with, what guarantee do we have that you're not going to start shooting at us when we try to leave the parking lot?"

Cesari was trying to buy time. They had no intention of handing Emily over to anyone and Gerry was gradually inching her back toward the school bus in case somebody got trigger happy. The whole reason for the meeting was to see how many were arrayed against them and how heavily armed they were. All they saw were two handguns, a fat guy with a baseball bat on one side, and two Secret Service agents at odds with each other on the other. Only God knew what that was about, but that had to be good for team Cesari. At this point, Cesari just wanted to maintain the status quo and keep everyone talking.

Rufus said, "Why would we do that?"

"Because you're an asshole?"

Rufus grinned. "Granted…but look at it from my point of view. You have as many weapons as we do, and there's more of you. In military terms, it would make no sense for me to break the truce."

"Fair enough, but what about down the road? Assuming that Secret Service guy over there doesn't kill Emily immediately, how do we know you won't track her down a month from now or a year?"

"You don't, but I would have no reason to. This game is over from my end. Until tonight, there was some discernible gain for me to kill her but that is no longer the case. I don't just run around the globe murdering civilians for no good reason. There has to be some benefit."

"That's very comforting."

"I'm not going to hurt Emily," Morehouse said, finally joining the conversation. "I flew over here for the sole purpose of protecting her. I know that's hard for you to believe, but it's the truth. I plan on taking her from here to the American Consulate where she'll be surrounded by a platoon of Marines until I can arrange for an Air Force jet to fly her home. Any and all of you are welcome to join her. I just want to debrief her personally on everything that has happened, but if she doesn't want to, then I will accept that and walk away."

"Why can't we just walk away now?"

"Because I don't trust Rufus any more than you do. He'll kill Emily in a heartbeat just because he can. He has to. It's in his DNA. I'm the only one here that can provide her the kind of protection she'll need to make it back home alive."

The earth began to shake again only more forcefully than before causing them all to wobble and jockey to maintain their balance. This was followed by a thunderous explosion from the center of the crater. They all turned to watch as an orange glow suddenly appeared, and flecks of lava spat up into the night sky as if from a fountain. Pebble-sized rocks splattered on the ground around them, followed by fiery bits of lava. A piece of lava no larger than the size of a quarter hit Tullio in the cheek. At two thousand degrees, it instantly melted a hole in the side of his face. He began screaming and clutching at the wound. The piece of lava rolled onto his polyester warmup suit igniting it instantly, and he threw himself to the ground in a flaming ball of lard. Consumed by utter panic, he began frantically rolling around and flailing his arms trying to put himself out.

In the confusion of the spectacle, everyone spontaneously stepped forward to get a better look. Burke took advantage of the unexpected distraction, quickly pulled his gun from the small of his back and pressed it against the side of Morehouse's head. Just as suddenly as it came, the eruption died down, leaving in its wake an ominous radiance from the center of the crater. The entire parking lot felt a few degrees warmer. Booker helped Tullio to his feet groaning in pain and dismay. His teeth and gums could be seen through the gaping wound in his cheek. The man was obviously in agony and Cesari surmised that he would no longer be a factor. By the time everyone refocused their attention, it was apparent that the dynamics on the Secret Service side of things had dramatically changed. Somehow, Burke had got the drop on Morehouse.

Burke said, "Drop your gun, Grayson."

Chapter 52

As Morehouse tossed his gun to the ground, tiny movements were taking place as everyone readjusted to the shifting balance of power. Cesari signaled Gerry to get Emily inside the bus to relative safety. He didn't like the way things were starting to shape up. Tullio who had been leaning against the side of the van began vomiting and fell to his knees. Booker joined Rufus to stare at Burke's sudden ascendancy to power, momentarily neglecting Jaskaran and Teresa behind them. Jaskaran seized the opportunity to take an additional step back from his captors. As he did so, he slowly raised his hands to his head.

Worried that Munoz might take a shot at him from inside the car, Burke positioned himself so that Morehouse's back was to the Mercedes. He said, "It doesn't look like Munoz wants to come out and play."

"Would you?" replied Morehouse. "She's probably dialing the Carabinieri. Besides, you heard me tell her to stay in the car. I hope she drives away as fast as she can."

"Good luck with that. We'll shoot out her engine block long before she makes it out of here although I'd hate to waste the ammunition. As for the police, by the time they arrive I will have already disposed of America's enemies, having uncovered a conspiracy to assassinate the president of the United States involving no less than Deputy Director Grayson Morehouse himself who unfortunately refused to surrender when confronted with his sins. I haven't decided whether Munoz was a collaborator and died alongside you or by your hand trying to bring you to justice. I need to think on it a little."

"You would kill me and Munoz after I trusted you?"

"As they say in the movies, it's just business, not personal. I always liked you, Grayson."

"Thank God for that, but at least grant me the satisfaction of telling me why."

Cesari and the others listened, not sure of the best course of action other than to wait it out. They still had Jaskaran and Teresa which was problematic. It turns out Morehouse was one of the good guys after all but there was little they could do to help him at the moment without turning the parking lot into a shooting gallery. Further complicating the situation was Etna's ill temperament. Everyone with a high school education knew that it was the poisonous gases spreading silently and rapidly from a volcanic eruption that would kill you long before the heat wave, molten lava, and spewing rock. They needed to get out of there before they became mummified like the artifacts at Pompeii.

Burke said, "Morehouse, are you really that naïve?"

"Was it money?"

"Money was a factor, I won't deny it. The bad guys always pay better, but that's not the main reason."

"Then what?"

"You're looking at the next Director of National Intelligence, Morehouse, but that's only if Taylor becomes president."

"This is about getting a promotion?"

"Are you serious? Mandatory retirement versus DNI? That's like saying would you like a gold-plated watch and a kick in the teeth versus the keys to a brand new convertible Bentley, the hot blonde included. The DNI is the holy grail of intelligence, Morehouse. You know that. Every bit of information from every intelligence agency in the world gets funneled onto the desk of the DNI. Think of it. The CIA, the FBI, the NSA, the Army, the Navy, Homeland Security, and a slew of others all will have to kiss my ring. Information is power, Grayson, and as DNI, I would have all the information including every dirty little secret, every dirty little politician thought no one knew anything about. Now, that's power you can sink your teeth into. Compared to the DNI, the presidency is nothing but a show horse, a figurehead. As DNI, I'll make J. Edgar Hoover seem like an altar boy."

"Taylor promised you the DNI if you helped get him elected. So he really was behind all of this."

"The first part was right, but if you're asking again did he order Claire's death, the answer is no. He didn't know anything about it, although I'm sure he's pieced it together by now. It was Rufus's idea and I gave him the green light because, Grayson, there's something else you should know. I told you in the car on the way up here that Mr. Big was here personally supervising things. That was the truth. What I neglected to mention was that I am Mr. Big. Now where do you want it? The back of the skull or a direct heart shot?"

Cesari recoiled as he listened, and Vito whispered, "Holy shit. He's going to murder his own guy right in front of us."

"That's why I'm cringing. He's never going to let a bus load of witnesses just walk away."

Tierney added quietly, "You're right about that. Maybe he doesn't have enough firepower to take us on tonight without taking casualties himself, but as the DNI he'll authorize every intelligence agency at his disposal to track us down like animals. We'll be on the run forever."

Vito said, "We'll be like Jason Bourne minus all the survival skills."

"One step at a time, boys," counseled Cesari. "Let's just get through tonight."

Burke said, "Well, Grayson? Do you have a preference of where you would like to be shot or would you like me to pick for you?"

"I can't even begin to tell you how sad I am to hear all this, Travis."

"We all have to grow up some time. Now, don't make me say it again."

Morehouse held up a hand. "Can I show you something first?"

Burke looked puzzled and perhaps even a little amused. "Like what?"

"It's in my pocket."

He slid his jacket to one side to show Burke there were no surprises. Burke gripped the gun a little tighter. "Slowly, Morehouse. Very slowly."

"Not to worry."

Morehouse slipped his left hand into his left pocket and came out with a handful of 9mm bullets. He held them up for Burke to see and then let them spill onto the pavement. As they bounced around, he said, "You see, Travis, the problem with sitting at a desk all day is that you lose your edge, like the ability to tell what a loaded gun feels like versus an unloaded one. I removed the bullets from your Glock when I put Bernardo in the trunk."

Burke stared in disbelief at the ammunition rolling in all directions on the ground, and as he did, Morehouse quickly slipped his right hand around to the small of his back and came back with Rosemarie's Beretta. Burke's eyes went wide, and he pulled the trigger, once, twice, three times. The hammer clicked harmlessly, and Burke's jaw dropped in defeat.

"When did you know?" he asked.

"There were a lot of little things, but what pushed me over the finish line was when Rosemarie searched me for my gun. She was more than a little surprised that I didn't have one and gave you a questioning look which I thought was odd until I realized it was because you had told her I was carrying one in a shoulder holster. During that whole exchange she kept her pistol pointed at me and never once aimed it at you. Because she knew you weren't a threat. Very shoddy, but that's what happens when you get used to killing defenseless civilians. But I still had enough doubt that I felt I should at least give you one last chance to prove your veracity, and now here we are."

Burke stared ahead blankly, and after a deep breath said, "Back of the head for me if you don't mind, Grayson."

"Turn around and face Rufus. I'd rather keep you alive as a human shield for the moment."

As Burke turned, there was a blood curdling scream from behind Rufus and Booker. In the dark and unattended, Jaskaran had managed to slip the Colt and twelve-inch kirpan out from under his turban undetected. Now, standing protectively in front of Teresa, he held the curved blade up in his outstretched right hand and the Colt revolver high up in the air in his left hand. His demonic shriek was designed to paralyze his opponents and did so successfully. Booker turned and flinched at the fearsome sight of a full-on Sikh warrior who was now armed and ready for combat, his face contorted with rage.

Unprepared for the attack and startled by Jaskaran's fierce appearance, Booker reflexively backed up into Rufus whose weapon discharged accidentally and innocuously into the ground as Jaskaran plunged the kirpan into Booker's abdomen up to its hilt, slicing through vital organs including his aorta. The blade emerged out the other side of Booker, and Jaskaran pushed the man backward with all his might and with such force that several inches of the steel pierced into Rufus's torso as well. Rufus yelled out in pain and anguish, but before he could react, Jaskaran pressed the muzzle of the Colt into Booker's nearly lifeless body and fired twice. Both bullets tore through Booker into Rufus killing them both instantly.

Burke saw an opportunity in the mayhem and seized it. He bolted away into the darkness, his shadowy form rapidly disappearing behind the van in the direction of the crater. Morehouse considered taking a shot at him but decided he was more valuable alive than dead and took off after him with Munoz close behind. Cesari decided to help them while Vito and Tierney attended to his cousin and Jaskaran. Tullio lay helplessly on the ground, much of his back covered in blistering third degree burns.

Running up the path, they reached the crater's ridge and saw Burke's outline sprinting along the rim ahead and gaining ground. He was wearing dress shoes and the going was tough along the rocky path, but he was energized by fear and desperation. The desire to avoid incarceration was highly motivational. The crater spanned approximately one hundred yards in diameter, and the freshly spewed pool of lava thirty feet below in the center glowed and bubbled like a witch's cauldron. It was no more than twenty feet in diameter with an extended rim of hot rock and ash a short distance beyond that. How close one could get and survive was an interesting question. It was already starting to feel uncomfortably warm where they were.

Morehouse shouted, "Burke, you can't escape. Make this easy on yourself."

Burke stopped and turned around, sucking wind and exhausted. He hadn't sprinted like that in decades, and although he'd had a good start, he was out of gas. He was in great shape years ago, but now he was pushing sixty and a dedicated desk jockey for the latter part of his career. He was no match for his pursuers.

He stared at them and knew that outrunning them wasn't an option. Where would he go anyway? On top of a volcano in a silk suit and no weapon. Even if he made it back to civilization, Morehouse would have cut off his credit cards, and he would be the most wanted man in the world. There was no way anyone in the States would allow him to live long enough to stand trial. He knew way too much about way too many powerful people. Would anyone have the gumption to throw him a lifeline, claim national security, obscure the facts, blur the lines, and let him just sail away on some peaceful ocean current, never to be seen or heard from again?

Not a chance he assessed. He'd be a pariah. When it was revealed that he had pursued a twenty-two-year-old girl around the globe just to murder her for political gain, the public outcry would be vehement and severe. Nothing less than his head on a platter would placate the jackals nipping at his heels. He'd be sitting in a cell in isolation for many months awaiting trial, but in reality, they'd be waiting for his name to finally disappear from the front pages to be replaced by the next high-profile scandal. That's when they would come for him, in the middle of the night, with ropes or syringes filled with untraceable poisons.

He called back, his voice echoing, "The truth is, Grayson, I am making this easier for me, and for my country. There's no point in dragging the agency I love through the mud. I'll let you work out the details on how best to spin things, but I suggest you let your anger simmer down some first."

He turned away from them and began to slowly trek down the side of the crater toward the center. Munoz covered her mouth in horror. Cesari couldn't believe what he was seeing.

Morehouse yelled, "Don't do it Grayson! There's no need for this."

Ignoring the plea, Burke walked inexorably downward, tripping and stumbling on the craggy, irregular surface. He looked haggard and wretched as the ground beneath his feet warmed and the ambient temperature rose to unpleasant and nearly intolerable levels. Slowing his descent as he reached the outer perimeter of intense heat, where scattered rocks burned bright red, he looked as if he was having trouble breathing, but he staggered onward, dragging his feet and willing himself forward. Despite the enormous effort, he couldn't quite make it to the fiery pool in the center and collapsed onto a pile of embers twenty feet from the percolating lava. They watched his body burst into flames, and they assumed he must have lost consciousness because he didn't scream in pain or thrash about. Cesari looked at the two agents who appeared numb.

He said, "I think we have a lot to talk about."

Morehouse retorted, "To say the least."

They went back to the parking lot and held a quick conference with Tierney and Vito, exchanging the highlights of recent days and agreeing to a more detailed briefing later when time wasn't as much of a factor. Then they brought Bernardo out of the trunk of the Mercedes and flung him onto the ground next to Tullio where they sat dejectedly. Both men were acutely aware they had no right to expect any leniency. In fact, they were sure they were dead men. Rufus's briefcase with the money lay between them. It might as well have been thirty pieces of silver.

Cesari, Morehouse, and Vito glared down at them. Tierney had taken Stonewall out of his carrier and held him on a leash. The cat didn't like Tullio and relieved his full bladder on the man's outstretched leg. No one voiced an objection, not even Tullio.

Vito finally said, "You can keep the money, Bernardo, but this is what I want in return."

Bernardo looked up with raised eyebrows as if he didn't hear correctly. A glimmer of hope that he might survive the night had just appeared on the horizon.

"Anything, Signore. I am your man."

"We'll see… First, I need you to get rid of these bodies," Vito instructed, indicating the corpses of Rufus and Booker. "As soon as Tullio stops feeling sorry for himself, he can help you. I assume you know how to do something like that."

Bernardo looked skeptically at Tullio but agreed. "Of course, but you don't want that we just to throw into volcano?"

"No, after that eruption, there will probably be a team of scientists up here come daylight to examine the place. They're going to find one body already. Hopefully, they will just attribute that to some foolish hiker who got unlucky. If they find three bodies, it will trigger national attention, and there will be a greater chance that one of the bodies will be identified."

"And we definitely don't want that," interjected Morehouse. "Plus, you have to go back and pick up that woman, Rosemarie, from the side of the road."

Vito said, "Then do what you guys always do over here."

Bernardo nodded, suddenly eager to please and thankful to be on the team again, said, "I understand. We dump in Mediterranean. I have do many times."

"Yes, and you never saw any of us."

"Naturally…"

Vito looked sternly at him. "Why were you at Ernesto's house the other night? Did that greaseball call you?"

Bernardo shook his head. "No, Ernesto is peaceful man… Is Aunt Rosaria make call to me. She was fear that you would hurt Ernesto and want me to protect him from you."

Vito shook his head in exasperation. "I should have known… Did the witch tell you to rough me up too?"

"No, no, Signore. She was my idea. I no like you."

Despite his sour mood, Vito laughed softly. "All right, I can appreciate honesty so let me be honest as well. I'm not a fun guy to piss off. I almost never let rats like you live, and I could change my mind in a heartbeat, so listen carefully." He paused a moment, took the sawed-off shotgun he was holding, and pressed it against Bernardo's forehead. "My cousin, Teresa, is coming back to the States with me to be with her family. She's going to try to put this all behind her, and when she returns to Palermo, I'd better not find out that you or any of your friends have been bothering her… Now nod your head and tell me you understand."

Bernardo nodded vigorously, saying, "Capito, Signore. I no bother anyone ever again."

Vito relaxed and removed the gun from Bernardo's head. "I bet."

Morehouse stepped close and crouched down to look Bernardo straight in the eyes. "Because if you do harass or threaten or do anything to harm this man's family, I assure you that the full weight of the United States Secret Service will come crashing down on your ass like lava from Etna itself."

Bernardo didn't say anything. The fear in his eyes said it all. He had tangled with the wrong people, and he knew it. Morehouse stood and joined Munoz in the Mercedes who was waiting with the engine running. Vito and Cesari hopped onto the school bus with the others and Gerry hit the gas just as the first rays of dawn were starting to break over the horizon.

"Where to?" asked Gerry.

Cesari replied, "Follow the Mercedes to the American Consulate."

CHAPTER 53

Arlington, Virginia
Two days Later

Cesari showed Morehouse the text he had received earlier in the day from Tierney. The fingerprint analysis of the love letters they found with Claire was inconclusive. Claire's prints were all over them, but the only other set of prints found were not in the national database. Morehouse was expressionless as he nodded. They had just pulled to the curb in front of the seven-thousand-square-foot mansion nestled on five pristine acres in the Country Club Hills section of Arlington in full view of the Washington Golf and Country Club. Gerry drove the Cadillac and Vito rode shotgun. They had picked up Morehouse from his office on the way so they could compare notes and be on the same page.

Morehouse shook his head and said, "Well, that neither rules in nor out the possibility that the senator wrote the letters. His prints are in the data base. I already checked, but he might have been smart enough to wear gloves or have someone else handle them. I guess we'll have to use some old-fashioned sleuthing and see how far it gets us. I used to be a cop. Did you know that, Cesari?"

"No, I didn't."

"A pretty good one too. Metro P.D. for ten years. I had made detective like your boy Tierney before I entered the Service. Sometimes, I wish I'd never left," he said wistfully. "The grass is always greener. You know what I mean?"

Cesari nodded. "I do."

"Anyway, how's Emily?"

"She has a hundred years' worth of post-traumatic stress to deal with but she's with her father who's home now and recuperating nicely. That's helping. They at least can mourn the passing of her mother knowing that the people responsible have been brought to justice. Detective Tierney is going to stay with them for a few days."

"With that cat?" Morehouse asked, grinning.

"Yeah, with that cat."

"He's a good man, Tierney… C'mon, Cesari, let's get this over with. Follow my lead, and don't forget the briefcase."

Cesari and Morehouse walked up the brick path to the front portico leaving Gerry and Vito to mind the car. Two Secret Service agents stood guard at the entrance and nodded at Morehouse.

"How's it going guys?" he asked.

One of them opened the door and said, "All quiet on the Western Front, boss. They're expecting you both inside."

A butler ushered them into the living room where Senator Remington R. Taylor and his wife Lorelei were waiting. It was three in the afternoon, and she wore a formal navy dress with heels and a pearl necklace. She was in her early fifties but appeared much younger although her hair looked like it may have had a little help from a bottle because Cesari didn't notice any graying. The senator however seemed to revel in the silver streaks of his distinguished coiffe. He wore a black two-piece suit and red, striped tie. His shoes were shined to a glassy reflection and a Rolex flashed on his wrist. They stood to greet their guests.

Morehouse began the introductions. "This is Dr. John Cesari. Senator, Mrs. Taylor, I told you about him. Cesari, this is Senator Taylor and his wife Lorelei."

They all shook hands, exchanged a few perfunctory pleasantries, and then sat down opposite each other. Lorelei offered them coffee from a sterling silver coffee urn sitting on a sterling silver platter resting in the center of an eighteenth century beechwood coffee table. They politely declined. This was not that kind of visit. While superficially polite and respectful it was clear that both the senator and his wife didn't appreciate Cesari's presence in their home. He was an outsider, an ordinary citizen with no skin in the game that was known as beltway politics. The senator in particular studied Cesari as if he were some kind of bug that had evaded the exterminators. He was only there as a result of Morehouse's insistence. This was a critical juncture in the senator's career trajectory and Morehouse held most if not all the cards. It would have been grossly impolitic to deny his request. Still, it puzzled him and bordered on impertinent. Something that would have to be dealt with after the election.

The senator asked, "I know we discussed this already, Grayson, and I don't mean to be rude, Dr. Cesari, but what exactly is your involvement with all of this?"

Morehouse answered for him, "Dr. Cesari and his friends very nearly lost their lives trying to protect Emily Hoffman from assassins sent by Travis Burke to silence her. I felt strongly that he and his colleagues earned the right to hear firsthand and unedited what may or may not have happened to cause such upheaval in their lives. At the other's request, he represents them here today."

"And you have proof of what you say about Travis?"

"I have his verbal confession to me just before he committed suicide to escape justice."

"That's quite an accusation, Grayson, and I might add, one which appears to be unsubstantiated. I would tread lightly before slinging mud at the memory of such a highly decorated public servant."

"I agree, and for public consumption, I'm preparing a statement lauding the director for his bravery and outstanding career. The statement will read that Burke single-handedly uncovered an international plot to assassinate the front running presidential candidate, you, and went to Italy with your chief of staff, Rufus Youngblood, to personally investigate certain delicate leads. They were in the process of rounding up those involved when they were ambushed and summarily executed. Thanks to their sacrifice, however, the plot was foiled, and the conspirators are on the run with the authorities close behind. For reasons of national security, the details of the conspiracy need to be kept secret. Both men will receive commendations and hero memorials. I understand the need for discretion when dealing with the media and the public, Senator, but I've already briefed the president on what really happened in Sicily and why it unfolded the way it did. He is also fully aware of my visit here today with Dr. Cesari, and gave me full authority to pursue this matter to its ultimate conclusion."

"I am fully aware of your visit with the president. He called me right after you left… Are you telling me that you don't believe it's over?"

Morehouse replied sharply, "It's not over until I understand why it happened in the first place, Senator, and that's where you come in."

Taylor reached over to grasp his wife's hand for support. "Then how can I help you?"

"It all started because Clair Tompkins left D.C. in an emotional mess to go to Miami ostensibly to visit her family. She knew something she wasn't supposed to, and Rufus Youngblood ordered Agent Mills to murder her. Whatever she knew must have been pretty important because Travis Burke approved the hit. He told me so himself. Emily Hoffman got caught in the crosshairs and then simply became a loose end which needed tending to. Are you with me so far?"

The senator nodded. "I am."

"Good, because in Claire's possession, we found more than two dozen love letters and cards sent to Claire by an unknown but ardent lover. I'm not a cynical man by nature, but it seems awfully cliché for a powerful man's beautiful secretary to be run out of town just before election season."

The senator became red in the face but managed to control his temper. He said slowly, "Please make your accusation perfectly clear, Grayson."

"Emily Hoffman told me that before Claire died, she seemed to be singularly disenchanted with you and the misfortunes of love. Claire was vague, but she also warned Emily to not trust you. Why would she do that?"

The senator let out a deep breath and murmured. "I have no idea. I never treated either women with anything but the greatest respect. Specifically, I never made any, and I mean any, kind of sexual advances toward either one."

"Cesari, give Senator Taylor the letters."

Cesari reached into his briefcase and came out with the stack of cards and letters they had found in Claire's luggage. He placed them on the coffee table where the senator and his wife just stared blankly at them. After a moment of inaction, Lorelei reached out and picked them up.

The senator said, "If no one signed the love letters, and I deny being the author, then I would say that any further accusations or questions along this line are bordering upon inappropriate."

Morehouse countered, "I never said the letters weren't signed."

The senator turned crimson again and stammered, "You said the lover was unknown."

"Unknown, yes, but I never said the letters were unsigned. There might have been pet names or secret codes or symbols."

"You're playing semantics, Grayson. It's beneath you."

"Would you care to know where these letters have been for the last few days?"

The senator was beginning to get frustrated and annoyed. "Where?"

"Detective Tierney, one of the men who aided Emily Hoffman, submitted them for fingerprint analysis at the NYPD. The results should interest you greatly."

The senator stood suddenly. "I think it's time for you to leave. My wife and I do not have to allow ourselves to be subjected to this kind of harassment and quite frankly, plebeian abuse."

Lorelei touched his hand in a calming way. "Please sit, Remy. I think we both know whose fingerprints are on the letters, Deputy Director."

The senator sat down close to her and seemed as if he were truly sad as he looked at his wife. Cesari and Morehouse glanced at each other, suddenly curious at this new development. Morehouse was clearly trying to bluff the senator into a confession. Failing to do so, he would have had to back down and walk away. That was the original plan anyway.

Lorelei said, "It was my idea. Claire Tompkins left her job at the Capitol because I asked her to leave it."

"Would you care to explain that further, Mrs. Taylor?" asked Morehouse.

"I would think the letters are fairly self-explanatory, but if you want to hear it straight from the horse's mouth, then fine. Claire and I were lovers. We had been for some time, but I had promised Remy long ago that if he ever decided to throw his hat in the ring for president, then I would back him one hundred percent, and that included distancing myself from any and all damaging relationships such as having a lover employed in his office."

The look of anguish on the senator's face was indescribable. Years of personal torment were now being exposed in a raw and unadulterated fashion. Cesari and Morehouse were so stunned by this unexpected revelation that they couldn't even think of anything to say for a full minute.

Cesari eventually asked, "May I help myself to coffee, Mrs. Taylor?"

"Of course," she sighed.

Cesari leaned forward and filled a cup to the brim.

Lorelei continued, "It wasn't easy, and I tried to be as gentle as I could when I broke it off with her, but she was badly hurt, distraught even. She didn't believe that I would do such a thing and she blamed it all on Remy, that he was forcing me to get rid of her. I arranged a job for her at a prominent law firm in Miami where she had family. The job came with a hefty pay increase and a significant signing bonus per my request. It was nothing to sneeze at but only if she left quietly. It was her idea to tell everyone here she had a family emergency to avoid having to tell people the truth."

"How did Emily get involved?" asked Morehouse.

The senator answered this time. "That was Rufus's suggestion, and it made sense at the time. Claire was upset, angry, hurt, sad, depressed. All of the above wrapped into one. Rather than have to take a cab by herself where she would brood the whole way, perhaps stoking her feelings to the boiling point, he suggested that having a woman she knew and worked with drive her might be comforting. You know, allow her to vent and decompress a little lest she explode. It seemed logical but I guess none of us were thinking too clearly at that particular moment. Certainly the notion that Emily was being set up never occurred to us. We are not evil people, Grayson."

Morehouse nodded, processing the information, making sure it fit with the facts as he knew them, and so far it did. "When did the letters come into play?"

Lorelei spoke softly, "Obviously, Claire was upset but I figured she'd settle down in time, but one day, her emotions spilled over. She barged into Remy's office where we were having lunch with Rufus discussing the political landscape. She was hysterical and waved the stack of letters and cards in my face, demanding to know if I ever really had any feelings for her. Unfortunately, the best kept secret in Washington just landed in the lap of Rufus Youngblood. In a moment of weakness after she left, I told him everything. The next thing we knew, Travis Burke was sitting exactly where you are now, Dr. Cesari, explaining to us the harsh realities of having an inflamed lover running around with incriminating love letters which, if you read any of them, were quite passionate not to mention graphic. The potential for scandal or future blackmail was too great. He asked us to allow him to retrieve the letters which we interpreted as meaning to bribe or steal them back.

In retrospect, it seems naïve, but we honestly had no idea he was going to murder Claire."

The room fell quiet for a long minute as the senator's eyes welled up, and for the first time in many years he spoke from the heart and not with measured words aimed at political gain.

"I love my wife, gentlemen. I always have and I always will. I know this might sound strange to your ears after everything you've just heard, but she's been wonderful to me in so many ways and a fantastic mother to our children. I can't possibly imagine not spending the rest of my life with her in any capacity that she will permit, and I would gladly give up any political ambitions I have to protect her from public scorn."

She turned to him tears streaming down her face. "And I love you too, Remy. I know it's not the kind of love you hoped for when we married, but I do cherish you and the life we've built together."

Cesari wasn't interested in the lovefest and asked bluntly, "And the price tag for getting the letters back was the DNI?"

The senator held his head low and nodded. "By the time Rufus and Burke finished with us, we were convinced that Claire was going to be our ruination, but once she was found dead, I knew that we had made a pact with the devil, and you don't break those kinds of deals. That much was made clear to us by Travis Burke himself, and some troll of a woman he sent named Rosemarie, who we found sitting in our living room one night at two in the morning listening to Mozart on our stereo system in a singularly repulsive act of intimidation. She was sipping our best cognac and holding a framed photo of our youngest grandchild."

Morehouse took that in and said, "I'm going to ask you a direct question and I want a direct answer. You only get one chance to tell the truth, and if I don't believe you, I'll slap handcuffs on you right here and now… Did you know beforehand that Travis Burke and Rufus Youngblood had ordered Agent Mills to assassinate Claire Tompkins and Emily Hoffman?"

The senator shook his head emphatically. "No, I did not. I swear. It wasn't until after Claire's body turned up behind the Lincoln Memorial that I became suspicious of what had really happened. I suppose I could have said something after the fact, but by then I was afraid for my family's safety."

Morehouse looked at the two broken people in front of him and said, "Let's go, Cesari."

Chapter 54

They dropped Morehouse off at Secret Service headquarters on H Street NW, and then picked up I-95 northbound to New York. Cesari and Vito sat in the back while Gerry negotiated the big Caddie.

Vito said, "So, what's going to happen?"

"I don't know. Morehouse has a lot to think about. He's probably going to consult with the president and the attorney general. There's a lot of legal ramifications that have to be explored. My guess is Senator Taylor is going to have to bail out on his presidential bid. There are way too many dead bodies to explain away, and both he and his wife have admitted to being involved in the conspiracy."

"But they didn't know anybody was going to get killed."

"Try telling that to Fred and Emily Hoffman. Besides, that's what they say. Maybe some people will believe them, but I bet a lot won't. Remember, they're the ones who stood to benefit the most by Claire's death, and the court of public opinion can often be the harshest."

Vito nodded and then lit a cigarette. He opened his window a crack allowing highway noise and wind to whistle in as he blew out his first puff.

"I guess I don't really care one way or another," he concluded. "It's not like I vote."

Cesari asked, "You don't care who runs your government?"

"No, I don't. They're all liars. I know it sounds cold, but a handful of people get killed, and we force some senator to fall on his own sword as if that will make the world a better place. You can't be serious? In the big scheme of things, this doesn't amount to a hill of beans. Meanwhile, some asshole gets us involved in Vietnam for twenty years and no one even remembers who it was, how it happened, or how many thousands of guys died for nothing."

Cesari looked out his window thinking about that. He hated when Vito was right. It didn't happen often, thankfully. "So that's it? You think we should just let a guy who participated in a conspiracy to murder his wife's lover run for president?"

"You don't think much worse has been covered up in the pursuit of the most powerful office in the world, Cesari? You're being naïve.

Besides, I don't want to talk about this anymore. I already said I don't care, and I really don't."

"What do you care about?"

"Right now I'm pissed off because someone almost murdered my only living aunt and I still don't know who or why. But trust me, I will find out, and I don't care how long it takes."

Cesari said, "I think you should let sleeping dogs lie. Your aunt survived and fully recovered. She looks great and Teresa talked her into spending another week here with you. You can show them around and really get to know your family. Why would you want to ruin that with dark thoughts? Just forget about it."

"She does look great, and so does Teresa... By the way, what was that going on with you and her in my apartment yesterday? While I was having coffee with Sofia, you were in Teresa's room alone with her for almost half an hour. You thought I didn't notice, but I did."

"You were timing us?"

"Damn, right. That's my cousin. I warned you about that. You're lucky I was enjoying Sofia's company. So what were you talking about?"

"I was just telling her that I was grateful to her for letting us use her apartment in Palermo and for her helping out in general, and that I thought she was very brave."

Vito's eyes narrowed into slits. "Did you try to have sex with her?"

Cesari laughed. "No, I did not."

"You better not have. I'm going to ask her later to find out."

"You won't find out anything. I made her swear not to tell," Cesari joked.

"And what do you mean, let sleeping dogs lie? I don't let attacks against me or my family just lie."

"Sometimes not knowing the truth is better all-around for everyone than knowing."

"What the hell is that supposed to mean?" Vito asked suspiciously. "Do you know something I don't?"

"No, I don't... Just forget I said anything."

"Gerry, stop the car."

"But boss, we're in the middle of I-95."

"I don't give a rat's ass where we are. Pull over now."

Gerry drove onto the shoulder and came to a stop. Cesari glanced around as tractor-trailers whizzed by at unhealthy speeds. He said, "Vito, this is unnecessary and dangerous."

"What do you know about the attack on my family?" he demanded.

"I only know what you know."

"You're a lying sack of shit, Cesari. Get out of the car."

"I'm not getting out of the car."

"Get out of the car so I can beat your ass properly."

"I'm not getting out of the car, and you haven't been able to beat my ass since the fifth grade."

Gerry turned around with his pistol out. "You want me to cap him, Vito?"

"Gerry, put the gun away and turn around. Now, what happened to my family, Cesari? Is that why you were talking to Teresa for so long? What did she tell you?"

Cesari took in a deep breath and exhaled slowly. "Look, I'll tell you what I know but only if you promise not to lose your mind."

"Keep talking."

"I went back to that trattoria we ate at after our visit with Ernesto and Rosaria. There was something Teresa said that night or maybe it was just the way she said it that made me curious. I had lunch with the owner, a nice guy named Pasquale DiGiovanni…"

"Keep talking, Cesari."

"He and his family have owned the restaurant forever and he remembered Enzo and Teresa very well. He thought it was very sad about what happened."

Vito's features went from brooding anger to puzzlement. "What happened?"

"Well…" Cesari said slowly. "Teresa, it seems has been a very good cook her entire life. She took to it as a little girl and had a flare for it. Enzo it seems not so much."

"So what? She told us all that."

"What she didn't tell us was that she was feeding him her own secret recipes not just cooking techniques. He was using those recipes without giving her any credit to make a name for himself in the Italian culinary world, but she didn't mind standing in his shadow."

"Okay, she didn't mind it. Again, so what?"

"Why do you think a woman would do something like that?"

"Tell me," he growled.

"She was in love with him, Vito. Pasquale told me she was head over heels in love with him."

"Did Enzo take advantage of her? I'm going to kill him."

"No, the problem was he didn't take advantage of her. If he had, I don't think any of this would have happened. She let it all hang out, and he didn't even see her. According to Pasquale, as far as Enzo was concerned, Teresa was the invisible woman. They didn't even hold hands. Then Angelina showed up and all hell broke loose, but it gets worse."

Vito had calmed down and sat back in the plush leather upholstery. "I have a feeling I'm not going to like this, but go ahead."

"Enzo submitted Teresa's recipe for caponata as his own to a national cooking competition…"

"Let me guess… he won."

"A full ride to Rome's most prestigious cooking school."

"When he graduated, he authored a cookbook featuring?"

"Teresa's caponata?"

"Damn, you're smart. The book was moderately successful which was bad enough, but then he committed the worst crime of all. He asked Angelina to marry him and move to New York."

"Are you trying to tell me Teresa nearly murdered her own mother because she wanted to ruin Enzo?"

"First of all, she wasn't trying to murder anyone, and I don't really think she was trying to ruin Enzo so much as spoil his big night, maybe knock him down a peg or two. She was unaware of the potential complications of ipecac and the risks it posed. She read about it on the internet, but didn't know anyone personally in the medical profession she could consult with. She thought people might get a little sick, complain about the food and go home pissed off. When she offered to help prepare the caponata that day, she made two batches; one for the family and one laced with ipecac for the other restaurant guests. She made it clear to the staff which one was for which, but your family ate so much of it they quickly ran out and the staff didn't see any harm in serving them from the tainted batch."

Vito was very quiet for a minute before asking, "And Teresa told you this herself?"

Cesari nodded. "That's what we were talking about in her room. I confronted her with what I had found out, and she confirmed every word. For what it's worth, she's very contrite. She loves her mother and her sister very much and would never deliberately try to hurt them. It's just that…"

"It's just that she was angry at Enzo."

"And maybe a little jealous. Even though Enzo didn't know it, she had been in love with him a long time ago and now he was marrying her sister and rising to fame using her caponata recipe. That had to be very frustrating for her."

"I'll bet… so I'm just supposed to pretend I don't know anything when I see them."

"I would. There's no good going to come over opening that wound. Let everyone heal and let Teresa put it behind her. No one died, and she more than redeemed herself by risking her life for Emily. She has nothing to prove to anyone. You have to let her figure out what's best for her and her family. I promised her I wouldn't tell anyone."

"And Enzo never saw any of this coming? He had no inkling that she's been harboring a grudge all these years?"

"Not a clue, and he still doesn't."

"How stupid can one guy be?"

"Is that a trick question?"

Vito threw his cigarette butt out the window and said, "Damn…I've been waiting my whole life to meet my Sicilian family and now I find out they're all nuts."

"They're just people, Vito. It's not their fault you romanticized them in your mind."

"I guess I did. You know what's funny? I'm not sure whether to be mad at Enzo or feel sorry for him. I mean, according to what you just said, there could be some woman out there right now unbeknownst to me, angry as a hornet over some perceived offense I know nothing about, plotting her revenge."

Cesari nodded. "That about sums it up, but the good news is that we're all in the same boat."

"That doesn't reassure me… I'm not embarrassed to admit that I'm feeling a little vulnerable right now. I mean, how can a guy tell if a woman is angry at him?"

Cesari said, "Well, sometimes they'll frown when they're angry but sometimes they'll smile too. And sometimes they'll yell and scream but then again, they can also be very quiet. Not infrequently, they'll throw sharp objects at you but it's also not uncommon for them to be super affectionate so you don't know they're upset. I've seen women act like wildcats when they're pissed, and at other times I've seen them act totally normal as if nothing was wrong."

Vito laughed. "There's no way of being sure, is there?"

"I'm afraid not. They're much better at this stuff than we are. You're only hope is to avoid making them angry in the first place."

"And how do I do that?"

"I'm not sure you can."

The End

THE AUTHOR

About the Author

John Avanzato was born and raised in the Bronx, New York and is a practicing physician in upstate, New York. Inspired by authors like Tom Clancy, David Baldacci, John Grisham, and Lee Child, Avanzato writes about strong but flawed heroes. His stories are fast-paced thrillers with larger than life characters and tongue-in-cheek humor. He enjoys interacting with his readers and can be reached on Facebook or by e-mail, johnavanzato59@gmail.com for further discussion.

A Sicilian Cat

Made in the USA
Columbia, SC
01 April 2023

14d09d04-7853-4081-a8a4-d97f18b9bfd6R01